Hope for the Good Time Girls

Hope for the Good Time Girls

Fiona Ford

embla
books

First published in Great Britain in 2023 by

 **embla books**

Bonnier Books UK Limited
4th Floor, Victoria House, Bloomsbury Square, London, WC1B 4DA
Owned by Bonnier Books
Sveavägen 56, Stockholm, Sweden

A CIP catalogue record for this book is available from the British Library.

ISBN: 9781471415395

This book is typeset using Atomik ePublisher

Embla Books is an imprint of Bonnier Books UK
www.bonnierbooks.co.uk

For all those who served on the Home Front

1

June, 1942

The thrum of the music underneath the maple-sprung dance floor sent a shiver down Renee Hammond's spine. She had always loved listening to the first few bars of the orchestra as they tuned up, but now that she owned the Hammersmith Palais de Danse she made it a priority to hear each and every band warm up. Not only did she believe that it sent a clear message that she was interested in their performance but she also believed that, as owner and manager, it got her excited about every dance.

Not that Renee needed an excuse to be excited. It had been six months since the death of her husband Ronnie, who had taken over the Palais. The two had never seen eye to eye and so it hadn't come as a huge surprise to learn that Ronnie hadn't left the Palais to her. What had come as a surprise was that Ronnie had an older brother named Roger he had never mentioned, and that it was Roger who had inherited the Palais.

However, with Roger being a vicar, he felt he wasn't best placed to run a dance hall but he knew a woman who was. And so he had handed the Palais over to Renee, just like that. Since then, Renee had taken to the Palais like a lost lover returning home. The moment she had set foot in the Palais over three years ago, she had felt as if she had found her place in the world. Now that she owned the venue, she couldn't imagine ever being anywhere else. The Palais had always been her happy place and the dance floor had always soothed her soul.

As she closed her eyes and leaned against one of the ornate Chinese pillars that dominated the dance hall, Renee gave herself permission to lose herself in the music.

'Eh, up, Dolly Daydreamer. You're wanted.'

A sharp, female, Mancunian voice caused Renee to swiftly open her eyes. Blinking she brought herself back into the moment and grinned as she caught sight of the new Palais Master of Ceremonies, Janice Dobson, walking towards her.

'And what the hell d'you want disturbing my peace?' Renee gave the MC a mock glare before her face broke out into a wide grin.

Renee had always been fond of Janice, from the moment they first met at the Manchester Dance Hall eighteen months ago, when Renee had briefly moved away from London. In her fifties with a wit as sharp as a blade and a down-to-earth streak so grounded you could practically see the soil on her back, Janice had been the perfect MC, and an even better friend.

When Renee had taken over the Palais and the former MC, Bill Cain, had chosen to retire, Renee had known without question who she wanted by her side. And Janice, with family away at war, had immediately agreed to help her old friend out, becoming an instant hit with staff and regulars alike.

At the question Janice rolled her eyes and reached into her pocket for a Player's Light. Lighting up, she inhaled sharply and then addressed Renee.

'Them Yanks are causing trouble on the doors.'

'Again?' Renee asked.

'Afraid so.'

'What's the problem this time?'

Janice stifled a grin. 'To be fair, it's not really their fault. It's the local lads that are upset.'

'We haven't got that many local lads to be upset,' Renee said brusquely. 'They're all away at war.'

'Well, the ones that are left are upset the ladies outside are more interested in the Yanks than them.'

As Renee met Janice's eye she let out a whoop of laughter. Ever since the American soldiers had arrived in Britain in January they had caused a staunch divide amongst the locals.

The women loved their exotic accents and handsome faces, not to mention the seemingly never-ending supplies of stockings, chocolates and cigarettes the Americans could obtain. Naturally, the local lads had been upset to be usurped by such a good-looking bunch and hadn't been afraid to let their feelings on the matter be known. In the past few months they had complained directly to Renee, pleading with her to ban the Americans, and when all else failed had begun queueing up even earlier to discourage the GIs from entering the Palais, suggesting they sling their hook and go elsewhere.

'What are they doing now?' Renee asked with a shake of her head.

'Old Jimmy Bell's son, Arthur, has threatened to flatten one of the Yanks for talking to his sister.'

'Oh, for crying out loud.' Renee let out an exasperated sigh. 'The same thing happened last week with Harry Salter when his wife was talking to one of the Yanks.'

'That was a bit different,' Janice offered. 'Harry's wife was inviting the lad round for his tea. Harry didn't want him nicking his rations. Jimmy's lad thinks the Yank wants to ruin his sister's reputation.'

Renee raised an eyebrow. 'If I know Jimmy's daughter I should say that ship sailed a long time ago. Come on, then, let's have a look at the show outside.'

Leaving the band to continue tuning up, Renee followed Janice outside into the warm June sunshine. Just as she expected, she saw Arthur pressed up against the wall by one of the American soldiers. At the sight she tried not to smile; Arthur looked like a scrappy little dog, trying to do battle with a great big Alsatian.

'All right, then, lads,' she called in a tone that brooked no argument. 'What the hell's going on outside my dance hall?'

At the sound of Renee's voice, the soldier dropped Arthur like a stone and mumbled an apology.

'Sorry, ma'am.' Taking off his cap, he held it in his hands and looked at the ground with contrition.

Eyes still sparkling with anger Arthur refused to do the same and took a step forwards towards Renee and Janice.

'You wanna hear the things he was saying about my sister. It ain't right these Yanks coming over here and getting away with murder.'

'From what I can gather, Arthur, love, your sister's more than capable of taking care of herself. And judging by the way she's standing next to the Yank rather than you just now, I should say she's picked her side.'

Turning around to see the pairing, Arthur clenched his jaw, about to walk towards the American, when Renee rested a hand on his arm.

'That's enough,' she said firmly. And then, taking a step back to address the small crowd gathered outside waiting for the doors to open, she clapped her hands. 'I don't know how many times I have to keep saying this,' she called. 'But the Palais is welcome to all of you who behave yourselves. I don't want any trouble, and if you do cause any, Janice here will have no trouble throwing you out on your ear.'

At the mention of Janice some of the lads tittered at the idea of the older woman throwing them out. But one sharp look from Renee and her MC caused them to stop chuckling immediately, correctly sensing Janice wouldn't put up with any nonsense regardless of the fact she was female.

As the noise died down, Renee eyed the crowd. 'Like it or

not, we're all grateful these American lads have turned up here to do their bit and help us beat those pigging Germans. So give 'em a British welcome, eh – and that includes you, Arthur. I mean it, I don't want no trouble here, and if that's what you've got in mind you can go somewhere else. Now, have I made myself clear?'

With that, the small crowd nodded and murmured yeses and Renee smiled. Looking to Janice, who gave a quiet nod of her head, she turned back to the crowd.

'Right, well now all that's sorted I suggest we all get on with our evenings. Welcome to the Palais, everyone, and behave yourselves.'

As the group filed past her, Renee smiled at each of them, but as the line came to an end she let out a little bark of surprise at the sight of a tall, slender man, with a thick mop of curly black hair and dressed in a well-fitting black suit, complete with dog collar.

'Roger,' she breathed. 'What on earth are you doing here?'

Dressed in his clergy uniform, Roger beamed. 'I've been meaning to pay you a visit for a while. See how you're getting on. Though, if the way you dealt with this lot is anything to go by, I should say you're doing rather well.'

As he leaned forward to kiss her cheek Renee felt a rush of emotion. She was delighted to see the vicar, of course she was. But as she pulled away and stared into the eyes that were the spit of her late ex-husband's, the one overriding emotion pulsating away at her heart was guilt.

2

The sound of excited voices floated through the open window of the bar. At the exchange, Violet Millington and Temperance Adams swapped knowing looks.

'What's all that about, do you think?' Violet asked.

Reaching for another glass to polish she checked there were no smears or rim marks. Since taking over, Renee had been particular about the state of the glassware, insisting the Palais's standards were high at all times. Clean glassware was just one of the things she had singled out.

'The usual,' Temperance replied. 'We had fights between the regulars and the Americans last week, as well. I hope someone can nip this in the bud soon.'

She wiped a finger across the bar and Violet watched her carefully assess it for dust and grime. She smiled. Under Renee's stewardship, every one of them had taken an even greater pride in their roles at the Palais. It was as though Renee was now representing each one of the Good Time Girls and they all wanted the place to shine.

'I hope so, too.' Violet sighed and leaned back against the bar for a moment. 'We had all that complaining from folk that America hadn't joined the war, but now they have, people don't want 'em here.'

'That's not quite true,' Temperance replied with a wry smile. 'There are plenty of people who are grateful they're here, but just not our local lads. Don't want to be deprived of a night out with a lady.'

'Then they want to sharpen up their ways,' Violet said, not

altogether unkindly. 'After so long at war, it'll be nice for the girls to be treated by a fella.'

Temperance wiped a small smear from the bar tray. 'I agree, Vi, but you know what they're like round here. They've had it too good too long. Now there's a bit of competition and they don't like it.'

'Well, we can't carry on like this every night,' Violet announced.

'I couldn't agree with you girls more,' a loud Brooklyn accent called from behind them.

Spinning round, Violet smiled at Nancy, their general manager and friend. With her thick brown hair, thicker American accent and lavish eye make-up, Nancy always exuded a tough exterior, but the girls knew she was as soft as butter underneath it all.

'So, what's your plan?' Temperance asked.

Nancy pursed her lipstick-red lips and ran a hand through her hair. 'Honey, if I had an answer to that I'd be a rich woman. I don't know. I wondered if we could hold some sort of social night for the locals and GIs.'

General Issue was a term the American soldiers used for themselves due in part, the rumour mill claimed, to the fact that 'GI' was stamped all over their uniforms and kit.

'Won't that be difficult when we're so short-staffed?' Temperance countered.

'Honey, I can't lie, yes. But there's a war on; we've all got to do our bit. And even though half our girls have joined up alongside our menfolk now we can't let that get in the way of our problems.'

'And the fights between locals and GIs are a problem.' Violet sighed.

'So is our lack of staff,' Temperance muttered before turning to Violet. 'Any word from Maisie?'

At the mention of her sister Violet felt a flame of affection unfurl within her heart. She had never been close to Maisie growing up, but since she had been conscripted into the ATS back in March Violet missed her more than she could ever have expected. It was a wonder Maisie was the only woman at the Palais to have been called up. Temperance after all was eligible, but she was registered as her mother's carer: Enid suffered with her nerves following the death of her husband and son. Violet, together with her mother Betty, was also a carer for George, Betty's husband and the man who had raised Violet since she was a baby. George was disabled since losing his arm in Dunkirk.

'She's fine. She wrote to me last week. She's doing well up in Northampton. Made friends with a girl called Kitty.'

'That's good.' Temperance looked pleased for a moment and then bit her lip. 'I keep expecting my call-up papers any moment.'

Nancy shook her head. 'Honey, it's not going to happen. You're both listed as carers for your family; they're not going to conscript you.'

'I hope not.' Temperance shook her head then, realising what she'd said, blushed. 'I mean it's not that I don't love my country. Course I do, I'd do anything to serve and fight Hitler, but I worry about Mum; she'd never cope if anything happened to me . . .'

As her voice trailed off Violet squeezed her hand. 'And that's why they won't conscript you. Your mum's got you around for a long time.'

'That's what Archie keeps saying.'

At the thought of her sweetheart, butcher Archie Ledbetter, Temperance grinned and Violet couldn't help but join in. The two had been courting for several months now and made a perfect pairing.

'Then listen to him,' Violet assured her. 'I've been worried about the same thing, but Betty's had me listed as George's official carer so I can keep baby Eamon.'

The fact that she'd had to lie about giving birth to her

baby boy, pretend that he was an orphan, abandoned when his mother had been killed in childbirth during a raid in the capital, broke Violet's heart. She hated that on his birth certificate she'd been forced to put 'mother and father unknown', when the truth was that she had wanted to sing from the rooftops that little Eamon was hers and hers alone. That he had a mummy, and a daddy who would have loved him very much had he been given the chance. Violet shook her head, trying to free herself from the pain of thinking about the death of her own sweetheart, Temperance's older brother Eamon. He had died during the first bomb attack on London and as she came to terms with his death, Violet had been both delighted and terrified to discover she was pregnant with his child.

'How's he doing, honey?' Nancy asked.

'He's doing well.' Violet felt herself light up. 'He's started sitting up on his own and you can see him getting more curious. He loves it when I put the light on.'

'Don't we all after a night of blackout,' Nancy quipped. 'Seriously, I'm pleased. Bring him down to the Palais sometime. I've love to see him, and I know Ruth would. She's so fond of him, she'd relish the chance to babysit.'

'Do you think she's old enough?'

'She's fifteen. You know what kids are like.' Nancy shrugged. 'But she's very responsible.'

Despite the nonchalance Violet knew that Nancy was touched Ruth was confiding in her and creating a bond. The general manager had taken in two Kinder Transport children, Peter and Ruth, from Vienna just before Christmas last year. And although Nancy had always longed to be a mother, she had found it difficult initially to bond with the children. Thankfully, in recent months they had turned a corner and now Violet was pleased to see that Nancy and the kids were so close you could barely put a pin between them.

'All right,' Violet said. 'If she'd like to then I'll bring him down one evening. That way I'll be around in case there are any problems.'

'There won't be any problems.' Temperance laid a hand on her shoulder and gave an affectionate squeeze. 'Eamon's an easy, lovely baby. Ruth will be fine.'

Violet flushed. Was the worry over her child that obvious to spot? She thought of her baby every waking moment of every day. She physically ached for him when she couldn't be with him, even for just a moment. She had no idea how she would cope when he grew up and left her to start his own life. Violet shuddered; it didn't bear thinking about.

Instead she took a deep breath and nodded at her friend. 'You're right,' she said, then turned back to look at Nancy. 'So, you really think we need to do something to get everyone to stop fighting?'

'I do.' Nancy nodded.

'And what have you got in mind?' Janice barked from the doorway.

As she walked towards them Violet smiled at their latest recruit. The older woman had been a very wise hire as MC on Renee's part and had fitted in seamlessly with the rest of the team.

'Janice, honey, there you are.' Nancy smiled. 'I was hoping to talk about this with you. I wondered if we might have a sorta getting to know you dance?'

'Getting to know you dance?' Violet echoed.

'Yes, we had one of them back in Manchester when we had a load of Liverpudlians causing trouble,' Janice replied.

'Did it work?' Temperance asked.

Janice paused as she considered the question. 'It didn't solve everything but it certainly helped. I think it's a good idea, Nancy. You know, get people talking.'

'I like that,' Nancy mused. 'And I think Renee would, too.'

'Where is she by the way?' Temperance asked, suddenly looking around for Renee.

'She's with a vicar.'

'A vicar?' Nancy asked, her face turning a ghostly shade of white.

'Some fella Renee seemed to know,' Janice explained. 'Perhaps he can help us find a way through this, if he's a pal?'

Violet smiled. A vicar would certainly help, and it seemed to her that someone with God's ear could only help them work wonders in the community.

3

As Nancy galloped up the stairs towards the office she and Renee shared above the Palais's dance floor, she took a moment to steady herself. Leaning against the wooden bannister she breathed heavily, trying to calm down. Between them they only knew one vicar, and though Nancy might like to pretend that was because she was Jewish and regularly attended synagogue, not church, she knew fine well who it would be – Roger Newsham. Ronnie's older, wiser and far kinder estranged brother.

For a second the thought paralysed her. Roger had never played a part in their lives until Ronnie died and left the Palais to his brother in his will. Nancy was sure this had been purely to upset Renee, but of course Roger, being the good, Christian soul that he was, had signed the Palais over to Renee in the blink of an eye. It was a situation that had made Nancy feel overwhelmed at his generosity of spirit, and worried. For months the Palais had been chaos – largely due to the war effort, which had seen so many of their own dancers and customers called up to serve their country, a fact that had a huge impact on the Palais's coffers.

It hadn't helped either that when Renee had first arrived at the Palais from her native Liverpool, she'd been on the run from her abusive husband, and then stolen from the Palais to pay him off when he inevitably caught up with her. Desperate to try and leave her past behind once and for all, Renee had come up with the bright idea of stealing cigarettes and alcohol totalling hundreds of pounds to pay off the debts Ronnie claimed she owed him.

Nancy knew Renee had been desperate and in her madness had convinced herself that stealing from the Palais she loved was the answer. Naturally it hadn't been; Renee hadn't been able to raise nearly enough and Ronnie had caught up with her, forcing her to flee again, this time to Manchester. Renee had eventually managed to repay all the money she had taken before she left, but the damage had been done and the Palais's books were in serious need of balancing.

Naturally, Nancy had done her best to steer the Palais back on course, but her mother-in-law, Edna Goldstein – together with Bill Cain, Edna's comrade in arms, former sweetheart and the Palais MC – had thwarted Nancy's every attempt, even agreeing with the board to sell a majority share of the Palais to Ronnie Newsham. The moment Ronnie had taken the reins, the Palais had fallen into an even greater state of disrepair. Rather than try and build the Palais up, Ronnie had turned it into his own personal playpen, hoping eventually to sell it to the highest bidder for a tidy profit.

Now that Ronnie was dead, Nancy knew that Renee hoped all their problems were over, but Nancy, who had never left her New York cynicism behind since leaving America for England over a decade earlier, wasn't convinced. True, under Renee's stewardship the Palais had begun to thrive once more, but Nancy wasn't sure how long that would last. Then of course there was the part she and Renee had played in Ronnie's death. The thought of what she and Renee had done still gave Nancy sleepless nights and she often woke up in a cold sweat, anxious they would be found out. Now Roger was here, surely that meant she was about to be proven right. The vicar hadn't visited since the day he handed the Palais over to Renee back in December. Did he know?

Heart still pounding, Nancy squared her shoulders and braced herself for whatever lay ahead as she walked up the short flight of stairs towards the little room at the top. Lightly, she rapped on the door and walked inside. At the sight of her, Renee and Roger broke off their conversation and welcomed her with wide smiles.

'Nancy, love, we were just talking about you,' Renee said, gesturing to the small wooden chair beside her to sit down.

Anxiously, Nancy took a seat and primly crossed her legs as she smiled at the vicar.

'I heard you were here. Thought I'd come and say hello,' she said, aware that her breathing was a little uneven.

Roger smiled broadly at the New Yorker. 'Pleasure to see you again, Nancy.'

He reached across the table for a glass of whisky and Nancy tried to hide her surprise. Only it was too late as the vicar looked apologetically at the glass.

'I'm afraid I drink so much tea that when Renee offered me a whisky I couldn't refuse.'

'I can't stand tea myself,' Nancy replied. 'For me, it's coffee every time.'

Roger wrinkled his nose. 'I'm afraid that's one drink I've never cared for. It seems to jolt me wide awake.'

'I think that's why we New Yorkers love it so much,' Nancy quipped. 'We haven't got time to wait for the gentleness of tea to get us going in the morning.' She stopped babbling and got to the point as calmly as she could. 'So, Roger, what brings you this way?'

Roger cleared his throat. 'Can't I pop in for a social call?'

'Well, you can, love,' Renee said easily, 'but as I've not seen you since Christmas I'd say it was unusual, unless you happened to be just passing.'

'Fair enough.' Roger smiled. 'It's true I am in the area and thought I'd see how you were getting on, but the truth is I was hoping you might be able to help me with something.'

Nancy braced herself. Here it was. There was no such thing as a free Palais.

'If I can, love, I will,' Renee said. 'What is it?'

'I want to do more to help the homeless who've been bombed out. I'm working with an East End parish over in Bethnal Green. Together we're laying on schemes to give mothers and children somewhere to get a good meal and a rest, and for the bombed out we offer free meals, as well as entertainment on occasion.'

'Commendable,' Renee said. 'They've been bombed to high heaven over there, the poor beggars. But I'm not sure what we could do. We're already involved in the National Restaurants scheme and some of our staff do volunteer work there. I don't know if we could spare anyone else for something new, Roger, love.'

'But of course we will look into it,' Nancy said smoothly. She shot Renee an irritated glance. What was she doing? They needed to keep Roger sweet; the last thing they wanted was him asking questions.

'That's not actually what I want help with, but thank you, Nancy.' Roger lifted the glass of whisky to his lips. 'No, I know the Palais is more than doing its bit. But there's something else. As you know, Ronnie left me some of his estate, besides the Palais.'

'Yes, the clothes shops and properties back in Liverpool? That's right, isn't it, love?' Renee confirmed.

Roger nodded. 'It is. I've just sold them. They were never going to be of any interest to me, and I'm delighted to say I've made a handsome profit.'

'That's a feat with there being a war on,' Renee exclaimed. 'So what are you going to do with the money? Take yourself off on a mission? That's what you vicars call your holidays, isn't it, when you help the needy?'

Roger chuckled. 'Are you always this cheeky?'

'She's famous for it, honey.' Nancy rolled her eyes.

'I don't see any point beating about the bush when there's a point to be made,' Renee said.

'Quite right,' Roger said, putting his glass on the table and leaning back in the old chair. He surveyed the women and Nancy felt a flash of discomfort as he fixed his eyes on her for what felt like far too long. Could he read her mind? Did he know all the secrets that lay buried in her heart?

'The truth is, I have seen the good the ministry in Bethnal Green is doing. The people there are benefitting hugely from the sense of community.'

'So what's your point, Roger?' Renee asked, her eyes twinkling. 'You said you were getting to it.'

Roger shook his head at her teasing. 'All right. The point is I want to use the money from the sale of Ronnie's properties and businesses to open a new dance hall in the East End. I've found an old theatre, The Regal, I like the look of not far from the church in Bethnal Green and I want the Hammersmith Palais de Danse to open a second dance hall with community at its heart. I'll be paying for it; I just need your know-how.'

As the vicar finished his sentence he sank back in his chair looking pleased with himself, while Nancy was left reeling. Of all the things she was expecting him to say, the idea of opening another dance hall in the East End definitely wasn't one of them.

4

An hour after the vicar had left, Temperance stood in the corner of the dance hall, her eyes trained firmly on the dancers she taught day in, day out. The American soldiers, or GIs, had booked dances with almost all the girls in the pen for sixpence a time and they were keeping the girls on their toes.

As the music of the orchestra changed from a quick, upbeat tempo to a slower waltz, Temperance expected the soldiers to instinctively know what to do and hold the girls in their arms as they waltzed across the floor. Yet, to her surprise, they clung to the dancers in the same way but moved their feet in a small, confined space with their hips doing most of the work.

Temperance felt her pulse quicken. She had danced this dance herself but it wasn't something she routinely saw in the Palais. It was one of the newer dances that came from Cuba and was brought to the US in the 1930s and, like so many popular dances, had developed and been turned into something new and unique.

She glanced nervously around the floor. The dancers, like Temperance, knew the steps, though they weren't as familiar as the GIs. The Brits, however, merely stood back on the sidelines watching in disgust or carried on dancing the waltz as best they could.

'Have you seen this?' Temperance whispered to Renee, who had woven her way through the throng of people to stand next to her.

Renee sniffed. 'It's a long way from sequence dancing.'

'But don't you think it's beautiful?' Temperance breathed.

Renee paused for a moment and Temperance tried to see the steps through her eyes. Renee was a renowned dancer, and had won more trophies than she'd had hot meals. Renee wasn't just her friend and now her boss, she was her dancing mentor and her opinion mattered.

'I think it's incredible, love,' Renee said eventually. 'Look at those tight turns those GIs are making with their hips, and the exaggerated movements – yet they're barely moving across the floor.'

'Our girls are keeping up, though,' Temperance said, a little defensively.

Renee raised an eyebrow. 'Nobody's picking fault. I think the fact they know it at all and can hold their own is a miracle in itself.'

'Well, I suppose some of them have seen them in that Ginger Rogers and Fred Astaire film, *Flying Down to Rio*. And we did run through some of the steps this week in practice,' Temperance admitted.

Since taking over as dance instructor Temperance liked to ensure she stayed ahead of the current dances.

'That, I can see,' Renee replied, affection rippling through her tone. 'You've done an excellent job.'

Allowing herself to bask in this praise for a moment, Temperance grinned. 'Do you think we ought to learn more of these dances that are so popular with the GIs, then?' she asked.

For a second, Renee paused, and Temperance watched her survey the dance floor again. The Brits were largely curious, though some looked cross.

'Yes,' Renee said, quickly now. 'I think that's a good idea. I'll help with instruction. Our lads might not like it, but we have to cater for everyone. Time doesn't stand still and that means change.'

'Sounds like you're talking about something else,' Temperance ventured.

Renee fixed her green eyes on her and Temperance saw that familiar warmth.

'Can you come in early tomorrow? I'm asking everyone. I want to discuss something important.'

Temperance felt a flash of concern. 'Is everything all right?'

'Everything is fine. Just some business to discuss. Can you get here about eight?'

'Course.'

As Temperance agreed she saw Renee's face flood with relief.

'Is everything really all right?' Temperance asked. 'Only, I saw Ronnie's brother.'

'Yes, Roger's got a proposal for us and I want us all to talk about it tomorrow.'

'What sort of proposal?'

But Temperance's question was drowned out by the sound of applause ricocheting through the room as the dance finished. As she joined in to show appreciation she became aware of the man standing next to her.

'We ought to have a go at that,' he whispered in her ear. 'We'd knock spots off this lot.'

Turning to him, Temperance's heart swelled with love at the sight of her sweetheart, Archie Ledbetter. No longer just the son of the butcher, Archie's dad had retired after ill health, and now Archie was the one running his own butcher's business in the day and dancing his way across the floor and into her heart by night.

'Maybe we ought to have some private lessons?' Temperance giggled.

Archie grinned as the dancers filed off the floor while the band announced a break.

'Thought you'd never ask.' Quickly kissing her on the cheek, he smiled up at Renee, Nancy and Violet who had now joined her on the dance floor. 'How's tricks?' he asked. 'I heard there was a fight earlier?'

Violet rolled her eyes. 'Course there was. It's the only way some of these lads know how to behave.'

Temperance frowned. Ever since her brother Eamon had died in a bombing raid at the docks last September, Violet never had a good word to say about another fella. She could understand that Violet was rightly grief-stricken to lose her sweetheart, but that didn't mean that all men were useless. Temperance worried that Violet was becoming slightly bitter and about the impact that would have on little Eamon, her nephew.

'Come on now, honey, they're not all bad. They're just confused and hurting,' Nancy said. 'We got the argument sorted out in the end, didn't we?'

'Yes, but we don't want to have to go through that all night. I think it's a good idea to put on a dance to bring everyone together.' Renee turned to Temperance. 'Have a think about some styles we can bring together. Perhaps the American lads can teach the Brits and vice versa, that sort of thing.'

Temperance nodded. She would get to work immediately, and was about to ask more questions when she spotted Peter, one of Nancy's adopted Kinder Transport children, taking to the floor.

'Look,' she said, beaming. 'Has Peter got a sweetheart?'

Nancy followed her gaze and chuckled. 'That boy has changed since he turned seventeen. He's got girls following him everywhere. So, no, honey, that's not a sweetheart, that's some girl he's just met and taken a shine to. I can't complain; he works hard now and he plays hard, too.'

Temperance chuckled, feeling Archie wrap a hand around her waist. As she leaned into him she felt a flush of pleasure that she had such a wonderful man by her side.

'What does Alex say? He must want to meet these children?'

'Oh, sure.' Nancy beamed. 'In fact he wrote me last week. He's coming home for a visit at the end of July.'

Renee looked at her in surprise. 'You never said.'

'Didn't I?' Nancy looked wrong-footed for a moment. 'I meant to, but there's been so much going on.'

But as Temperance watched Nancy relax her features she noticed her jaw was still clenched. Nestling in closer to Archie, Temperance got the feeling that a visit from her husband home on leave wasn't something as joyous as Nancy was making out.

5

The following morning, after a sleepless night of feeling grotty, Nancy woke tired, in a way that only a night of tossing and turning can make you feel.

Throwing the eiderdown off her slender frame she padded to the kitchen and set about making herself a coffee. It was only six; Peter and Ruth wouldn't be up for at least an hour. This meant that, although she felt wretched, at least she had some time alone to gather her thoughts.

As she waited for the kettle to boil, Nancy reached for the by now well-worn letter that she had hidden in the bread bin and began to read.

15th June, 1942

My dearest Nancy,

How are you? How are the children – and of course the Palais? Mother says she paid a visit last week and was astonished and delighted in equal measure to find the place so full of gaiety, with so many Americans taking to the floor—

It was at this point that Nancy grimaced. Who spoke like that? It was as though she had married someone from some upper-class British family with several bags of plums in his mouth, rather than a guy who was brought up in a dance hall alone by his mother. Alex had never spoken like that before he went away. When they had first met, when he'd been working as the Palais barman, Alex had sounded more like an East

End barrow boy than some British gent, with a great sense of humour to match – was it any wonder that a straight-talking New Yorker had felt an instant attraction? Shaking the nostalgic thought from her mind, Nancy picked up the letter again and continued reading.

I understand that the new MC, Janice, is settling in well, which is of course marvellous news. Mother tells me that Bill is spending much of his time in the garden, tending to his roses. Perhaps you could visit him one day Nancy, dear – and take the children. He was such a part of the Palais for so very many years, I do consider him family.

Speaking of visits, I write with what I hope is welcome news. I have been granted leave at the end of next month and will be returning to Britain for a few days. I will let you know the exact date nearer the time. I simply cannot wait to see you and meet the children. Will you come and meet my train?

Take care my darling
Your loving husband, Alex

Nancy finished reading, sighed, and stuffed the paper back into the envelope. It had been a week since she'd first read Alex's letter, and with every reread, she hoped she would find some new connection, some way of feeling that she knew the man behind the words. She didn't. Instead, she only felt more irritated and more full of dread. If she didn't recognise this man in his letters, what hope was there for them when he returned home? *Returned home.* There were two words that caused Nancy to feel sick. As the kettle boiled she reached for the jar of instant coffee she had been forced to resort to and dug out a teaspoon of the pungent brown powder. It wasn't coffee as she knew, but it would have to do.

Pouring the boiling water onto the powdered mix she allowed herself to enjoy the aroma of the java flooding her nostrils. The first coffee of the day was always the best. Taking her cup she sat at the scratched wooden table and tried to think. Since moving to England, Nancy had managed to make a good fist of starting a new life. She had originally followed her sister Esther to London, but when Esther returned home to New York two years later, Nancy hadn't wanted to go with her, breaking her mother's heart in the process. And though, in the eight years that had passed since then, Nancy never once regretted her decision, finding everything she wanted right here in West London – the perfect job at the Palais, then marrying who she thought was the man of her dreams – as her eyes fell back on the envelope inscribed with her husband's familiar hand, she allowed doubt to creep in. Alex felt like a stranger to her these days. And the Palais she loved so much was changing beyond recognition. Yes it was wonderful to have Renee run the place, and Janice Dobson sure made a terrific MC. The place was making positive changes, but the trouble was Nancy wasn't sure they were changes she recognised.

If she was honest with herself, change wasn't the only reason she was feeling so conflicted at the Palais. The truth was, that dreadful night when she and Renee had been responsible for the death of Ronnie had started to haunt her. She was now sure that one day they would be found out and she dreaded what that meant.

For the past few months she had allowed herself to feel a false sense of security. The police weren't interested, and Ronnie was six feet under in the churchyard a mile down the road.

But now his brother Roger had appeared. With fancy ideas for a new dance hall on the opposite side of town. A cold shiver ran down Nancy's spine. Was that really all he wanted?

* * *

Later that morning Nancy still wasn't convinced of the vicar's intentions as she sat in the Palais bar. Renee was dishing out tea and coffee to all the Good Time Girls, as well as Violet's mother, Betty, who had gathered to discuss the latest plan. Spirits were high.

'So, Roger has the money to open a new dance hall?' Violet asked, her tone rightly incredulous.

Renee nodded as Janice spoke up.

'It doesn't seem like the best of ideas when there's a war on. For all he knows we could be up and running, and within a day Hitler'll put the mockers on it.'

There was grim laughter, and even Nancy raised a smile. Janice's no-nonsense ways were a welcome addition to the group and she enjoyed the older Mancunian's dry sense of humour.

'Well, we could say that about this place,' Renee pointed out. 'Who knows what Hitler's bloody game is these days.'

'Rumour is, even Hitler doesn't know,' Temperance muttered.

'Well how would this work, then?' Violet asked now, steering them back on track. 'And where exactly is this place Roger's earmarked?'

'Near Bethnal Green, and from what Roger told me it will run slightly differently to the Palais. This new dance hall would be a bit less luxurious and a bit more community-minded. By day, it would be a place for those poor souls who have been bombed out to find food and shelter, fresh clothes for the kiddies and that.'

'And by night?' Temperance asked.

Renee gestured to the grandeur of the maple-sprung dance floor that lay opposite the bar.

'And by night we put on a dance for them to enjoy themselves.'

'With a band?' Violet asked.

'Of course with a band,' Renee replied impatiently. 'You're not expecting me to start singing like Vera Lynn are you?'

'I hope not,' Janice quipped. 'You're tone-deaf.'

25

The girls laughed, including Nancy, who then felt Renee fix her gaze on her.

'And what do you think, Nancy? You've been very quiet on the subject.'

Nancy sighed. 'I don't know that it's the best time, Renee, honey. I admire the vicar's intentions, truly I do, but where would we even get the manpower to start something like this?'

'Roger says there's money for new staff, but we would perhaps need to oversee it ourselves, the dance part anyway, to ensure it's as successful as the Palais.'

'It would be a lot of work,' Betty said, quietly now. 'The church is badly overstretched as it is. They'll have good intentions to help out with hot food, but now the National Restaurants scheme is well underway do people need hot food from the church?'

'Roger says yes. And with your experience setting up the National Restaurants I was hoping you'd help out, queen.'

As Nancy looked at Betty, she thought she saw a hint of colour flood her cheeks.

'Me?' she echoed.

'Better you than Violet,' Nancy teased. 'That girl can barely boil water.'

'Hey!' Violet chuckled good-naturedly then nudged her mother. 'It'd do you good to get out of the house a bit,' she said softly.

Nancy couldn't help but agree. Betty had a lot to contend with. Her husband George was a well-known womaniser and gambler. He had joined the army, then lost an arm in battle in Dunkirk. Betty had worked tirelessly to support him, only to discover that before he went away to war he had got another woman pregnant, a woman who happened to be Renee's sister, Lizzie, who'd tragically died in the same blast that had killed poor Eamon Adams.

Last year, Betty had started working for the Palais and

later had been seconded to Howell & Smart, the posh department-store chain, whose management had the bright idea of setting up a group of restaurants that were heavily discounted, so the needy could benefit from a hot meal. It had gone swimmingly, until the job had led Betty back into the arms of her childhood sweetheart, Alan Hopkins, who had in fact turned out to be Violet's real father.

Now Alan had started a new job in Birmingham heading up the National Restaurant campaign from the heart of the country. He had invited Betty to join him but she had refused, insisting she was a married woman and wouldn't desert her injured husband, no matter how feckless he was.

An honourable choice, but as Nancy watched Betty drink her tea, eyes downcast, she couldn't help feel it was the wrong one. It was obvious how much Betty missed Alan and Nancy wondered if this new dance hall might be the making of her.

'I think we ought to give it a go,' she found herself saying now. 'It would be good for us to give back to the community, to extend the Palais brand, surely?'

'But what if it goes wrong?' Temperance asked.

'Aren't you little miss doom and gloom?' Janice said with a shake of her head, but an affectionate tone. 'It's called life, sweetheart. And in life, sometimes things go wrong and sometimes things go right. You can never know, you just have to do what you think is best at the time.'

Nancy nodded at Temperance. 'She's right, honey. We all have to take risks in life, otherwise you're just sat around waiting to die.' She turned to look at Renee. 'I don't think we have a choice, do we? Roger's offering us a chance to help the community and for that reason alone we have to say yes.'

As she finished speaking she was pleased to hear murmurs of agreement. But that wasn't what surprised Nancy the most. The thing she was most amazed by was the complete about-turn she herself had made since earlier that morning. Whether a second dance hall was a good idea or not, Nancy wasn't sure, but she knew that whatever lay ahead, if there was a chance to help with the war effort it was only right they do their bit, whatever it cost.

6

Later that evening as Violet sat in the kitchen, with her grand-mother, Queenie, in the corner and her mother at the stove making dinner, she couldn't stop thinking about what Nancy had said earlier on: that they had a duty to help those in need. Glancing down at Eamon, fast asleep in the makeshift cot that stood next to the old stone hearth, she wondered what sort of a future he would have. Violet knew he would already have a tough road ahead of him being half black and fatherless, but whilst she felt that some of Eamon's future had already been written she knew that she had a duty, no, more than that, a desire, to give her son everything she possibly could. And if that was a new start in the East End where nobody knew them, perhaps that was what was best.

'What do you think of this new dance hall idea then, Betty?' she asked her mother, raising her voice above the din of the stove. Violet had never called Betty by anything other than her first name, probably because they hadn't been close while she was growing up. And now, even though things had improved since the truth about Violet's real father, Alan, had come out, old habits stayed firm.

'New dance hall?' Before Betty could reply, Queenie lifted her head from the socks she had been knitting and peered at Violet questioningly.

'Yes, the Palais are thinking of opening a second branch near Bethnal Green.'

'A second branch?' Queenie echoed.

'What are you, the family parrot?' Violet teased, with a soft twinkle in her eye. She and her grandmother had always had an easy relationship, and even though Queenie was George's mother, which in turn meant she was not Violet's biological grandmother, Violet loved her as much as she always had, refusing to see her as anything else but her beloved nan.

'You just be glad I'm taking an interest,' Queenie replied.

Shoving her knitting in the bag beside her she didn't bat an eyelid when some of the stitches fell off the needles.

'You making string vests?' Violet enquired.

Queenie sniffed and gave a wry smile. 'Socks for soldiers. All them holes'll probably give their feet a bit of an airing.'

Violet broke into peals of laughter, and it felt so good. She hadn't laughed for months after Eamon, her sweetheart and Temperance's brother, had died. Now, although she felt a flash of guilt when there was a bit of joy amongst the clouds, she mostly felt a little lighter. She knew that whatever happened she didn't want to bring her own misery into her son's life. He had done nothing to deserve it, and for her sweetheart's sake Violet would do everything in her power to ensure that her son had the best upbringing she could provide.

'So is someone gonna give me an answer or what?' Queenie said over Violet's giggles.

'It's something and nothing,' Betty replied at last, not turning around from draining some boiled vegetables.

'It's a bit more than that,' Violet cried. 'They've got premises.'

'Premises?' Queenie repeated again, earning herself a glare from Violet. 'Sorry.' Queenie put her hands up. 'I thought the Palais was in trouble, though. Where's all this extra money come from for an extra dance hall up east?'

Sensing her grandmother wouldn't stop asking questions until she was satisfied, Violet explained everything that had happened in the meeting earlier that day.

'Well, stone me!' Queenie exclaimed. 'This Roger's not a

thief 'n' all like his brother is he? He could be anyone! Renee's only met him once.'

'He's a vicar,' Betty said.

Queenie shifted in her seat. 'That doesn't mean anything. You can still be religious and up to no good.'

'Gran!' Violet admonished. 'This is a good thing. Be pleased, eh? Besides, Betty's going to help, aren't you?'

'Well I haven't said yes yet.' Now it was Betty's turn to look disgruntled. Setting down the plates of Mock Cheese on Toast with leeks on the side, she turned to Violet. 'Shout your father please? He's upstairs doing heaven only knows what.'

'I've been trying to repair your watch,' George said, thundering downstairs.

Violet looked up at him and tried to feel some sort of emotion towards him as she did every time she saw him. This man had brought her up, provided for her. But he was also the man who had made her mother miserable with his bullying and womanising, never mind that he'd nearly left her in debtors' prison with his gambling.

'Well, that's very nice of you,' Betty said in an overly bright voice. She pulled out a chair and gestured for him to sit down.

'It *is* very nice of you,' Queenie said, taking a seat opposite her son. 'You planning on selling it for extra money?'

'Queenie!' Betty admonished her mother-in-law yet again, only for the older woman to shake her head. Since the truth about her son had come out, Queenie made no bones out of making her disappointment and frustration with George clear.

George said nothing, choosing instead to rip into his meal with his one good hand.

'Did I hear right? You and Violet working up this second dance hall, then?' he asked his wife, with his mouth full.

Betty took a seat at the table, and gestured for Violet to do the same.

Shooting George one last reluctant look, Violet got up to

join them. At Temperance's aunt Winnie's flat, which Violet called home, she usually ate and read with Eamon right next to her, wanting to make the most of every moment she wasn't working to be by his side.

'Yes, I will be. I'm off to look at the site next week,' Betty told George.

'And what are you going to be doing?' he asked, his eyes never leaving his plate.

'Just what I was doing for the National Restaurants.'

At the mention of the charitable scheme set up by Howell & Smart, George's face darkened, and Queenie and Violet exchanged concerned looks.

'And will that old flame of yours be involved?'

Violet glanced at her mother, who she was pleased to see wasn't rattled by the question.

'Alan?' she replied loftily. 'No, he's up in Birmingham running things from there.'

'Ruining other people's families besides this one?' George put down his fork and glared at the table.

Violet said nothing. George knew Alan had admitted to being Violet and her twin brother Roy's father, but the fact that Betty and Alan had rekindled their romance, just temporarily, was something Betty had managed to keep from him.

'Alan didn't ruin anything,' Queenie pointed out. 'He only told the truth.'

'Over twenty years too late,' George thundered. 'Where's my thanks in any of this? I gave your kids a home, food in their bellies.'

'And a lifetime's worth of trouble,' Violet shot back. She had heard enough. Yes, it was true she did have a certain amount of sympathy for the man who had raised her, but at the same time George had treated them all with such a lack of respect, such disdain, she wasn't about to have him play the victim.

'Don't you cheek me in my own house.' George slammed his fist down on the table causing Eamon to stir.

As her baby son's cries filled the house Violet got up to attend to him.

'Where do you think you're going?' George thundered again.

'To see to my child.' Violet sighed.

'We're having our tea,' George pointed out. 'Let him wait. He'll stop when he's ready. You women are too quick to pander.'

'It's called being a mother,' Queenie said shortly, then turned to Violet. 'Do you want help with him, love?'

Violet shook her head as she scooped the mewling infant up into her arms and took him out into the warm summer's air. The moment they stepped outside, Eamon immediately stopped crying, looking up at her with his bright brown eyes full of mischief.

'Did you do that on purpose?' Violet half whispered, half giggled. 'Did you cause a fuss to get me out of sitting opposite that awful man any longer?'

'Heeeheeeheeheee.' Eamon gave a little giggle in his mother's arms, and then without warning threw his head back on Violet's shoulder and snuggled in close.

Breathing in his sweet, milky scent, Violet kissed him lightly on the top of his head and made a silent promise to always put him first, no matter what.

Violet knew her mother had done her best, or at least what she thought was her best, in finding a man who would take on two illegitimate children. And Violet commended her for that. But Betty's best wouldn't be anywhere near good enough for her own son. Violet was determined to give Eamon the future he deserved. Kissing his head once more, she felt peaceful and content. Aware that there was just one thing that would make this moment complete – if her sweetheart, Eamon Adams, could somehow, suddenly appear by her side.

7

A week later and Temperance found herself sat at the bar of the Palais before it opened, engrossed in an article in the *Dancing Times* about the new craze of American dances. She had of course already built up some knowledge of them, but the technical aspects were so different compared to British dancing that Temperance had her work cut out getting to grips with them.

At the sound of footsteps walking across the floor towards her, she looked up from reading and smiled at Renee.

'What you doing, queen?' Renee asked, in her Liverpudlian drawl.

Temperance lifted the magazine to show her. 'I thought it would be nice to teach some of these dances in the pen, like we talked about. That way some of our customers won't feel so lacking when the Americans come in and start taking over the dance floor.'

Renee gave a wry smile and pulled a pack of Craven A from the pocket of her tea dress.

'The hardest part you'll have is convincing folk round here that these new dances aren't just an excuse for canoodling,' she said, lighting her cigarette.

'I've seen how close some of them get!' Temperance exclaimed. 'That'll set a few tongues wagging.'

'Like they need any excuse round here.' Renee rolled, sharply inhaling her smoke. 'As I said, I'll help you out at first. You might meet a bit of resistance.'

Temperance said nothing. She was more than used to resistance from people around here. She knew most people meant well, but there were a few who still thought her black face didn't fit. She pushed the unwelcome thoughts from her mind and, hearing the sound of footsteps in the foyer outside, smiled and got to her feet.

'Showtime.' Temperance grinned.

With that, Renee walked back across the floor leaving a trail of cigarette smoke, and Temperance watched her leave. Renee epitomised the glamour of the Palais in a way Temperance wasn't sure she ever would.

When she had first started working at the Palais, she had been overawed by the sheer beauty of what had formerly been a tram shed transformed into the most luxurious dance hall in Europe, famous for its maple-sprung dance floor and Chinese-influenced interior design.

Temperance glanced upwards at the giant pagoda roof, complete with brightly coloured silk lanterns that hung from the ceiling and lacquered glass panels, each one elegantly decorated with Chinese scenes. Tall, black columns with intricately painted gold letters stood at each corner, and the central mountain, with a replica mountain range, which stood in the centre of the floor. But for Temperance it was the replica temple at the front of the dance hall that was the Palais's showpiece. Providing the perfect stage for whichever band was entertaining the crowds, the temple was impossibly exotic. She glanced at it now and smiled, remembering that it was when they'd been dancing before that little temple that she and Archie had realised they had feelings for one another.

But all daydreams of Archie were knocked clean from her head, as an influx of people, largely GIs, suddenly made their way through the doors. Temperance felt a shiver of excitement, as she did before every Friday night dance. There was something special about this first night of the weekend, the anticipation of all that lay ahead.

And it was then she saw her sweetheart walking towards

her. Dressed in a lounge suit, his hair pomaded neatly away from his angular face, Archie always had the power to take her breath away. But as he approached her, his face full of smiles, she couldn't help notice his usual grin didn't reach his eyes.

'Everything all right?' she asked, as he reached her side.

'Fine,' Archie replied a little brusquely. 'Just a busy day at the shop.'

Temperance wrinkled her nose. She knew how hard he was finding managing the shop on his own. 'Have you thought any more about taking on a junior?'

Archie gave a hollow laugh. 'Chance'd be a fine thing. All the lads who could come and do that job have been called up.' He sighed. 'I'll just have to manage . . .'

His voice trailed off as he looked around the room and gave a bemused shake of his head. 'I just hope our lot are having as good a time as these lads.'

Temperance followed his gaze and saw how it looked. Hordes of Americans in smart uniforms and cheery smiles laughing and shouting in the confident way they had. She saw a group of them now looking her way, then exchanging whispers. She knew why, and that they were part of the problem she faced too often.

It was well known that the GIs believed that whites and blacks should be kept apart, that they had separate armies for each race; they'd even lobbied the British government when they arrived here, for them to do the same.

Thankfully, the government had refused but the message wasn't lost on black people across the country. Americans thought blacks weren't worthy of mixing with whites. The thought of those men, now, talking about her, judging her, criticising her purely because of the colour of her skin, made Temperance not only feel angry, but also alone.

She looked up at Archie. He was engrossed in conversation with Violet, laughing about something, and to her surprise she felt a fresh wave of anger. How could he stand there laughing with his friend when it was so obvious that a group of men opposite them were making pointed, cheap jibes about her? Temperance wanted to scream, to say something to these men, but most of all to Archie. But she knew there was no point, that there were some battles you couldn't hope to win. As she ran her eyes across Archie's face, as familiar to her as her own, she felt a pang of regret. There was so much they shared, so much they understood about one another, but there was one thing that they would never understand about each other – what it was like to live in each other's skin.

8

As a gaggle of GIs walked past her, loud with their never-ending stream of laughter, Nancy felt a wave of homesickness. In all the years she had lived in Britain she thought she had got used to English eccentricities and an English way of life. In fact, if it weren't for her parents and siblings, she rarely thought of her native New York at all. But now, hearing those familiar accents and the way the American boys laughed and presented themselves to the world – proud of who they were – Nancy felt a surge of homesickness, in a way she never had before.

She shook off the feeling, and turned back to the pile of papers that stood in front of her. She had a lot of work to go through before the first site visit to the new Bethnal Green hall tomorrow, and she wanted to be prepared.

'Buy you a drink, honey?'

Honey. When was the last time anyone had called her that? Nancy looked into the twinkling blue eyes of the GI who had interrupted her and smiled as she gestured to her water.

The GI made a face, his aquiline nose crinkling in disgust. 'Where's the fun in water?'

'When you're working, there's plenty of fun in water,' Nancy said pleasantly.

At the sound of her accent he beamed, and lifted his glass of beer.

'American.' It wasn't a question.

Nancy nodded. 'New York. You?'

'Colorado,' he replied. 'You're a long way from home. What

brought you here? It couldn't be the weather.' They laughed in the knowing way foreigners did at the British weather, famous for its rain. 'So what's a pretty girl like you doing in a place like this?' he added.

Nancy couldn't help herself and threw her head back with laughter.

'Oh, wow. I've missed that American arrogance.'

The GI raised an eyebrow. 'Arrogance, huh?'

'Honey, you're sweet but I'm old enough to be your very big sister, if we were being kind.' Nancy wiped the tears of laughter from her green eyes and looked at the GI. She was pleased to see now that he looked more relaxed and less like he wanted to play a game of courtship. He was probably a good five years younger than she was and he seemed almost apologetic.

'Sorry. I got carried away . . . chatting to a pretty American girl. Reminds me of home you know?' When Nancy smirked, he shook his head. 'You *are* pretty.'

'But probably not a girl,' Nancy quipped.

At that, the two clinked their glasses and laughed. For a moment Nancy lost herself in the light relief of talking to a man without pressure or judgement. Someone who knew her reference points. America and England may share a language but that often seemed to be where the similarities ended. To Nancy it sometimes felt as if they were worlds apart.

'So what are you doing here, if you don't mind me asking, ma'am?'

'You can quit the ma'am stuff,' Nancy said, extending her hand. 'I'm Nancy.'

'John,' the GI replied, taking her hand and shaking it.

'And now that we're acquainted, I can tell you I run this joint.'

John looked at her, impressed, his blue eyes quizzical at a woman in authority.

'It's a wonderful venue,' he said.

'I like it,' Nancy replied. 'I've been running it almost ten years now.'

'You've been here that long!' John exclaimed. 'Tell me, do you ever get used to the food here?'

'No!' Nancy shook her head and laughed. 'There are days I'd kill for an ice-cold Coca-Cola.'

At the thought of the fizzy drink she had grown up with Nancy's eyes closed with delight.

'Well, then, you should come over to the Rainbow Rooms sometime,' John said pleasantly. 'I'll treat you to as much Coca-Cola as you like.'

Nancy narrowed her eyes. She had of course heard of the club in Piccadilly where many American soldiers relaxed and let loose. Best of all, there was no food rationing there, so GIs could indulge in all their homeland favourites: juicy burgers, sodas, beers and doughnuts. Up to now, the Rainbow Rooms had been the stuff of legend, but now, here she was, being invited in to enjoy food and drink she hadn't tasted in years. It seemed too good to be true, and she was about to say as much when she heard a commotion across the dance floor.

She looked apologetically at John and turned to the sound of the disturbance, spotting a group of white GIs remonstrating with two black soldiers. At once, anger burned; Nancy knew what the problem was.

The look on her face must have said it all as John got to his feet. 'Goddammit. I told Hoover and Glen not to get into this tonight.'

'Get into what?' Nancy asked.

John shook his head. 'They've got a bee in their bonnet about the Palais allowing black soldiers in. They said if they saw any tonight they were going to make a noise.'

Nancy bristled with anger. There had been enough trouble

in her dance hall over the years: she wasn't about to allow a group of numbskulls to cause problems over the colour of people's skin.

Spotting Janice making her way towards the group Nancy was hot on her heels. Together they rounded on the men.

'What's going on?' Janice asked briskly.

'We were just telling these fellas here they have no place in this dance hall,' the man Nancy guessed to be Hoover replied.

'And why is that?' Nancy asked.

At the sound of her accent she saw the man's face relax.

'OK, so you're American. You get why us and blacks can't and *shouldn't* mix.'

Running a tongue over her teeth she glared at the men.

'I might be American, but you're wrong, I don't understand and I don't want to. I'm sick of you trying to ram it down our throats. This is England, honey, and in England we mix.'

Hoover bristled and drew himself up to his full five feet five inches. 'Sweetheart, this doesn't concern you. Let me speak to the manger.'

'She is the manager, you cheeky little twerp,' Janice growled, her cheeks now as red as the tea dress she was wearing. 'And let me tell you, if you don't like it here you are more than welcome to take your custom elsewhere.'

As the women squared their shoulders, Nancy was pleased to see Hoover and Glen look outfoxed. She turned back to see the black soldiers' reaction.

'Are you guys OK?' she asked.

The taller of the two nodded. 'Yes, ma'am, and thank you.'

'No thanks necessary,' Nancy replied. As her eyes caught sight of the bar manager, Sybil Hancock, scurrying past, she waved and caught her attention. 'Sweetheart, fix these two fellas up with whatever they want to drink for the rest of the night.'

'Oh, no, ma'am, that's really not necessary,' the other black soldier said, looking hesitant.

Nancy could see he was embarrassed and immediately felt guilty. But, no, manners were everything and she was ashamed of her countrymen in that moment.

'Please,' she said softly. 'Let me help make this right.'

Then she turned back to Glen and Hoover, whose eyes were alight with irritation.

'You can't mean that. Surely you can see these guys have no place here. They shouldn't be mixing with us.'

How dare they?

'I decide who comes in this dance hall, not you,' Nancy said, her own eyes flaring with anger now. 'And for now I've decided who's welcome in here and it certainly isn't you. Now get out and climb right back under whatever rock it is you crawled out from.'

Hoover let out an angry grunt and look beyond Nancy's left shoulder. She turned and saw John hovering nearby.

'Lieutenant, please talk to this woman. You can see I was doing nothing wrong. It's them that should be thrown out, not us.'

John narrowed his eyes at his charges. 'You are guests not only of this lady's establishment but in this country. If she has asked you to leave then you do as she says. That's an order.'

'But, sir,' Hoover wheedled.

'He said, that's a bleedin' order!' Janice snapped, so abruptly and so loudly that Nancy nearly jumped. 'Now get out of here before I crown the pair of you. And don't bloody come back either.'

With that the two soldiers slunk away, muttering to themselves and each other about how they would make sure the place was ruined, but Nancy didn't care. She hated racial segregation and wanted no part of it in her dance hall.

She turned back to look at the black American soldiers but

saw they too had disappeared. The only person left standing was Temperance, a mix of anger and hurt on her face, and for the first time in her life Nancy felt utterly helpless.

9

Standing on the corner of the proposed new East End dance hall, Renee tried to ignore the sinking feeling in the pit of her stomach. She rarely ventured to this side of London; she had no reason to. But although she knew of the bomb damage – it would be impossible to live in the city and not know how bad the East End had had it – Renee felt nothing short of desperate at the site before her.

Bombed-out ruins of houses nestled against those that hadn't been touched. Bricks and debris lined the streets, despite the fact that volunteers had done their best to clear up, whilst signs of lives torn apart in the form of unclaimed treasures and abandoned household essentials – photographs, washing lines, even a teddy bear – lay amongst the wreckage.

Of course, Renee had seen this before. They'd suffered enough damage over west, no matter what the East Enders thought. The difference was, that the damage in the east was so brutal, and worryingly it surrounded the proposed new dance hall site, not five minutes' walk from the unfinished Bethnal Green Tube station.

As the sun shone on the disused theatre that had narrowly escaped ruin, Renee narrowed her eyes and tried to picture its potential. It hadn't been used for years, and had a general air of neglect. But there was still something beautiful about it. The stained glass windows were a beauty as were the columns that framed the flat-roofed building. The wide front doors with arched entrance were also inviting. Yet there was something about it that made Renee feel uncomfortable. It wasn't the devastation surrounding the would-be dance hall, it was the church, which stood just feet away. For some reason, Renee couldn't take her eyes off it.

As a child she had been brought up with religion, taught to believe in God, say her prayers and go to Sunday school each week. Yet after her mum died and her father had brought nothing but trouble to her door, Renee had stopped believing somewhere along the line, likening God to just another fairy story, a nice thing to believe in but not relevant for the likes of her. But as she looked up at Roger now, tall and dressed in his clerical dog collar, he looked over the moon surveying the new site, and she could see why it was perfect for him. This dance hall would only be yards from the church, so the ministry could keep an eye on the place; prevent young couples from getting up to too much mischief. Though at the thought, Renee had to smile. In her experience, young couples who were hell-bent on mischief-making would always find a way.

'What do you think?' Roger asked, turning to meet her gaze. His face was full of pride, as if he had just asked her to dance with Fred Astaire himself.

Renee smiled and turned to the Good Time Girls, who she'd convinced to come over to the East End with her. 'I think there's a lot of work to do.'

'Not that much!' Violet exclaimed. 'A lick of paint here and there, maybe.'

Renee shook her head. Violet was fast coming up through the ranks, proving herself capable, no mean feat with a baby to look after single-handedly, but she still had a heck of a lot to learn about the dance business.

'Nancy, what do you think?' Renee asked.

'I think if we're going to make it the sister site to the Palais we've got our work cut out,' Nancy said brusquely.

'I agree,' Janice offered. 'You've got a good one here, Vicar, but there's a lot to do. When were you thinking of opening?'

Suddenly surrounded by these questioning women, Roger looked overwhelmed.

'I don't know . . . I was hoping before Christmas.'

At this the Good Time Girls laughed, even Temperance, who up until now had looked sympathetic towards the vicar.

'Is there really that much to do?' Roger asked, a little deflated.

'We'll need to repaint the front,' Violet said firmly, sticking to her paint theme. 'And there's the repairs to the render, too. This will be the dance hall's shop window; we want people to be excited about coming inside.'

'But it'll be dark,' Roger pointed out, looking slightly aghast. 'Will that matter?'

At this the women scoffed and shook their heads.

'People will pass this place in the day,' Temperance explained. 'If they see a tatty-looking outfit they're not going to want to come inside.'

'And when they're inside they'll expect to find a maple-sprung dance floor,' Renee mused. 'Needs to be done by someone who knows what they're doing as well, not just any Tom, Dick or Harry.'

'And then there's the band pit,' Nancy put in. 'Though as this was a theatre, there's a chance there might be something already in there we can use.'

At this the women murmured in agreement.

'But if we're looking for this place to be a bit more than a dance hall, more of a community place, we'll also need to make sure there's a good kitchen,' Betty declared.

'Very true, that, queen.' Renee nodded approvingly.

She turned to Roger. 'As you can see, we've got a lot to think about, and that's before we've even got inside.'

'Then perhaps we should go in?' Roger suggested.

'Are you sure, Vicar?' Janice cackled. 'You never know what else we'll find to do when we get inside.'

The women laughed again in unison and Renee was reminded of just how much she adored them and appreciated their company.

As they trooped inside, Renee tried not to let out a shiver of despair. The place stank of must and the dust was an inch thick. Reaching what had been the auditorium she did her best to look around through the half-light.

'I'm guessing there's no electricity in here?' Nancy asked.

The vicar shook his head. 'We expect to get that put in imminently.'

Renee said nothing, but glancing at Roger, she saw he looked quite defeated, his eyes downcast, as if he were a little boy who had just discovered there was no such thing as Santa Claus. It was a look she had never seen her late husband wear, and seeing it now on Roger reminded her of just how different the brothers were.

'I'm sure between us all and with the help of people who know what they're doing, we can get this place ready in good time,' she said, though not really believing it.

But the moment the words left her mouth, Renee knew she had said the right thing as his face brightened immediately. 'Do you really think so?'

'Course, love,' Betty said in a no-nonsense fashion, quickly sensing what Renee was trying to achieve. 'You just wait, we'll get this place together for you.'

'Though it might take a bit longer than a few months, honey,' Nancy said cautiously. 'We have to remember there's a war on. Not only are materials hard to find but all the fellas will have been called up.'

'Which is why we can do some of this ourselves,' Renee said determinedly. 'We'll beg, borrow and steal manpower.'

'And perhaps we can run a slightly smaller-scale version of the Palais in the meantime?' Temperance suggested.

Renee looked at her friends gratefully. They were saying

just what the vicar needed to hear, even if they did have serious doubts.

'There, we'll have this place sorted, don't you worry,' Janice said cheerfully.

Roger smiled in relief, and clapped his hands together happily. 'I knew you'd see the vision for this place. And think how much good we can do the community from here.'

'Course, Roger.' Renee nodded. 'Together you can rely on us.'

'Well, I think this calls for a cup of tea to celebrate,' Roger announced.

'Good idea, Vicar,' Janice agreed. 'As long as it's not in here. A mouse just ran over me foot, and I don't mind telling you it's right turned my stomach.'

10

Later that morning, the Good Time Girls arrived back at Hammersmith Tube and wandered over to the Palais. They hadn't stopped talking since they'd left, and kept going over the topic of the new dance hall.

'Roger can't honestly expect us to recreate the Palais in that old theatre, can he?' Janice asked for the umpteenth time.

Violet smiled. They may not be able to perform the impossible, but since she'd started working at the Palais the one thing she'd discovered early on was just how determined each of the women who worked there was, no one more so than Renee. Violet knew that Renee would shift heaven and earth to make the new East End dance hall the second coming.

'I don't think we can ever hope to recreate the Palais, honey,' Nancy said now. 'But we can do something different.'

'Perhaps something more community-minded,' Betty put in helpfully.

Violet smiled at her mother, and linked her arm through hers. She knew how hard she was finding life at the moment. With Violet's twin brother Roy killed in the war, Maisie away in the army, and Alan back in Birmingham, Betty was having a tough time. This show of support for the Palais's new venture was Betty's way of coping.

'Have you thought how we might help?' Violet asked, worried she wouldn't be able to commit enough time to the project. Her work at the Palais, not to mention the fact she cared for Eamon, was bound to slow her down. She bit her lip. She hated not being able to do as much as the others, that she wouldn't be thought of as a team player, but she wanted to try. That had to count for something.

'Don't worry, honey,' Nancy said, turning back and smiling over her left shoulder. 'We can work that out in plenty of time.'

'Where's little Eamon today?' Temperance asked.

'Your mum's got him,' Violet replied, with a hint of affection. Eamon and Temperance's mother, Enid, had been nothing short of helpful since the baby's arrival. Violet checked her watch. 'In fact, she should be at the Palais with him now. I said I'd pick him up at two and it's ten past.'

'Don't worry,' Temperance soothed. 'You know how besotted Ma is with Eamon.'

'I know, but I don't like to take advantage,' Violet replied earnestly.

It was true. She hated feeling like she owed people favours. As a mother raising a child alone she was already far too reliant on other people for help. But at the same time, if it meant Eamon had the best possible life then she would do it. The thought of her precious child left her with a rush of love as it always did. She would walk over hot coals for that boy.

As they rounded the corner of Brook Green Road and the white neoclassical Palais came into sight it was all Violet could do not to run down the road, find her child and scoop him up in her arms.

But, as was proper, she restrained herself. Walking into the bar where she had agreed to meet Enid, her eyes landed first on her son sleeping soundly in his pram. And secondly they alighted on Enid who, to her surprise, was enjoying a cup of tea with Edna.

Violet and Nancy exchanged wary looks, but Nancy was the first to recover as she walked towards her mother-in-law, arms outstretched in welcome.

'Edna, I didn't know you were popping in to see us today,' she exclaimed, giving the older woman a light embrace.

Violet smirked. It was well known amongst the Palais folk that there was no love lost between the two women, but good old Nancy was acting as though Edna was a much-missed friend.

Edna released herself and patted her elegant grey chignon. 'I was just passing, dear. Thought I'd see if Ruth and Peter were around. But of course Ruth is at school and Peter at work, so Enid here took pity on me and suggested we have a cup of tea together.'

'How lovely,' Nancy said brightly.

'It has been lovely.' Enid beamed. 'I don't get to go out much so when I saw Edna I suggested we have a little gossip. Catch up on our news.'

'Not that I've got much news,' Edna said, with a sigh. 'Not now I'm retired.'

Violet saw a flicker of irritation cross Nancy's face.

'Honey, that was your choice, but you know that you're welcome back here any time.'

'Nancy's right, queen,' Renee put in. 'Especially now we've got this second dance hall to open. It'll be all hands on deck; I wondered if you might be interested in showing off your talents.'

At the mention of the word *talents*, Edna's blue eyes lit up. 'I could, of course, but do you think that the East End is really where we ought to be opening a second dance hall?' She shivered as she uttered the word *east*. 'I mean, it's got a certain charm that side of London of course, but is it really the best place? What about Kensington, or even Chelsea?'

Nancy bristled, but Renee smiled. 'Come on, Edna, even them up the East End have a right to a night out.'

'And besides . . .' Violet paused in peppering her boy's face with kisses as he giggled in delight. 'This second dance hall is more of a community project. You know how the people are suffering over there.'

'We've hardly got off scot-free ourselves,' Edna protested. 'Jerry's sent plenty of bombs up west.'

'But he started over east, don't forget,' Violet said sharply. 'I was there that night he bombed the docks.'

At that, everyone fell silent for a moment. Nobody could forget how Violet had been called upon to help the WVS that fateful Saturday night in September two years ago and how her sweetheart had died in her arms.

'Hmmm,' Edna said non-committally, breaking the silence. 'I'll think about it.'

But Violet knew Edna would do more than just think about it; she would hound Nancy and Renee until she was given star billing on opening night. Some things never changed, and for that Violet was grateful.

'And if there's anything I can do, I'd be more than happy to be involved,' Enid said in a small voice.

Violet looked at Enid in surprise. Since the death of her son, baby Eamon's father, Enid had become something of a recluse, not venturing out much beyond WVS duties. Queenie had tried to take her under her wing, recognising how grief-stricken the woman was, losing both her son and her husband in the space of two years, but although Enid had gone through the motions she always seemed grateful to return home. The only time Violet ever saw Enid smile these days was when she was in the company of her grandson.

'Would you really, Mother?' Temperance asked now in surprise.

'Yes,' Enid said with an air of determination. 'I think it might do me good to get out. Course, I can't dance.'

'You're a wonderful dancer,' Temperance said softly. 'You and Dad used to dance all over the house to his calypso tunes.'

A wistful look passed across Enid's face at the memory. 'We did,' she said, looking down at Eamon who was still sleeping in his pram. 'But I think my dancing days are over for the moment. There must be other ways I can help, though?'

Betty pulled up a chair beside Enid. 'If you're interested, I'm taking on the cooking. Unlike this place, the new dance hall is going to be a refuge for those what have been bombed out, so the least we can do is give folk a hot meal.'

'My cooking skills are a bit rusty.' Enid looked doubtful, but Betty patted her hand.

'Don't you worry. I'll be keeping it simple. Perhaps we can chat through recipes one night, when one of us is looking after this little lad?'

Enid nodded, looking pleased, just as Eamon began to stir as if sensing he was being talked about.

'How has he been?' Violet asked now, as she picked him up out of his pram for another cuddle. She leaned in and inhaled the scent of his fuzzy head. How she wished she could bottle that smell.

'Lovely as always.' Enid clucked. 'He's just like his dad was at that age, full of fun.'

'How on earth would you know that?' Edna asked, her eyes shrewd with suspicion. 'You didn't know Eamon's father, did you?'

Panic rose within Violet at Enid's slip-up. She adored Eamon's grandmother, of course she did, but this wasn't the first time Enid had nearly given the game away. Eamon's true parentage was only known by a discreet few within Violet's inner circle. Edna wasn't a part of that circle, and never would be, as far as Violet was concerned.

'Well that's just it,' Enid said calmly. 'We think of baby Eamon so much as our own lad, that I just think of my son as his father. Maybe it's the colour of baby's skin, too – like mine and my family's. It's no secret how much my boy and Violet were in love, and that marriage and family was the way their relationship was heading. That's how I like to think of it, anyway. So I see baby Eamon here as much my grandson as if he were my flesh and blood.'

'And that's a lovely way to think,' Betty said smoothly. 'I'm sure your boy would be proud if he could see you now.'

Enid's eyes filled with tears. 'I hope so. It's just it's a wonderful thing Violet's doing and this little baby means the world to me.'

'He means the world to all of us,' Temperance said gently.

'That, I can see.' Picking up her cup, Edna took a gulp of her tea before looking around at them all. 'But be careful, Enid,' she said. 'It would be a terrible thing for Violet if you said something like that in the wrong company. Misunderstandings can lead to dreadful complications, you see.' She stood and put her coat on. 'I must get off now. Bye all.'

As Edna sashayed out of the bar, teetering on three-inch heels, Violet felt a surge of worry and pressed Eamon close. Edna was right. One wrong word could have terrible ramifications for her and the life of this child she loved more than anything else in the world. She glanced at Enid who looked as if nothing had happened. She was going to have to talk to her to ensure she took more care over what she said. Not just for herself, but for the life of her grandson.

11

Later that night Temperance found herself in an old and almost forgotten position of cloakroom assistant. Two of the girls were off ill and so Temperance had volunteered her services. For some, she knew that a demotion, even for one night, would be seen as a slur, but not for Temperance. She enjoyed every aspect of her work and was always happy to lend a hand at the Palais. As far as Temperance was concerned, the Palais wasn't just a job, it was a second home, and she would always go out of her way to do whatever the place needed.

Still, though, as she looked around at the sea of dancers waltzing across the dance floor, she wished she could be in the pen. Temperance had never overtly refused the opportunity to work as a professional dancer, and certainly after winning the dance competition over eighteen months ago with Archie as her partner it would have seemed then possible that attitudes had changed, that the time was right for a black dancer in the pen.

But Temperance had never even thought of it. Instead she had chosen a life in dance behind the scenes, preferring instead to flex her dancing muscles away from prying eyes. Already in the short time she had been a qualified dance instructor, her expertise and skills had become renowned, not just locally but within the dance community. It was a role Temperance was largely happy with; she had never had ambition to be a top-class dancer like Renee. But looking at the pen dancers now, all showing their American GI partners a thing or two about English dancing, Temperance couldn't help wondering if her life as a backstage expert had been chosen for her, rather than what she'd chosen for herself. After all, how many of the dancers here now would have paid their sixpence to dance with the black girl? With so many American GIs in the country, Britain may not have segregation in effect but it's more than likely a dancer for hire like her would have caused a stir.

'Hey, there, could I please swap my shoes?'

A young American voice made her jump to attention.

'So sorry,' she said smiling in apology at the handsome black soldier who was handing her his hobnail boots. Automatically, she took his shoes and checked the size. Shortly after the outbreak of war the Palais had started to run a shoe swap scheme for soldiers where they could exchange their hobnail boots for a pair of dance shoes for the evening. To many it seemed a selfless endeavour, but Temperance knew it was because the Palais board – the group of directors that owned the Palais alongside Renee and her lion's share – were concerned about the expensive maple-sprung floor being damaged by hundreds of pairs of thick, heavy boots.

Seeing the soldier's shoes were a men's size eleven, Temperance winced apologetically. She was out of a lot of the larger shoe sizes.

'I'm sorry,' she said. 'I can offer you a ten or a twelve?'

She watched as the man did a quick calculation. 'That's a US forty-three or forty-five, right?'

Temperance nodded hesitantly and the man laughed.

'OK, honey, I'll take the twelves. My feet are so crunched up in those boots all day, they'd appreciate the chance to breathe.'

Handing the soldier his shoes, Temperance took a moment to look at him and realised he was one of the soldiers who had been at the heart of all the upset the other week. The soldier who had been ridiculed by the whites simply for his skin colour.

Feeling her eyes upon him, the soldier looked up and smiled as he did up his shoes.

'You OK? Have I gotten something on my teeth?'

As he flashed a good set of teeth at her, Temperance felt embarrassed. He was tall, with broad shoulders and large eyes that Temperance could see were full of fun. She shook her head, and was about to turn away when curiosity got the better of her.

'Doesn't it upset you?' she asked, bluntly.

The soldier looked confused for a second. 'Doesn't what upset me?'

'All them out there.' Temperance waved her hand absent-mindedly towards the dance hall.

'People?' the soldier guessed.

'White people,' Temperance lowered her voice.

A look of understanding flashed across his face. But instead of answering straight away, he took a second to examine her. Temperance was surprised to see compassion pass across his features as he drew himself up to his full height.

'Does it upset *you*?'

Now it was Temperance's turn to feel confused.

'Why would it upset me?'

The soldier shrugged. 'You tell me why you think I'd be upset.'

Temperance already regretted asking the question, but her curiosity had burned so brightly she couldn't ignore it now.

'Because of the way the white soldiers treat you. Because of the way they think you shouldn't be here, the way they think you should be segregated just because of the colour of your skin.'

The soldier paused for a moment and then spoke.

'What's your name, honey?'

'Temperance Adams,' she replied.

'I'm Sergeant Stafford Gilkins,' he said, extending his hand. She took it and smiled, as he gently pumped it up and down. 'Well, Temperance, this seems like a mighty big conversation for a fella who just popped into this here dance hall for a little fun.'

'I'm sorry,' Temperance said. If nothing else Stafford was a soldier and a customer. Renee would have her guts for garters if she caught her upsetting the clientele.

'No need to be sorry.' Stafford shot her a smile. 'All I'm saying, is maybe it's not an easy question to answer.'

'No,' Temperance agreed.

'I mean, yes, of course I get upset and angry that white folks judge me on the colour of my skin. I wouldn't be human if I didn't feel that way. But to get through this life I've learned there's injustice all over the place, and if you can't get used to that, well, you're going to spend a lot of your life miserable.'

Temperance felt warmth bubble up inside her. It felt so refreshing to hear someone speak like this other than her Aunt Winnie.

'You remind me of my aunt,' she said. 'She's always telling people to stop moaning and start doing.'

Stafford nodded knowingly. 'Sounds an awful lot like my mother.' He looked at the shine on his newly polished dance shoes. 'The thing is, I just try to live my life and rise above it. We're supposed to be kept separate, just as we are in work, but there are places . . . like here . . . that turn a blind eye.'

Temperance shook her head. 'I don't know how you can stand it.'

'Temperance, sweetheart, I've only been in this country a few weeks, but already I'm amazed at how different things are here. There's no coloured parts of town, no coloured bars or restaurants. You don't even have coloureds-only drinking fountains or signs saying no coloureds to sit on the bus.'

'That's what you have in America?' Temperance said quietly.

Stafford nodded. 'In some of the southern states, yes. And there of course we're called trash and beaten by the whites.'

The way Stafford spoke was so matter-of-fact that Temperance thought her heart would break. She had thought things were bad enough in Britain, but to discover how terribly black people were treated across the pond was shocking. She knew, of course, that her father had suffered racial injustice all his life, right up until the day he died. And that when he had married her mother, a white woman, both of them had suffered racial abuse and beatings. Then there was Nancy, who Temperance had heard hold forth on the subject of racism in her homeland many a time. But to hear Stafford be so clinical with his language was something that shocked her to her very core.

'I don't know what I'd do,' she said at last. 'I think you're brave.'

Stafford laughed, and Temperance realised how much she liked the sound.

'Honey, I'm not brave. I'm just like you, doing whatever I can to serve my country and get us safely out of Hitler's way. But Britain is like a breath of fresh air for guys like me.'

Temperance raised an eyebrow. 'We've got our share of problems, believe me.'

'That may be so,' Stafford said. 'But you ain't gotten no colour bar, and that in itself is a blessing.'

Pausing for a moment she looked him in the eye. 'You should come to a meeting of the League of Coloured Peoples sometime, led by Dr Harold Moody. It's a movement he set up for equality between all races.' She reached for a pen and paper behind the desk and wrote down the Camberwell address. 'If you ever get time, it's worth coming. People from all walks of life are there.'

Stafford surveyed the card and put it in his pocket. 'I might just do that. Equality, you say?'

Temperance nodded enthusiastically. 'It's something we're working hard to strive for. My brother was a big believer in Dr Moody and I'm ... well, I'm trying to do the same as him.' At the thought of Eamon she felt a pang of sadness that she tried to push out of her head. She couldn't afford to break down now, not in front of a perfect stranger.

He smiled and looked at the address before pocketing the card.

'My buddies are waiting, but thank you for this. Maybe I'll see you there.'

And as he walked away Temperance found herself hoping that she would see Stafford and she hoped it would be soon.

12

As Nancy sat at the bar beside Betty, she observed the exchange between the young American GI and Temperance. For some reason a sense of unease crept its way through her body and she couldn't place a finger on why. The soldier seemed perfectly nice; in fact, when she had spoken to him the other day following the altercation, he had apologised to her for causing trouble. It was unthinkable. The man was kind, well-mannered and, right now, he seemed mildly besotted with Temperance.

'You think there's trouble there?' Nancy asked, turning to Betty.

Betty frowned as she followed Nancy's gaze. 'Temperance? Good Lord, no. She'd never give a saint a day of trouble.'

Nancy smiled and took a sip of her gin and tonic. She found these days she was drinking more frequently, and given spirits were becoming increasingly hard to get hold of she knew this was a dangerous game. She shook her head and let the warmth of the alcohol seep through her soul. This wasn't the time to worry about her gin intake.

'Perhaps you're right,' Nancy said now. 'I mean, I'm hardly the greatest judge of relationships.'

Betty shot her a shrewd look as she took a sip of her port and lemon. 'Well, I'm certainly not.'

'Where is George this evening?'

'Out with the tote man, or some of Ronnie's friends.'

'Ronnie's friends?' Nancy echoed in horror. 'He still sees some of them?'

To everyone's surprise, last year George had become very

friendly with Ronnie Newsham. After his death, however, Nancy had assumed that all his friends and associates had crawled back under whatever rock they came from. Learning that George was still knocking about with some of them came as something of a surprise.

Betty shrugged. 'I think so. George keeps telling me they're continuing Ronnie's work. Something about "leaving a legacy"?'

'What?' Nancy spluttered. 'You can't be serious.'

'Unfortunately, I am.' Betty sighed.

Nancy couldn't miss the look of resignation on her friend's face. She took another slug of her drink, trying to shake the shock.

'And how do you feel about that?' she asked Betty.

'I don't care either way,' Betty said with a sigh, then, realising what she had said, covered her mouth in horror. 'I'm sorry. I shouldn't have said that.'

Nancy patted her knee reassuringly. 'Don't worry. I won't say a word.'

'I want to care,' Betty said now, desperation in her voice as she struggled to make sense of her feelings. 'But I don't. The only thing I care about is how long will George be out of the house and away from me.'

'That's not easy,' Nancy said sympathetically.

Betty's eyes filled with tears and she wiped them quickly away with the back of her hand. 'It's not. All I ever wanted was to be a good wife and mother. I never thought it would end up like this.'

'None of us ever do,' Nancy said softly. She let out a breath she hadn't realised she had been holding. 'Since we're swapping confidences, I might as well tell you Alex is coming home for a visit next month.'

Betty smiled now. 'You must be thrilled.'

'I should be, but I'm not,' Nancy admitted. 'I'm dreading it.'

'Why?' Betty asked, her mouth falling open in surprise.

'Because we're like strangers in our letters now,' Nancy explained. 'I feel like I'm reading notes from a long-lost uncle, rather than my husband.'

'Sure, that's natural,' Betty exclaimed. 'You've been apart so long now, and war does terrible things to a person.'

'Exactly,' Nancy said, brushing a piece of imaginary lint from her A-line, navy skirt. 'Honey, I've a feeling Alex and I are total strangers to each other now, and this visit of his is only going to highlight that.'

'You don't know that,' Betty consoled her. 'It could be just what you both need. And he'll get the chance to meet the children and spend time with them.'

At that, Nancy relented. She had to admit she hadn't given the children a lot of thought in this; too busy thinking about herself. She shook her head. Some mother she would have made! Perhaps it was a blessing she had never had children.

'Maybe you're right.' Nancy sighed. 'I just can't think how to talk to him, how to *be with him* anymore.'

'It'll come back,' Betty reassured her. 'You just have to give it time. The moment he returns you'll feel like you used to around one another.'

Nancy sighed again, and pushed her brown hair out of her eyes. It was in desperate need of a cut, but there never seemed to be the time to look after herself like she used to. She examined a nail; it was chipped and broken. The old Nancy would never have walked about like this. What was happening to her? If beauty was apparently a duty, she wasn't performing her duty very well.

'He's only here for three days,' she told Betty. 'Time is the one thing we don't have.'

'Then you'll have to do the best you can with the time you have,' Betty said firmly. 'You're married, Nancy. Lots of couples feel this way. How many women do you think waved good-bye to their husbands and now feel they're married to a total stranger? We get on with it because it's marriage. It's all part of the promises we made.'

Nancy considered Betty's wisdom. She was right. In a way it didn't really matter what she thought about this, and worrying wasn't going to help. The simple truth of the matter was that she and Alex were married and they had to make it all right. She glanced at Betty. Knowing that whatever she felt about her own marriage, Betty's was on a cliff edge.

'Was that how you felt when George came back from Dunkirk?' Nancy asked, gazing into Betty's pale face.

'No,' Betty said shortly. 'Because any hint of love in my marriage to George had disappeared long before he were injured. But I knew as his wife it was my place to make sure he was well looked after. It wasn't a choice or a question, it was just something I did.'

Nancy shook her head in disbelief. 'It makes marriage sound like an awful chore, honey.'

'If I were you I'd have some things planned for when he gets home,' Betty said brightly, pointedly ignoring Nancy's last assertion. 'Maybe a trip to the pictures, so if you're worried about conversation you don't have to talk much. Send him out to bond with the children without you, a walk in the park, something like that. If it's too much there will be ways for you to cope, Nancy. Trust me, I've managed to find them.'

A wave of sadness coursed through Nancy as she gazed at her friend. When Betty's daughters had first started working at the Palais, Nancy had been dismayed and amused in equal measure to discover Betty thought that working there was nothing short of dancing with the devil. But after a while Betty had come to see the Palais for what it was: a place for everyone to relax and let their hair down. And in time, it had become Betty's salvation, when she started to work there herself; a precious escape from her husband when she was struggling to cope.

She was about to say how brave she thought Betty was, when the sight of Roger strolling into the bar caught her by surprise.

'That Roger?' Betty asked, squinting to see.

Nancy nodded. 'And it looks like he's not alone.'

Behind the vicar, laughing and joking, were three men Nancy thought she would never see again – acquaintances of Ronnie Newsham. The question was why were they with the vicar, and what on earth were they doing at the Palais?

13

As the group of men filed into the dance hall, and the music of Oscar Reyburn and his band providing the perfect soundtrack to her thumping heart, Renee was very tempted to run and hide.

Like Nancy, she thought she would never see those men again, especially after the last time. Shutting her eyes, she remembered that horrific night when she had last seen her husband. The violence these men had been a part of. The sound of her heels connecting with the wooden stairs as she raced up to the office, desperate to get away. And then, what came next. Ronnie, lying in a pool of his own blood. She and Nancy standing over him, horrified at the events that had played out before them, events that when she thinks of them now, Renee can't believe she was a part of.

Not that she had ever felt any guilt. Ronnie was a terrible man. He deserved his fate. And these friends of his, strolling into her Palais as if they owned the place, smiles on their faces, deserved never to feel joy again. And they certainly didn't deserve to feel it in *her* Palais.

Striding out of the dancers' pen from where she had been watching, Renee couldn't help herself. Weaving her way determinedly through the throng, she set her sights on Roger and walked towards him. Seeing her, Roger lifted his arm and waved.

'I was hoping I'd find you here tonight,' he said smoothly.

Renee said nothing and glared at the trio of men behind him. As she surveyed them, she let out a start of surprise at one of them in particular, who had been mysteriously absent since the death of her husband.

'Mick. You're looking well,' she said. 'Certainly compared to the last time I saw you crumpled in a heap on the floor covered in your own blood.'

Her tone was sour, but she didn't care. Renee had worked too hard to put that night behind her, and she wanted nothing more than to forget the horror of what it was like being married to Ronnie. Now that his brother had brought her late husband's business associates into the bar, the memories of all she had endured came crashing down around her like a tidal wave.

At least Mick had the grace to look embarrassed. 'Nice to see you, Reen,' he mumbled.

'I wish I could say the same,' she snapped. 'I could swear you were on the run from the police? They thought you'd had something to do with Ronnie's death.'

Mick waved his hands as if he was swatting a fly. 'All a misunderstanding. Sorted out now.'

Renee frowned. She highly doubted that anything in Mick's world was sorted out, but she chose not to dwell any further. Turning to Roger, she saw the confusion in his eyes. 'Why have you brought these men here?'

For a moment he said nothing, and then turned to the men behind him. 'Order whatever you want, lads. I'm just going to have a chat with Renee.'

Taking her elbow in his hand he steered her away from the bar and out towards the foyer.

'Whatever is the matter?' he asked.

Renee looked at him. She could see he looked hurt, embarrassed even. She shook her head and let out a shaky breath.

'I'm sorry.' She paused. 'Actually, I'm not sorry. I'm angry you've brought these men into my Palais.'

'A Palais I gifted you,' Roger said, with a surprising hint of steel to his voice.

Renee looked at him, taken aback at his tone. She had never heard him talk that way before. To be honest, she didn't think he had it in him. She felt wrong-footed, but quickly recovered herself.

'A Palais I *earned*,' she said, meeting his gaze.

As her eyes fixed on his for a moment, she saw a flicker of irritation pass across them and for a second she thought she was looking into her late husband's face. With a jolt she found she couldn't stop staring; his expression seemed so familiar.

Then Roger sighed, and immediately the spell was broken.

'I'm sorry, Renee, you're right, of course you are,' he said, a familiar and kindly expression returning to his face once more. 'But there's a reason I brought these men here – and no, it wasn't to rub you up the wrong way,' he added, correctly sensing she was about to suggest as much.

'So why have you all come, then?' Renee asked, sulkily. She was aware she was behaving like a truculent child, but she was feeling distinctly rattled.

Roger frowned. 'I wanted to talk to you about the new dance hall. The adjustments you said we would make, the work that needs doing.'

Renee now felt a pang of guilt. It perhaps had seemed as though she and the rest of the Good Time Girls had poured cold water all over his dreams.

'We don't need to do everything,' she said gently. 'We just need to do some of it. Make sure Betty has a good kitchen, ensure there's a well-repaired and smooth dance floor.' She looked lovingly at the Palais's own maple-sprung floor and felt a pang of longing.

Roger laughed. 'I'm sorry, Renee. Our budget dance hall must be a disappointment.'

Renee quickly rallied. 'Not at all, love. I've danced all over the country and I can tell you, floors like this one—' she jabbed at it with her toe '—are a luxury few can afford.'

'Good.' Roger clapped his hands together and glanced at the men behind him. 'Because that's why I wanted to talk to you.

I know my brother was a bad apple, Renee, and I feel terrible I didn't do more for you. If I'd known, if I'd helped . . .'

His voice trailed off as Renee clamped her hand around his forearm.

'He's gone now, Roger,' she said gently. 'It's all in the past. We need to look forward.'

At this, Roger brightened. 'That's why I invited Mick and his friends here. When they heard about what I was doing in the East End they offered their services.'

'They've what?' Renee exclaimed.

'Come on, Renee,' Roger said gently. 'They want to make amends. It's important we turn the other cheek. They want to help. They've offered to get stuck in, rip up floors, that sort of thing.'

'You must want your head testing,' Renee scoffed. 'They'll swipe the lot. You can't trust them.'

As if to further emphasise her point she glared at the men still stood at the bar, who admittedly looked abashed as her gaze fell upon them.

'Renee, you know what I do,' Roger tried again. 'I'm a vicar, and part of being a vicar means I believe in second chances. These men heard about our plans, and I see it as an offer to make amends. They know their behaviour was less than exemplary, and Mick, I know, had a dreadful part to play in Ronnie's death.'

At that he broke off and Renee felt a pang of guilt at her own involvement in Ronnie's demise.

Roger took a deep breath and smiled at her. 'Now that Ronnie has gone, I think it's given them a chance to look at the way they have lived their lives until now. These men have expressed a desire to atone for their sins and I want to be able to help them do that. You should want the same, Renee.'

'Why?' she demanded.

'Because not only will it mean we get the Palais up and

running quicker, but also because I believe it will help you heal from the years of hurt Ronnie inflicted upon you.'

Renee looked away. Uncomfortable with Roger being so nice to her.

'My brother put you through a lot. I hoped that gifting you the Palais would help you come to terms with everything that went on, but I think the mental damage is too great,' Roger continued. 'By extending forgiveness to those closest to Ronnie, maybe you'll start to heal yourself.'

Renee turned back to look at him. She saw nothing but hope in his eyes and knew she didn't want to let him down.

'Fine,' she said with a sigh.

And as Roger smiled she was sure she had made the right decision.

But as Roger turned back towards Ronnie's old friends, Renee's gaze landed on Nancy. The look of fear in her friend's eyes was unmistakeable. In that moment Renee knew that there was no amount of forgiveness in the world that would help her come to terms with the fact that – no matter the excuses or justifications she routinely employed – she had killed a man to save herself.

14

July

As June marched into July, Violet and Queenie walked up the road towards the community centre. Violet lifted her face towards the sun and enjoyed the warmth. Since Eamon's birth, she'd been so rushed off her feet that she found she rarely had time to appreciate the small things in life, so feeling the sun on her skin was a simple pleasure she found she savoured all the more because she could share it with her boy.

She peered down at her son, who was beaming up at her contentedly. Her heart swelled with love at the adoration in his eyes. Eamon reminded Violet of his father in so many ways and the fact his eyes were the perfect replica of the man she had adored was a treasure Violet felt blessed to have every day.

'He looks like he's got wind,' Queenie said, interrupting Violet's train of thought.

Violet frowned. 'He does not have wind. I burped him before we left. He's smiling.'

As if keen to support his mother, Eamon gurgled in delight and pointed at her.

'See,' Violet said, with an air of triumph.

Queenie snorted with laughter. 'I'll say one thing, he's got your stubborn streak.'

Violet shook her head, then laughed. She felt lighter than she had for some time. Eamon was becoming easier now he was getting a little bit older. But there had been heartbreak, too, as she knew that her Eamon, her boy's father, would have delighted in watching his son grow and develop. She watched him now; a part of her couldn't help wonder if he would take after his father and she couldn't wait to find out.

As Violet and Queenie approached the community centre for their regular knitting circle, Violet couldn't wait to show Eamon off as she did every week. The ladies there always clucked over the baby, letting him play with the balls of wool and laughing as he tangled himself up in the yarns as if he were a cat rather than an infant.

'You seen your mother this week?' Queenie asked.

Violet shook her head. 'Not since we went east last Tuesday. Why?'

'Ah, it's nothing,' Queenie said evasively, removing her jacket and slinging it over her arm. 'Warm, isn't it?'

'What's nothing?' Violet asked.

'I'm just a bit worried about her. She's lost all her old sparkle.'

'Did Betty ever have any sparkle?' Violet asked, not unkindly.

Queenie considered the question as they strolled along the road.

'She had fire. She at least used to challenge George about his comings and goings. Now she just says nothing. It's as though she's completely given up.'

'Well, it's not really a surprise. Alan moving away has hit her hard,' Violet said.

'She should have gone with him. Made a new start.' Queenie sighed.

'She should,' Violet agreed. 'But she would never leave George; you know that.'

'I do.' Queenie sighed again and undid the top button of her tea dress.

As she did so, two women passing them tutted, and Queenie rolled her eyes.

'It's a top button, it's not as if I'm showing me knickers off in the street,' she snapped, angrily.

'Gran!' Violet admonished through giggles. 'You can't say things like that.'

'Well.' Queenie grimaced. 'You can say whatever you like at my age. It's one of the perks of getting old.'

There was a pause then as the two continued walking, Eamon's gurgles the only sound that could be hard.

'What about Alan? D'you hear from him much?' Queenie asked now.

'A bit,' Violet said. 'I think he's miserable without Betty. He keeps saying he could do with a fresh start himself.'

'You mean Birmingham isn't enough of a fresh start?' Queenie asked.

'I think he feels a bit lost. He invited me and Eamon to go and visit him.'

'You should,' Queenie said. 'Be good for you to spend time with your father.'

Violet said nothing.

'What's wrong? Don't tell me you don't want to?' Queenie pushed.

'It's not that,' Violet said uneasily. 'I think it might hurt Betty.'

'There's no reason for her to know, is there?' Queenie said as they rounded the corner. As the community centre came into view, they slowed their pace.

'I wouldn't feel comfortable lying to her about something like that. It's how this whole mess got started in the first place,' Violet said.

'True.' Queenie pushed open the door to the centre and hung

her coat up on one of the pegs. 'But your mother wouldn't want you missing out on a relationship with Alan on her account. Go and see him; it would be good for you.'

'Perhaps,' Violet said non-committally.

Lifting Eamon out of the pram, she balanced him on her hip and followed Queenie into the small room that was earmarked for the knitters. She smiled and waved at the little group of women already assembled on hard-backed chairs around a small table. Each had their own stash of wool, pilfered from old jumpers or blankets they had unravelled so they could knit socks for soldiers.

Violet set Eamon down on the floor and grinned at him as he gazed up at Mavis, the old lady Violet always sat next to.

'I think you've got a fan there,' Violet told her.

Mavis raised an eyebrow and turned away. 'If you say so.'

Violet frowned and glanced at Queenie, who shrugged and shook her head. Instead she encouraged Violet so sit down and pull out her knitting.

'How come there's not so many of us this week?' Queenie asked, settling herself in her own chair on one side of Violet. 'Was it something we said?'

'More like something you've brought,' Mavis said glaring down at Eamon.

'What did you say?' Violet's voice shook with anger.

She looked down at her baby, who was still gurgling up at Mavis, blissfully unaware that his presence was causing so much concern.

But Mavis only pursed her lips and returned to her knitting. Violet looked again at Queenie, wondering if she'd misheard Mavis. But judging by the look on Queenie's face it was clear she hadn't.

Queenie surveyed the rest of the room and saw the women had their heads bent low and were all very focused on their knitting.

'All right, girls, out with it. What's going on here?' Queenie barked sharply, causing the women to look up.

Mavis shifted uncomfortably in her seat and coughed, before Jean, one of the other women in the group who Violet knew to be kind, met her gaze.

'Violet, I'm sorry, but we don't think it's right you come here anymore.'

'What?' Violet felt as if she had been slapped. 'Why?'

Jean looked down at this point, but Queenie refused to let her get away with it.

'What are you on about, Jean? You've started now so you might as well finish. What's Violet supposed to have done?'

As if emphasising Queenie's point, Eamon let out a loud burp. It was all Violet could do not to giggle. Her son had perfect timing.

At the noise, Mavis rolled her eyes. 'And that is little more than we can expect from a *bastard*.'

She whispered the last word as if saying it would cause her to spontaneously combust, and any hint of humour that Violet might have been feeling was gone in an instant.

'What did you just call Eamon?' she hissed.

Glaring at Mavis, she balled her fists. It was all she could do not to leap up and slap the sanctimonious smirk from the woman's face.

'Violet, Mavis may not have put it the right way, but the truth is we know about Eamon's parentage. This pretence has to stop. We know that you're his mother, and that Enid Adams is that boy's rightful grandmother,' Jean said.

'You've the morals of an alley cat,' Mavis added nastily. 'Your kind don't belong here, and we'd thank you not to sully us with your presence. Now get out and get that boy away from me.'

With that, she looked down at Eamon and seeing he was blissfully playing with her ball of wool snatched it angrily from his hands.

A heady mix of anger and shock coursed through Violet. How did these women suddenly know the truth about Eamon? She had said nothing. And up until recently the women she had knitted and gossiped with for weeks, if not months, hadn't known anything either.

But how they had discovered the truth wasn't important now. The only thing that mattered was getting her son away from these poisonous women. She scooped him up and pressed him to her body as if wanting to shield him from all the hurt that they wanted to inflict on her innocent child.

Queenie, though, had no such reservations. Violet glanced at her and saw her grandmother was puce with rage.

'Never in my life have I been so ashamed as I am in this moment.'

'You should be,' Mavis cried, clearly warming to her theme. 'With a granddaughter like Violet here, I'd be ashamed, too.'

'Not of Violet, of you, you spiteful old bitch,' Queenie roared.

At the sound of his grandmother's shrieks Eamon began to cry, but Queenie hadn't finished yet.

'Whatever you think you know about this little boy, you don't. And even if the vile things you're saying *are* true, what sort of a way is that to speak about a child who has done nothing wrong? It's *you* lot I'm ashamed of. *You* with your hypocrisy. May I remind you, Mavis Adcock, that your daughter was caught round the back of my allotment in a knee trembler a few years back with a fella that weren't her husband. And as for you, Jean Pitt, you're not as green as you're cabbage-looking, neither – don't think I ain't seen you helping yourself in Archie's butcher's to an extra egg when you think his back's turned. We all *know* you're a thieving little toerag, but we don't say nothing because we feel sorry for you, what with your Harold passing away, and we know times are hard. But you lot, you can't wait to stir up trouble can you? And for what? To cast judgement on this poor little mite. Knickers to the lot of you!'

The women let out a gasp of shock, but Queenie didn't care. Her whole body was quaking with rage – Violet had never seen her so angry.

'Come on, Violet, we're going. And God help me if I see any one of you horrible lot again.'

15

Meanwhile, in Brook Green Road, Temperance Adams found herself sharing a cup of tea and a sandwich with Archie during her lunch break. They'd both been working too hard lately, so Archie'd taken matters into his own hands by closing the shop for half an hour so that they could spend time with each other.

Temperance knew he was right. And so not only had they agreed to meet for a quick bite in the café across the road from the Palais, but they were also planning their next night out together.

'Do you want to see *One of Our Aircraft is Missing* or *The Foreman Went to France*?' Archie asked, peering at Temperance over the top of his newspaper.

'Eh?' Temperance grunted. She had been trying to focus on what Archie was saying but she was sure that the man standing at the counter ordering a strong black coffee was Stafford. As she peered at his back she was surprised to find how much she wanted it to be the American soldier. She hadn't seen him for almost three weeks, not since the night that she had given him a pair of shoes that were too large and they had swapped stories and thoughts about race. It wasn't that she was fixated on him, more that he had made her think. Although she had done her best to continue her brother's work and legacy with the LCP, Stafford had taken her back to a time when debates about the colour of their skin and their worth were commonplace at home, and she realised how much she had missed it. She suspected that race was a subject Archie felt uncomfortable about. Maybe because he was such a sunny, happy person by nature, who didn't like to dwell on anything too serious, but focused on the positive instead.

'Temperance? The pictures . . .' Archie prompted, with a hint of irritation in his voice as he rustled the paper at her. 'Any preference? Both are showing up the Ritzy.'

Temperance tuned back into what her sweetheart had been saying. 'What about *Mrs Miniver*? I love Greer Garson.'

'Me, too,' Archie said, leaning over the Formica table and kissing her nose. As he did so Temperance felt strangely shy.

'Arch,' she protested, pulling away and glancing around the café. 'People are looking.'

'Who cares?' Archie shrugged. 'They're just jealous I'm courting the prettiest girl in West London.'

'Not all of London, then?' she teased.

Folding his paper Archie shook his head in mock seriousness. 'Not all of London, no.'

Temperance swiped playfully at his hand and almost knocked her tea all over his newspaper.

'Steady,' he said. 'What's up with you this afternoon? You seem a bit on edge.'

'I'm all right,' she replied.

Fixing his steely blue eyes on her, Archie pursed his lips. 'I know you well enough to know when something's up. Now what is it?'

'Nothing,' Temperance said. She rested her chin in her hand. 'I'm just feeling guilty that I haven't been going to any LCP meetings lately.'

'Oh, sweetheart, don't feel guilty about that,' Archie said. 'You know your brother would understand how busy you are. Don't be so hard on yourself. You've ever such a lot going on at the moment. What with work, the new dance hall opening, not to mention baby Eamon and helping your mum out.'

'I know,' Temperance said. 'But I feel I ought to be doing more. My brother would have been appalled at the way the

American GIs are treated. I can't stop thinking about all the trouble we've had at the Palais lately.'

'But that's not your fault, Temp,' Archie said kindly.

He leaned over and squeezed her fingers. She looked at his pale hand for a moment, such a contrast with her own skin tone. Were they equal? Did Archie see her skin colour and not care, or was it something he didn't want to talk about?'

'Arch, don't you ever worry we're not the same?' she asked bluntly now.

'The same?' Archie tugged the peak of his cap over his brow and looked at her, clearly puzzled. 'What do you mean?'

Temperance felt a pang of regret that she had started this conversation. But she didn't want to back down now. This was the first time she had really broached the topic of race between them, and she knew that whatever was said now was important. She wanted Archie to understand that they were different, that they would have challenges in the future to face. She needed him to understand and not want to bury his head in the sand.

'I mean you're white and I'm black,' she pointed out.

Archie laughed and squeezed her hand. 'I know that, Temp. I'm not blind.'

'But you act as if it doesn't matter,' she replied.

'It doesn't matter to me,' Archie replied. 'All that matters is you're you and I'm me and we care about each other.' He leaned across the table and brought his face close to hers. 'Skin colour, height, weight, all that stuff – none of it matters, you know. Just you and me, we're what matter.'

Temperance opened her mouth about to say something else when she became aware of a figure standing by their table. She looked up and saw Stafford grinning at her. Her heart leapt at his smile, and she snatched her hand from Archie's.

'Dancing queen!' Stafford exclaimed. 'I thought it was you.'

Temperance felt her cheeks colour. 'Stafford. Hello.'

'How are you?' Stafford asked.

'I'm well. I haven't seen you at the Palais for a few weeks.'

Stafford sighed. 'You know how it is. White soldiers keeping us blacks on our toes.'

Temperance inwardly grimaced, mindful of the conversation she and Archie had just been having. Archie turned to the soldier and extended his hand.

'Archie Ledbetter. Nice to meet you.'

Stafford took Archie's hand and shook it. 'And you, sir. You work with Temperance at the Palais?'

'Sometimes,' Archie replied, taking back his hand. 'We do dance together.'

'And I bet you're a sweet mover,' Stafford said, turning back to Temperance. 'You'll have all the moves those white girls don't.'

Temperance chuckled. 'Actually, I mostly teach.'

Stafford looked impressed. 'I didn't know that. Good for you.'

'Temperance is a marvellous teacher,' Archie said. 'Thanks to her, we won a dance contest a couple of years ago.'

'I don't doubt it,' Stafford said. 'You'll have to let me have a dance with you next time I'm at the Palais.'

'I'm mainly behind the scenes,' Temperance said hurriedly. 'And I don't work every night.'

'I guessed not,' Stafford said. 'But me and some of the other boys will be in on Friday, if you're around? It'd be nice to see you.'

'Of course,' Temperance said quickly. She felt awkward, aware that she was gushing too much and that Archie was looking at her with curiosity in his eyes.

Stafford tipped his hat. 'Well, I'll look forward to it. Bye now. Nice to meet you, Archie Ledbetter.'

Archie waved politely goodbye. 'And you, Stamford.'

'Stafford,' Temperance corrected, when the soldier was out of earshot.

Archie shrugged. 'If you say so.' He paused and pursed his lips for a minute. 'Who is he?'

'I told you. Just a customer,' she said hotly.

Archie nodded then folded up his paper and got to his feet. 'Funny. I've never seen you so hot and bothered over a customer before. I'll see you tonight after work, providing of course you're not too busy talking to customers.'

With that, Archie left, and Temperance felt guilt surge through her as her sweetheart left the café without looking back. She leaned back in her chair. She loved the bones of Archie, had done since the moment they started courting. So why was Stafford suddenly having an effect on her? If her heart was entwined with Archie Ledbetter's, why was a GI soldier getting in her way?

16

Upstairs at the Palais, Renee was feeling as confused as Temperance. She hadn't stopped running through Roger's proposal since he suggested it. And now, as she discussed it over a strong cup of tea with Nancy in their shared office, she found herself choking on the words as Nancy looked at her aghast.

'Honey, are you sure you heard him right?' Nancy asked, her eyes filled with horror. 'Roger wants Ronnie's friends to help out with the new Palais?'

Renee nodded. 'That's what he says. Reckons that's the best way for the new dance hall to get off the ground.'

Nancy pinched the bridge of her nose and exhaled loudly. 'Are you sure? You don't think there's something else going on?'

'Like what?' Renee asked sharply, as though she had not wondered the same thing herself.

'Like, maybe he knows what really happened that night,' Nancy hissed. 'Maybe he's using Mick and his cronies to draw the truth out of us.'

'Don't be so flamin' daft!' Renee exclaimed, with more bravado than she felt. 'You've been reading too many Agatha Christie books! Of course he doesn't know. Even the police don't know. They closed the case, didn't they? As far as everyone was concerned it was a fight that got out of hand.'

'But what about Ronnie's friends then, huh?' Nancy continued. 'The police may not know, and let's say Roger doesn't know and he really is offering redemption to Ronnie's friends, but half of them were actually there that night. What if they don't believe it was a just a fight between Mick and Ronnie that got that out of hand?'

'Christ, queen, I'm confused just listening to that, but even if it's true, none of them would want to reopen old wounds,' Renee said.

'Mick threatened Ronnie with a knife,' Nancy said.

Renee shook her head so violently a strand of red hair fell from the bun pinned at the top of her head.

'Nancy. Mick fled the scene, remember, and for good reason. I'm telling you, he's not going to want to bring this up.'

Nancy said nothing and leaned back in her chair, observing Renee, who had to admit that she was hoping Nancy would calm her worries, not exacerbate them. Because behind her bravado, she shared Nancy's concerns.

Before he'd left the other night, Roger had invited her out to dinner for this evening, and Renee was still half tempted to cancel. Something she said to Nancy now.

'Don't be dumb, honey,' Nancy said bluntly. 'If he wants to take you to dinner, then you let him, and find out what else he knows. I thought you two were friends, anyhow.'

'We are.' Renee frowned.

'He seems smitten,' Nancy said sullenly.

'Smitten!' Renee exclaimed. 'He's a man of God.'

'Still a man, honey,' Nancy muttered darkly.

'And it's obvious your fella's been away too long if that's where your mind's going,' Renee said. She helped herself to another cup of tea from the pot on the little wooden table. 'When is Alex coming back, anyway? Couple of weeks, you said?'

Nancy sighed and Renee felt a pang of guilt she had been so insensitive. She knew her friend was worried about her husband's impending visit. But she had to admit she thought it would be good for Nancy to see Alex for the first time in almost two years; visits like this were a rare thing.

Not only that, but morale in the country was poor as the

Allied forces looked as if they were in trouble across Europe. German U-boats had attempted to destroy British ships, meaning UK ports were almost at a standstill. Then there was the battle in Egypt's El Alamein, which had begun this month after the Allied troops had been badly defeated by the Axis powers at Gazala a month earlier. From what Renee could gather from the papers Churchill had been full of fire, insisting that this was the battle that would win the war for Britain. So far, it wasn't going well and the Prime Minister had taken rather a battering in parliament for the British Army's lack of progress.

There was no doubt, from Renee's perspective, anyway, that Alex was probably as worried about this visit as Nancy, and, she imagined, he'd be needing reassurance – a bit of a lift – from her. What he would think about Nancy's big promotion at the Palais, Renee hadn't thought about. One problem at a time was her motto, and one she intended to stick to.

Just as Renee was about to say as much to her friend, there was a sharp rap at the door.

'Come in,' she barked.

Violet pushed the door open, looking badly shaken.

'Sweetheart, whatever is it?' Nancy asked.

Renee got to her feet and rushed to Violet's side, guiding her gently to the chair in the corner and nodding to Nancy who took the hint and busied herself arranging for more tea to be sent up.

'What the hell's happened?' Renee asked gently.

Violet shook her head and tried to still her breathing. At first glance Renee had thought she had been crying. It was only now she could see that her face was red and pinched with fury, not tears.

'Those witches,' Violet finally managed to get out. 'Those horrible women are spreading rumours about me.'

Nancy, who'd just come in with a tea tray, exchanged a worried glance with Renee as she set it down. 'What do you mean, honey?'

'I mean the secret's out. The women at the WVS knitting group know that baby Eamon's mine. And the worst thing is, they think I should feel ashamed of my lad. They treated him like he was a bit of dirt rather than my son. He's just a child, a defenceless child.'

'OK, OK, try and calm down and tell us exactly what's happened,' Nancy instructed.

As she set about pouring them all tea, Violet told them both what had happened at the knitting group and Renee found her blood boiling. She was staggered at the cruelty. The spiteful way women could be with each other never failed to amaze the dancer.

'I've a good mind to give that Mavis a backhander, myself,' Renee snarled, as she handed Violet her cup. 'She can think twice about coming in here again.'

Violet shook her head and raised a smile. Renee was pleased to see that the younger girl hadn't lost all her spirit.

'You must be feeling awful, sweetie.' Nancy sighed, watching as Violet took a sip from her cup.

Violet nodded. 'I am. Hurt, shocked . . . but also, not surprised. I should have known the cat would be out the bag soon enough,' she said quietly.

Sitting in the battered chair beside Renee's, Violet's nails were bitten to the quick, Renee noticed.

'Who do you think told them?' Renee mused.

Violet let out a long sigh. 'I'm guessing Enid. She won't have meant to, but she's so proud of her grandchild – she's bound to have let something slip. You heard her in the bar the other day when we got back from the East End.'

Renee thought for a moment. Yes, Enid had been full of glowing praise for her grandchild, and it had been troubling. Still, if there was one thing Renee knew about secrets it was that without careful management they didn't stay secret for long.

'The thing is, not everyone knows about this,' Renee said carefully. 'It's just a select group of busybodies who haven't really got much to go on at all, and they're only guessing. They don't have proof. This'll just be a bit of drama for them, something to gossip about when *It's That Man Again* isn't on.'

'So, you think just carry on as normal?' Nancy asked. She pursed her lips as she thought. 'I think that's a good idea. For all Enid's enthusiasm she won't have actually come right out and said that Eamon is her grandson.'

'And if she had, she would have been mortified and told you about it,' Renee suggested, carefully. She set her cup down on the table and leaned forwards. 'I think what you need is a little break.'

'A break?' Violet echoed.

'Yes. Do you good. Take Eamon with you.'

'But where would I go?' Violet asked, puzzled.

'Birmingham,' Renee said decisively. 'You can do some research for us.'

Nancy smiled and nodded. 'Good idea.'

'But what research would I do in Birmingham?' Violet asked, clearly perplexed.

'Well, we need to work out what's going where and how we're going to manage the charity side of things along with the new dance hall,' Renee said.

'And how am I going to do that in Birmingham?' Violet asked, still confused.

Nancy rolled her eyes. 'Honey, you're the daughter of the man who helped spearhead the National Restaurants campaign. If that's not research, I don't know what is.'

'That way the air can clear here and we can have a word with Enid and get her to stop mouthing off,' Renee added bluntly.

Violet looked unsure. 'I don't know. I mean I don't know

Alan that well. He may not want me around for a few days. I'd hate to get in his way. And Eamon can be very noisy.'

'All babies are noisy and I have a feeling that Alan would love nothing more than the chance to spend a few days with his family,' Nancy put in wisely.

'But what about this place?' Violet said. 'We've got all the prep for the new venue, not to mention the dance we're trying to organise to bring the GIs and the community together.'

Renee got to her feet. 'Not for you to worry about. And besides, I've got a plan for the GI dance.'

'Have you?' Nancy asked in astonishment.

'Yes.' Renee grinned. 'I'm sick of all this messing around, so when Alex is back we're going to ask him to organise it.'

'What?' Nancy and Violet exclaimed in unison.

'That's far too short notice,' Nancy said.

Renee shrugged and walk towards the phone. 'I think it'll do both you and him good. It'll give him something to do if you aren't getting on, Nancy, and it'll also remind him that he still has a place at the dance hall, even though I'm in charge now. Reassure him what's important. Trust me.'

Nancy and Violet exchanged doubtful looks, but Renee didn't care. She loved the feeling she got fixing other people's problems. If only she could apply the same pragmatism to her own.

17

Two weeks later, Nancy was drinking a strong cup of coffee in the café opposite the Palais and trying not to wince at the tasteless liquid. She had said it many times, but it was impossible to get a decent cup of Joe in this country and she had almost given up trying. But the proud American in her refused to sacrifice her morning java ritual and so she stuck with it, no matter how disgusting the taste, rejoicing in the fact it was still better than tea!

Setting her cup down, Nancy gazed across at the Palais and tried to feel lightness in her heart. Today was the day of Alex's return and she was a ball of nervous energy. She kept telling herself that of course she wanted to see him, that it was just nerves. And besides, the children were beyond excited to meet this mythical man. They'd written to him and introduced themselves, but beyond that knew nothing about him.

Peter, Nancy knew, was keen to have a male role model in his life and she recognised he was at the age where he needed it. Peter was a good lad, but at the end of last year Nancy had been worried about how close he'd gotten to Ronnie Newsham, who'd owned the Palais. Being at an impressionable age, Peter had looked up to Ronnie, and had the older man not died, there was every chance that Peter would have done something stupid, even illegal, under his influence

Nancy closed her eyes, remembering how Peter's hero-worship of Ronnie had pained her. Thankfully, Peter had finally seen the monster for who he truly was, and for that she was grateful.

Now Peter had the opportunity to learn from someone with kindness and honour in his heart. No matter the distance between her and her husband, Nancy knew that Alex had goodness at his core.

Finishing her coffee, Nancy got to her feet, squared her shoulders and took a deep breath. She was made of strong stuff. She could get through the reappearance of her husband.

But pushing the door of the café open, she took one look at the Palais, then checked her watch and decided to walk in the opposite direction. There was roughly two hours before Alex was expected. Could she gather herself together in the time before he arrived? She fervently hoped so.

It started to rain, and picking up her pace Nancy found her mind began to race. How on earth had Alex even orchestrated home leave anyway? She knew other women with husbands in the army who hadn't seen their men since they joined up. Alex had gone in as an officer and had fought in the Great War, which had somehow given him an advantage, but even so. There was a huge great battle going on in North Africa. Shouldn't he be there?

If truth were told, when Alex first told her he was leaving, she could hardly bear the idea of being without him. Funny, she thought now, as she rounded the corner on Hammersmith Broadway, that the idea of him being back here seemed almost unthinkable. So much had changed. She was optimistic, though, that Renee's plan to give Alex the dance to oversee at the coming weekend would work. Alex had always relished a challenge. She hoped he still did.

Head down, mind still racing, Nancy wasn't focusing on where she was going, so intent was she on trying to make sense of her feelings. It was only as she narrowly sidestepped out of a passer-by's way and ran headlong into someone else, bashing her head as she did so, that she realised she wasn't thinking straight at all.

'I'm so sorry!' she said. Looking up, she found herself staring into the eyes of a familiar-looking GI.

'Hey, there.' John grinned. 'Fancy seeing you here.'

Nancy rubbed her forehead. 'Yes. Sorry. Not looking where I was going.'

'I can see that,' John said, not unkindly. 'You all right?'

Nancy paused for a moment. Was she all right? 'Oh, I'm fine,' she lied.

John smiled as if he didn't believe a word.

'You sure? That forehead of yours looks a little red.'

As John leaned down and touched her forehead, she flinched at the contact of his skin against hers.

'Sorry,' he said. 'Did that hurt?'

'A little,' Nancy replied, knowing that any pain she felt wasn't from John's unexpected touch.

She took a step back, wanting to put some distance between the two of them, and ran her eyes across him. He looked different somehow. He was dressed in his usual blue uniform but his eyes had an unexpected twinkle in them.

'What are you doing here? Shouldn't you be fighting a war, or living it up in the Rainbow Rooms drinking gallons of Coca-Cola?'

John gave her a lazy grin that spread across his face. 'Running an errand, as you Brits say.'

Nancy raised an eyebrow. 'Cut me open and you'll find nothing but stars and stripes,' she quipped.

As John laughed, Nancy found herself relaxing as she joined in. It was a relief to let out some of her frustration and stress.

'So, what are you really doing out here pounding the streets in the rain?' he asked.

Nancy looked at him, and felt a sudden urge to unburden herself. 'If I said I was avoiding my husband, would you judge me?'

John looked bemused rather than shocked, Nancy was

pleased to note. And for a second she remembered how good it felt to spend time with someone who was from her own neck of the woods, someone who got her references, her humour and the way she spoke.

'Not my place to judge, ma'am,' he said gently.

Nancy observed him again. His brown hair was greying at the temples and with the lines around his eyes, John looked almost wise.

'No,' she said gently. 'Not my place, either. Sorry, John, it's a difficult time. My husband's returning after almost two years away and I'm nervous.'

John nodded. 'I can imagine. I don't know when I'm next going to see my wife and how things will be when I do.'

'You're married?' Nancy exclaimed.

'Why is that such a surprise?' John laughed.

'I don't know,' Nancy faltered. Why was it a surprise? Because she had the impression that most of the GIs in Britain were footloose and fancy-free. What was the expression in the papers? Oversexed, overpaid and over here.

'We've been married almost fifteen years,' John said lightly. 'I miss her every day, but I don't doubt our relationship will have altered when I go back. I hear it in her letters sometimes. She's changing without me, and I guess I am too.'

Nancy nodded as she looked into his eyes. She could see sadness there and she supposed it was no surprise. The impact of this impossible war was being felt by people everywhere around the world. It wasn't just the raids, the danger, or even the rationing. It was the long separation from loved ones and the consequences of that. People returning home as strangers, forever marked by the experience of war. It wasn't healthy, Nancy mused, and the ramifications of this would be felt for decades: of that she was sure.

'I'm sure things will be fine for you when you get home,' she said softly as the rain eased up and the gentle summer breeze tickled the back of her neck. She tugged at the ruby silk scarf she had been wearing, causing it to fall. Stooping to pick it up at the exact same time as John, they brushed hands, and Nancy now felt a sudden jolt in the base of her stomach at his touch, which sent shock waves through her body. Looking up at John, she could tell he'd felt it, too; she caught the hint of surprise and fear in his blue eyes.

'I'm sure you're right,' he said evenly, handing back her scarf.

Taking care not to touch him again, Nancy took the scrap of silk and smiled as she took a step back.

'Well, it's been good to see you again,' she said brightly.

John tipped his cap. 'And you.'

With that, Nancy turned and began to walk, her heart racing. She had only managed a couple of steps when she heard John call her name. She spun round and saw him beaming at her.

'I just wanted to say. I'm sure it's going to be fine with your husband,' John said. 'Give it a day or so and you'll be back to normal.'

Nancy nodded. 'Thanks,' she said.

'And if not, you're always welcome at the Rainbow Rooms,' he said with a grin. 'I'll be there all weekend helping settle in some new recruits. And the offer of free Coca-Cola still stands.'

And just like that, the tingle Nancy had felt as she'd brushed fingers with John returned, and this time more strongly. She opened her mouth to speak, but he waved and turned to walk away. Standing in the street watching him go, Nancy felt sick with worry. She fervently hoped he was right. That Alex would return and that all her worries about her marriage would disappear. That she would have no need at all to accept John's invitation.

18

Back at the Palais, preparations were well underway for Alex's return, with a special exhibition dance that Temperance and Renee had been organising; Renee and Archie were working out a sequence of steps they were due to perform, including a waltz that went into a frenzied jive.

'Perfect!' Temperance exclaimed as their dancing drew to a close, and was about to declare practice finished when Edna appeared, standing in the doorway of the practice room with a face like thunder. Temperance was the first to spot her and smiled hesitantly at the former dance champion.

'Everything all right, Edna?' she asked, over the blare of the gramophone.

'Well, that depends what you call all right.' Edna sniffed.

Renee, standing with Archie, resisted rolling her eyes at the older woman's tone, then turned off the gramophone and smiled over at her.

'I dunno, Edna,' she said brightly. 'But given you've a face like a busted clock, I'd say you're far from all right. So out with it, queen.'

Edna scowled and turned back to Temperance. 'My dear, Alex will expect something more traditional. This was *his* dance hall for such a long time.'

'And still will be, Edna, love,' Renee said briskly. 'I may have taken it on, but we'll make sure there's still a place for Alex when he comes back.'

'I should think so.' Edna drew herself up to her full height. 'I know you've got this dance you want him to organise whilst he's here, but honestly, Renee, I do think my son is capable of a little more than that. This place *thrived* when he was in charge.'

'And the country wasn't knee-deep in war when he left, either,' Renee shot back.

There was silence as Edna pursed her lips, while Renee looked unperturbed as usual.

Temperance felt like knocking their heads together. There had never been any love lost between Edna and Renee when Edna had worked at the Palais, but there was always the hope that things would change between them when Edna retired. No such luck. If anything, they had become more critical of one another, and Temperance dreaded Edna's appearance at the Palais.

She glanced across at Archie who gave her a wink and walked towards Edna.

'Now, how about you and me show these two how it's done?' he said, taking her smoothly by the hand and leading her back onto the dance floor.

Without waiting for an answer, Temperance queued up the music and watched as Archie and Edna expertly took to the floor. The sight made her smile. Edna was well into her early eighties now but, dressed in a Chanel-style two-piece, she still moved with all the grace of a woman in her twenties. True, her hips didn't move quite as smoothly as they once had, but her timing was faultless. Despite the older woman's crankiness, Temperance could watch Edna dance all day.

'Well, well, well, what's all this?' a voice thundered from the doorway.

Temperance looked up just as Edna let out a loud shriek and practically scampered towards the entrance.

'Alex,' she cried. 'My precious boy, you're home.'

Taking a moment to stand back and look at him, Temperance could see how much he had changed since she'd last seen him. His face was more lined, his skin weather-beaten and there was a weariness to his brow she had never seen before. The thick crop of blond hair he had sported was now noticeably greyer, and he was thinner, too – not that that was any great surprise. She knew how arduous life was in the army, despite the extra rations for soldiers.

'Alex,' she said warmly, walking over to greet him as Edna put him down. 'How are you?' She kissed him on the cheek and saw how sharp his cheekbones had become. There was not enough flesh on him, that was for sure.

'I'm just fine,' Alex replied, his eyes sparkling as they pulled away from each other. 'Really, I am. Good to see nothing around here has changed.'

Renee and Edna let out a sharp laugh, as Archie and Temperance exchanged knowing looks.

'I think you'll find a lot has changed, and not necessarily all of it for the better.' Edna couldn't help herself.

Renee rolled her eyes. 'Change the record, Edna. Your son's only here for a few days; I'm sure he doesn't want to hear it.'

Edna scowled as Alex cleared his throat.

'I don't know,' he said with a grin. 'It's nice to hear you two snapping at one another like old times. I've missed it.'

Renee let out a bark of laughter. 'About as much as I miss the warts I used to get on my fingers as a kid. Anyway, enough of all that. Why don't you go upstairs and settle yourself? Nancy's just popped out, but I'll get Sybil to send you up a tea, or a whisky, if you fancy something stronger?'

Alex raised an eyebrow. 'Can you spare the alcohol?'

Renee waved his concerns away. 'Course we can.'

'Then in that case, yes please.'

He picked up his kitbag and walked away. 'You coming, Mother? You can fill me in on any gossip before Nancy gets back.'

Temperance hid a smirk as she saw Edna trot after Alex out of the door and up the stairs.

Renee shook her head. Reaching for a packet of cigarettes

from the pocket of the satin slip skirt she always wore for dance practice, she pulled one out and lit up.

'I think that's more than enough for today. Do you two mind tidying up and I'll check that the bar's in order before we open?' Renee didn't wait for an answer and scampered away, leaving Archie and Temperance alone.

Temperance took a deep breath. Things between her and Archie had been strained for the past fortnight, ever since their conversation about race. More than anything, she wanted things to go back to how they were, and she was hoping that she might have found the solution for that.

'I've been thinking,' she said lightly. 'Perhaps you and me could put on a dance tonight?'

Archie looked at her in surprise. 'Really? Won't that set tongues wagging?' he said, a little defensively.

'Don't be daft.' Temperance felt weary. 'Don't you think it would help set things in motion? You know, get things in the right mood for the dance tonight and bring people together.'

A flicker of annoyance passed across Archie's face.

'Oh, this is a political thing? You want us to dance together to show the Palais doesn't agree with segregation?'

'No,' Temperance said hotly. 'I thought it would be nice for us, too, actually. Doesn't have to be an exhibition dance – if Edna has her way there wouldn't be time, anyway.' She took a step towards Archie and ran a hand through his wavy hair. 'I miss you, Arch. I feel like we're growing apart and I don't know why.'

Archie's face softened and he leaned down to kiss the inside of her wrist. His lips against her skin sent butterflies scurrying around her stomach and she smiled, relieved. Her Archie still loved her, no matter what had been said between them.

'We won't,' he said gently. 'I love you, Temperance, always have always will. I won't let something as daft as skin colour get in our way. All that matters is you and me. If you think a dance tonight will fix things, then I'll give you all the dances you want.'

Archie might not yet understand just how important her race was to her, but with his hands now snaked around her waist as he leaned down to kiss her lips, Temperance decided to pick her battles as the familiar surge of love crept through her heart. They'd work it out somehow. And with Archie by her side, she knew all would be well – it had to be.

19

As the train crawled along the track to Birmingham, Violet tried to settle a noisy Eamon. They had been lucky boarding the busy carriage, as two soldiers had helped Violet with all her belongings and even given up their seats so that she and Eamon could travel in comfort to the Midlands.

Violet had been more than grateful for the assistance as she settled her son. But what she hadn't been prepared for was the multiple times their train had pulled into sidings to allow another train to pass.

As she gave Eamon the parchment from the paste sandwich that Betty had made for the journey, she tried to swallow her nerves. She knew she was being silly, that there was no reason at all to feel worried about this trip, but all that she'd felt since Renee made the arrangements with Alan – and Howell & Smart, too, of course – was worry.

It had been a good idea of Renee's to send her away for a bit, get her away from the gossip that had started to circulate. Queenie was the only one who had been outraged.

'I don't see why you should have to go anywhere,' Queenie thundered when Violet broke the news. 'It's those witches that should be cast out, not you.'

'Nobody's casting anyone out,' Betty said with a weary sigh.

Violet watched her mother fold the tea towel she was holding into a neat square and place it on the kitchen table.

'This what you want, Vi?' Betty asked, her voice even. 'To go away for a bit? I can see the merit in Renee's wisdom, but you know we'll support you if you don't want to go. We'll help you stand up to these gossips.'

Violet had felt torn. When Renee had made the suggestion, she'd quickly thought it was a good idea. Violet wanted nothing more than to get away from the forked tongues and whispers that seemed to follow her everywhere she went. What she really wanted was a chance to start again, to be Eamon's mother, even if it was just for a few days. She knew that not everyone would understand her decision. Queenie obviously thought she was running away, but it wasn't until she looked now into her mother's pale grey eyes that Violet questioned whether it was the right thing.

Betty had walked this path before. Pregnant with Violet and Roy, Betty had borne the scars and stigma only an unwed mother can wear. It wasn't just your own standing in the community that being an unmarried mother would bring, it was also the standing of your child. The stares, the judgements and taunts would taint him for the rest of his life.

And then there was the rest of Violet's family to think of. If word got out Eamon was hers, they would be shunned in the street, shops might refuse to serve them. She bit her lip. She was lucky the girls at the Palais had been so supportive – she had heard horror stories of others who had lost their jobs. Some under the age of sixteen had even been forced into lunatic asylums.

'What do you think?' Violet had asked her mother, then.

'I think it's a good idea, love,' Betty said smoothly, shooting a pointed glare at Queenie, who was still smarting. 'And you're not running away, you're working. Something those terrible old women wouldn't understand.' At the vitriol in her mother's voice, Violet had smirked. Betty never usually had a bad word to say about anyone. 'But I worry that staying with Alan will add more of a burden to your shoulders.'

'I'd have thought you'd have wanted your daughter to get to know her birth father,' George suddenly piped up.

Violet spun around to look at him standing in the doorway. He looked dreadful. Hair sticking up, and the empty arm of his jacket tucked into the pocket.

She remembered visiting George in hospital when he had first been injured. She had hoped that he would change, that they would become close. But that hadn't happened. If anything, since his accident George had got worse. Violet reasoned that discovering the daughter you've brought up as your own suddenly wants to build a relationship with her long-lost father was a shock. And George never dealt with bad news well. She wasn't surprised by his reaction.

'I think that's a very good idea,' Queenie said firmly. 'About time she got to know a real man who'll do right by her. My point is, she shouldn't feel as if she *has* to go anywhere.'

And so the reasons for and against had gone round in circles. In the end, Violet had just slipped out of the house, taking baby Eamon with her. Now, here she was on the train, almost in the centre of Birmingham after a five-hour journey, and she still wasn't sure if she had made the right choice.

The platform at Birmingham New Street came into view and Violet tried not to wince as she took in the scenes of devastation. Birmingham had been badly hit in a raid back in April, with the station roof taking a battering, thanks to the Luftwaffe.

Naturally Violet was accustomed to signs of bomb damage in her home city, but seeing it somewhere outside of London really brought it home to her how cruel the Jerries were and how much pain and destruction they had caused.

As everyone around her scurried to get off the train, grateful to be on firm ground after such a long journey, Violet waited. She was of course as keen to get off the train as everyone else, but not only did she have Eamon to carry, she also needed a moment to gather her thoughts.

She felt as if she knew Alan well enough – their relationship had been brought forwards fairly quickly after she had given birth to Eamon. But it had been some months since she'd last seen him and she wondered if he would be pleased to see her or if he was too busy with work. She shook her head as the last of the passengers around her got off. It was time to deal with whatever lay ahead.

Scooping Eamon expertly into one of her arms and holding her small case in the other, she emerged from the train. And there, waiting for her, just a few yards away wearing a warm and familiar smile, stood her father.

'Alan,' she cried, wanting to wave but unable as her hands were full.

He rushed towards her and immediately took her case and kissed her cheek in one fluid movement.

'It's so good to see you, Violet,' he said, then. Peering down at Eamon, he stroked the little lad's cheek. 'How was your journey? Are you hungry? We must get you something to eat. My house is in Solihull but I thought it easier for you to come here. I've brought the car – well, it's not my car, it's the company's car – but I've borrowed it as I wasn't sure how much help you'd need or how many belongings you'd have.' He paused for a moment and then looked at her apologetically. 'I'm sorry. I'm babbling. I've been so looking forward to this day.'

Violet felt all her fears disappearing in an instant as this lovely man said everything she needed to hear in that moment.

'We're fine,' she assured him. 'Betty made a sandwich for me for the train and we're in no hurry to get anywhere.'

At the mention of Betty, Violet saw Alan's eyes light up.

'How is your mother?'

His voice was even, but Violet knew the pain he'd felt at leaving Betty behind in London, having wanted to start a new life with her. But Betty had obstinately refused; standing by her marriage vows meant she was wedded to George until death parted them.

'She's well. She sends her love,' Violet said.

That message made him break out a smile, and Violet knew in an instant that no matter what lay ahead, and no matter the reasons that had brought her here, spending time with her father, Eamon's grandfather, was always going to be a good decision. As they exited the station towards the Standard Alan had managed to park right outside, Violet could feel it in her bones.

20

As Nancy made her way back to the Palais, she felt a new sense of resolve. Bumping into John in such an unexpected way had given her pause for thought.

All couples faced tests, and if she and Alex were strong enough they would get through this one. Who could forget the poignant images of the King and Queen walking through the East End after their own home, Buckingham Palace, had been hit during a raid? No matter that they lived in a mansion that most could only dream of, the two had faced their own trauma but still came together and leaned on each other for support. That's what marriage was.

So Nancy squared her shoulders, lifted her chin, and pushed through the double doors that led to the Palais's foyer. As she did, she could hear laughter coming from the bar. Her mother-in-law and, if she wasn't mistaken, her husband.

Suddenly, excitement flared within her, and Nancy found herself rushing towards the source of the noise, pausing only to drink in the sight of Alex. Dressed in his army uniform, hair slicked back as it usually was with the thick pomade he favoured. Her heart sped up as she looked at him unobserved. He had certainly changed. He was a lot thinner; his hair was greyer, too. But the essence of him was still pure Alex, and she felt her body pull towards her husband like iron to a magnet. She looked down at her slightly crumpled green tea dress and wished she'd had time to change before he saw her. Her legs weren't even dressed in stockings, painted instead with gravy browning as some of the dancers had taken to doing, since stockings were now so hard to come by. But she'd have to do.

At the sound of her shoes on the parquet floor, Alex turned to look at her and as her eyes locked with his sparkling blue ones she was transported back in time to when she had first met the handsome Palais barman.

Every concern she'd had for their marriage vanished in that instant as she rushed towards him and felt her husband's arms around her waist.

'God, I've missed you,' he said burying his face in her neck.

'And I've missed you,' she sobbed, tears streaming down her face as she pressed her cheek into his army jacket. Inhaling his familiar scent, she felt the knot in her stomach loosen – what had she been worrying about? Her Alex, the man she had loved for so long, was right here with her.

Just over two hours later, and the pair of them were still in the bar, giggling like youngsters in the grip of first love. Nancy had been surprised at the strength of her feelings, having been worried for so long. After their initial excitement at seeing one another again had died down, Nancy was happy to find she was relaxed in the company of her husband, even taking him up to meet the children for a bit, before they'd returned to the bar to carry on catching up.

'So what do you think of Peter and Ruth?' Nancy asked now.

Alex grinned as he picked up his glass of beer. 'I think they're wonderful. But you knew I would.'

Nancy nodded. She had been delighted to see that the children were an instant hit with Alex, and vice versa. He had been interested, warm and engaged, just as she knew he would be. In turn, Peter and Ruth had been thoughtful, asking appropriate questions, delighting in his answers.

'They're great kids. But Peter, he's of an age now where he needs a man in his life.'

Alex frowned. 'I don't disagree, but it's hard, Nancy. I don't know when this blasted war will be over and I can come back again.'

'How long are you here for?' she asked.

'I have seventy-two hours' leave. Then I must report for duty.'

Nancy swallowed a large gulp of her port. It seemed such a short amount of time. How were they to properly get to know each other again in just three days? And what if, when he went away again, he never came back? As the dark thought entered her mind she did her best to push it away. Thoughts like that were far from helpful, especially now.

'Is there anything you would like to do while you're here?' she asked instead.

'Be with you.' Alex slipped his hand across the table and squeezed her palm. 'I can't tell you how I've longed for you, Nancy, how I've missed you.'

'Me too,' she whispered, realising that amongst all her worry about the state of their marriage she had missed her husband, too. 'What can you tell me about what you've been doing?'

'Precious little,' Alex said. 'All I can tell you is I'm looking forward to this one day being all over so I can come back for good, pick life up just as I left it.'

That familiar feeling of anxiety returned to the pit of Nancy's stomach.

'Well, things will look a little different, but Renee has assured me that your job will be here for you when you come back, honey,' Nancy said softly.

At the statement, Alex looked perplexed. He reached for his glass and took another pull on his pint.

'Well of course it would be. I mean, when all the men come back we'll all go back to how things were. You women are just holding the fort for a little while, but no doubt all these extra responsibilities are difficult for you. We need to get back to normal, for the sake of the country.'

Annoyance burned in the pit of Nancy's stomach and she struggled to hide it. He was making it sound as if women were unable to cope without men, as though they were whimpering on street corners, desperate for their men to come home. If anything, the opposite was true. Nancy had seen with her own eyes the way women had come together to do their duty by their country and take on the challenges war brought, all without any help from a man. She wanted to say as much, but Alex clearly hadn't finished.

'I'm saying all that, but that's assuming there's anything left to come back to, of course.'

'You mean London? The country? The Palais?' Nancy asked, a little exasperated now.

A sigh escaped Alex's lips. 'I don't know, Nancy. All of it, I suppose. I mean, look around.' He gestured to the Palais. 'I don't recognise it here anymore.'

'It's still the same. Nothing's changed,' she said defensively.

Alex let out a hollow laugh. 'Everything has changed. Renee owns it now. Who could have predicted that one coming? And that she has by all accounts become friends with a vicar. I certainly couldn't have predicted that either.'

Following Alex's gaze, Nancy saw Renee sashay across the bar towards them, lipstick as bright as her hair, with Roger trailing just a little behind her. She looked delighted to see Alex and greeted him warmly, throwing her arms around his shoulders and kissing him theatrically on both cheeks and introducing him to Roger.

'How are you, kid?' she asked, taking a seat beside Nancy, Roger pulling up a chair beside her.

'Can't complain,' Alex said good-naturedly.

Renee raised an eyebrow. 'Makes a change; you did a lot of that when you were in charge.'

At the quip, Alex laughed. 'You haven't changed, Renee Hammond. But this place has.'

'Like it?' Renee asked, getting to the point.

Nancy smiled inwardly. Renee always did have a way with words, and it was something she had long admired in the fiery redhead she was proud to call her friend.

'I don't dislike it,' Alex said, looking around. 'I mean, the essence is still the same. But you've made changes to the running order of bands, I see, and you don't seem to have an exhibition dance planned for later.'

Renee tapped the side of her nose. 'You wait, love. Not everything has been revealed.'

Roger chuckled. 'She's a woman of mystery, Alex, you have to give her that.'

'She's that all right,' Nancy chimed, earning herself a reproachful look from Renee, who then turned back to Alex.

'Has Nancy filled you in on our new dance-hall venture?' she asked.

At the question Alex frowned. 'Second dance hall?' he echoed.

'Yes, near Bethnal Green,' Renee explained. 'It won't be like this one. No maple-sprung floor, for a start. But it's a chance for people to come together, have fun, pick up a hot meal when they're in need.'

For a moment Alex said nothing, and Nancy could see the set of his jaw as he struggled to make sense of the news.

'Do the board know about this?' he asked eventually.

'They do, and they're very supportive,' Renee said brightly.

'And what's your involvement in all this?' Alex asked Roger.

'My idea, I'm afraid,' he said, looking sheepish. 'I think it will be wonderful for the local area to have a dance hall they can call their own, come together as a community.'

'I don't disagree.' Alex nodded as he drummed his fingers against the table.

'Why don't you come along to the new site tomorrow afternoon?' Roger suggested. 'You can see for yourself what we're doing.'

Nancy smiled at the vicar. He really did know how to soothe troubled waters, and this was the perfect way to ensure her husband felt involved.

'I'm not sure.' Alex's expression darkened. 'The truth is, I don't think now is the best time to open up something like this. You're exposing the Palais to huge risk, Renee, not to mention the fact we must be careful to protect our brand. The Hammersmith Palais de Danse has a reputation for being the most luxurious of dance halls, not just in England but in Europe. I'm sorry, Renee, but I can't support this.'

Nancy opened her mouth to speak, but thought better of it. How she longed to say to him that times had changed, and that like the rest of them, Alex was better off getting used to it.

21

By nine o'clock that night the Palais dance floor was packed. It was a sight that always made Renee smile. She had worried when war broke out that dancing would be the last thing on people's minds, but it seemed that the opposite was true, with everyone grateful for an escape from their troubles. Whether it was the handsome GI far from home or the lonely housewife who wanted a night off from the drudgery of housework, the Palais had always been a welcome refuge for everyone. No matter what Alex thought it would always be the same.

She looked over at him now, where he was still sitting beside Nancy, his brow furrowed. Renee hadn't meant to upset him, but he had to see that times had changed. And while she was happy to ensure he still had a role at the Palais when he returned from war, she wasn't about to stand in the way of progress.

'You look deep in thought,' Roger said, pulling her back into the present.

'Something like that.' Renee sighed. 'Nothing for you to worry about, though.'

She patted his knee and got to her feet. There was only one cure for her misery and that was to take to the dance floor. She looked at Roger expectantly.

'Fancy a waltz?'

Roger looked surprised for a moment. 'I don't usually dance.'

Renee laughed. 'Well, you're about to pay for a second dance hall – I think you ought to know a thing or two about it.'

With that, she led Roger by the hand towards the dance floor and in one fluid movement pulled his arm around her waist and held his hand. Together, Renee made it look as if he were doing the leading rather than the other way around as she guided him around the floor and Oscar Reyburn played a lively waltz.

'How do you do this every day?' The vicar struggled to keep up, as Renee continued to twirl him around the floor.

'How could I not?' Renee laughed. 'Makes me feel alive.'

A bead of sweat gathered at Roger's brow. 'If you say so. I can't imagine my brother was too interested in dancing.'

At the mention of her late husband, Renee felt a shadow fall over her happy mood.

'No,' she said briskly. 'He wasn't.'

'But he must have liked you doing it,' Roger said, as Renee pulled them both into a reverse turn.

'He didn't mind the money and the admiration he got as a result of me doing so well,' she said carefully.

Though she and Roger were becoming friendly, Renee wanted to be careful about how much she divulged about her relationship with his brother. She was sure Roger knew just what sort of a person Ronnie was, but she didn't want him to start being suspicious. Renee was sure he was already getting enough of a picture from Ronnie's former colleagues, having lined them up to help with the new Palais.

'I'm sorry about Alex,' she said, changing the subject.

Roger looked unperturbed. 'Oh, there's nothing to be sorry about. He'll come tomorrow.'

'What makes you so sure?' Renee asked.

'Because curiosity will get the better of him.' Roger grinned as he spoke. 'He's just doing what all men do – putting his stall out, letting you know he's not happy, but he'll want to be involved, if only so that he can have a say.'

Renee smiled, and as the dance came to a close, allowed Roger to lead her towards the bar.

'How did you get so wise?' she asked.

Roger's face flushed. 'I don't know about wise, but I've picked up some things along the way.'

Lighting a cigarette, Renee said nothing as she took a sharp pull. 'Not sure I've picked up anything worth sharing.'

'Oh, I don't know,' Roger said. 'I should say you've got some great gifts.'

'If it's how to deal with a rude punter, then yes, I've got that well and truly covered,' she quipped. Turning to Roger she saw he was looking at her, concern written across his face. 'What?' she asked. 'Have I got lipstick on my teeth?'

'No,' Roger said gently. 'I was wondering if you're ever serious?'

'Course I'm serious,' Renee said. 'How else d'you think I run this place?'

'There you go again,' Roger said. He reached for his pint and took a sip. 'You make light of everything, Renee. I understand you've been wounded, but not everything is a joke.'

Renee shook her head. She was in no mood for this. If Roger had been a soppy Southerner, like most of the people she worked with, she could have understood his interest in feelings. But Roger had been born and bred in Liverpool, just like she had. Granted, he'd lost the accent, and she imagined that a life living in nearby Kent keeping an eye over a parish in Bromley wasn't the same as Toxteth, but had Roger really forgotten what life was like as a Northerner?

She looked at him coolly. 'I've always been one for just getting on with things, Roger. I appreciate that might not be your way but it's mine.'

'And there's nothing wrong with that,' Roger said. 'But I worry that because you don't open up you're carrying pain that needs to be released. You're a good woman, Renee; you deserve better than my brother ever gave you, that's for sure. As your friend, and former brother-in-law, let me help you.'

At this, Renee felt wrong-footed. Her brain scrambled for something sharp to say but she couldn't find the right words.

'I know how my brother treated you,' Roger went on, 'and I'm ashamed. As a boy he was always so thoughtful. I don't know where it went so wrong. From our uncle, I imagine. I'm sure you know he was a petty crook. When I left home, he took Ronnie under his wing. I didn't like the violence, the criminality, but for Ronnie . . . Well, I could see how it made him light up inside.'

Renee looked at the vicar, aghast. She knew precious little about her late husband's childhood. He had never shared much when they were together and she had been happy to leave it like that. She knew the obvious things – that both his parents were dead – but beyond that Ronnie never said much.

'But you took a different path?'

'Indeed.' Roger set his glass down. 'I found religion and the church at thirteen. I liked the comfort it gave me and I was fortunate that the pastor's family looked after me. I'd all but moved out of the home by the time I was fourteen. Nobody minded, and Ronnie was a baby.'

Feeling her blood run cold as she remembered the look Ronnie used to get on his face before he hit her, Renee could well understand what Roger meant by a dark side,

'And I know you know what that looked like,' Roger said gently. 'Renee, I know my brother put you through hell.'

She opened her mouth about to make a joke, protest even. Renee was many things, but she wasn't a victim.

'I'm not here to get you to talk if you don't want to,' Roger said, holding up his hands. 'But if you change your mind, I want you to know I will listen. I may not be married—' he gave her a wry smile '—but I know something of what goes on.'

'You know more than you think.' Renee smiled again, grateful they were now on more familiar footing.

'With that in mind, I want to talk to you about another

idea I've got for the new dance hall,' Roger said, looking nervous now.

'Go on,' Renee coaxed.

Drumming his fingers on the bar, Roger paused then spoke. 'One of the things I want to do at the new dance hall, as you know, is offer more help to the community. And something that has been on my mind is the problem some wives have.'

'Some wives?' Renee narrowed her eyes.

'Yes.' Roger looked uncomfortable, and Renee almost felt sorry for him. 'I don't think you're the only person who has been treated badly by their husband, Renee. I think a lot of women go through what you went through, and I wondered if you might talk to these women about your experiences.'

'My experiences?' Renee exclaimed. 'Whatever for? I don't go around airing my dirty drawers in public, and most women feel the same.'

'I know that, Renee,' Roger put in. 'And that's not what I'm asking. I want you to give these women hope. Look at you. You're a successful dancer and businesswoman, and you live your life by your own rules.'

'Only because Ronnie's dead!' she exclaimed. 'If he was still here, I wouldn't be living this life.'

'Perhaps not,' Roger said. 'But you were still a successful dancer during your marriage. You made something of yourself, despite being put in a terrible position, and I think that there are plenty of women who could benefit from hearing a story like that.'

Renee took another frantic pull on her cigarette. Her brain was whirring into overdrive now. It was tempting to give other women comfort. That much was true. But she also knew that the more she talked about Ronnie, the more she left herself open to be questioned, and she couldn't face that. Yes, she was happy to offer support to these women with the chance of a night out, a drink even. But she couldn't talk about her own experiences. Her eyes strayed to Nancy, who was trying to get Alex to smile. She didn't just have herself to think about.

'I can't, Roger,' she said flatly.

'Please, Renee.' Roger looked at her pleadingly. 'Just think about it.'

'No.' Renee shook her head and stubbed out her cigarette. 'I'll help any other way I can, but I'm not talking about me marriage, and please don't ask me again.'

With that she walked away from Roger and tried to steady the beat of her pounding heart. Even in death Ronnie had a hold over her. When would it ever stop?

22

Early on Monday morning as the kettle whistled on the stove, Alan picked it up and poured hot water into the teapot. Watching him then set it down on the tray, Violet couldn't help smiling as he brought it across to the table.

'Thanks,' she whispered.

'You're welcome,' he whispered back as he began to pour.

As Eamon made gurgling noises in her arms Violet looked down at her son and smiled. He'd had been no trouble until about four that morning, when he had finally stirred. Violet had done her best to settle him, but by five she had given up and brought him downstairs to sit in Alan's little kitchen.

She hoped she had done her best to be quiet, but Alan had appeared within minutes, offering to make tea. She had tried to encourage him back to bed but he wouldn't hear of it, insisting that she was his guest and he wanted to do all he could to make her and his grandson feel welcome.

'He doesn't usually wake up like this,' Violet said apologetically. 'I've got him to sleep until at least six these days.'

Alan reached out a forefinger and stroked Eamon's cheek, who was now looking up at him with an almost angelic smile.

'It'll be a change in his routine. Being somewhere new,' he said. 'I remember when our two were born, they were terrible to settle whenever we took them out of their home.' At the mention of his other children, with his estranged wife Vera, Alan looked suddenly abashed. 'Sorry.'

Violet shook her head. 'You don't need to apologise. Everything that's happened . . .' She waved a hand as her voice trailed off. 'What I'm trying to say is we've got to look forwards, not back. Besides, I'd like to meet them one day, if they wanted to . . .'

'Would you?' Alan looked at her in delighted surprise as he splashed tea into her cup.

Violet nodded. 'I don't know if you've told them about me?'

She realised as she spoke she was probably being hugely presumptuous. There was every chance Alan wanted to keep her and her twin brother Roy's existence a secret. But Alan shook his head.

'I told them all about you soon after we met . . . the moment you knew I was your dad.'

Violet reached for her tea, steeling herself for her next question. 'And how did they react?'

'Vera always knew, of course,' Alan said. 'The children were surprised, but they took the news well. They're living with their mother in Canada now, becoming adults in their own right, forging their own life and path, but they've expressed a desire to meet you.'

Excitement bubbled up inside of Violet at the prospect of a new family somewhere who wanted to get to know her, but then reality crashed down around her as she realised how far away they were.

'Can't see a trip to Canada in my future, but nice to know they feel the same.'

'You could always write to them,' Alan said. 'I know they would be delighted to hear from you.'

'Would they?'

Alan nodded. 'Of course. I'll give you their address before you leave and you can write when you want to.'

She thought for a moment, enjoying the silence – apart from the sweet song of a skylark hovering somewhere nearby. She wanted Eamon to have as much love in his life as she could give him, and if that meant cousins in Canada she would take the opportunity and write to them.

'I'd like that,' she said, then changed the subject. 'What do you have planned for the day?'

'I rather thought we could go and look at the shadow factories over in Lode Lane.'

Violet frowned. 'Why?'

'Because we have recently opened a National Restaurant nearby that is used by all the workers. We offer them one hot meal a day, free of charge, because they're doing essential war work. I thought it might be good for you to see how we do that so you can report back for your second Palais opening.'

Eamon gurgled delightedly in his arms causing both Violet and Alan to laugh.

'Eamon seems to think it's a good idea,' Violet said brightly.

'Then that's settled,' Alan said, reaching for the pot again. 'I'll take you to lunch afterwards.'

'In the restaurant?' Violet asked.

'No, there's a pub around the corner that does a brilliant meat pie,' Alan said. 'I think it might be mock duck, but the landlord swears its pure beef and I'm happy to live in ignorance.'

At the suggestion, Violet laughed. Solihull seemed a world away from London already. It was so peaceful and quiet. When Alan had driven them back to his home from the station, Violet had taken time to examine her new surroundings, which was easy to do as Alan's car was the only one on the road. Everyone else seemed to travel by bus and bike, and stared at Alan as he drove past.

'Why did they house you here?' Violet had asked him.

'It's much quieter than Birmingham itself, and I travel all around the area so it was seen as a better move,' Alan explained. 'Must admit I like the feeling of safety. We've even got evacuees here, and some families have taken in the American GIs, you know.'

Violet nodded and looked out of the window, drinking it all in. Yet despite her initial reflection, it was obvious that Solihull had suffered. The arcade opposite the station was black from fire damage, and a nearby street had clearly taken a battering with most of the street decimated. As Alan drove past a street of houses, she saw one that bore a large Waste Paper Salvage Drive sign hanging from the window, and underneath a little girl was dropping off scrap paper at a collection point.

'It feels like a real community here,' she said.

'It is,' Alan said, as he waved at one of the women walking past holding a little girl's hand. 'You know, I wasn't sure when I left London if this was the right place for me to be, but I've settled in well and I think it was good for me to take on something new, especially after everything with your mother.'

As they'd pulled up outside his house, Alan's words had hung in the air and Violet hadn't liked to broach the topic again until now.

'You and Betty still write to each other though, don't you?' she asked now as she poured a second cup of tea for them both.

At the question, Alan looked ashen. 'No,' he said quietly. 'I did write to her shortly after I left, and she replied and said she thought it best if we put this behind us. Move forwards.'

Typical Betty, Violet thought. What a mess it all was. Alan deserved better and sadly, Violet thought in that moment, so did Betty.

She was about to say as much when the piercing, telltale wail of the air-raid siren echoed through the house.

Violet raised an eyebrow. 'Is that what I think it is?'

'Probably just a false alarm,' Alan said, reaching for his tea.

But as the sound reverberated around the small kitchen again Violet got to her feet.

'I don't think that's a false alarm.'

She peered out of the window and, to her horror, saw a long bomber heading their way, the familiar drone studding the air with the unmistakeable sign of its intentions. Heart pounding, she turned to Alan, Eamon still in her arms.

'Have you got an air-raid shelter?'

Alan shook his head. 'I've never thought we needed one. It's so safe here.'

She looked around the room and saw the stairs to the basement. It wasn't perfect, but it would have to do. The last time Violet had been caught in a raid she had given birth – she wasn't about to let something as dramatic as that happen again.

Holding Eamon, Violet followed Alan through the front room and down towards the stairwell that led to the basement. They were just inches away when there was suddenly a huge explosion and glass from the windows was fired across the room.

Violet watched in horror as a piece of shrapnel narrowly missed her baby's head, boomeranged around the room and embedded itself on the floor.

'We need to get out of here,' she shrieked.

By now Eamon was screaming and she wrapped her arms around his head, doing all she could to protect him.

'We'll be fine in the basement,' Alan shouted above the noise. 'We just need to get to safety. Crouch down and stay low. We're nearly there.'

Legs trembling, Violet did as instructed, holding Eamon tight.

'We're all right, my love,' she crooned, over the noise. 'Everything is going to be all right.' Reaching the door that Alan had wrenched open, she ran down the stairs and into the dark basement.

'We'll be all right in here,' Alan promised.

He reached for a lamp and lit the candle inside. As the flicker of candlelight filled the small, damp room Violet reached for an upturned box and sat on it. Eamon looked up at her, his brown eyes blinking trustingly as his cries calmed.

'He's settled down,' Alan said cheerfully.

The sound of the ack-ack guns answering the gunfire echoed above them.

Violet smiled. 'He usually sleeps right through the air raids.'

'Lucky lad.' Alan raised an eyebrow in surprise. 'Wish I could say the same.'

'Well, I suppose he was born in an air raid. Perhaps he feels at home amongst the drama.'

Another round of gunfire echoed overhead and Eamon continued to close his eyes, looking drowsy. Violet leaned her head back against the damp brick wall. This basement felt small and cramped. She longed to be back in the comfort of Alan's home upstairs. But if it meant they were safe, she could cope. She leaned down and pressed a kiss to Eamon's forehead.

'I so wanted to do that with you and Roy,' Alan suddenly blurted. 'It's my biggest regret that I never got to know my first-born son. But I never forgot about you both. I spent years wishing things were different, that I were a better man, that I could have been a better, proper father to you both. When I think about what I missed out on . . .'

His voice trailed off and Violet reached out a hand to pat him on the knee.

'We can only ever do what we think is right. At the time you thought you were doing the best thing. It's not for me, Betty, or Roy even, to judge you for that.'

'Maybe not,' Alan said. 'But I judge me. I wish I could have been stronger. I wish I could have seen you both grow up.'

Violet thought for a moment. How different her life would have been if Alan had been her father, brought her up instead of George. But then who's to say where she would be now. Who's to say things would have worked out with her and her baby. Because no matter what, having Eamon was the best thing that had ever happened to her.

'I don't think there's any point going over the past,' she said gently. 'It's the here and now that counts. And I know I'm grateful you came into my life and you're my father now.'

Alan shot her a wan smile. 'I feel the same, love. I can't tell you how happy it's made me that we're finally getting to know each other.'

'It goes to show, it's never too late—'

But Violet's voice was drowned out by the sound of an ear-piercing whistle. As the whistling grew louder, Violet's pulse quickened and she readied herself for what was undoubtedly coming next.

'Alan, brace yourself,' she shouted, covering Eamon with her body in a bid to protect him.

They were just in the time, as the bomb she had heard whistling through the air rocketed to the ground. Debris and rubble immediately rained down around them; a brick flying through the air before striking Alan on the back and sending up clouds of thick dust.

Violet glanced up, shaking. To her horror, a bomb had all but devastated Alan's house, and the one next door.

'Alan,' she croaked, through clouds of dust. 'Alan, are you all right?'

'I'm fine, love,' he called. 'Are you and the baby OK?'

'Think so.' She sat upright and used the sleeve of her cardigan to breathe. Then, when she had control of herself, she fished into her pocket and placed a hankie over Eamon's tiny mouth and nostrils.

Casting an eye upwards, her heart was in her mouth as she saw the clear early morning sky directly above them, and a lone German Heinkel circling. Anger coursed through her. Did this pilot have no shame? Didn't he have a family of his own? Loved ones to protect?

'We have to get out of here,' she said.

Alan looked around and nodded. 'There's a shelter two streets down – if we hurry, perhaps we'll make it.'

Violet didn't wait for an answer. Glancing down at Eamon, she saw that he was breathing normally and seemed fairly content. It was now or never. Gingerly, she made her way through the rubble towards the basement staircase, which was thankfully still intact.

Pressing one foot against it, she held her breath as she moved determinedly up the stairs to the ground floor. As her eyes fell on what had once been the living room, she tried not to wince at the devastation. Alan's house was beyond repair, as was his neighbour's. The only blessing was that it looked as if next door had made it to shelter in time as there was nobody around.

'You still all right, Alan?' she called behind her.

'Yes,' he said, his voice shaky.

She glanced back and saw her father had a large cut on his forehead.

'You're bleeding,' she said.

'And we'll die if we don't get out of here,' he replied.

That was all the incentive Violet needed. Holding Eamon in her arms she picked her away through the knee-high bricks, and the furniture that had been destroyed in a second.

Outside in the street, the silence was eerie. For a moment Violet wondered if she had imagined things, but then she heard the faint whine of the bomber. The Jerries clearly hadn't done enough damage.

'This way,' Alan shouted, in front of her now.

As he ran along the street, Violet blindly followed him, Eamon still in her arms.

A few minutes later, Alan halted at the sight of an ARP warden.

'Get inside,' the warden yelled, holding open the door to the public shelter.

Violet didn't have time to register what sort of building it was. Instead she blindly rushed inside, and found a seat beside an elderly couple who cooed delightedly at Eamon.

Sinking into her seat, Violet felt the weight of her father as he sat down beside her, and allowed him to pull her into his arms. Breathing out a sigh of relief, she allowed her heartbeat to slow and looked down at her son. He had snatched the hankie away from his mouth and nose and was now holding it happily in one hand instead.

Violet felt tears pool at her eyes. To think she could have lost this precious bundle. Her world would have been wiped out in an instant if they hadn't been so lucky against the Jerries.

Wordlessly, she pressed her lips to Eamon's forehead. From now on she would move heaven and earth to protect this child.

23

In London that evening, Temperance was making her way across town to Camberwell by bus, and dealing with a mixture of feelings. She hadn't been to a meeting of the League of Coloured Peoples for several weeks now, citing work and family as an excuse.

That hadn't been the real reason, though. Temperance had in fact felt conflicted about going to these meetings since Archie had dismissed them in that café.

In the months following her brother Eamon's death, both she and Violet had made a point of regularly going to meetings and carrying on his work. But Violet's commitment had understandably tailed off when baby Eamon was born. Temperance had no such excuse, other than that she still felt conflicted. With Archie uncomfortable when she talked about race and tried to point out the differences between them, it was increasingly difficult to balance their relationship with the duty she had to her heritage and its impact in this country. Archie might think that if they loved each other it didn't matter, but Temperance knew it wasn't that simple and never would be, not until serious change was made and prejudice overcome.

Temperance's first conversation with Stafford had been on her mind for weeks. He had reawakened her identity, made her realise that she owed it to herself and her brother, to continue his work. Finally with a Monday off, Temperance had decided to go back to Camberwell and start as she meant to go on.

She hadn't been able to tell Archie the truth about where

she was going, when she'd popped in to see him at lunchtime. When he had asked her what she was doing with her day off, she had lied and said she was running errands for Renee.

As the bus reached her stop on Church Street, Temperance disembarked and walked along the busy tree-lined street, trying to justify herself. She didn't have to tell Archie where she was every moment of the day – it wasn't as if they were joined at the hip.

Having convinced herself, she strolled towards the meeting hall, feeling more buoyant as she got closer, glad that she would be able to mix with like-minded people, folk who knew her struggles and where she had come from.

Pushing open the door and waving hello to Una, one of the group leaders, Temperance made her way inside. The place was busy for a Monday evening, but the din of chatter was comforting. Taking a place near the back, she set her bag down and felt the knot in her shoulders loosen.

'Hey, there, Dancing Queen.'

The voice made her jump as she turned around and came face to face with Stafford.

'What the devil are you doing here?' Temperance said, blindsided.

Stafford's face broke into a wide beam. 'I could ask you the same thing. I've been coming here for a few weeks now, ever since you told me about the place. Not seen you here before, though.'

At this, Temperance felt her cheeks redden. 'No, well, I've been busy at work.'

Stafford nodded and turned to look at the front. 'What made you decide to come today then?'

'I've got a day off. Thought it was time. I knew my brother would be pleased.'

'Is he here today?' Stafford looked around him as if expecting to be introduced.

'No,' Temperance said. 'Though sometimes I feel as if he is. He's always in my heart I suppose.'

As Stafford furrowed his brow looking confused Temperance explained.

'Eamon was killed during the first raids on the city in September 1940.'

Stafford looked stricken. 'Oh, Temperance, I am sorry.'

Temperance shook her head. Almost two years had passed by since she had lost her older brother. She carried the pain with her every day and always would, but it was getting easier to bear. Yet the moment strangers passed on sympathy, she struggled to hold on to her emotions. The last thing she wanted to do was break down in front of Stafford now.

Instead she gave him a weak smile. 'Thank you.'

'They're a good crowd here,' Stafford said appreciatively. 'I can see why you like it.'

Temperance nodded as Una walked up to the centre of the stage. The crowd fell silent, with last-minute stragglers hurriedly taking a seat so they could listen to the speaker.

'Friends, it's wonderful to see so many of you here today,' Una said warmly. 'We have a lot to discuss. But first of all, I would like you to officially welcome Sergeant Stafford Gilkins, who has been coming here for a few weeks now and is going to talk about life as an American GI – and the differences he has experienced with attitudes to race in America and England.'

A round of applause broke out as Stafford got to his feet and gently pushed past Temperance who looked at him in astonishment. A million questions whirred around her brain, namely why on earth Stafford had been asked to speak.

Taking to the small stage, Stafford smiled shyly at the crowd.

'Good evening, ladies and gentlemen. Thank you for welcoming me here today.'

A small round of applause broke out as he spoke.

'I know that many of you don't know me; I've only been to a

127

few of these meetings. But the moment a wise young woman told me about them, I knew I wanted to come, to be a part of you all. Being an American in England has been a humbling experience. In my country we experience segregation to an extent that most of you won't have experienced here. And I'm glad that you haven't. So many back home and within my own coloured regiment accept that this isn't right and that this isn't the way things should be, but believe there's nothing we can do about it. Meeting some of you, talking to you all has shown me that we can do something about it, and we can act if we come together, that there is a chance for equality for all.'

At that, Stafford earned a rousing round of applause and even Temperance was on her feet clapping.

Looking abashed, Stafford waited for the applause to die down before he continued with his speech. As Temperance listened, she felt not only moved by the power of his words but also drawn to the fact someone was echoing the way she felt, sharing emotions that she understood.

Just over an hour later, the meeting was wrapping up. Stafford hadn't returned to sit next to Temperance, and had instead taken a seat at the front until proceedings were over. But as Temperance got to her feet and put on her jacket, she saw the handsome soldier walk towards her and she smiled.

'You never said you were giving a speech,' she teased.

'You never asked,' he quipped.

Temperance felt suddenly shy as she gazed into Stafford's eyes. He had said so many things that had resonated with her, it felt suddenly strange to occupy the same space as the sergeant now.

'I liked what you said,' she managed, feeling woefully inadequate as she tried to find the right words. 'I mean to say . . . I thought what you said captured people's feelings perfectly.'

Stafford played with the rim of his hat and nodded in thanks. 'Una asked me to talk last week, and honestly, I wasn't sure what

I was going to say when I got up there. Somehow seeing you in the crowd, knowing how important this fight for equality is for everybody at every level, gave me the confidence to say what needed to be said.'

'Well, I'm glad I could help,' Temperance managed. 'Though I'm not sure I did anything.'

Stafford placed his hat back on his head. 'You did more than you know. I'd love to take you for a drink, if you have the time?'

At the question, Temperance hesitated. Would Archie mind her going for a drink? She shook the thought off. She and Stafford were only friends, after all – where was the harm?

'I'd like that.' She smiled up at Stafford and was relieved when she saw a look of delight pass across his features.

'Great. You can introduce me to a pint of stout.'

Temperance wrinkled her nose as they filed out of the hall, bidding goodbyes and nice to see yous as they went.

'Not for me, thank you. But a port and lemon will be lovely.'

'Your wish is my command,' Stafford said as they stepped outside in the cool summer air.

As they walked along the road, conversation flowing easily between the two of them, Temperance became suddenly aware that she felt hot and her heart was pounding. As Stafford pushed open the door to the nearest pub, she took a deep breath. There was no need at all for her to be feeling this nervous, no need at all.

24

An hour or so earlier that day, as their bus pulled into Bethnal Green, Nancy found herself feeling increasingly nervous. She looked around, sure someone could tell that her heart was racing, but everyone was getting on with their day, reading the paper, chatting to their friends.

Nancy glanced at Alex beside her, looking for some sign that he was happy, excited even, to see the new dance hall, but his jaw was set and his mouth fixed in a grim line. He looked handsome in his army uniform, she had to give him that, with many a woman running their eye over him as if sizing him up for their own home.

Usually, Nancy would have found something like that amusing, but not today. The weekend had been a bitter disappointment. During their initial few hours together when Alex had first arrived, she had hoped she'd been wrong, that the distance between them could be overcome. But the souring of Alex's mood when he'd learned of the second dance hall had persisted all weekend, with him asking to see the books, making curt suggestions for how to improve takings behind the bar, increase prices on the door – and even worse, advising that they stop swapping servicemen's shoes for free.

'Every dance hall does it,' Nancy had protested on the Saturday night, whispering because the children were in bed. 'If we stop how does that make us look?'

'As if we understand how to run a business,' Alex replied shortly. 'Which at the moment, with all these discounts, it doesn't.' He jabbed a forefinger at the accounts ledger. 'Look, you're even letting women in for half price on Saturdays.'

'Only if it's a ladies' event,' Nancy said calmly. 'We find that draws the crowds, as you'll see from the sales column. It's a loss leader.'

'And what about the bar?' Alex continued, as if she hadn't spoken. 'What are you doing about that?'

Nancy frowned. 'What do you mean?'

'You're charging precious little for a pint. There's a war on, supply is limited, prices should be going up.'

'And where's the sense of community in that?' she had argued. 'Why on earth do we want to punish our customers? They're loyal, happy and coping with a lot. As you say stocks are low, we can't always offer everybody the drink they would like, so we've kept our prices the same to reflect that. To say, hey, you know what, times are tough we're all in it together.'

As Nancy finished her speech Alex had practically slammed the ledger on the table, making her jump.

'You'll wake the kids,' she hissed.

'Good,' Alex snapped. 'They need to learn that with you and Renee at the helm there will be no business for them to fall back on when this war is over.'

Looking at him coolly, Nancy had then left the room and taken herself downstairs to the Palais. The place was closed but she knew she couldn't be in the same room as her husband. And there she had stayed until the small hours. Sipping a port and lemon, wishing things were different.

Since then, things had been strained between the couple. They had been cordial with each other in front of the children, but the moment they were alone they barely spoke, and Nancy could feel the resentment between them building, as if they were two countries about to embark on a war, rather than a married couple.

She had half expected Alex to pull out of this visit to the new site today, and she and Renee had decided to keep quiet about involving him in the dance organisation, given his mood. Yet, when she had suggested he stay behind, he had looked at her so aggrieved she had hastily backtracked. Now, with the train pulling into Bethnal Green, the moment was here.

Wordlessly, the couple disembarked, and as the warm summer breeze whipped around her neck, Nancy felt tempted to reach for her husband's hand, but resisted. In the old days she wouldn't have thought twice about it, and that made her sad.

'Is it far?' Alex asked now, pulling Nancy from her thoughts and into the present moment.

She shook her head and continued with her brisk pace. 'Just up here on the left.'

As the white building came into view, she paused to allow him to take in the sight. It looked better bathed in sun, she thought. The Palais itself could have something of a foreboding atmosphere in winter, but the place really did cheer up in the light. She imagined scores of people queuing outside as they did in Hammersmith, the line full of excited chatter about the night ahead. And she pictured those in need coming in for a hot meal during the daytime, to line their stomachs and a have a good chat with a friend and neighbour. People coming together in times of crisis, each moment warming the body and soul.

'You can't be serious,' Alex said. He scratched his head as he took a walk towards the old theatre. 'Look at it.'

'I am looking,' Nancy said calmly. 'It needs a bit of work but it's already come on leaps and bounds since we saw it a few weeks ago.'

Alex shook his head. 'It doesn't look anything like a dance hall.'

'But it's not just a dance hall. Look, come and see what they've done inside.'

She patted her bag for the keys Renee had entrusted her with for that afternoon's visit and fished them out.

Unlocking the heavy wooden door, she smiled as she breathed in the heady mix of fresh paint and wood shavings, and paused to look around. The foyer had received a lick of paint, and the doors had been freshly sanded and planed. She was able to finally see the vision Renee and Roger had. She didn't want to admit to Alex that she too had struggled to see this place as another dance hall, but now with the light flooding through the windows at the back, Nancy could see the possibilities.

Craning her neck upward, she smiled in delight as she saw a small chandelier, commandeered from heaven knows where, taking pride of place in the ceiling rose.

She then looked down at the hardwood floor; that too had been sanded and prepared for hundreds of feet passing through each day. She continued on into the dance hall. Walking into the main space, she could see the improvements there already. The sanded and varnished floor and the walls that the lads had started decorating. There was just a small bar area left to create, and she could see work had already started on that, too, with carpenter's tools lying in the far corner.

'It's a mess,' Alex said, aghast.

'It's a fine hall that doubles as a dance floor and canteen,' Nancy said ignoring his dour words as she explained the dual purpose.

'It's not maple-sprung,' Alex complained, jumping lightly on the floor and wincing slightly as his ankle absorbed the shock. 'And where will the band go?'

Nancy gestured towards the orchestra pit in front of the stage.

'There. It's perfect.'

As Alex said nothing, she could see that he agreed but was too stubborn to say so.

She smiled as she walked around. Now that the chairs had been removed and casual seating, a ramshackle collection of mismatched furniture creating a bar area and place to sit down and chat, had been added, she realised the place had a warm, inviting feel. She could imagine mothers coming together to knit and chat as they made socks for the services and equally she could see men coming together in the evenings to play dominoes – and even young sweethearts taking their first strides towards romance. This place wasn't the Palais but it didn't have to be; it just had to echo its heart and soul.

Not waiting for Alex to offer more criticism, Nancy strode towards the door on the right and flung it open. The makeshift kitchen hadn't been touched yet, clearly the last thing on the tradesmen's minds. She frowned; she had hoped to be able to show Alex how the essence of the Palais was being transferred to the East End.

Turning around to look at her husband, she could see the disdain in his eyes and knew that before he had even set foot in the place he had already made up his mind.

'You hate it, don't you?' she said.

In that moment, Nancy regretted opening her mouth in such an obvious display of vulnerability. Alex often deplored her direct nature – an American attribute, he felt. And now, seeing his mouth set in a tight line, she could see that she'd gone too far.

'I don't *hate* it Nancy,' he said coldly. 'I merely think none of this reflects well on the Palais. You and Renee have done an admirable job of running things there in my absence, but you're allowing your hearts to rule your heads. The Palais is a business, and community has no place in business. I'll be making my feelings clear to the board tomorrow before I leave.'

And then, without a backwards glance, he turned to walk away. Nancy watched him go, not wanting to follow. He had no idea of the war being fought at home. Yes, she knew the boys who were serving their country had it tough and she could only imagine what they had been through, but life was tough at home, too. As far as Nancy was concerned, if you could do something to help, you stepped up to the plate. Now, as she watched her husband's retreating back, Nancy knew in her heart that they had become poles apart. She had lost her husband, and she wasn't sure how they would ever find their way back to one another.

25

A week after the attack on Birmingham and back in London, Violet sat in the Lyons Corner House in Piccadilly, the cup of tea in front of her growing colder by the second. She looked up at Queenie and Betty who were both fussing over baby Eamon, and felt as if she wasn't really present, but miles away.

She reached for her cup and turned her attentions back to her family, desperately trying to tune in to the question Queenie was asking her.

'Is that something you'd want to do, Vi?'

Violet looked at her grandmother quizzically, only for Queenie to roll her eyes.

'Do you want to help your mother get that kitchen set up in Bethnal Green on Saturday?' Queenie shook her head. 'Where's your head at, girl? You left it in Birmingham?'

At the mention of the city and the recent devastation she'd experienced, Violet gave an involuntary shudder. The memory of it still haunted her. The burning, the screaming of those in pain and the utter powerlessness of being unable to help – and Violet had been able to do nothing more than raise the alarm, apply bandages and offer words of comfort. Alan had told her she had gone above and beyond, but had she really? When she looked at those injured, even dying, amongst the debris, she had seen only her sweetheart Eamon's face and the pain of losing him had hit her all over again, harder than any bomb Hitler could drop.

'Leave her,' Betty said gently, laying a hand on Queenie's forearm. 'She's had a tough time.'

Violet gulped her tea and winced. 'I'm fine,' she said unconvincingly.

'You don't have to be,' Betty said.

'And you don't have to be, neither,' Queenie said sharply.

Queenie turned to the passing nippy and gestured that she wanted a fresh pot for the table.

'You haven't really talked about what happened up there,' she said to Violet, her tone gentler now that she had ordered tea.

Violet shrugged. 'You know . . . We've been through it before down here,' she said, trying not to make too much of it.

Betty frowned. 'Violet, you've had a hell of a time up there. You couldn't have known there was going to be a raid.'

'We none of us can know that,' Queenie said.

As the nippy set the pot down, Queenie smiled gratefully and began to pour fresh tea out for them all. Violet felt her mother's eyes on her as she reached for a cup.

'And how's Alan?' Betty said lightly.

Violet looked up at her mother. Her tone might have been casual, but she knew there was more to Betty's question.

'He is well,' Violet replied. 'He sends his love.'

Queenie gave her a piercing look to suggest this was not enough information.

Violet sighed. 'He seems to be getting on well,' she managed. 'He's moved into temporary accommodation and looks to be doing all right at work. The National Restaurant roll-out is seemingly successful too, with more being added. They're really proving popular in the communities.'

'I bet they are,' Queenie offered. 'And look how popular your attempt to feed the people of the East End will be. Poor devils.' She took a sip of her tea. 'They've had it ever so tough.'

Violet thought again of Eamon Adams, her baby's father, and the flames that had engulfed the docks that fateful night he had been killed. Queenie was right, the war was ripping the heart out of people. She wanted to help, of course she did, but in this moment Violet just felt worn out and broken.

'Like your gran said, you could just help me get the kitchen ready,' Betty said gently, now. 'Queenie's going to help out, too.'

'For me sins,' Queenie muttered, as she took another sip of tea and eyed Violet sharply. 'You had any more trouble off that bunch of old crones since you've been back? Is that why you're so quiet?'

Queenie looked so fierce, Violet couldn't help laughing as she shook her head.

'No, I haven't been to the WVS since I got back.'

'Good.' Queenie looked satisfied.

'But will you go back, Vi?' Betty asked now.

Violet paused. She hadn't actually given it much thought, being honest, but the idea of seeing those women again made her shudder.

'Probably not,' she admitted. 'I'll find another group to join if I can. I can't bear the way they treated baby Eamon.'

Eamon then stirred in his pram, as if giving his own support to his mother.

'While you were away I had a word with Temperance's mother,' Queenie said softly now.

Violet raised an eyebrow. 'Gran, tell me you didn't. The poor woman didn't mean any harm.'

'I know that.' Queenie raised a hand. 'But your life and Eamon's life are going to be a misery if she doesn't watch what she says.'

'Did you say that to her?' Betty laughed.

'Not in so many words,' Queenie said, looking non-committal. 'I simply told her it'd be a shame if you and baby Eamon had to move away to Birmingham, or somewhere else, because of wagging tongues.'

'And what did she say to that?' Violet had to admit she was intrigued now.

'She was horrified, course she was. It helped Winnie was there 'n' all, mind.'

Violet clamped a hand over her forehead. Just how much worse was this going to get?

'And what did Winnie say?' Betty asked.

'She agreed with me. Said that grandmotherly pride was one thing, but not at the expense of the grandchild itself.'

'So, did she admit that she was the one who said Eamon was her grandchild, then?' Violet asked.

Queenie shook her head. 'No. But she went a bit pink in the face when she insisted she'd never said nothing to anyone who might spread unkind rumours.'

'So, she did say something, then?' Betty said with barely concealed disgust.

'Betty!' Violet exclaimed, looking at her mother in surprise.

'What?' Annoyed, Betty reached for her cup of tea. 'We all agreed that we'd stick with the story that Queenie came up with. You found that baby in a raid after his mother died, and are selflessly raising it as your own. We'd all love to go about shouting that's really our grandchild, and yes, people might suspect that's the truth, but they can't go around saying it's gospel if they don't know. Enid's had a lot of hardships to endure, but haven't we all? I won't have her making your life a misery as well, whether she means to or not.'

As Betty brought her speech to a close Violet gaped at her mother. She hadn't known she had such strong feelings. But she was right. Violet couldn't bear the idea of having to move away, or worse give up her baby, because of nagging tongues.

'Both Winnie and Enid did raise one important point, though,' Queenie said now.

Violet looked at her grandmother expectantly, who glanced at Eamon and smiled affectionately at the little boy.

'They did say that as he gets older it's going to be harder to keep this lie going about his parentage. It won't be long before people start noticing that he looks like you and his father.'

'Nonsense,' Betty cried. 'Folk around here won't look that closely.'

Fear studded Violet's heart. 'Course they will.'

She turned to look at Eamon. Already she could see traces of both her and his father reflected in the baby's features. He had his father's eyes, for definite. And the same-shaped mouth and chin, and the slope of Violet's nose. Queenie was right. There would come a time when it would become difficult to keep their secret. And what would that mean for her? And more importantly what would that mean for her son? Instinctively she clamped a protective hand around her son's chubby forearm. Mavis's recent behaviour was a warning sign of things to come if she didn't do more to protect her boy.

'People see what they want to see.' Betty was still countering defensively, pulling Violet back to the present.

'And sometimes what people want to see is the truth,' Queenie rebutted, sagely.

As Violet leaned over the pram and stroked her son's soft cheek, she felt a sinking feeling in her stomach. Time was running out. Sooner or later she'd have to make a decision about how best to protect her baby.

26

November

Months passed, in which time each of the Good Time Girls had found themselves caught up in their own problems. It didn't help that, to Renee at least, the world seemed to be going to hell in a handcart. Every time she listened to the news or flicked through the newspapers she was constantly faced with misery.

In recent weeks, she and the rest of the country had endured the death of Prince George, Duke of Kent, who was killed in Scotland during a military air crash, Luxembourg had been annexed by Hitler, a British ship had been torpedoed and sunk by a German U-boat killing two thousand people, and the RAF had bombed Bremen. Whether this was in retaliation, Renee wasn't sure, but she wouldn't have been surprised. Yet, most miserably of all, the war had further escalated in Egypt. To Renee, it seemed never-ending. Only last week, a second battle in El Alamein had broken out between Allied and Axis forces and Renee knew that this was a huge worry for her clientele, most of whom had sons and husbands fighting out in the desert. As if that wasn't enough, the milk ration was due to be cut to two and a half pints from next week. Just how much worse were things going to get before they got better?

Hearing the sound of footsteps now, Renee folded her newspaper shut and slid it back across the bar.

'Not interrupting, am I?' Roger asked now as he approached.

At the sight of her new friend, Renee's face broke out into a wide smile. 'Not at all. Lovely to see you.'

Roger had become a regular visitor to the Palais these past few weeks, popping in every couple of days. At first Renee had worried about the frequency of his visits, sure it meant he was checking up on her and the new East End dance hall – or worse, wanting to probe her about Ronnie. But since that time he'd talked about their upbringing, Roger never uttered a word about his late brother. Instead, he concentrated on Renee, the Palais, their plans for the second dance hall, and even on occasion, their hopes and dreams for the future – when the war was finally over.

'I think I'd like to settle down by the sea somewhere,' Renee had said one day.

Roger had looked at her, surprised. 'Really?'

She'd chuckled. 'Why is that so shocking?'

'What about your dancing?'

'What about it?' Renee had given a soft shrug of her shoulders, Glenn Miller's 'In The Mood' playing on the gramophone behind them. 'I can't dance forever, no matter how much I might want to. And I have to admit, these days I can't go on as long as I used to.'

'Stuff and nonsense,' Roger had protested.

'It's true. A couple of waltzes and I'm nearly done for. You throw in a jive or cha-cha-cha, and I'm bound to get one of me heads.'

'You're a funny one, Renee Newsham.'

'I'm Hammond, now,' Renee reminded him. She had gone to great trouble to legally take back her maiden name once Ronnie had passed, and felt much better for having done so.

'And what will you do in this house by the sea?' Roger asked. 'Husband? Children? Pet dog?'

Renee had chuckled, allowing the sounds of Glenn Miller to

wash over her. 'Who knows. I'm happy in me own company, though; don't need anyone else about me. And you can find pals in folk anywhere.'

'I can see that.' Roger had nodded. 'As my old mother used to say, Renee Hammond: you'd make a friend in an empty house.'

At the shared joke from their hometown, they'd both thrown back their heads and roared with easy laughter.

'And what about you?' she asked. 'You wed to the church till the day you die?'

The vicar thought for a moment before he spoke. 'I saw the violence around our family, Reen,' he explained. 'Course I had girlfriends once, but I liked the easy company the Lord gave me.'

'Are you allowed to say that?' Renee gave a wry smile.

'Probably not,' Roger admitted. 'What I mean is, that I liked the stability of the church; I liked helping people. It felt natural to me. I feel as if I've found my calling. Like you with your dancing.'

Renee had nodded at this, then rested her head back on the chair, allowing the sweet music of Glenn Miller to wash over her. It had been a lovely moment, and Renee had felt at ease with Roger ever since, their friendship growing by the day.

Still, she hadn't been expecting him today, and she had promised Nancy she'd go down the pictures with her later that night. Noël Coward's *In Which We Serve* was finally showing at the Ritzy, to much excited chatter, and both women were looking forward to a night spent away from the Palais watching the silver screen.

'I'm not interrupting?' he asked now, gesturing at the paper on the bar.

Renee wrinkled her nose at it. 'I dunno why I bother reading it. It's always the same, full of doom and gloom.'

'I can't say as I disagree,' Roger said, taking a seat beside her. 'Anyway, I wanted to show you something.'

Renee raised an eyebrow. 'Careful vicar. Folk'll talk.'

'Oh, you!' Roger waved her quip away with a grin. 'Can you come to Bethnal Green?'

'Now?' Renee checked her watch. 'I said I'd go to the pictures with Nancy in an hour.'

'Bring her with us.' Roger grinned as he got up and did up his coat. 'I promise, you'll want to see this.'

An hour later, Renee and Nancy found themselves back in Bethnal Green with Roger, a chilly, late autumn wind biting at their heels.

'Honey, this better be good,' Nancy said as she stalked along the road next to Renee and behind Roger, who was gathering pace. 'I thought we had a date with Noël Coward.'

'We do,' Renee said briskly, aware the afternoon light was beginning to fade. It would be dark in an hour. 'Nancy, show a bit of patience. We won't be long and this means a lot to Roger.'

'Fine,' Nancy said shortly. 'But if we're not in that cinema in an hour, I'm holding you responsible.'

Renee said nothing. Nancy had been in a foul mood in the months since Alex had returned to the army. But from what Renee had gathered, Alex had been a misery while he'd been home; surely the fact that he'd gone away now would have put a smile on Nancy's face? But if anything, it had done quite the opposite. Nancy had been withdrawn, quiet and moody, only ever managing a smile when the GIs came to visit, or rather one GI in particular. Nancy had struck up a friendship with a fella named John, which Renee thought was far from wise, but it wasn't her place to say anything. After all, what right did she have to tell anyone how to live their life? She'd made that many mistakes of her own, you could write a book about them.

Suddenly Roger came to an abrupt stop outside the new dance hall.

'Ta-da!' he said theatrically.

As he did so, Renee and Nancy gasped in unison. The old theatre was unrecognisable, transformed into a glittering dance hall fit for royalty. Gone was the tatty sign advertising the theatre, and in its place stood a cinema-style plaque bearing the words *Bethnal Green Regal* in big red letters, and then underneath *All Welcome for Dancing, Food and a Good Time.*

Renee clapped her hands together. 'It's wonderful. Roger, love, you're so clever. I had no idea we were at this stage; I thought there was still some finishing off to do before the grand opening next month.'

'Thanks, Renee, but this isn't what I wanted to show you,' he said. Walking towards the newly christened Regal's door, he pointed to a smaller sign above.

Renee Hammond, licensee, and champion dancer of the Bethnal Green Regal.

Tears pooled at Renee's eyes. She had seen herself credited dozens of times in her career as a dancer, but never more than just her name. This finally felt good: she had achieved something, her *name* meant something. After all she had been through, it finally felt as if she had turned a corner – the old very definitely being seen out with the new.

Renee turned first to Nancy, who was gazing at the sign in awe, and then to Roger.

'I can't believe you've done this.'

'I hoped you might like it,' he said. 'I know you have your name over the door at the Hammersmith Palais, but I wanted to do something a little extra here. I wanted everyone to know it's not just a name behind this door, it's a real person, with a real passion for dancing and community.'

'I don't know what to say,' Renee said, genuinely speechless.

Roger grinned. 'Well, I think your next question is obvious.'

'Is it?' The redhead looked confused.

'It is to me, honey,' Nancy said gently, as she tightened the scarf around her neck. 'The next question, I'm guessing, is when the heck are we opening?'

'Thought you'd never ask.' Roger smiled in anticipation. 'I know we said we'd open next month, but I thought we'd get locals in early next week, let them see what it's all about.'

'Next week?' Renee echoed, shocked. 'But . . . we're not ready.'

'We are more than ready,' Nancy said. 'Look around you. The place is finished. The exterior has been painted to within an inch of its life, the kitchen is in, the floor is finished, as is the bar area, which we know is fully stocked. The adverts in the local papers have gone out so everyone's expecting us, Betty's been prepping her best recipes for weeks in readiness, Queenie's organised a dominoes night for the fellas and a make-do-and-mend night for everyone else. And now your signs are up. What else is there to do?'

'Well . . . staff, for a start,' Renee said falteringly.

'Easily solved. We can get some of the community around here to help out with cleaning and general maintenance, while the Palais staff switch between the two,' Roger said calmly.

'What about stocks then? And dancing shoes?' Renee countered. 'It takes time to get them in.'

'Sybil's been doing that. And as this isn't a maple-sprung floor it doesn't matter if some of the lads don't change out of their hobnail boots, though we do know it's not ideal,' Nancy said with a grin. 'Now, anything else?'

Renee looked over at the Regal before her. It had a very different feel to the Palais in Hammersmith, but it already felt like a second home. She felt at peace here, as if she knew it was a place to start again, ensure some happy memories were made. It was just what she needed. And it was all thanks to Nancy and Roger, who she was lucky enough to count as friends. She owed them both so much in so many different ways.

'You know what?' she said then, as she linked arms with Nancy and gave her a squeeze. 'Since the two of you have thought of everything. Let's get this place open!'

27

Ten days into November, and Violet, together with Temperance and Betty, found herself on her knees scrubbing the kitchen floor of the Regal in Bethnal Green.

'I really don't see why we have to do this, Betty,' she groaned. 'The place is spotless; it's brand new.'

'It's a kitchen; you can't be too careful,' Betty insisted, as she sloshed more hot water onto her brush and scrubbed in earnest.

Violet resisted the urge to say anything else, and instead looked over at Temperance. As her friend locked eyes with her, it was all Violet could do not to break into laughter. She felt like a kid at school again, being caught out for messing about in class.

The truth was her mother was fussing about nothing, as she always did when she was anxious. Violet decided to let it go. Things weren't easy for Betty at the moment, and she was determined to make more of an effort. Violet was very aware that Betty's life was being made more difficult by George, who was in the next room helping out Ronnie's old friends. George insisted he was on excellent terms with the men, though Violet suspected they were merely tolerating him – humouring him, as they had with Ronnie when he was alive. She could only hope the presence of Archie with them might help keep things on the straight and narrow. George had always had a lot of time for Archie, though the feeling wasn't mutual, particularly after Temperance's brother, Violet's sweetheart, had died. A fellow auxiliary fireman, Archie had blamed George for Eamon's death, convinced that if Eamon hadn't gone to rescue George from a burning building at the docks, where her stepfather had been attempting to steal money, then he'd still be alive.

'Well, now look at that,' Temperance said brightly as she got to her feet. Staring at the floor, admiring the shine, she stood with her hands on her hips and smiled. 'It's gleaming.'

Violet got up to join her. 'I should say so. Last job of the day.'

'And tomorrow we open.' Temperance rubbed her hands together in glee.

Betty joined them. Brushing the dirt from her knees she gazed around the kitchen, looking for flaws.

'I'm not sure. We should never have brought the opening forwards; we're not ready.' Betty frowned. 'I still haven't got all my stocks in.'

'Your butcher is out there,' Violet said. 'Hasn't Archie promised you that he'll have all your meat rations ready for you first thing?'

Betty nodded. 'He has. He's been ever such a good lad.'

Temperance flushed at the praise. Since the news of the second Palais had broken, Archie had worked overtime trying to help get the place ready. He had spread the word, lent his time and carpentry skills for any outstanding work, and had even offered to help Betty prepare the meat the next day, though Betty had assured him she would be fine on that account.

'And of course it's nice to see George helping out,' Violet said carefully. Much as she resented George, now that she had been living out of the family home for a while, she could see that her mother was never going to leave him, no matter how much she might want her to. Therefore, it was in everyone's best interests if Violet was as encouraging as possible, especially since her mother was so unhappy these days that even a cuddle with baby Eamon only went so far. Violet looked around the kitchen again: perhaps this new challenge in Bethnal Green would help bring her mother some fulfilment. She could only hope.

'Yes, George is trying his best,' Betty agreed, joylessly.

Looking at her mother, Violet felt helpless. Since Alan had left, Betty seemed to have aged a good five years. Her shoulders slumped, almost as if she were apologising for herself, while the lines on her face made her look permanently in despair. After Maisie had left for service, Betty seemed to have all but given up. She had never been the happiest woman on earth, but she had always had a bit of life about her. When Alan had reappeared in her life, Violet had got a glimpse of how things might have been for her mother. Happier, easier, that was for sure. Betty had transformed with Alan's love. Now, with both her youngest daughter and her long-lost sweetheart far away, Betty seemed to have reverted to her old ways. More than that, she was a shadow of her former self. She was a ghost.

Violet opened her mouth, about to try and say something to cheer and chivvy her mother along, when the sound of footsteps behind her caught her attention. Turning round, Violet saw Janice, Nancy, and, to her surprise, a black GI.

'Hiya, kid,' Janice said, smiling at Violet then looking around the kitchen. 'By heck you've done wonders in here.'

Betty sighed. 'We're getting there, Jan. But I do wish we weren't opening tomorrow.'

'There's never a good time for these things,' Janice said. 'But you're as together as you'll ever be.'

'Janice is right, honey,' Nancy said. 'Besides, I've brought reinforcements. Kids, come in here.'

At the sound of Nancy's voice, Peter and Ruth – who was still in her school uniform – appeared at the doorway.

'These two are yours for the week,' Nancy said triumphantly. 'Well, Peter will be here full-time; Ruth will come down after school. Right, honey?'

Ruth nodded enthusiastically. 'It was so much fun dressing the tables like we did for the National Restaurants. Will we do that again?'

Everyone laughed at the youngster's enthusiasm.

'Not quite,' Betty said. 'This place will be a bit more relaxed.'

'Still plenty for you to do to help Betty, though, love,' Janice said, before turning to Peter. 'And the same for you, young man.'

Nancy laid a hand on Peter's shoulder. 'We're going to have Peter continue his training at this branch. Renee thinks it'll be good for him to see a project from the beginning.'

'And it will give me more experience in other areas, too. Alex said that was vital if I wanted to be a good manager one day,' Peter added.

At the mention of Alex, Violet saw Nancy visibly stiffen before she made herself relax.

'Well, it'll be a pleasure to have you both here,' Betty said warmly, her eyes then drifting to the handsome soldier. 'And what about you . . . Stafford, isn't it?'

The soldier tipped his hat. 'That's me, ma'am.'

'I'm guessing you're not here to help out?' Betty asked, a rare twinkle in her eyes.

Violet grinned. Her mother seemed almost animated.

'No, ma'am.' At this, Stafford almost looked shamefaced.

'Found him loitering outside,' Janice said.

'He's here for me,' Temperance said hurriedly. 'We're going to a meeting together.'

'An LCP meeting?' Violet asked, already knowing the answer.

Temperance nodded and Violet felt a flush of guilt. Like Temperance, she had made a silent promise to her sweetheart, Eamon, after he died that she would carry on his work. But after only a handful of meetings she had given up. What did that say about her?

'We're all finished in here,' Archie said now as he walked into the kitchen followed by George.

'Fit for a king out there,' George bellowed, his chest puffing up with pride. 'That bar will keep many a happy man in a pint.'

Violet buried her irritation at George's bragging, and smiled at Archie instead.

'Thanks, Arch.'

'We're all so grateful to you,' Nancy said brightly. 'You'll be guests of honour at our official opening on Saturday night.'

'That mean free drinks all night?' George bellowed again, and laughed at his own weak joke. The assembled group ignored him and Archie instead locked eyes with Stafford.

'Hello, lad,' he said. 'What are you doing here?'

'We're going to a meeting,' Temperance explained hurriedly. 'I'm sure I did tell you.'

Archie frowned and wiped his hands on his trousers. 'Did you? I can't remember.'

'I'm sure I did,' Temperance said again. 'I won't be long.'

'She's giving a speech tonight.' Stafford looked at Temperance proudly as he spoke. 'About her late brother's commitment to the LCP.'

Now it was Violet's turn to look surprised. 'Are you? You never said. I'd have liked to have come to that.'

'So would I,' Archie said quietly. 'You standing up and making a speech is a big deal, Temp.'

With all eyes on her, Temperance's cheeks flushed. She looked for all the world as if she wanted the earth to swallow her up whole.

'Oh, you wouldn't want to come to anything as boring as me wittering on.'

'Yes, we would,' Archie said calmly, though there was a certain grit to his voice. 'You didn't give us the chance, Temperance. You assumed we wouldn't be interested, or we wouldn't understand.'

Violet shot a look at Archie. She seemed to be witnessing a private argument and she wasn't sure she wanted any part of it.

'Hey, come on, man.' Stafford spoke softly to Archie now, but in a tone that brooked no argument.

'I'm sorry, what did you just say?' Archie exclaimed, turning to Stafford and gazing at him in incredulity.

'I meant leave her alone, man. She'd have had her reasons

for not mentioning this stuff to you. All good ones I'm sure. But still, it's not like you'd understand the same way we would.'

'I wouldn't understand what it's like to hear my sweetheart stand up and tell a room how brave her brother, my friend, was?'

Violet watched in horror as Temperance fled the room, tears pooling at her eyes. She looked at Archie who seemed frozen, unsure what to do next.

'Go after her, you silly sod,' Violet hissed.

But Archie stood rooted to the floor, unable to move, and it was Stafford who ran after Temperance. As he did so, Violet turned to Archie and shook her head. Temperance and Archie had their differences, but falling out over this felt needless. Archie was letting jealousy get to him. She just hoped he'd come to his senses, before it was too late.

28

'Temperance, slow down, please,' Stafford pleaded, as he struggled to keep up with the dance instructor. 'What's wrong?'

At the question, Temperance felt anger bubble up inside her. 'What's wrong? Are you serious? You embarrassed me in there, that's what's wrong.'

Stafford caught up to her and reached for her arm, only for Temperance to snatch it away. She had managed to ignore him for the entire bus ride to Camberwell, fury coursing its way through her veins. Now that they had disembarked she couldn't contain herself any longer.

'I'm sorry. I was just trying to make a point.'

'You made a point all right,' she snapped, coming to an abrupt halt outside the LCP meeting room. 'You made me look a fool, and you made Archie lose his temper as well.'

Stafford held his hands up in defence. 'Hey, that ain't nothing to do with me. If a man can't control his temper that's not my fault.'

'You provoked him.'

'I did not,' Stafford protested. 'The bigger question is why you weren't straight with your man, Temperance? And your friends?'

Defeated, Temperance sank miserably to the floor. The concrete was cold, and the chill seeped through her skin and into her bones but she didn't care. These days she felt so confused by her life, so worried about everything. This new dance hall was exciting, but it would mean even less time with her already beleaguered family. Then there was Archie. Things had become more strained between them lately. All she wanted was for them to go back to the way they were. She rubbed her head, unable to make sense of anything. Worse, she felt alone, as if she had nobody to talk to. Her mother was too wrapped up in baby Eamon, and her Aunt Winnie was busy trying to get her theatre back on an even keel. Renee was tied up with Palais business, as was Nancy. Maisie had left to go to war, and Violet had her hands full worrying about her own mother, as well as caring for the baby. Tears pooled in her eyes and Temperance brushed them angrily away. The last thing she wanted was to start crying in front of Stafford.

At the sight of her tears, the soldier crouched down in front of her and offered her his hand.

'Come on, Temp,' he said. 'Crying's going to get you nowhere.'

As he pulled her gently to her feet, she felt the strength in his hand and the warmth from his palm as if it were a balm to her soul. Once she was up, he put a hand on the small of her back and guided her away from the meeting room and towards a bench further down the road.

'Now, talk to me?' he asked after they'd been sitting a few moments.

Temperance sighed. 'I don't even know where to start.'

'The beginning,' Stafford suggested helpfully. 'Always works for me.'

Smiling in spite of herself Temperance began to talk to him. First about her family and her worries over little Eamon and Violet. Then, crushingly, how scared she was that she was drifting apart from her sweetheart, Archie.

'We just don't have anything in common anymore,' she said, then thought for a moment. 'No, that's not true. It's just getting harder and harder for the things that we have in common to keep us together.'

'And why do you think that is?' Stafford asked.

'I don't know,' Temperance said.

A couple walked past them chatting and laughing in that natural, easy way a couple can when they're right for each other. Temperance envied them. She knew things between her and Archie had been like that – where had they gone so wrong?

'Do you really not know?' Stafford asked gruffly. 'I mean there has to be a reason you didn't tell him about tonight.'

At the statement, Temperance said nothing. She didn't want to say the words aloud. But as she looked up at the darkening skies she knew that she had to admit the truth: it would set her free.

'I think we're too different,' she said.

'Why?' Stafford asked.

'You know why,' Temperance said again.

'I want to hear you say it. Understand that you get it,' Stafford insisted.

'Because he's white and I'm not.'

'You're black, honey,' Stafford said, more gently now. 'You can say you're black and you're proud.'

Looking at the soldier she saw the gentle smile on his face and laughed.

'I am proud of who I am. My father taught me to always be proud of who I am. Maybe with him and Eamon gone, it's been harder for me to stay true to that.'

'Your mother's still here, though, right?' Stafford frowned as he asked the question.

Temperance nodded.

'Surely she drums it into you the importance of who you are.'

For a moment Temperance though about her mother. Yes, Enid had always encouraged her to be proud of who she was, but she had never actively encouraged her to fight for who she was, not in the way her brother and father had.

'My mother's white,' Temperance said bluntly, recognising

that was the fastest way to get Stafford to understand. She was right, as a look of comprehension passed across Stafford's features.

'That must have been tough for her, being a white woman being married to a black man.'

Now it was Temperance's turn to look surprised. Nobody else ever had really understood that.

'It was,' she said. 'My mother was sometimes beaten black and blue, and by complete strangers who thought she should be taught a lesson for marrying someone from another race.'

Stafford shook his head frowning.

'But she and Dad had this bond, you know?' Temperance cast her mind back to how her parents had been with each other. 'They had this incredible love for one another that was stronger than anything anyone outside of that bond could throw at them. Dad respected their differences, he knew their lives, but especially Mum's, were harder because of it, but he was so proud of his heritage.'

As Temperance finished speaking Stafford let out a long sigh. 'If only we could persuade the rest of the world to see things that way, huh?'

'That would be nice,' Temperance agreed.

There was a pause and then Stafford spoke again.

'So, ain't it like that for you and Archie?'

At the question, Temperance gave a start. It was, wasn't it? 'I don't know,' she said in a small voice. 'Archie loves me and I love him, that's true. But I think Archie wants to pretend there are no differences between us, that we should forget about all that and just be who we are with each other. He thinks that by acknowledging we have different skin colour, we're creating a problem. *I'm* creating a problem.'

Stafford nodded. 'But if you embrace your differences, you can come together and face challenges from others. There ain't nothing wrong with being different.'

Temperance smiled. It had been a long time since she'd heard someone say that.

'What do your family think of you courting Archie?' Stafford asked now.

'They love him. Mum, especially. I think she worries, though. My Aunt Winnie, my father's sister, she's always worried about me or my brother courting outside of our own race. She knew how hard Mum and Dad had it. But I'm not just black, I'm white, too. It's confusing.'

'I can see that,' Stafford said lightly. 'It's not easy. But it sounds like your mom and pop had their own way of working things out.'

'They did,' Temperance said. 'Mother would often come here to support Dad, listen to him speak. Though she wasn't too comfortable when my brother Eamon wanted to do it.'

'Why?' Stafford asked.

'Because Eamon was a lot more forthright, more angry than Dad about the way people of colour were . . . are . . . treated. Eamon was sure that the reason he was turned down to fight in the army was because he was being discriminated against.'

'I thought England removed the colour bar years ago?'

'We did. But Eamon was convinced that was the reason, and not the fact that as a docker he was in a reserved occupation. I think Mother worried Eamon was too sensitive about it all, and didn't have enough tolerance.'

'Well, sometimes tolerance ain't what's needed,' Stafford said. 'But I can see your mom's point. And what about you? Does she know you're involved now in the LCP?'

'She does. But she doesn't know I'm here regularly again. I think she'd worry.'

Stafford nodded and checked his watch. Temperance got the feeling that he wanted to say more, but instead he got to his feet.

'Time for you to go inside and knock 'em dead,' he said instead.

As Temperance followed him into the hall, she tried to gather herself for the evening ahead and the speech on tolerance she had prepared. Yet all she could think about as she nodded polite hellos and good evenings at her LCP friends, was just what Stafford thought about all she had revealed, and why his opinion mattered so much to her.

29

The following day, Nancy sat in the office at the Regal gazing out of the window. She hated to admit it, but the room needed more sprucing up. It was colder than the office in Hammersmith, and the walls were bare brick as it hadn't been deemed essential to get the staff areas as polished as the rest of the place. Then there was the fact it was the size of a shoebox, and a kid's shoebox at that, with a tiny desk pushed up against one wall and a cramped easy chair in the corner for guests.

Nancy looked across her desk at Janice sitting opposite, hands wrapped around a cup of tea, a quizzical look on her face.

'What's wrong, honey?'

Janice chuckled and took a sip of tea before she spoke. 'That obvious, eh?'

Nancy lifted her own coffee to her lips and looked at the older woman. 'You could say that. What's on your mind?'

'I'm wondering what we're going to do about an MC? I know we're all working across both venues but talented as I am, Nancy, even I can't be in two places at once. We need someone else, surely?'

Nancy sighed and shook her head. 'You're damn right, honey. I can't believe we've been so stupid. We open tonight and we don't have an MC!'

Panic set in. They couldn't open tonight without someone to handle proceedings. What would people say? And what would people do if there was trouble? The MC not only handled the music but also the guests if any of them stepped out of line.

'Well, I have been giving it some thought,' Janice said gently, 'I had a feeling you'd forgotten.'

Nancy raised an eyebrow. 'Don't sweeten the pill, will you, honey?'

Janice smiled wryly. 'I had a cuppa with Bill Cain last week,' she began. 'Lovely fella, though I can see why he'd ruffle a few feathers.'

'That's an understatement,' Nancy said. 'Why did you meet up with Bill?'

'He popped in to the Palais,' Janice explained, setting her empty cup down on the floor. 'Said he'd heard about the new dance hall through Edna and wanted to find out more about it. You lot were all over here, so I filled him in myself.'

Nancy could well imagine how that had gone down. She imagined Edna had delighted in telling Bill what a nightmare Alex thought the whole venture was, and could picture her and Bill sat around Edna's spacious West London kitchen, rubbing their hands together in glee as they thought about how quickly it would fail. How she and Renee would be forced back to Hammersmith with their tails between their legs, waiting for Alex to return home and sort it all out.

Remembering the look of disgust on Alex's face as Roger had outlined the plan to him, and the subsequent rows with her over the rest of his visit, Nancy felt a chill run down her spine, along with a bolt of steel. There was no way on earth she would allow this new dance hall to become a failure. No way she would allow Alex and his mother the satisfaction of knowing this plan hadn't been as successful as Nancy, Renee and Roger had hoped.

'And what did Bill have to say about it?' she asked Janice now.

'He was actually quite interested. Thought it'd be good for the area,' Janice said thoughtfully. 'He asked who your MC was, and when I said I didn't know he offered up his services if you needed.'

Nancy nearly choked on her coffee. Well, that was a turn-up. But there was still no way on earth she would allow Bill Cain anywhere near the Regal. The place was unsullied, best to keep it that way.

'We don't need him,' she said firmly.

'But you do need someone,' Janice said firmly. 'And I can't do it.'

There was a pause as Nancy gathered her thoughts. Janice was right – being an MC was a skilled job; you couldn't just get any Tom, Dick or Harry off the street and every dance hall needed one.

'Would you be happy to be the Bethnal Green MC as a temporary measure?' she asked Janice. 'Till we find someone of your calibre.'

Janice looked surprised at the question. 'But surely you need me at the Palais?'

'I need you here more, right now,' Nancy said. 'The Regal is new, we want to start off with a bang, establish a reputation for quality.'

At the compliment Janice beamed. 'And what about the Palais?'

Nancy got to her feet and pulled on her wool coat. 'You leave the Palais to me.'

Just over an hour later, Nancy was walking down a road full of untouched two-up, two-down terraces in West London. She had only ever been here once before but it didn't take long to find the house she wanted. It was the best kept house in the street, and its owner was busy out the front pulling weeds from the path.

She paused to watch him for a moment. Stooped over the path, Bill Cain looked a lot older than the last time she had seen him. He still sported a thick head of grey hair, but he'd lost a lot of weight. Then again, with rationing, who hadn't?

Bill stood up and at the sight of Nancy he smirked. 'Wondered how long it'd be before you came crawling back.'

'I'm not crawling back, honey,' Nancy said briskly. She meant it, too. She would rather the Palais have no MC at all rather than beg Bill Cain for a favour. 'I need an MC. You up to the task?'

'Bethnal Green?' Bill sniffed. 'That's a hell of a way from here every day.'

'It is,' said Nancy coolly. 'But the Palais is just ten minutes' walk.'

'You want me back in Hammersmith?' Bill looked surprised as he set down his trowel.

'You know it like the back of your hand.' Nancy inhaled briskly, as she took in his mud-stained trousers. 'And I wouldn't give you the run of a new dance hall where people don't know you or understand you like they do around here. No, I wondered if you'd help out at Hammersmith until we get ourselves sorted. Janice can take over at Bethnal Green in the interim.'

Bill rested his chin on his wooden hoe and thought for a moment. 'My old job back, eh?'

'A temporary position,' Nancy cautioned. She didn't want Bill getting the wrong idea.

'And what about Edna?' Bill suddenly barked.

'Edna?' Nancy echoed. 'What's she got to do with it?'

'She'll want to come back as chief dancer.'

Nancy laughed. 'Honey, Edna can come back in an advisory capacity but she can't run the pen, or dance, for very long these days. You know that as well as I do.'

Bill said nothing. Nancy knew he couldn't argue with that.

'All right,' he said. 'But I want me old rate. I'm not taking a pay cut just because you're having trouble finding someone else.'

'You'll get your old rate of pay,' Nancy promised.

'Good,' Bill said gruffly. 'I'll be up at five.'

With that, he bent down to start tending to his path once

again and Nancy took it as her cue to leave. She had only managed a few steps when she heard her name being called.

Turning around she saw Bill straightened up again. 'Thanks Nancy,' he said solemnly. 'I'm grateful you've come to me.'

Nancy felt shock course through her. Wonders would never cease. Bill Cain had actually said thank you! As she continued down the road a huge smile spread across her face. Finally, a true miracle had happened in the world: Bill Cain was a changed man!

30

As the band warmed up in the pit, Renee walked up and down the dance floor and addressed her staff.

'Now remember, we are not the Hammersmith Palais, we're more relaxed, more low-key, but I still want to make sure we offer the same service and standards,' she said earnestly. 'Tonight's a big night. Not only are we opening, but word has got out that the battle in El Alamein has been won by Britain. No doubt there'll be a few celebrations tonight, so brace yourselves.'

Renee watched as heads nodded up and down in unison, and felt a stab of pride. Each one of her girls had worked tirelessly to bring this new venture together, with some facing greater hardships in their quest. She glanced at Violet who looked pale and tired. She resolved to talk to her after the first night and see how she was faring.

'Janice will weed out any troublemakers as our MC,' Renee continued.

Janice nodded sagely.

'And I'll be here, too, making sure everything is going well. I'll also be introducing the Ladies Excuse Me tonight, and as a special treat, Roger here will be announcing the raffle.'

At the mention of his name Roger took a little mock bow and Renee nearly doubled over with laughter. The vicar looked so solemn.

'All proceeds go to the National Savings Week's Spitfire Fund, of course,' Renee continued. 'The prize is a month of free dances at the new dance hall.'

At the generosity, there were a few exclamations amongst the staff.

'And one more thing. Edna will be doing the exhibition dance tonight with Archie.'

At this, nobody said a word, but all eyes turned to Archie, who didn't look bothered. Nobody could forget the last time he and Edna had performed an exhibition dance, almost two years ago, when they'd taken a very public nasty tumble.

'I am sure it will all be a great success,' Roger said smoothly as he came to join Renee's. 'And on behalf of the church, I would like to thank you for all your hard work, and the wonderful job you have done. Thank you all.'

With that, the staff disbanded and Renee turned to Roger. She was keyed up and anxious. She desperately wanted tonight to be a success, not just for her but for Roger, too. She smiled. 'Thanks for all your support with this. You've created something really special here. And we're going to make sure it's a triumph.'

Roger smiled back and was about to speak when Mick, one of Ronnie's former henchmen, arrived. At the sight of the man, in a jacket two sizes too small and hair so heavily pomaded that it looked like it had been dipped in lard, Renee shivered. She still hated to be near anything or anyone that reminded her of her late husband.

'What do you want?' she said icily.

Mick shrugged, seemingly untroubled by Renee's attitude. As he did so, Renee could still see the scars that lined his face, the result of multiple beatings from Ronnie, she assumed, given when Mick hadn't done his bidding.

'Just come to wish you and the vicar well,' he said.

Roger beamed. 'Well that's kind of you, Mick.'

At the praise, Mick looked uncomfortable and shot Renee a wary look from beneath his bushy black brows.

'You're welcome,' he managed, and then, appearing to find

his footing, said. 'But whilst I'm here I want to talk about a business opportunity.'

Renee groaned inwardly. Whatever it was Mick had in mind, she knew that it wouldn't be on the straight and narrow and would come at a price.

'Oh?' Roger asked, pleasantly.

'I've got a friend of a friend,' Mick said now, his voice low. 'He reckons he knows a bloke what's making beer on the side. He could get you a job lot for this place, if you want? Everyone knows it's getting harder to come by. It'll be at a big discount, seeing as this is a bit of a charitable operation.'

Roger looked doubtful. 'He's making beer, you say?'

Mick nodded enthusiastically. 'Got extra crops on his farm, too: fruit, veg and that.'

'Extra crops?' Roger queried. 'That doesn't sound quite right to me.'

'No, no vicar, it's all above board.'

At that, Renee couldn't help herself and laughed.

'You don't think he's genuine?' Roger asked turning to her.

'No, I don't, and neither do you,' Renee said bluntly. She fixed her gaze on Mick. 'We're not selling knock-off goods here, Mick, do you hear me?'

'It ain't knock-off,' Mick insisted. He drew himself up to his full six foot. 'All that's in my past. I just want to help you and the vicar.'

'If you say so,' Renee said coolly. 'Forgive me for speaking me mind, son, but if a deal sounds too good to be true, then it usually is.'

'It's not like that, Reen.' There was a hint of panic in Mick's voice and Renee wondered what exactly he'd got himself involved in.

'It does sound like a marvellous idea, Mick,' Roger said. 'But my feeling is that if your pal does have these extra crops, as he says he does, he really ought to turn them over to the government. They could be used to help our military effort, at the very least, as our men continue fighting this dreadful war.'

'I see your point, Vicar,' Mick began, 'but I don't think that's what my friend wants to do.'

'Well, I rather think you might have to persuade him,' Roger said in a gentle but firm tone. 'We can't take anything that might not be completely above board.'

'It's all honest,' Mick tried again.

Roger shook his head. 'I'm sorry, Mick. I appreciate the offer, I really do, but I wouldn't feel right taking something like that. Now, if you'll excuse me, I want to make sure I'm outside ready to greet our parishioners when they arrive.'

With that, Roger made his way across the dance floor and disappeared through the double doors. When he was gone Mick rounded on Renee.

'Can't you have a word with your mate?' he muttered, jerking his head in the direction of Roger.

Renee looked at him, incredulity spreading across her face. 'You want me to try and convince the vicar to buy dodgy goods?'

'They ain't dodgy,' Mick insisted.

'Pull the other one,' Renee scoffed.

Mick set his cold dark eyes on her, then reached into his jacket pocket for a cigarette. As he lit up, he cocked his head to one side, a plume of smoke trailing upwards from his left hand.

'I see why you might think like that, Renee, I really do,' he tried again. 'I ain't always been honest, and as you know, when I was knocking about with your late husband things weren't always on the regular.'

'You're preaching to the choir here, lad.' Renee rolled her eyes.

Mick offered her a cigarette, which she gratefully took.

'I was fond of your old man, Renee.' Mick appeared to change the subject as he lit her cigarette. When Renee inhaled and said nothing, he added, 'Ronnie's missed by a lot of people. Not just here and up north, but all over the country. Anywhere he was known.'

'He was known, all right,' Renee said, taking another sharp pull on her cigarette.

'That's the thing. When people are known, they're missed. And when they're missed, people start to wonder . . .' Mick let his words hang in the air.

Renee narrowed her eyes. 'What's your point, Mick?'

He shrugged, then stared down at his cigarette. 'It's just some people can't make sense of what happened that night. Like I said, they wonder about it.'

'There's nothing to *wonder*,' Renee said, more casually than she felt. 'Ronnie was tired after that scuffle he had with you.'

'See, I don't buy that,' Mick said again. 'Ronnie knew how to handle himself. It weren't the first fight he'd had. There are rumours circulating. Thought you should know, is all.'

'Rumours?' Renee felt goosebumps starting to rise along her flesh, and her heart began to race.

'Yeah, thing is folk are wondering if maybe what happened to Ronnie wasn't an accident. That maybe someone bumped him off, like.'

Renee gave a short little laugh. 'Don't be so daft. He fell and hit his head. He was disorientated. The busies said so themselves.'

Mick scratched his chin, his cigarette smoke now billowing into Renee's face.

'Coppers are busy at the moment. There's a war on.' He gave a half laugh. 'They ain't got time to look into things properly.'

'It was a tragic accident, Mick.'

'Was it, though?' Mick asked, fixing his gaze on Renee again. 'I can't believe you thought it was too tragic.'

'Come again?' Renee exclaimed.

'We all know things weren't right between the two of you.

169

You buggered off and left him for years, for a start. That's not the sign of a happy marriage.'

'I had to help me sister,' Renee said defensively.

'And it was common knowledge Ronnie used to knock you about a bit,' Mick continued, as if she hadn't spoken. 'Never thought that was right, myself. Should never hit a woman. No excuse.' He leaned forwards now, as if warming to his theme, and Renee did her best not to recoil. 'Thing is, I wouldn't blame you if you'd had enough of him that night and done something about it. Knocked him off yourself.'

Though all the nerve endings in Renee's body felt as if they were on fire, she let out another little laugh.

'You've been reading too many fairy stories, Mick.'

Mick threw his cigarette to the ground and shrugged. 'Maybe. Maybe not. Thing is, Reen, folk are talking. And after all you've been through I'd hate for trouble to start knocking at your door.'

'That a threat?' she asked, her tone flinty.

Now it was Mick's turn to laugh. He held up his hands in mock defence. 'Me, threaten you? Never in this world.' He looked away and paused. 'It would be a shame if that nice vicar started asking questions, though. You know, if rumour spread that you'd done something to his beloved brother.'

'Hardly beloved,' Renee pointed out. 'They hadn't seen each other for years.'

'Even so,' Mick said in a casual way. 'Blood's blood, Renee. If word got out there'd been a bit of foul play, as it were, then no doubt Roger'd be upset. Who knows, he might even be upset enough to go to the police. Start asking questions.'

Renee's heart was banging so loudly against her chest that she was sure Mick could hear it.

'But if the vicar could be persuaded to take my pal's beer, I've got a feeling, Reen, that I could personally put a stop to these rumours meself. Make sure nobody ever heard anything about them.' He turned to look at her and smiled. 'I'll leave it with you. Just something to think about. We'll catch up in a couple of days.'

And with that, Mick walked away.

31

'He said what?' Nancy exclaimed. She paced the little office in Bethnal Green, sure her brain was about to explode with what Renee was telling her.

'He said that he'd heard rumours about what had happened to Ronnie,' Renee said again, her voice thick through the cigarette she was smoking.

'But how can this have got out?' Nancy babbled. 'Nobody knows what happened to Ronnie, apart from you and me.'

'He's bluffing,' Renee said, though her hand was shaking. 'He has to be.'

'But what if he's not?' Nancy ran a hand through her dark hair. She couldn't take the risk, not with two children to look after. Something had to be done; they had to find out for sure just how much Mick knew, and if indeed he was bluffing.

She stared at her friend and sighed heavily. Renee had burst into her new office an hour earlier and told her about Mick's blackmail attempt – because that was exactly what it was – and Nancy had felt as if her world had imploded.

She and Renee had never really spoken about the night Ronnie died. It was as if they had each tried to bury themselves in work, and everything in between, so as to forget what they had done. That didn't stop the nightmares that regularly haunted Nancy, though. She would often wake up cloaked in a sheen of her own sweat, her pulse racing, as the horrors of that fateful night, when Renee had finally stabbed her own husband, tormented her.

Nancy had no doubt what would happen to them both if

word ever got out. At first, she had been so relieved that the police were ready to accept their story, that she'd convinced herself they'd gotten away with it. But even though it had been self-defence – Ronnie had been about to overpower Renee, do God-knows-what to her – the fact that they'd covered it up, kept the truth from the authorities, did not look good. Who was to say that the police would even believe the truth after all this time? They could insist it was murder. And when you were an accomplice to murder, did you ever really get away with the crime? If you didn't pay the price with a public trial and then imprisonment, or your own life, then you paid in other ways. The blood that had spattered all over the walls, the scrubbing and cleaning it had taken to get rid of it once and for all, haunted Nancy, and she was sure it always would.

Gazing across at Renee, she swallowed before she spoke. 'Do you ever think about that night?'

Renee's jaw clenched as she stubbed out the cigarette in the silver ashtray Nancy kept on her desk.

'Course I bloody do,' she said. 'Every bloody day. That man tortured me in life and he still does it in death. I'll never forget the look on his face as I lifted up that shoe and stabbed him with the heel, and I'll never forgot how it made me feel. I was like a woman possessed, I could taste freedom once and for all and I wasn't going to let Ronnie take it away from me again—'

She broke off, and Nancy was about to say that she knew just how Renee felt, but Renee wasn't done.

'I've never seen so much blood though, Nancy. In all my life, I thought I'd seen it all. In the fights Ronnie made me bear witness to, the scuffles on the dance floor, and the look of horror in his eyes as I finally did what he never thought I was capable of.'

'But you were,' Nancy said slowly.

She walked around to Renee's side and crouched down beside her, putting a hand on her knee. She had no idea of the burden and the pain her friend carried with her each day. A trickle of guilt passed through Nancy. When Renee had told her of Mick's attempts to blackmail her, Nancy's first thought had been for herself. But the simple truth was that Renee had been through enough at the hands of Ronnie Newsham, and Nancy wasn't about to let her suffer alone. She had always known the day would come, that they would be found out, but she'd hoped that it wouldn't be at the hands of one of Ronnie's thug mates.

Nancy stood up, walked across to the filing cabinet in the corner of the room and fished out a notepad and pen.

'Time to make a plan.' She sat in the chair and flipped open the book to find a clean page.

Renee lifted her head in surprise. 'What on earth are you doing?'

'We need to sort this out, Renee honey,' Nancy said kindly.

But Renee snatched the pen from Nancy's hand and threw it across the room.

'If we're going to survive this we need to get smart, you dozy cow,' she hissed.

Nancy jumped back, startled. 'What the hell is wrong with you?'

'What the hell's wrong with you, more like?' Renee snapped. She got to her feet, retrieved the pen and pad, and put them both back in the filing cabinet. 'I worry about you sometimes, Nancy Blum, I really do. Much as I appreciate the sentiment of you wanting to help in this situation, you start writing things down and we're done for. What were you going to do? Call it the "how to get away with blackmail and murder" plan?'

Nancy wriggled in her seat, feeling uncomfortable. Renee was right. It was a dumb idea to start writing things down.

'So what do you suggest we do, then, Einstein?' she asked. Renee might be right, but Nancy's pride was bruised.

'Well, we've got a few options from what I can see,' Renee said. She paced up and down the office in the way Nancy had.

'Go on,' Nancy encouraged.

'We can ignore it, assume he's bluffing – after all, he doesn't really know what happened – and hope he goes away,' Renee suggested.

'Or?' Nancy asked, not wanting to put all her faith in one idea.

'Or we can assume that Mick's not bluffing and that he will tell Roger what we did, so we tell Roger ourselves.'

'Absolutely not, honey!' Nancy exclaimed. 'Roger's a man of the cloth. He'll have to go to the police; he'll have no choice.'

As Nancy finished speaking the sound of the orchestra starting up could be heard below. Opening night had begun, and neither she nor Renee were there to welcome their new guests. As the orchestra came to a close, Nancy heard Janice's voice boom across the room. She couldn't hear exactly what she was saying, but her tone was jubilant and the excited applause from the crowd told her that their experienced MC was handling the job with aplomb.

Nancy sank her head in her hands. How had her life come to this? How was she sat here in a tiny little office, trying to work out how to deal with a blackmailer, when her priority right now was the new venue. That, and her kids. She should be excited and happy that their hard work had all paid off. Instead, she was here dealing with more of Ronnie's never-ending mess.

As she lifted her head, she heard the sound of Peter and Ruth laughing outside as they made their way down the stairs towards the dance hall. Nancy had promised them both that they could stay as long as they wanted at the dance that night, as the evening was purely celebratory. After all, there wasn't just the new opening for people to be jubilant about, but emotions would be high because the long battle in Egypt had finally come to a successful conclusion, with the British defeating the Germans once and for all.

As Peter and Ruth's voices ebbed away, Nancy knew she

had too much to lose to let Mick get away with his threats. As unpalatable as it might seem, there was only one option.

'So we'll have to accept Mick's offer and let him blackmail us,' she said miserably.

Renee stopped pacing and grinned. 'Or, we play him at his own game.'

'Why are you smiling?' Nancy looked at her hesitantly. Whenever Renee had a plan, trouble wasn't usually far behind.

'Because I am sick and tired of letting men like Mick and Ronnie get one over on me,' she said. 'I made a promise to myself, the moment Ronnie died, that I wouldn't let men treat me like dirt anymore, and I'm not breaking that promise. No, we'll let Mick think we're going along with his scheme while getting something on him. He's going to wish he'd never been born by the time we're finished.'

As Renee trailed off, her face full of excitement, the crowd below erupted with a huge round of applause. Nancy looked into her friend's face and could see there was no changing her mind. Renee had the bit between her teeth, and nothing Nancy could say would get her to think twice. She leaned back in her chair and sighed heavily. Though she was almost excited at the idea of exacting revenge on someone who wanted to harm them, the more rational, sensible side of Nancy told her that this was surely the path to trouble. And hadn't they all had enough of that in their lives?

32

'Welcome to the Regal,' Violet chorused as she greeted visitors in the foyer of the Bethnal Green establishment. She had been on the door for the past hour, though she had been due to work behind the bar.

She checked her watch for the umpteenth time and wondered where on earth Renee and Nancy were. They were the ones who were supposed to be here, welcoming customers and showing off the new venue.

Catching Edna's eyes on her, Violet put on a broad smile and looked away. Whatever the reason that was keeping Nancy and Renee out of the way, she knew it had to be a good one. She turned then to usher in two guests, who like almost everyone else had, oohed and ahhhed at the transformation of the old theatre.

Violet had to admit they had done a good job. In one corner of the room, many of the old, red velvet seats had been repurposed and turned into fancy bar stools rather than be thrown away. The remainder had been put into storage, ready to be used for the dance hall's daytime restaurant.

And although money hadn't stretched to a proper maple-sprung dance floor, Renee had refused to compromise on the centrepiece chandelier. One had been sourced – Violet didn't like to ask where from – and hung proudly above the dance floor, glittering like a jeweller's window, causing the stir Renee knew it would amongst the guests.

'Violet, love.' The sound of Temperance's mother's voice caught her attention and Violet whirled around to greet her.

'Hi, Enid, how are you?' She leaned forward to kiss the older woman on each cheek and caught a whiff of talc-scented skin.

'I'm all right.' Enid beamed. 'Winnie'll be along in a minute.'

Violet raised an eyebrow in surprise as she released Enid from her grasp.

'I didn't know she was coming. Thought she was too busy at the theatre.'

'You know what Winnie's like.' Enid chuckled. 'She wants to see the competition.'

'Do I hear my ears burning?' Winnie Adams called now, sweeping towards her sister-in-law and Violet as if she was a woman of twenty rather than sixty-five.

'Only a bit.' Violet grinned. 'Enid says you're here to size up the competition.'

Winnie sighed. 'Well, you might be onto something with this new budget dance hall.' She prodded the wall with her stick as if examining for hidden treasure. 'You're certainly busy enough.'

Violet followed her gaze out towards the bar and dance hall. Word had got round and the place was packed – with locals and American GIs.

'I expect everyone has come to see what the fuss is all about,' she said.

'No Renee or Nancy?' Winnie enquired, looking puzzled.

'Er no, they're showing some bigwigs the offices I think,' Violet said, thinking on her feet.

'Never mind all that, where's my grandson?' Enid chirruped, and looked around for him as if she expected to see him suddenly appear from behind Violet's shoulder.

'Enid. Shhhh,' Violet hissed.

'Oh, stop it,' Enid chuckled. 'Nobody knows you here.'

'Some do.' Violet frowned and gestured at the crowded dance hall. 'A few of the Palais regulars are here tonight.'

'You sound as if you're ashamed of being his mum,' Enid grumbled.

Winnie shook her head and nudged Eamon's grandmother with her stick.

'Don't be so stupid, Enid,' she scolded. 'You know how difficult things are for the girl. Tongues have only just stopped wagging since your last outburst. What are you trying to achieve by constantly mentioning the relationship between you and Violet's boy?'

Winnie's voice was getting louder and Violet was becoming increasingly uncomfortable. She knew Winnie meant well, and Violet was grateful. But she wished both women would just keep quiet and go inside. She was about to try and persuade them to have a drink at the bar, when she saw Temperance and Archie appear at the entrance to the foyer.

'Oh, look, Temp's here,' Violet gushed, and all three of them turned to look, as Violet waved at the couple. But their eyes were downcast, she noticed, and neither of them seemed to see Violet's gesture.

'They've been arguing again, no doubt,' Winnie observed, giving a gentle tsk. 'I don't know what's the matter with those two at the moment. They never seem to see eye to eye.'

'That's not true,' Enid said defensively.

But as the couple walked towards them, nobody could deny that both Archie and Temperance looked as miserable as sin. Archie's hands were in his pockets and his expression was tense, while Temperance was clutching her bag with both hands, holding it so tightly her knuckles were pale. And her chin was lifted defensively, even a little defiantly, Violet thought. But as Temperance's gaze finally found Violet standing with her family, she managed a smile and a wave.

'Hello,' she said, overly brightly. 'What do you think? Isn't it wonderful?'

'It's lovely,' Enid gushed. She linked her arm through her daughter's and gave it a squeeze. 'Have you got time for a celebratory drink before you start work?'

Temperance shook her head.

'Sorry, Ma. Me and Archie need to check the dancers are ready, and of course Archie's dancing with Edna tonight, to celebrate the new opening, so we need to run through the steps one final time.'

'Oh, yes, don't want a repeat performance of the last time you danced with poor old Edna in public, Archie,' Winnie chuckled.

At the mention of the time Edna had twisted her ankle after a nasty fall when she partnered Archie as part of an exhibition dance, the butcher didn't laugh. Instead he only clenched his jaw.

'No. Well, if you'll excuse me, I need to go and get ready. See you all later.'

And with that he disappeared through a crowd of GIs, looking all the more furious with every one that he passed.

'Whatever was that about?' Enid exclaimed.

Temperance shrugged, and Violet couldn't miss the look of exhaustion across her face.

'I think he's just had a bad day at work.'

'That boy's had a lot of bad days at work, if you ask me,' Winnie mused.

'He's busy,' Temperance said defensively.

'If you say so,' Winnie said pointedly. Then, turning to Enid, she gestured towards the bar. 'Come on, let's get a drink and celebrate, even if nobody else feels like joining us.'

Smiling apologetically, Enid allowed herself to be led away by Winnie, leaving Violet and Temperance alone.

'Archie really just have a bad day at work?' Violet asked quietly.

'Of course,' Temperance snapped. But as Violet looked at her, startled, her face softened. 'Sorry,' she said, before her beautiful dark eyes filled with tears.

'Temp, what on earth is the matter?' Violet begged.

She led her to a quiet corner of the foyer. Hidden behind a

heavy damask curtain, she knew they would have some privacy for a few minutes at least.

'I don't know,' Temperance sniffed. 'It's Archie and me. We're just not getting on.'

'Oh, Temp,' Violet soothed. 'Everyone goes through bad patches.'

'This seems like more than a bad patch.' Temperance sniffed. 'We can't even talk to each other.'

'But what's caused all this?' Violet asked.

Temperance shook her head sadly. 'It feels as if we're worlds apart at the moment. I can't even open my mouth to speak without us falling out,' she said.

'But what's happened?' Violet persisted.

She knew that they were perfect together. There was no way they would fall out like this without good reason.

'It all began months ago,' Temp started haltingly. 'When I started talking about race, and the work I'd been doing at the LCP.'

'And? What's wrong with that?' Violet asked.

'Archie doesn't understand. He doesn't see why we can't all just get along, or why there has to be a discussion about race, or about a black woman being a white man's girlfriend. I'm sure he thinks I am looking for reasons to be different.'

'Ah,' Violet said, knowingly. Whilst she was very aware of her position as a white person, she also remembered how Eamon had waxed lyrical when he was alive about how well-meaning white folks often just wanted everyone to get on and stop making a fuss. Violet wasn't educated enough to feel she could comment on that, other than to say that she sympathised with both parties.

'So, does Archie not want you volunteering with the LCP anymore, is that it?' Violet asked.

'I don't know.' Temperance shrugged. 'I don't think he minds. I just think he doesn't understand why it's necessary. I suppose it doesn't help that Stafford – you know, my GI friend – is so supportive, and involved in the LCP himself.'

The pieces of the jigsaw quickly slotted into place as Violet remembered the filthy looks Archie had been giving the GIs just moments earlier. Temperance might have thought this was about differences to Archie, but from what Violet could tell, this was good old-fashioned jealousy.

'Perhaps Archie just wants to feel included. I mean, you didn't help matters when you didn't tell any of us about that talk you did recently,' Violet offered. 'We'd have all loved to hear you speak, but you never gave us a chance.'

'Didn't think you'd be interested.'

'That's plain daft,' Violet chided. 'You know I'm supportive, always have been. I've even written articles for the LCP magazine. I've only pulled back lately because of baby Eamon.'

'I know,' Temperance said quietly.

'So, don't go assuming people think something they don't. Ask first. We all love you, we're here for you and want to support you. Try and include Archie a bit more and maybe he'll start seeing where you're coming from.'

Temperance wiped away her tears with the back of her hand and smiled at Violet.

'I've been silly, haven't I?'

'A bit,' Violet agreed. 'But show me someone who's never made a mistake in their life, and I'll show you a darned liar!'

Temperance laughed.

'Thanks, Vi.'

Violet squeezed her friend's arm. 'Any time. It's what friends are for.' She checked her watch. 'Time to get back to it. It's showtime.'

33

By nine o'clock that night, everyone at the Regal was in full party spirit. It was a sight for sore eyes for Temperance, and she was delighted to see all the guests, some she knew and some she didn't, having such a good time.

As well as the locals that Roger had rounded up and encouraged to come to the Regal to celebrate not just the opening but also the British victory in El Alamein, many of the Palais clientele had come over from Hammersmith to see the new venue and toast its success.

They included, to Temperance's surprise, a fair few of the GIs, who were chatting away with each other by the bar. Though many, she noted, were more interested in chatting up the women from the area. Temperance shook her head and smiled. Since the GIs had arrived from America, women flocked to them as readily as they flocked to the end of a queue – all hoping for something a bit extra they didn't usually find with British men.

'You look lost in thought.' A voice came from behind her, and she turned to find Archie. Standing inches away, hands in his pockets and a sheepish look on his face, was her sweetheart. At the sight of him, Temperance's heart melted.

'Not really.' She shrugged. 'Just looking around, enjoying the moment.'

Archie nodded shyly.

'I'm sorry, Temp,' he said, sincerely. 'I didn't mean to argue with you earlier.'

Temperance hung her own head. 'I'm sorry, too. I hate rowing with you, Arch.'

He moved closer to her and reached for her hand.

'I don't know why we can't get on like we used to,' he said softly.

Temperance sighed. She knew the reasons. They were too different; that she was sure of, but to say so now felt churlish, and besides, to voice those fears would mean she would have to do something about it and she couldn't face that, not now.

'I miss you, Temp,' he said at her touch. 'I just want to be with you and for us to get along.'

'That's all I want, too,' she said sincerely. 'I want us to go back to the way things were.'

'Then let's try.' He reached for her other hand and squeezed it. Just then the band launched into a lively quickstep, and he smiled. 'Care to join me?'

He gestured towards the dance floor and Temperance felt a flash of guilt.

'I'm supposed to be working,' she said.

'Nobody's going to mind,' Archie went on. 'You deserve a moment off for yourself.'

Temperance smiled. She had to admit that the quickstep was one of her favourite dances.

'Go on, then,' she said, allowing Archie to lead her across the dance floor. He wrapped his hands around her waist and she enjoyed the closeness of his body. As they danced their way across the floor, she felt all their problems fade as the combination of music and steps took them to another world.

Looking up at her beau, she saw Archie smiling down at her and knew he felt it, too. No matter what problems they were facing, surely they could get through them together? They had to. They were Temperance and Archie.

Allowing her eyes to meet his, she gave him the first genuine smile she had felt in a while, and was just resting her cheek against him, when a sudden shout from somewhere broke the spell. Temperance jerked up, looked around and, to her horror, saw a fight had broken out on the dance floor.

'What the hell did you call me?' one of the GIs was shouting.

'Only what you deserved,' came a voice Temperance recognised well. Shock coursed through her as she took in the sight of Stafford squaring up to a white GI.

A small crowd had gathered around the pair, a sea of faces both anxious and curious, as the band stopped playing. Then the white GI began to laugh nastily.

'You bastards just don't understand,' he sneered at Stafford. 'You don't belong here.'

'Says who?' Stafford snapped. He jutted his face at the white man, who took a hesitant step back, though his jaw was still clenched in anger. There were several black GIs gathering behind Stafford now, on his side. While Temperance saw some white men in uniform were pledging their support to his opponent.

Fear shook her. Temperance might not have been particularly worldly, but she had seen enough of life to know when a fight was about to ensue, and she was about to witness something ugly. Then Stafford caught her eye, and she saw the look of anger in his features. He'd reached breaking point.

'We say,' the white GI snarled. 'Just because the Brits aren't clever enough to keep a colour bar, that doesn't mean things have changed. You don't mix with us. Or to put it another way, you stay on your side of the street, and we'll stay on ours.'

At this, Temperance felt anger burn from deep inside her soul. The crowd had swollen now with many of the Regal's invited guests gathering near to see what was happening. She glanced at them anxiously and saw her mother and aunt in the throng, both caught up with those onlookers who were gawping at the display as if it were all part of the entertainment. With the sudden hostility in the air, Archie stepped closer to

Temperance and laid a protective hand on her shoulder. As he did so one of the GI's friends gave a snort of disgust.

'And this is what happens without a colour bar in this country,' he said, gesturing towards Archie and Temperance. 'This filthy lot are allowed to infiltrate our race. You're disgusting.'

As if to further demonstrate his point, he spat on the floor at Temperance's feet, and she shrank back in horror, not before she saw the satisfied smirk on the white soldier's face.

After that, everything happened so fast Temperance struggled to keep up. One minute Archie was beside her; the next he had flown at the soldier and wrestled him to the ground.

'You're a piece of scum,' Archie snarled. Drawing his fist back, he landed a punch squarely on the white soldier's jaw.

Archie's punch acted as a physical invitation for the rest of the soldiers. And before Temperance could draw breath, hell seemed to have literally broken loose as soldiers and guests alike took it as an opportunity to vent inner frustrations as they began landing punches on one another.

Cries of 'bastard' and 'you lot have had this coming' echoed through the old theatre, while others reached for chairs and glasses and started smashing them against the bar or worse, throwing them at each other.

Temperance felt sick. All the hard work, the effort that had gone into restoring this place, and it was being destroyed in an instant by sick thugs who didn't care about anyone or anything but themselves.

She looked at her mother and Winnie, and saw the disgust in their eyes. Auntie Winnie was banging the floor with her stick, shouting for them to stop, but her words had fallen into the abyss of noise as the crowd continued to fight.

This wasn't right. None of this was right. For Temperance, for her family and certainly not for the hard work that people had put into restoring this place. She thought of Roger and all the effort he had put into ensuring the Regal was a place of refuge and salvation.

A fire deep within Temperance burned as she thought of her father, who'd told her to always stand up for herself. Then she thought of her recent talk at the LCP, when she had spoken about the importance of remembering your self-worth.

Enough was enough. Without even thinking, Temperance walked around the outside of the baying mob and towards the bar. Pulling open the cupboard under the sink, she reached for one of the metal buckets they kept underneath and filled it with water. When it was full, she marched back to the throng, climbed up on one of the wooden tables, and without hesitation hurled the icy, cold water into the crowd.

As the water hit the people below her, they looked up in astonishment at her holding the bucket aloft.

'You lot are the ones that are disgusting,' Temperance cried. 'Look at you. Look at each other. Look at what you've done to this beautiful dance hall. A new venue, with community at its heart, and you thugs have ruined it, and over what?'

There was silence but Temperance wasn't finished yet.

'I hope I never see any of you again. None of you deserve a place in the Regal. But I'll tell you this, before I kick your sorry backsides out onto the street you're going to clean this place up and pay for what you did.'

When she'd finished speaking, the crowd looked up at her, open-mouthed in shock, for what felt like an eternity. Until the sound of applause from someone behind her caused Temperance to look round.

Renee was standing there, shaking her head and clapping. 'You took the words right out of my mouth, Temperance, love,' she said. 'You lot are flaming pigs. You heard what she said, get this cleared. And after that you're barred.'

The white soldier who had started it all walked towards Renee.

'Now, just a minute, honey. I wanna speak to the boss,' he said, glaring at her.

'I *am* the boss,' Renee said. She gestured towards Temperance who was still standing on the table, bucket in hand. 'And if you don't do as she says, I'll get her to fill another bucket of water and throw it all over you.'

With that, Renee swept out, pausing only to give Temperance a wink, leaving her feeling that, finally, she was beginning to find out what she was capable of.

34

The next day, Temperance walked into a hero's welcome at the Hammersmith Palais. Renee led the charge, getting to her feet and stamping the ground.

At the sound and the celebration of all her friends smiling and cheering, Temperance looked abashed. But as far as Nancy was concerned there was no time for modesty, not today. Temperance had single-handedly stopped a fight and saved the Regal from a disastrous first night and possible future ruin. She pulled her friend into her arms in a rush of affection. Nancy had always known that despite her gentle nature, Temperance was capable of standing up for herself and letting people know she was someone who mattered. Last night in Bethnal Green she had done that and more. She deserved all this praise that was being heaped on her.

'Enough,' Temperance said eventually, pulling herself from Nancy's grasp and smiling as she did so. 'I don't deserve all this.'

'You certainly do,' Betty said. 'I'm proud of you for standing up for yourself.'

'You, lady—' Renee stepped forward '—are a heroine. I've never seen anything like it.'

'That fire in your eyes, honey,' Nancy said, casting a glance at Ruth and Peter who were looking at Temperance with the same admiration in their eyes. 'It was quite something to behold.'

'Must admit, I've never used the water technique on a crowd before,' Janice said earnestly, as she pulled on a freshly lit Craven A. 'Very effective. Might try it myself next time.'

Renee shot her a sharp look. 'Not in here you won't, lady. Think of the floor.'

Janice chuckled, as Violet came towards Temperance with a pretty bunch of purple stocks, which she thrust into her hands. Nancy could see how touched Temperance was.

'Vi, you shouldn't have.' Temperance looked overwhelmed.

'I didn't,' Violet told her. At Temp's confusion she explained, 'That GI, Stafford, who you've been going to LCP meetings with, he dropped them round earlier. I think they're apology flowers.'

'Stafford?' Nancy was sure she saw a flicker of delight pass across Temp's face for second, before her eyes became wary.

'Well, it wasn't all his fault,' Temperance said now, a little haughtily.

'No but, honey, he didn't help matters,' Nancy said, then pinched the bridge of her nose and let out a long sigh. She had a lot on her plate and the last thing she or any of the other Good Time Girls needed was to deal with American race politics, as well as clear up the mess that had been made at the Regal. For the umpteenth time since war had broken out, Nancy found herself wondering when she would get a break.

Temperance's cheeks flushed with displeasure at Nancy's rebuke. For a moment, she looked like she was on the verge of saying something else, but thought better of it.

Renee then clapped her hands together and gestured for them all to sit round the bar where Sybil had made a big pot of coffee, before disappearing to the cellar. As the group pulled up chairs and helped themselves to hot drinks, Nancy looked earnestly at her friends.

'Renee and I stayed late at the Regal last night, as you know,' she explained. 'We wanted to try and see how bad the damage is. Today was supposed to be our first official day opening.'

'And how bad is it?' Betty asked, nibbling nervously on a thumbnail as she spoke.

Nancy grimaced. 'I've seen worse back in Brooklyn.'

'That's not very comforting,' Renee cried. 'From everything you've said, it sounded more like they were animals that went to your clubs in Brooklyn rather than humans!'

'Must admit I've heard similar myself,' Janice chipped in, earning a wink from Renee.

Nancy chose to ignore them both as she continued.

'Betty, honey, the kitchens are thankfully still intact. So we wondered if you might want to go over and offer an early evening meal, as planned? It's a cold but at least not a wet night, so perhaps we can encourage people to sit outside. We can put together some makeshift furniture and the like.'

'Yes, all right,' Betty agreed, as she turned to Peter and Ruth. 'Will you two help me?'

Ruth nodded eagerly. 'I can come after school.' She checked her watch and then got to her feet. 'I'd better go. See you later.'

'Take care, honey,' Nancy called. 'And go straight to Bethnal Green when you're done. I know Granny Edna wants to take you out for tea tonight, but I'll let her know you're going to the Regal instead, OK?'

'OK.' Ruth nodded, and Nancy smiled. She knew it was daft, but she enjoyed hearing the young girl say the odd Americanism.

'I'll come with you now. How busy do you think we'll be?' Peter asked.

Betty frowned. 'I don't think we'll be too bad. It's, what, Thursday today, and Hitler's behaved himself so we shouldn't have too much of a rush on. Perhaps we'll just do something simple like a mutton soup. Least that's hot and nourishing.'

'Sounds delicious,' Nancy said reassuringly. 'And that will give us time to oversee the repair work going on there today.'

'You've done well,' Temperance said approvingly. 'Do you want us all to go over?'

Nancy and Renee exchanged glances.

'I don't think it's necessary for us all to go. Temperance, you'd better stay here, I think you've done more than enough to save the place. But, Violet, can you go over today?'

'Until three,' Violet said. 'Enid's got Eamon until then. She's got a WVS meeting after that.'

'Not with those witches?' Nancy asked, aghast.

Temperance's face was grim as she nodded. 'I've told her to keep her mouth shut, Vi, really I have.'

'And do you think she will?' Betty asked, her face a picture of worry.

Temperance shrugged. 'She means well, but she gets carried away. She's not doing this to hurt you.'

'I know,' Violet said miserably. 'But she will if she doesn't stop it.'

'So, I can be at the Regal all day,' Nancy offered. She squeezed Violet's hand in a show of sympathy. 'But I wouldn't mind a second pair of hands when you've gone. Just to keep the peace if nothing else.'

'That won't be necessary.'

A loud voice Nancy immediately recognised as belonging to John, her friendly American GI, boomed out from behind them. As he came into view, she felt her stomach do cartwheels as she drank in the sight of him, standing there in his handsome, neat-fitting uniform.

'What the hell are you doing here?' Renee snapped. 'Your lot did enough damage last night.'

John took off his cap and fiddled with the brim. 'Yes, I'm not proud of the way things were handled.'

'Not proud?' Renee echoed. 'You should be downright ashamed. I've never seen anything like it.' She jerked her head towards Janice. 'And neither has she, which, given she's been an MC up north for years, is something of an achievement in itself.'

Nancy couldn't help smiling. Even when she was angry, Renee's wit was knife-sharp. It reminded her that she too needed to exhibit wary caution, however irresistibly handsome John was.

'Is that all you have to say for yourself?' she asked him. 'That you're not proud of the way things were handled? Your boys nearly ruined the Regal, and they'd better be there today to clean up the mess they created.'

'That's why I'm here,' John told her. 'Yes, my boys didn't behave well and I can promise you, steps will be taken to put that right. But it wasn't just them. From what I can tell, some of the locals got involved, too, and I don't think it's fair to put the blame squarely on my fellas.'

Nancy felt anger flood through her veins.

'You don't think it's fair to put the blame squarely on your fellas?' Nancy echoed darkly, irritation coursing throughout her body. 'Your *fellas*,' she said, seething. 'Your men started this whole thing. Your men taunted other guests with their racist comments.'

'Come on, Nancy, you know how difficult this is for them. There ain't no colour bar here, and that's going to lead to trouble.' John looked at her beseechingly, but Nancy was in no mood.

'So now it's the Brits' fault that Yanks can't hold their tongues?' she growled.

John raised an eyebrow. 'Last time I checked, ma'am, you were a Yank, too.'

'Not one like you,' Nancy snapped. 'Not if you lot are an example of what it means. I'd happily trade in my US citizenship and call myself a Brit any day, if you guys are what it means to be American.'

At the outburst, a flicker of surprise danced across John's face, before he looked down and fiddled with the brim of his cap. He seemed to be thinking about what he wanted to say next.

'I'm sorry, Nancy,' he said at last. Lifting his chin, he met Nancy's eyes. 'You're right, my men were not a shining example of Americans last night. We'll make it up to you, and we'll make sure the Regal is good as new by the end of the day. I'll see you there later.'

With that he placed his cap back on his head and saluted Nancy, before turning and walking out of the room.

Once he'd gone, there was mostly a stunned silence. Only Renee had something to say as she playfully nudged her friend in the ribs.

'You and Temperance are your own army, Nancy,' she told her proudly. 'And it seems like you've got that GI wrapped right around your finger.'

35

It took a full week for the repair work to be carried out at the Regal, something that surprised everyone. Whilst it was true that the GIs responsible for the mess had turned out in full force and worked hard, there had been greater damage than first thought. A few of the windows had been smashed, furniture broken and heavy marks on the floor where chairs had been scraped. Added to that, a couple of the fighters had managed to put their fists through the walls, exposing crumbling plaster, and even the chandelier had been damaged, though God knows how. Consequently, the girls had rolled up their sleeves and worked tirelessly, helping clear, paint and scrub when they weren't working shifts at the Hammersmith Palais.

As the full chill of late November dawned, Violet tried to ignore the ache in her back, the bags under her eyes, and the fact her hands were red raw from scrubbing the last of the beer stains off the walls.

Standing up to inspect her work, she felt tears prick her eyes. Violet hadn't known exhaustion like this for a long time and the worst thing was that she had barely seen her little boy over the past days.

Enid had kindly offered to look after Eamon for as long as Violet needed while she was putting in extra hours. Violet had been beyond grateful, but missed her boy more than she could have imagined. A few precious hours at the end of each day simply weren't enough.

'Here you go,' Temperance said, sidling up alongside her and pressing a hot cup of tea in her hands.

Violet looked at Temperance gratefully. 'Thank you.'

'You all right?' Temperance asked, seeing the tears in Violet's eyes.

Violet gave her a weak smile, the din of work clattering all around them. 'I'm just tired,' Violet said. 'And I miss little Eamon.'

Temperance gave her a sympathetic smile. 'Look around you.' She gestured to the nearly complete dance hall. 'It's almost done.'

She followed Temperance's gaze and her eyes settled on Nancy's friend, John, who was currently up a ladder, painting the coving. He seemed to be doing a good job; and the bar area at least seemed to look a little less like a bomb had hit it.

Yet, as she watched him work, she felt a resentment deep within her. These GIs, with their ludicrous notions of right and wrong, their literal black-and-white attitude, they were responsible for keeping her from her child.

And when she saw Stafford walking away from the bar towards Temperance, Violet's eyes narrowed. It was him she blamed most of all.

'Well, hey there, ladies,' he said brightly as he reached their side.

Temperance smiled awkwardly. 'Hello.'

'You're not going to throw that at me, are you?' Stafford asked, gesturing to the mug of tea Temperance was holding. 'I've seen you with liquids.'

'Not today, no.' Temperance laughed.

'But I might,' Violet quipped.

Stafford looked at her in surprise. 'Oh. Sorry. Violet, right?'

'That's right.' Violet gritted her teeth.

'How are you getting on?' Temperance asked, sensing the awkwardness between him and Violet.

Stafford nodded and wiped his hands on his khaki overalls. 'I think we're almost done.'

'So you should be,' Violet snapped.

'You OK?' Stafford stared at her in surprise.

Irritation coursed through Violet's body at the question.

'Because of you, I'm having to work extra hours so we can put this community resource back to how it's supposed to be – all because of some stupid argument you and your friends got into. And that means I barely see my son. So, no, I'm not all right.'

As Violet stopped speaking, she saw Stafford's forehead crease in consternation.

'I'm sorry you feel that way, ma'am,' he said, in what Violet could tell was a very controlled tone. 'That row might have been stupid to you, but for me it was unavoidable. I was standing up for the right of all black people to walk the same God-given earth as you. So I'm sorry if you're inconvenienced by that. You're white, so I don't expect you to understand, but I do ask for your tolerance.'

As Temperance looked deeply uncomfortable, Violet felt the heat in her body begin to build.

'Don't tell me what I do and don't understand,' she snapped. 'Temp's brother was my sweetheart; our son is half black. Don't tell me I don't understand the importance of having this argument, of standing up for your rights. I believe in that more than you know. I want my son to have just the same rights as me, and I know his father would want the same. But there are ways and means of doing it, and what you and your GI pals did that night wasn't one of them. It was thuggish male violence.'

Beside her, Temperance was speechless, and pale with shock as Violet brought her speech to a close. And then Violet saw that everyone at the Regal was gaping at her. She nearly put her hand over her mouth as she realised what she'd just done.

Yes, she had taken a stand and stood up for herself, but she had also, inadvertently, done something far, far worse. She'd given away the identity of her son's father and revealed that she was little Eamon's biological mother.

Looking at the shocked faces gaping at her open-mouthed, Violet did the only thing she could. She turned and she ran.

36

As Violet pushed past, tears streaming down her face, Temperance started to rush after her, but Stafford reached for her arm and held on tight.

'Let her be,' he whispered. 'She needs time on her own right now.'

Temperance looked up at him. Stafford's brow was furrowed with concern and she felt a flash of understanding pass between them.

Above the clatter of tools and machinery, she let Stafford guide her out into the foyer. There they found a table in the corner and sat down.

'You all right?' he asked.

Temperance nodded. 'I guess the cat is finally out of the bag.'

'That little Eamon is your blood nephew?' Stafford gave her a rueful smile. 'To be honest, I think that secret was blown apart a while back.'

'Really?' Temperance was astonished. She knew rumours had abounded. But she never realised that everyone knew Violet had been lying about the identity of her son.

'The question is, how do you feel about it?'

'How do you mean?' Temperance felt wrong-footed by the question. She wanted to keep Violet's secret. To do otherwise would put her friend and her nephew at risk.

Stafford rubbed his chin, a gesture Temperance had learned he liked to do when he pondered a subject he thought difficult.

'Well, much as I appreciate Violet's predicament, I can't help wondering if it's in the baby's best interests being raised by her.'

'Because she's not married?' Temperance asked. 'My brother adored Violet. If he hadn't died, he'd have married her, regardless of whether or not she was pregnant. They loved each other.'

'I don't doubt it,' Stafford said. 'But without a father around that boy's going to be raised with nobody to teach him about his heritage. He's a black baby, Temperance. You must see that it's just unkind for him to be raised all alone by a white woman, whether she's his mother or not.'

At Stafford's assertions Temperance let out a gasp of horror. Who was this GI to talk about her family this way? Besides, there was one very important thing he was forgetting.

'He has me,' she said angrily. 'And little Eamon is half white, too. That side of his heritage is just as important.'

Stafford shrugged. 'But that's not what folks'll see. Look at you, Temperance. Your daddy was black and your momma's white, but the people around you, they don't see the white part, just the black part. Same for Violet's son. He's going to need a parent around him who can be there to support him, guide him, help him through that. Much like your daddy did for you. I don't mean no disrespect, Temperance, both my parents are from Jamaica so I've never known what it's like when two races collide, but what I do know is I'm glad my mom and pop both looked like me.'

Temperance let out a shaky breath as she thought about what Stafford had just said. Yes, she imagined if she hadn't had her father to lean on life might have been more difficult. The fact her mother and father had adored one another, that Enid had been out on the streets protesting with her father when they were youngsters, wasn't lost on Temperance. She knew how hard her mother had fought for equality, how she had always drummed it into her daughter that Temperance would have to work extra hard at being good, nice, polite, bright and clever. How she could never afford to put a foot wrong because there would be those in society who would expect it, who would say she couldn't do certain things because of the colour of her skin. *You mustn't give them the satisfaction,* Enid would always say, and Temperance knew she was right. But Temperance also knew that Enid had no idea what it was like to walk a mile in her shoes, that she would never know the pain of being judged and written off simply because of the colour of her skin.

'You're right,' she whispered. 'You're right about all of it.'

For the first time since her brother had died, she felt a sense of belonging, of a shared past with someone her own age. She had forgotten how comforting that could be. Maybe her brother had sent Stafford as a gift, a sort of second brother, there to help her through the times when he couldn't. She rested a hand on Stafford's forearm and gave him a gentle squeeze.

'What the hell's going on here?'

Renee stood over the two of them, hands on hips, glowering, and Temperance felt her stomach lurch.

'I can explain, ma'am,' Stafford said.

He got to his feet and held out a hand, but Renee batted it away.

'I don't want your explanations or your apologies,' the redhead snapped. 'What I want is for you to finish repairing the damage you've already caused before you start on causing more.'

'Yes, ma'am.'

Shooting an apologetic look at Temperance, Stafford walked back to the dance hall, and as she watched him go, Temp felt Renee still glaring at her at her.

'Care to explain what all that was about?' Renee asked, though her tone was gentler.

'It was nothing. He's just a friend.'

'You wanna be careful,' Renee fired back. 'I don't touch my friends like that.'

Exhaustion seeped through Temperance's veins. She wouldn't expect Renee to understand; she didn't expect anyone to understand.

Then Renee let out a long sigh. 'You're going to have to talk to the lad, Temp.'

'There's nothing to talk about,' Temperance said, miserably. 'Archie is my best friend, I love him more than I thought I would ever love anyone. But Stafford . . . well he understands me in a way that Archie doesn't.'

'Stafford is also likely to be going home to America the moment this war is over,' Renee reminded her. 'What may seem intoxicating now, some special bond with some fella, well . . . it probably won't last, even if he were to stay here. You'll just have different problems.'

'I'm not in love with Stafford,' Temperance said emphatically. 'He's like a brother to me.'

'And I can understand that,' Renee said now, taking a seat beside her. 'But fellas are temperamental. It might be innocent enough to you but Stafford may see it as something else. And I'll tell you this: if Archie had witnessed what I just did, he'd see it as something else as well.'

Temperance huffed, confusion swirling in her.

'It looks to me like you need to do some thinking, flower,' Renee said, getting up and squeezing Temperance's arm.

As Renee walked away, and left her with her thoughts, Temperance knew her friend was right. She needed to get her ducks in a row, if not just for herself then for those around her.

37

As Renee stalked back to the dance hall, her mind was full of Temperance. She wanted to shake the girl. Renee liked Archie, thought him to be as straight as a die. But she also knew that the pair, as a mixed-race couple, had more problems to face than any other. Yet that didn't mean they were insurmountable. Temperance only had to look at her own parents to see a successful mixed-race couple if she needed proof that colour didn't matter when it came to love.

Walking into the room and seeing Stafford now whistling as he repaired a shelf, Renee felt like giving him a shake, too. He was a good lad, of that she was sure, but he was confusing poor Temp. Renee had half a mind to say something when her eyes landed on a more worrying coupling – Roger and Mick. Heads bent low, they looked deep in conversation and Renee felt her stomach turn over as she wondered what they were discussing.

Since she and Nancy had discussed how to beat Mick at his own game, nothing had been done. Largely because of the unplanned disruption to the Regal, another thing that made her send silent curses Stafford's way. All they had been able to talk about in recent days was the fight. Yet looking now at Roger and her nemesis, Renee knew this wasn't a situation that could be left to fester.

Squaring her shoulders, she strode towards the men and plastered on a smile.

'Hiya, gents,' she said, in as warm a tone as she could muster. 'You two cooking up trouble?'

At the sight of Renee, Roger smiled. 'Something like that. Mick has been trying to convince me to take this surplus stock from his friend,' he said, a worried look across his brow.

'I know you said no, but look at this lot.' Mick gestured towards the bar with his head. 'You've been closed a week, you're losing money hand over fist. I can sort you out a deal, Vicar.'

Renee could see the worry on Roger's face as he stared at the assortment of tins and packages of food sat on the bar top.

'It just doesn't seem right, Mick. I'm sure everything with your friend is above board, but I can't take food that doesn't rightfully belong to us.'

'It's surplus,' Mick tried again. 'You're not taking anything off anyone. It's just good business.'

'Roger's got a point,' said Renee. 'It doesn't seem right.'

Mick set his flinty gaze on her. 'Come on. It's not as if you're committing murder, eh, Renee?'

At this, Renee's stomach performed a fresh round of cartwheels.

'No,' she agreed as calmly as she could, aware Mick's gaze wasn't leaving hers. 'I suppose it isn't.' She sighed, then turned to Roger. 'Perhaps it is something to consider, Roger,' she said quietly. 'We have lost a lot of money following the fight and the damage caused. And I know that the repair work is being done by volunteers like—'

'And the thugs what caused this mess in the first place,' Mick growled, cutting her off.

She regarded him icily over the vicar's bent head. 'Yes, the fact of the matter is we could do with a helping hand, Roger, love. Perhaps this friend of Mick's who has a bit of extra, could make all the difference to our success here? Just until we're back on our feet.'

Roger looked up at her, undisguised warmth in his eyes as he listened to what she was saying.

'Do you really think so, Renee?'

'I think so, yes.' Renee swallowed, hating herself for what she was about to say next. 'I mean, where's the harm, really? We'd be using this surplus stock to do a bit of good in the parish, and the community as a whole.'

'She's right,' Mick said, slipping Renee a wink as Roger looked as if he was seriously considering Renee's words. 'I promise you, Vicar, I'd never take advantage. Not of a man of the cloth.'

At the false sincerity in Mick's words, Renee nearly snorted with derision.

'It is something to think about,' Roger said, scratching his chin. 'We do need the stock here, and after our false start I can't help but feel we're due a bit of good luck.'

'Hear, hear,' Mick said looking delighted.

'Well, then.' Roger looked pleased, now that he had made up his mind. 'Thank you, Mick. Let me know when we can expect the first delivery.' He turned to Renee. 'I expect Betty will need to liaise on this? Rally her troops.' He smiled at his joke and Renee joined in, though she felt sick to her stomach. 'I'll go and talk to her now.'

With that Roger ambled off, leaving Renee alone with Mick.

'Glad you saw things my way,' he said, fishing in his pocket for a cigarette. He pulled out a Player's for himself and then offered Renee one. She shook her head. She didn't want Mick adding cigarettes to her tab, as well as murder.

'Didn't leave me much choice,' she said bitterly.

Mick laughed and lit his cigarette. 'I reckon your Ronnie would have been proud of you. I always said he underestimated you. The way he used to speak about you, the beatings he gave. As I said, I never agreed with it meself, Renee, love. Never saw the need to hit a woman; that's always been wrong in my eyes.'

'But blackmail's a different matter, is it?' she said bluntly.

Mick chuckled. He reached over and tried to push a lock of hair behind Renee's ear but she moved away, avoiding his touch and making Mick laugh all the more.

'I always said to Ronnie to be careful with you. I said the worm could suddenly turn at any minute. And you did, didn't you, Renee? You killed him. And, to be honest with you, love, I can't say as I blame you.' He smiled at her. 'Let's just hope the coppers don't find out, eh?'

As Mick took another drag on his cigarette Renee found herself feeling murderous for the second time in her life. She and Nancy were going to have to work hard to come up with something to get this louse off her back. She hadn't killed one abusive man only to be taken advantage of by another—

A sudden crash behind her threw her out of her thoughts. Whirling round, Renee saw that John had fallen from his ladder and was now lying in a crumpled heap on the floor.

Immediately Renee raced to his side, pushing through the throng of men who had gathered around him. Nancy was already kneeling on the floor next to John, checking his pulse.

'John!' Renee exclaimed. 'Are you all right? Where does it hurt?'

'I'd imagine everywhere,' Nancy said, gently.

'I'm fine,' John croaked. 'Looks worse than it is.'

He tried to sit up, but as he rubbed his head he winced and collapsed straight back down again, this time his eyes fluttered closed.

'John!' Nancy said, in alarm, as he lay on the ground, motionless. 'John!' she said again.

But the GI didn't wake, and as Renee locked eyes with Nancy, she saw the panic she felt mirrored in her friend's gaze. Renee felt a dark sense of foreboding and like she'd been here before.

Surely she wasn't responsible for another man's death?

38

The following day, Violet sat at Betty's kitchen table, baby Eamon in her arms and a plate of Woolton pie before her.

'Give that baby to me,' Queenie offered, reaching out her hands to take Violet's son.

Violet shook her head and held Eamon ever tighter. 'He's fine,' she said shortly.

'You need to eat your lunch, girl,' Queenie said, rolling her eyes at her.

'I'll manage,' Violet said, with a touch of obstinance.

She picked up her fork, snagged a piece of pie and put it in her mouth, spattering crumbs into Eamon's mass of black curls as she did so. Queenie sighed and nudged Betty in the ribs as her daughter-in-law sat beside her.

'Have a word with your daughter. She's gone soft in the head.'

'Sure, and when has she ever listened to me?' Betty chuckled.

Violet let out a sigh. But, truthfully, she didn't care about her family's teasing. She had her son in her arms and in that moment that was really all she cared about.

'Is the Regal all spruced up again now, then?' Queenie asked.

'Almost. I mean, most of it is done. Renee says we should open tonight, anyway,' said Betty.

'Course she does.' Queenie nodded approvingly. 'Not right you had to close at all.'

'Well, there's something in that,' Betty agreed. 'But at least those what damaged the place have helped mend it, too.'

'How's that poor fella what fell off the ladder?' Queenie asked in hushed tones. 'I heard he's broken all his bones and been left paralysed!'

At that both Violet and Betty looked at each other and roared with laughter.

'He's got a sprained ankle and a mild concussion.' Violet giggled.

As she regained control of herself, Violet felt relief flood through her. She had been in the toilets when John fell, but she had heard the shrieks and come racing back to the dance hall to see what had happened.

Seeing John lying under the ladder, refusing to respond to Renee's and Nancy's pleas, she had anticipated the worst. But thankfully the troop's medic had been on hand and, after diagnosing John with a sprained ankle and concussion, arranged for him to be taken back to the Rainbow Rooms, where he could be looked after by the resident medical team.

'Where on earth did you hear such a thing anyway?' Betty asked Queenie, through a mouthful of pie.

'Mavis up the WVS,' Queenie said mournfully. 'Silly woman, should have known she was talking out of her backside.'

'As she always does,' Betty muttered darkly.

'She did say one thing, though, that made me wonder if it was true,' Queenie put in.

'Oh?' Violet asked.

'She said you lost your rag yesterday at the dance hall and as good as told everyone that Eamon was your son.'

Violet's cheeks flushed with colour at the memory, as Queenie went on.

'Course I told her to shut her cakehole, that her gossip had no place at a WVS meeting and I'd slap her into the middle of next week if she kept up her lies.'

'What did she say?' Violet asked. Her mouth felt dry as she waited for her grandmother to reply.

'She said she'd heard it was gospel.' Queenie shrugged as she finished her pie. Pushing her plate away, she fixed her eyes on Violet. 'She was lying, weren't she?' she asked, her voice hesitant. 'You didn't shout your mouth off, did you, Vi?'

Violet pressed her lips to her son's head and peppered him with kisses.

'I lost my temper. Stafford said something about me not being able to understand my son because we weren't the same skin colour.'

'And you blew the whole thing 'cause you lost your rag,' Queenie fumed.

'I didn't mean to.' Violet had gone into a state of denial since her outburst and almost convinced herself that no one important had heard her. 'There was nobody there who would say anything.'

'There obviously was. Word got back to Mavis quicker than a rat up a drainpipe.'

'We can say she's got her wires crossed, can't we?' Violet said, panicked. 'She usually has, let's face it.'

'But for once she ain't.' Queenie sighed. 'I suppose there's a slim chance she ain't spread the word yet, not after I put her in her place.'

'But if she has,' Betty said, aghast, 'we'll soon know about it, and then Vi's life will be ruined. Poor little Eamon will suffer, too.'

Violet felt her heart turn over at her mother's bluntness. How could she have been so stupid? After all she had said about Enid, and she had done the same, but worse – loudly, and in front of everyone. Enid had been talking with pride about her grandson, while Violet had been defending her right to be his mother. Looking down at her baby, she held him more tightly, only acquiescing when Eamon wriggled in her arms.

'What do you think we should do?' she asked in a small voice.

Betty and Queenie exchanged worried glances and Violet felt a small knot of fear in her stomach.

'I don't know, love,' Betty said.

Violet could tell Betty's mind was working overtime. Perhaps she was thinking of those awful mother and baby homes in Ireland, where the nuns took your baby and arranged for them to be adopted by strangers.

The thought of never seeing her baby again, of having him palmed off to other people and never knowing his fate, was unbearable. Violet buried her face in Eamon's hair. She was already wildly proud of her son and felt she had nothing to be ashamed of. So, she was an unwed mother raising a baby alone – was that really the biggest crime she could have committed? Because she would have done it all again in a heartbeat if it meant another precious night with her sweetheart.

She cast her gaze to the laundry hanging on the makeshift line outside near the Anderson shelter. It was cold out, but Betty was still attempting to dry her washing with the gusts of cool November air rather than have sheets hanging about inside.

But the fact of the matter was that Stafford's words had struck a chord. Almost as soon as she had given birth to Eamon, Violet had worried if she, a white woman, was doing her son a disservice by raising him alone. That was why she had been so grateful for Temperance's involvement. Not only did she see it as a link between her son and the father who had been wrongfully taken from him, but it was also a way for him to maintain a hold of his black heritage. Violet wasn't stupid; she knew there were issues and problems Eamon would face that she wouldn't have a clue about. But the fact remained, she wanted to do right by her son; that was all that mattered.

'I think we have to see how things go,' Queenie said gently. 'Then we can take it from there.'

'You could always go back and stay with Alan?' Betty suggested.

'He's living with his boss at Howell & Smart after his house was blown apart,' Violet reminded her.

Betty frowned and Violet knew that the fact her mother had forgotten that was troubling to her.

'Perhaps you ought to write to Alan, though, let him know what's happened?' Queenie suggested.

Violet shook her head. Alan had quite enough on his plate without worrying about her.

'He is your father,' Queenie said. 'And I think he might be a good one, if you let him. He might have a decent solution to this problem, because I tell you now, Violet, now that the word's out your life won't be the same again.'

As the sounds of George lurching about upstairs echoed in the kitchen, Violet thought Queenie might be right, and that the new father who had come into her life could offer some perspective. Because, sure as eggs were eggs, the one she'd known all her life wouldn't be able to help.

39

While Violet considered her and Eamon's future at Betty's, Nancy was in the heart of London, standing outside the Rainbow Rooms.

Wondering what exactly she was doing there, Nancy stood with her hands in her coat pockets and watched a group of American soldiers standing outside, laughing as they smoked cigarettes down to the quick. A variety of accents whirled through the air: Deep South, New York and pure West Coast. The noise and just the very essence of them, their lack of apology for being who they were, made her feel homesick; a feeling that had grown since spending these past few months surrounded by the GIs. It hadn't helped that things seemed beyond repair with her husband, but that wasn't the only reason she was missing home.

When Nancy had moved to Britain she had never expected to stay. But stay she had, finding wonderful friends, family and a job to boot. Her wildest dreams had been exceeded but lately it didn't seem enough. More than anything now, she dreamed of going back home, doing simple things such as popping over to her mother's for lunch – always guaranteed to be a noisy affair if her sister brought her brood of children with her.

Nancy let out a long sigh and tried to push the thoughts away. Wishing for what could have been wasn't going to help. And truthfully, she wasn't sure if what she was about to do next was helpful either.

When she had stepped onto the Tube an hour ago, she had told herself that she was merely doing her duty as manager of the Hammersmith Palais and the Regal. After all, the GI had been injured on her watch; it was only right she find out how he was.

But she couldn't quite forget the way her body had reacted when she had seen John fall at the Regal. She had raced to his side as surely as if it had been Peter or Ruth who had been hurt, her heart racing as he lay there on the floor. It wasn't the kind of response you'd have for a friend, it was . . . Nancy shook her head. She'd been sure she had given herself away, that her body had betrayed her and given off signals to everyone around her that John was more than a casual acquaintance.

Inwardly cursing herself, she tried to pull herself together. She was here to check on an injured colleague, nothing more than that. Crossing the road, she was determined now as she smiled at the group of GIs and walked into the club. She didn't loiter at the soda fountain, or sniff the air appreciatively and enjoy the scent of hamburgers. She made her way to reception and asked if she could be pointed in the direction of John's room.

'First on the left, honey,' the woman said, in an East Coast purr.

Nancy smiled. It had been a long time since someone else had called her honey, and she savoured the word.

Climbing up the long, dog-leg staircase, it didn't take long to find John's room. She tapped lightly on the dark, wooden door and realised her heart was racing again.

'Come in,' John's voice called.

She rested her hand on the door handle and before she could change her mind, pushed the door open.

Walking inside, she saw John sat at a small wooden desk. His military jacket was undone, and she could see a white vest poking out from underneath. The sight distracted her for a second, and she nearly forgot what she'd come to say.

'Hi . . . there,' she eventually stammered.

John beamed at her. 'Nancy. This is a surprise.'

'I hope I'm not intruding.'

'You've been in the UK too long. Since when do us Yanks "intrude"?'

She laughed, and he got out of his chair and gestured for her to sit down.

'I don't want to keep you,' she said as she took the seat. It was still warm, she noticed. 'I just wanted to see how you are.'

John sat down with a wince on the bed opposite her, which, she noticed, was all made up properly, complete with hospital corners.

'I'm fine. Much better, thank you.'

She frowned as she peered at his ankle, which looked badly swollen. 'Honey, if that's better I dread to think how you were before,' she said.

John laughed at her dry humour. 'That's the Nancy Blum I've come to know!' He then propped his leg up on the stool beside the bed. 'Got to keep it elevated.'

'Is that all the medical advice you've been given?' Nancy asked as she leaned back in the chair, trying to make herself comfortable.

'The doc says it's a miracle I didn't do more damage,' John admitted. 'Reckons I managed to fall "the right way", whatever that means.'

'Well, I'm glad,' Nancy said easily. 'How long are you off work for?'

'Not long.' He smiled ruefully. 'I've been consigned to desk duties for a time. Doc wants me to take a couple of days to make sure this concussion's nothing serious.'

Nancy nodded then said, slightly hesitantly, 'I was . . . we . . . were worried about you.'

'I'm fine.' John waved away her concerns. 'Not the first scrape I've gotten into and it certainly won't be the last.'

'Still.' Nancy gazed down at her hands, feeling uncomfortable. 'I feel responsible. It happened at our dance hall.'

John was silent for a second before he leaned forward and, with his forefinger, tilted Nancy's chin upwards so his eyes met hers.

'Nancy, none of this is your fault. If my boys hadn't gotten into that stupid fight then none of this would have happened. It's me who should be apologising to you.'

As Nancy rested her eyes on John's she felt a tug of longing. She could sense John felt it too as he leaned towards her, his mouth so close to hers she could feel his breath against her lips.

'I've been thinking about you,' he said, croakily. 'I've done nothing but think about you, Nancy Blum, since the moment I laid eyes on you.'

A heady mix of guilt and joy tore through Nancy's heart, She wanted John; she knew there was no point denying it any longer. But she was married. She had made vows. In that moment she thought of Betty, who had given up her happiness when she had found it all in the name of duty. More committed to her marriage vows than she was to her own heart. Nancy shivered at the thought. She adored Betty but she didn't want to end up like her. And so, banishing thoughts of Alex, her children, her synagogue, and her vows, she gave in to temptation and leaned into John. The moment she felt the warmth of his lips against hers, she knew what she needed, what she had been craving for years. In John she had come alive.

40

December

As December rolled along, the Good Time Girls had only one thing on their minds – Christmas.

For Temperance, it was usually a joyful time of year. She adored nothing more than being with her friends and family and celebrating, though in increasingly simple ways thanks to the war.

Back in Hammersmith, she took a seat next to the band pit for the Saturday night dance and watched the dancers glide around the floor. Her eyes landed on Archie, who was grinning in that ever-professional way he had. She watched as he expertly led one of their regular customers around the floor. A housewife who had been left alone since her husband had been called up. The woman had a crush on Archie that was as obvious as one of Hitler's dawn raids. Temperance had never minded. In fact, she thought it was rather sweet. But then it struck her: should she have minded? Did it say something about them that she didn't?

She shook her head – life was complicated enough without worrying about things that like that. After all, there was every possible reason to feel hopeful about the future. Following the Allied troops' success in El Alamein, they had gone on to recapture Tobruk. At home, all anyone could talk about was the Beveridge Report. Developed by a social policy expert, the report was a way for the government to help everyone in the country stay fit, healthy and well. Temperance had been too busy to read as much about it as she would have liked, but, from what she could tell, the policy meant the government was creating a sort of safety net when it came to poverty. There was talk about universal healthcare, no matter your income, as well as more ease in finding work and housing.

If she was honest, it all sounded too good to be true. And the idea of a free healthcare system, where you no longer queued down the street and crossed the doctor's hand with sixpence before you were seen, seemed bizarre. She couldn't understand how it would work, how it would be paid for. But when she had tried to discuss it with Archie, he had shrugged and said that the powers that be would have considered all this, and she shouldn't worry about it.

But that was the thing about Temperance, she had begun to realise. She was a born worrier. She knew that she and her brother would have discussed the Beveridge Report and what it meant for society until the small hours. With a start, she thought of Stafford. Would it have been something that the two of them would have discussed, too, given the opportunity?

Temperance wasn't sure. The thought made her uncomfortable. She hadn't seen Stafford since that day a week or so ago, when they'd got too close at the Regal. Well, that wasn't strictly true. She had seen him from a distance at both the Regal and the Palais, but she had fled at the sight of him, embarrassed and ashamed after what had almost happened. And she didn't know what to say or how to be with him. Renee, thankfully, had come to her rescue last week, when Stafford had asked to speak to Temperance; the Palais owner had sent the GI away with a flea in his ear and Temperance had been grateful.

She was beyond confused and hoped that time apart from Stafford would help clarify her feelings. But the truth was Temperance also wanted time apart from Archie. She adored him, of course she did, but it seemed increasingly clear that Archie wanted to live in blissful ignorance all his life, pretending that the horrors of the world they lived in didn't exist – something that felt deeply wrong to Temperance – and reluctant to discuss or analyse anything important to their future.

As the dance ended, she got to her feet ready to direct the dancers to their new partners. She scrolled through her list; all had been booked apart from Archie. Her heart felt heavy at the thought. It would mean that she and her sweetheart would need to make small talk, and for once she didn't have the energy.

Sure enough, as the girls filed past her and she pointed out their next customers, she and Archie were soon standing together.

'You having a good night?' he asked pleasantly, as the band struck up a lively waltz.

Temperance nodded. 'Beats Bethnal Green. Last night we thought we had a good crowd because they were queuing to the bottom of the road. But then we realised they were all there for one thing only, Betty's—'

'—hotpot!' Archie finished for her.

'The one and only.' Temperance grinned, as Betty's hotpot was legendary.

Archie rocked back and forth on his heels. 'Course, it's the meat that makes it. Betty gets it from the best butcher in town.'

Temperance laughed, and playfully swatted Archie's arm.

'It's nice to hear you laugh like that,' he said softly. 'It feels like it's been a while.'

Temperance's smile faltered. She didn't know how to respond, so instead she set her gaze at the dance floor. Her eyes landed on Roger and Renee. Together the two were making quite a stir on the dance floor with their precise movements and timing, though it looked to the untrained eye as if it was Roger who was in charge, Temperance knew it was Renee, an expert at making the moves. It was a skill like no other, Temperance thought.

It was a shame, really, that Renee had given up professional dancing. She was such a natural.

'I wanted to talk to you about something,' Archie said beside her in a low voice, pulling Temperance back into the present.

'What about?' she asked, in as light a tone as possible.

'It's about Violet,' Archie said.

Temperance turned to stare at him in surprise. She saw the look of worry on his face and wondered what on earth had happened.

'This was left on my counter at lunchtime,' he said, reaching into his pocket and pulling out a folded piece of paper.

Puzzled, Temperance unfolded it and began to read.

Tell your friend Violet Millington she's no more than a cheap whore. If her and her filthy bastard don't get out of Hammersmith there are folk round here that will make sure they do. We don't want sluts like her corrupting our community.

Temperance stared at the note, shock coursing through her veins. Had someone really done this? Did someone really hate her nephew and friend enough to leave a nasty, threatening note? Unable to believe what she had read, Temperance made herself go through it again word by word before she silently handed it back to Archie.

'Why did they leave it in your shop?'

Archie shrugged. 'I don't know. Maybe whoever did is trying to be clever, sending it to me rather than any of you. Maybe it was just easier for them to get it to me, rather than you or Violet.'

'You didn't see who left it?' she asked, her voice trembling.

Archie shook his head. 'We were busy today with the lunchtime rush. I didn't see the note until after the queue had died down. At first I thought it was someone's shopping list, but then I read it and saw it was clearly meant for me to pass on.'

'I can't believe someone would do this,' Temperance exclaimed. 'Who is this sick?'

Archie shrugged as he pocketed the letter. 'There are a lot of sick people out there.'

His eyes darted across to the bar and Temperance followed them. There was Violet working behind the bar, doing her best as always to fill in and keep order. She was smiling at customers, but even from the other side of the dance floor Temperance could see the worry in her eyes. Temperance had already heard two customers say they would rather wait and be served by Sybil than have to deal with that cheap tramp.

It made Temperance want to weep with the injustice of it all. Violet didn't deserve any of this. She looked back at the note.

'Should we tell her?'

Archie shook his head, his mouth set in a determined line.

'I don't think so. She's got enough on her plate; it won't help her or the baby. Cowards like this get bored in the end. Whoever this was will find someone else to torment.'

Temperance said nothing. She didn't want to voice the fact that it wasn't just one person who had said terrible things to Violet. Since Vi's outburst with Stafford there had been a couple of dozen folk who had made their feelings about Eamon and Violet clear. And the trouble was that it didn't just impact Violet. Temperance's mother Enid was worried sick; Auntie Winnie, too. She bit her lip and watched Violet wipe the tears away with the back of her hand when she thought nobody was looking. How much more of this could she take and where on earth was it going to end? More than anything, she wanted to help Violet. The biggest question was how.

41

The following day, Sunday, Renee met Roger for a much-needed cup of tea in the Lyons Corner House on Piccadilly. She had invited Nancy to join them, but her friend had cried off, saying that she was taking the children out for the day.

So she was meeting Roger alone. Something that, until Mick's blackmail threats had materialised, Renee would have enjoyed immensely. Her unexpected friendship with Roger had come to mean a lot to her; she trusted his counsel and found him a lot of fun. Yet every time she was with Roger now she dreaded him telling her that he knew the truth about what had happened to his brother, that he was going to see that she and Nancy paid the ultimate price.

As Renee strode through central London, she did her best to banish these thoughts from her mind. After all, she had been looking forward to this treat for weeks, but now that the day was here, she felt impatient, as though time was being snatched away from her. Christmas wasn't far off, and there was a lot to do at both dance halls. Although there wasn't much evidence of the festive spirit around town.

If ever proof were needed that rationing was in full swing, you only had to walk around the centre of London. The shops had done their best, of course, but it was obvious stocks were low. There were no new clothes, so department stores had displayed summer outfits in their windows, suggesting this was the perfect time to get organised for the warmer months. Elsewhere, years-old decorations had been spruced up and hung in the windows. It felt disappointing rather than uplifting and, if Renee were honest, she couldn't help feeling it would have been better if the government had just said Christmas was cancelled this year.

A little later, Renee communicated her thoughts on this to Roger as they sat across the table from one another at Lyons, a plate of almond biscuits and pot of weak tea for two between them.

'Christmas is about more than presents, trees and Santa Claus,' Roger exclaimed.

Renee raised an eyebrow. 'Tell that to my customers. They're already complaining we've not got a Christmas tree up. I said to 'em, show me someone who can get hold of one, then!'

But as Renee said the words aloud, she realised she did know someone who could get her a tree, if she wanted – Mick. Though the less said about him the better, it was true that since he'd started making deliveries to the Bethnal Green dance hall, the provisions had gone down well. Queues had been snaking down the road as word spread of the fresh vegetables and hearty pies that Betty had thrown herself into preparing using Mick's stock.

'It's about the spirit of Christmas,' Roger said kindly, now. 'Come on, Renee, you know that. We can make sure that both dance halls convey that message.'

Renee smiled weakly, as she lifted her tea to her lips. 'I'm not sure, flower. It's not that long ago there was a brawl so serious in Bethnal Green we had to close down for a week. One poor bloke got injured, not to mention his concussion afterwards.'

'Yes, but that was because he fell off a ladder, not because he was caught up in the fight,' Roger reminded her.

'True.' There was a pause then as Renee reached for an almond biscuit. She cocked her head to one side and regarded the vicar. 'What are you doing for Christmas?'

'Me?' Roger laughed. 'It's one of the busiest times of the year for me. My parishioners will be keeping me on my toes.'

'But what about Christmas lunch?' Renee enquired. She was suddenly worried about her friend.

Roger frowned for a moment. 'I expect my neighbour Mrs Steeple will have me over as she usually does.'

They shared a smile at the woman's apt surname, before Renee spoke again.

'Wouldn't you like a change this year?' she asked. 'Spend Christmas with us, Roger. Betty was talking about doing a big communal spread over at Bethnal Green as a thank you to all those who have helped. Personally I think it's just an excuse to get out of spending the day with George, but it keeps her happy.'

Roger rubbed his chin and thought for a moment. 'That does sound tempting, I must admit. And I'm sure Mrs Steeple would like a year off from my terrible jokes. Will Betty have enough provisions, do you think?'

'I think so,' she said. 'Mick seems to be keeping her happy with supplies.'

At the mention of Mick, she saw another frown flash across Roger's face. 'I've been thinking about that, Renee. I don't think we can keep on taking supplies from Mick. The war doesn't look as if it's going to end soon. Our troops need those supplies; we can make do with what we can find without involving favours. I mean, look around.' Renee followed his gaze and took in the scores of people enjoying tea and cake sat opposite one another, white-clothed tables between them. 'If the Lyons Corner House can manage, then so can we.'

A wave of anxiety passed over Renee. To tell Mick now that his services were no longer required would mean he would be incredibly angry, and Renee had no doubt what that meant for her.

'Are you all right?' Roger asked, his voice rich with concern.

Plastering on a bright smile, she did her best to conceal her feelings. 'Fine. Just thinking how disappointed Betty will be.'

'Betty Millington is a good, God-fearing woman. I imagine

that, much as she is enjoying the stocks, she would enjoy the fact they were being routed to the relevant servicemen fighting for our freedom a lot more,' Roger said sensibly. 'Didn't you say her son had been killed in the war?'

'Roy,' Renee muttered. 'Yes, he was. Poor Betty. And now her daughter Maisie has joined the army.'

'Ah, yes.' Roger recalled the name. 'She used to work at the Palais, didn't she?'

Renee nodded. 'She did. A funny, bright girl. I hope she comes back in one piece. Betty'll be hard-pressed to forgive the Jerries if Hitler takes two of her children.'

Roger sighed. 'Yes, forgiveness is a tricky business. It's something most of my parishioners struggle with.'

Leaning back in her chair, Renee felt the hairs on the back of her neck stand on end. 'What do you tell them?' she asked.

Roger smiled benignly. 'I tell them that it takes hard work. That it sometimes feels impossible, but that it is the true spirit of Christianity to forgive, however serious the crime appears to be.'

Renee nodded furiously, her red hair skimming her her-ringbone jacket at speed as she did so. An image of Ronnie burst into her mind. Him on the ground, her leaning over him, shoe in one hand, the fear and amusement on his face as she raised her hand above her head – and then the disbelief in his eyes when he realised she was actually plunging the heel straight into his flesh. Would Roger count all that as something he could forgive?

'Of course, forgiveness is not always easy,' Roger went on, sending her back to square one.

'You're a man of the cloth.' She let out a shaky laugh. 'If it's not easy for you what hope have the rest of us got?'

Roger opened his mouth to answer, but then she saw his eyes travel to something behind her, and he got to his feet. 'Mrs Goldstein,' he called.

Renee turned around in her chair and saw, to her surprise, that Edna had walked into the café, Peter and Ruth trailing behind her.

'Hello,' she said as she walked towards them. 'Fancy seeing you here.'

'I could say the same,' Renee said.

Gesturing to the children behind her, Edna smiled brightly. 'Thought I'd bring these two here for a treat. We've been saying we'll enjoy tea in town for weeks, haven't we?'

Peter and Ruth nodded mutely, and then continued looking around the restaurant.

'I thought Nancy was spending the day with you today?' Renee asked them in surprise.

Ruth shook her head. 'No, Nancy's got a meeting.'

'On a Saturday?' Roger queried.

'She said it was the only day she could get business done,' Peter put in.

'Quite,' Edna said with a smile. 'Well, we'll leave you to it. Don't want to intrude.'

And with that, she steered the children away to another table. As she did so, Renee felt her mind racing, but there was one question overriding everything else – why had Nancy lied to her?

42

Meanwhile, across town, Nancy found herself peering through shop windows, the magic of Christmas all around her as she wandered through the West End with John by her side. As their hands occasionally brushed one another's, Nancy felt her stomach perform somersaults. She kept sneaking sideways glances at the GI, only to find him doing the same.

As they walked, the sharp December wind blew her hair this way and that, but Nancy didn't care. She also didn't care that all the window displays were scant and stocks scarce. She didn't care that there was hardly anything to buy for her loved ones, she didn't even care that there was nothing she could buy for the children, consoling herself with the thought that it didn't matter as none of them really celebrated Christmas anyway.

The simple truth was that Nancy's mind was full of nothing but John. It had been from the moment they had gone to bed together and Nancy was sure now that she would never be able to think of anything or anyone else again. John was all that mattered.

Now her heart banged against her chest. What was she doing? She was surely too old to behave like a giddy kid. She had responsibilities, she had children, a job, a family . . . *And love,* a little voice inside her head said.

At the thought, Nancy almost gasped out loud. She was in love. She had lived without the feeling for so long that she had forgotten what it felt like, but here it was.

When she had first gone to see John at the Rainbow Rooms, she could never have predicted that it would lead to a full-blown love affair. But of course, at the back of her mind, she knew that was what she wanted deep down. She'd felt a connection to John since the moment they met, and whilst she'd never thought she would act on it, in the end she was powerless in the face of it. The feelings they shared were too strong for her to ignore. And if she was honest, she didn't *want* to ignore them. In the time since they had been seeing one another, much as Nancy hated the clandestine nature of sneaking about, she had never felt more alive. She knew that she wouldn't change a thing even if she could. The meetings between them had become more engineered and elaborate, with constant excuses to her colleagues, friends and children about where she had to be. Last week, Nancy had told Renee she was hoping to interview a new cleaner for the Regal, but when Renee had asked her to rearrange it if possible, so that they could both be there, Nancy had felt furious at the interference. She wasn't letting anything or anyone get in the way of her time with this man, who was making her feel happier than she'd ever been.

As if sensing her eyes on him, John nudged her and smiled.

'What are you thinking about?' he asked, reaching for her hand.

At the touch of him, Nancy felt a fresh flush of excitement. Then, remembering where and who she was, she quickly looked around, as if expecting to see half of the Hammersmith Palais behind her, gawping at the spectacle that was her private life.

'There's nobody here who knows us,' John whispered in her ear, pulling her closer to him as he did so. 'Relax and enjoy yourself. We don't have long. Or do we?'

Nancy shook her head. 'I've got to get back to Hammersmith for the evening dance.' She checked her watch with her free hand. 'Which starts in two hours.'

'Then let's not waste what time we do have,' John murmured. 'Where does everyone think you are now?'

'Out with the kids, and the kids think I've got a meeting with the bank.' Nancy frowned. She hated this complicated lying.

John laughed. 'I told my commanding officer I had a meeting about a community event.'

'Which I guess you do,' Nancy reasoned. 'We could talk about the community. I mean, you did help repair the Bethnal Green dance hall.'

'Which is now all shipshape, thanks to my lot,' John offered.

'And was ruined in the first place, thanks to your lot,' Nancy quipped.

John gave her a playful nudge. 'Hey, if I wanted a roasting I could get one from my men, not you.' And then, before she had time to realise what he was doing, he had pulled her into a side street near Liberty's. 'I've been wanting to do this since I met you at the Tube.'

And with that, he pressed his mouth to hers, and they kissed as if they were long-lost lovers who hadn't seen each other for years.

As Nancy revelled in the sensation of his touch, she felt as if she were floating in another world. How had she only known this man a few short months, when she felt as if they were destined to be together?

Pulling apart from him, she felt breathless, gazing up at him expectantly. Whatever she was feeling he was clearly feeling it, too.

'Where have you been all my life, Nancy?' he asked throatily.

He ran a smooth forefinger down her cheek; she shivered at his touch.

'I don't know, but I'm right here now,' she whispered, her eyes locked on his. 'And I'm not going anywhere.'

'Neither am I,' John replied. He reached for both her hands and squeezed them. 'I mean, I don't know where this is going, but I know I don't want it to end.'

'Me, neither,' Nancy replied huskily.

Gazing up into his eyes, she suddenly heard the sound of her name being called far away in the distance. Jolted, she pulled away from John and saw, to her horror, that Roger was at the bottom of the street, coming towards them.

'Nancy, I thought it was you,' he said, brightly. 'I've just come from having tea with Renee at Lyons Corner House. Fancy seeing you here.' Stopping just yards from her and John, Roger took in the scene and narrowed his eyes. 'And John, too. This is a surprise.'

Nancy moved away from John as if she had been burned.

'I think I'm OK now.' She turned to Roger and shrugged her shoulders. 'This darned wind got something caught in my eye.' Dabbing dramatically at her right eye with her finger, she looked back at John, smiling. 'Thanks for your help.'

'You're welcome,' John said, bowing his head in acknowledgement. 'I'm just glad I happened to be here.'

She had to hand it to him, he was playing along like a pro.

'Oh.' Surprise and a fair amount of relief passed across Roger's face. 'You two aren't together?'

'Good Lord, no!' Nancy and John exclaimed in unison.

'I was out walking,' John added. 'Looking for something for my wife for Christmas, but there's not a lot of choice.'

'And I just snuck off to get some Christmas gifts for Peter and Ruth. I want to spoil them; they're such good kids,' Nancy explained. 'We ran into one another.'

'And then something nasty blew into your eye,' John said. 'Lucky I was there to help.'

'Wasn't it?' Roger said.

For what felt like an eternity nobody said a word. Then Roger, breaking the spell smiled.

'Well, I must be going.' He paused and then gave Nancy a knowing look. 'I'll see you at the Palais later.'

It felt to Nancy more like an order than a question. She nodded and smiled brightly. 'Of course.'

Nodding at John, Roger walked away, and Nancy felt her heart bang against her chest like cannon fire.

'Oh, my God,' she moaned, leaning back against the cold brick wall. 'We're done for, as Renee would say.'

John laughed. 'Don't be silly. He totally bought that line about your eye.'

'I don't know, John,' Nancy whispered. 'You really think so?'

'Of course,' John said soothingly. 'Look, the guy's a man of the cloth. He wants to see the best in people; he won't think you're lying.'

And with that, he pulled her back into his arms and held her tight. As she rested her head against his chest, the chill wind biting against her cheek, Nancy realised she didn't care if Roger knew, if he judged her, or even if he told everyone what she was doing. In that moment all she cared about was John, and she wasn't sure there was anything else in this world that could make her feel differently.

43

Christmas Eve

The day dawned bright and clear and, as she walked to work in the sunshine, Violet felt her spirits lift. It was hard to feel down about anything on these crisp days that made you think life could and would be good again. She beamed into the pram and felt a pang of love as she watched her son smile up at her. Eamon was becoming lovelier by the day, and her heart ached whenever she had to leave him these days, sure she was going to miss some vital part of his development.

Pushing the pram towards the Bethnal Green dance hall, Violet paused for a moment. Tonight was going to be hard work for all of them. Each venue was running special Christmas dances, and she and Temperance had been charged with ensuring everything ran smoothly at the Regal, while Janice would keep an eye on things back at Hammersmith. Renee and Nancy would be flitting between the two venues, ensuring they wished all their customers a happy Christmas. Betty, meanwhile, was serving up a simple Christmas meal to all those in need in the East End, and Violet and Temperance had offered to help.

Reaching the Regal, she was surprised to find Bill Cain standing outside. Dressed in a thick navy overcoat that was patched at the elbows, black twill trousers, and shoes that gleamed, he leaned back against the wall enjoying a cigarette, his face turned towards the sun, making the most of the winter warmth.

'Afternoon,' Violet said. 'I didn't think you worked out east?'

He opened his eyes and didn't immediately speak, preferring to take a sharp pull on his cigarette before he did so.

'You can't bring that baby in here.'

Violet sighed. She had hoped that Bill might have changed since he retired, but far from it. As far as she was concerned he seemed even more cantankerous than usual.

'That baby, as you call him, will come inside, just as you will in a minute,' Violet told him. 'Don't worry, he's not staying. Enid's coming a bit later on with Temperance, and she'll take him off again.' She observed him. 'But you haven't said what you're doing here.'

'Since Janice is working at Hammersmith tonight, I said I'd come up here.'

Violet nodded then checked her watch and saw she was ten minutes early. Still, she wasn't going to stand out here making conversation with Bill until the others arrived.

'Shall we go in?' She gestured to the door.

Bill merely grunted and threw the cigarette on the floor. Stuffing his hands in his pockets, he followed Violet inside, and she beamed at how the interior had been transformed into a place of wonder. When she had left last night, her mother and Archie had been walking around the foyer wondering how to make the place feel festive. Looking around now, she could see they had done it.

Paper chains, made from what appeared to be the wax paper that Archie generally used to wrap meat in, festooned the length and breadth of the foyer. Sprigs of holly and mistletoe studded the red velvet curtains that lined the entrance hall. Paper lanterns, made from old newspaper and painted red and green, lined the reception desk and ticket office, giving a lovely warm, Christmas look.

They had done so much with so little and it was an absolute triumph, she thought. As Betty and Archie appeared from behind the curtain that led to the kitchen, Violet rushed towards them both and flung her arms around them.

'I can't believe what you've done. It's incredible,' she exclaimed as she finally released them.

Betty and Archie looked at one another, abashed.

'It was nothing,' Betty said quietly.

'Besides, we had some help,' Archie said.

He pulled back the curtain and gestured for whoever was behind to come forwards. As the figure appeared, Violet let out another squeal of delight.

'Alan!'

He moved towards her, his face beaming with pleasure and pride. For a moment Violet took in his features and saw he seemed to have aged since the last time she had seen him. He looked more tired, his face lined with wrinkles. But the happiness in his eyes as he drank in the sight of her and little Eamon made her want to burst with pleasure.

As he pulled her into his arms, Violet felt tears prick her eyes. This was turning out to be the best Christmas gift of all.

'I didn't know you were coming,' she said as he released her.

Alan tapped the side of his nose. 'I didn't tell you. Wanted it to be a surprise.'

'Alan wrote to me and asked if Howell & Smart could help this place with Christmas,' Betty explained. 'He arrived last night.'

'And he's staying with me tonight,' Archie put in. 'Me and my parents have put him up in my room and I'm sleeping at the shop.'

'Archie!' Betty scolded. 'You can't sleep there.'

'It's fine,' Archie assured her. 'We've got a room out back with a settee in it where I can bunk down. I've slept in worse.'

Everyone laughed, and Alan threw an arm around Archie's shoulders.

'And I'm grateful. I'll be off tomorrow night, though, so you can have your bed back then.'

'On Christmas Day?' Violet felt a flash of disappointment.

'I've got to work on Boxing Day,' Alan said. Then he clapped his hands together and grinned. 'So we should make the most of what we have.'

Everyone cheered, except for Bill, who groaned instead.

'How about we just get on with what we've got to get on with? Helping people have a good time and get drunk on the very poor beer we're serving.'

Archie laughed and slapped Bill on the back. 'Glad to see the spirit of Christmas is with you, Bill.'

'Hmmph,' Bill growled, turning to Betty. 'Any chance of some of that grub for me?'

Betty frowned. 'It's for our guests.' When Bill's face fell she added, 'But I've a bit put back for each of you after we close.'

Bill's face instantly cheered. He reached into his pocket, about to say something, when Temperance and Enid burst through the doors.

'Oh, my days!' Enid blurted. 'Look at this place. Betty Millington, you've done wonders.'

Betty flushed with pride. 'It wasn't just me. Archie did the lifting and grunting.'

Temperance beamed. 'It's wonderful.'

As she walked towards him, she reached for his hand and Violet couldn't miss the look of delight on his face as he drank in the sight of his sweetheart.

Bill coughed. 'Touching as all this is, ain't we better get on with our jobs? The punters'll be here in a minute.'

'All right, Scrooge,' Violet groaned.

As everyone sidled into the dance hall, Violet bent to pick up her child, who was now gurgling with delight at the sight of his grandmother.

'Are you sure you don't mind taking him tonight?' she asked, handing Eamon over to Enid's waiting arms.

'You know I don't mind,' she said, planting tiny kisses all over

Eamon's head. 'You can leave him with me until the morning if you want to. Save you coming all the way over late at night and waking him up.'

At the suggestion Violet felt a stab of disappointment. She had wanted to wake up with her son on Christmas morning, but thinking about it now realised how impractical it was. Enid was right. Eamon's needs had to come before her own.

'Of course,' she said, shaking her head. 'That would be very kind of you, thank you.'

'Not at all,' Enid said, pulling the boy in close. 'We'd better be off. Get home before it gets dark. And in the morning, we'll see if Santa has been.'

With that, she expertly took the pram in one hand and gently lowered a still-smiling Eamon back down. Then, giving Violet a quick wave goodbye, she wheeled the pram outside. As Violet watched them go, she tried to ignore the tears pooling in her eyes.

'Everything all right?' Archie asked lightly now.

She turned around and plastered on a smile. 'I'm fine. Being silly because Enid's going to keep Eamon for the night. I wanted to wake up with him on Christmas morning to give him his presents. One of the regulars made him a yo-yo and I wanted to see his face as he unwrapped it.'

Archie smiled sympathetically. 'He'll see it later. And you'll have all the time in the world to spend with him and your own dad, too.'

Remembering Alan, Violet nodded. 'I know. It's wonderful to see him.'

Cocking his head to one side, Archie looked at her quizzically. 'How does George feel about all this?'

Violet sighed. It was something she tried not to dwell on. 'I don't imagine he's happy. But me and George have never seen eye to eye: at least now I know why we've never got on. I do my best to avoid him and he feels the same about me, especially since I had Eamon. George thinks I've brought great shame on the family.'

As Violet rolled her eyes Archie snorted. 'As if he can talk, the wickedness he's put you all through.'

Violet said nothing. George Millington's wrongdoings were well documented; she didn't want to bring them all up now. Especially not at such a special time of the year.

'Come on,' Archie said, offering his arm for her to take. 'Time to celebrate.'

And, for once, Violet thought it was. Gratefully she took Archie's hand and allowed him to lead her into the belly of the party, though her mind strayed to Maisie and Roy. How she missed them both. This time of year was particularly sentimental, and since the first decorations had gone up she had found herself thinking about her much-missed twin brother, wondering what he would have made of her situation. He would have made a fine uncle, of that he was sure. With his quick wit and fierce loyalty, he would have made sure that she and Eamon were always loved and protected. But her brother hadn't been fortunate enough to see any more Christmases and she had no idea how Maisie was spending this festive period. With a start, Violet realised how lucky she was, how she had to make the most of these precious moments while she could.

44

A little after eight o'clock, and Temperance realised she had never been happier. As she stood by the bar and watched the East End regulars – as she now thought of them – kick up their heels and take part in a lively jive, she realised that there was plenty to look forward to this Christmas. She was going to spend tomorrow with Renee over in Hammersmith, and had a feeling that there would be much merriment surrounded by her friends and loved ones.

'Temp!' Violet called, breaking the spell and pulling her back to reality. 'Can you give me a hand in the cloakroom? The queue's all the way round the foyer.'

Immediately, Temperance followed her friend towards the little booth and, together, they got into a routine of hanging up coats and handing out tickets. An hour later and the queue had almost subsided, Temperance was pleased to note.

'Merry Christmas, ma'am,' a loud American voice said.

She turned to see Stafford grinning at her, a parcel in his outstretched hand.

'I didn't know you were coming tonight,' she said, feeling her pulse quicken at the sight of the GI.

Temperance hadn't seen Stafford for several weeks. He'd been absent from all the recent LCP meetings, and she'd assumed he had been posted elsewhere, or had been too busy to come to them, or either of the dance halls, lately. She had to admit, in a funny way it was a relief. Stafford had been making her feel confused, prompting questions she didn't want to answer.

Stafford looked sheepish. 'I've been busy the past few weeks, but I wanted to see you tonight. I hoped you might be here.'

'And here I am,' Temperance said pleasantly.

She heard Violet behind her sorting through the hangers. The last thing she wanted was a repeat performance of the last time they had been together. Violet had a lot on her plate and Stafford telling her friend that she wasn't giving her half black child the best start in life was not something she or anyone else needed to revisit that night.

Instead, Temperance walked around the other side of the ticket desk and, without saying a word to Violet, gestured for Stafford to follow her out to the corridor by the kitchen.

'We can talk here,' she said. 'It's quieter.'

Stafford nodded approvingly. He held the parcel out to her. She took it and looked at him. Stafford was smiling expectantly, almost as if he couldn't wait for her to open it.

'This is for me?' she said. She knew that it was, but also she wanted to play for time. Get control of her feelings.

Stafford nodded. 'It's just a token. Something to say happy Christmas.'

Temperance ran her fingers over the shiny gold paper. She didn't want to know where he had got it. It seemed too good to tear off in a hurry.

'I didn't get you anything.'

Stafford shrugged. 'That doesn't matter.' He patted her hand. 'Open it.'

As the band played in the background, she heard the sounds of Betty organising the washing up in the kitchen behind her.

'Archie, they're clean,' she could hear Betty cry. 'Just rinse them and move on. We'll be here until next Christmas if you take this long.'

'All right,' Archie replied wearily.

Temperance closed her eyes, trying to block them both out. And then, opening them, gazed down at the gold-paper-wrapped gift in her hands. Delicately she ran a finger under the satin ribbon, found the knot and untied it. Seeing the fancy box inside, she gave a start of surprise. Opening it, she saw a fine gold bracelet that matched the paper.

'It's beautiful.' She pulled out the bracelet and held it up to the overhead light. It glinted satisfyingly each way Temperance twisted and turned it.

'I saw it in an antique store weeks ago. I wanted to get it for you, there and then. Knew it would suit you.' He paused, then said, 'And I wanted to say thank you. You've been a good friend to me since I arrived in London. Made a lonely soldier feel at home. I want you to know how much you mean to me.'

Temperance looked at him and saw the hope in his eyes. Reality set in. She knew that this bracelet wasn't a simple thank you to a friend, or even a Christmas gift. It was as loaded as any GI weapon. She shook her head. Dropped the bracelet back into the box, closed it and handed it back to Stafford.

'I can't take this, Stafford. I'm sorry. It's beautiful and I'm touched you're thinking of me like this, but I can't. It's too much. I don't think Archie would like it, and your friendship is too important to me to lose over a bracelet.'

'Please,' Stafford said pleadingly. 'I want you to have it.' He pressed the bracelet back into her hand.

'What the hell's going on here?'

Archie's voice, loud and indignant behind them, caused Temperance and Stafford to spring apart. Colour crept up Temperance's cheeks as she took in the fury on Archie's face.

'It's not what you think,' she began, desperation creeping into her voice.

Archie glowered at the pair of them. 'And what do I think?'

'Stafford here was just giving me a Christmas gift,' Temperance said. 'Truly, that's all it was.'

'I'll bet,' Archie growled. 'And if you think that's the only thing he wants to give you then you're a fool.'

'Archie!' Temperance cried.

'Hey, man . . .' Stafford said, taking a step towards Archie. 'Don't talk to a lady like that.'

'Don't tell me how to talk to my sweetheart,' Archie said in a menacing tone Temperance had never heard before.

The two men glared at each other and she felt a wave of anger rise up inside her. She had done nothing to deserve this. Even if Stafford wanted more, he was still her friend, and she and Archie may have their problems, but she adored him. Besides, it was Christmas; this was neither the time nor the place.

'All right,' she said. 'That's enough from both of you.'

Archie fixed his gaze on her. 'I know you think Stafford understands you in a way that I can't. And now this.' He gestured at the bracelet that was still in Temperance's hand. 'I'm not stupid – I can see what's going on here.'

'There's nothing going on,' Temperance said crossly. 'We're friends.'

He crossed his arms. 'It's him or me, Temp.'

'What?' Temperance breathed. 'You're telling me who I can and can't be friends with?'

'I mean it,' Archie said firmly. 'I can't do this anymore. I've seen the way he looks at you and I've seen how you're drawn to him. I've put up with it because I love you, but I won't be made a fool of. I don't want you to see Stafford anymore.'

'You can't ask her to do that,' Stafford said angrily. 'She's her own person. It's up to her who she sees. We're not standing for oppression anymore.'

Archie shook his head in disgust. 'I'm not here to oppress anyone, as well you know. What I won't put up with is being messed about.'

There was a silence then as Temperance felt Archie's eyes land on her. He was waiting for an answer but in that moment she felt paralysed. She could see how he felt, how this looked. But she couldn't have Archie start telling her what to do and crucially she wasn't ready to lose a friend in Stafford. She looked at the GI and saw him looking at her pleadingly. She couldn't leave him either, not when they had shared so much.

She turned back to Archie and looked at him helplessly.

'Archie, I can't,' she began. 'What you're asking me, it's not that simple—'

'It's all right, Temperance,' Archie angrily cut her off before she could finish her sentence. 'Let me make this easy for you. I won't stand to be disrespected in this way, so I'll leave you and the GI here to get on with whatever you want. But you and me, we're finished.'

With that, he turned on his heel and walked quickly away. Temperance watched him go, nausea and panic coursing through her body, making her feel lightheaded.

'Archie,' she called after his retreating back. 'Archie, please.'

But he ignored her and just kept walking. As her former sweetheart left through the double doors, Temperance knew that there was no coming back from this. She and Archie were through.

45

Christmas Day

Renee drummed her red, manicured fingernails on the bar and looked around. It was Christmas Day and she had the place to herself. Not surprising since it was the crack of dawn, but then over the last few days she'd been struggling to sleep. Renee would have liked to put it down to the stresses of work, but she knew that wasn't the case. If anything she felt haunted, with Mick's threats ever-present, and the fact that she needed to get Roger to change his mind about continuing to take in Mick's friend's supplies weighed heavily on her mind. That wasn't the reason she felt haunted, though. No, Christmas was the anniversary of Ronnie's death. Death. There was a word, she thought, as she reached for the strong cup of tea she had made herself, resisting the urge to pour herself a whisky on the grounds it was far too early.

Death wasn't really the right word, was it, she thought. Manslaughter was more accurate. Yes, it was in self-defence, but she had stabbed Ronnie with a shoe when all was said and done.

Her eyes strayed to the tree that stood in the corner of the bar. The shoe ornament – reminding her of her weapon of choice thanks to its sharp, thin heel – took pride of place in the centre of the tree.

Looking at it, she tried to muster some feelings of remorse as she recalled how the needle-like heel had connected with

Ronnie's flesh. She remembered the blood everywhere. But try as she might, Renee couldn't bring herself to feel guilty. Ronnie had deserved what he got; he'd had it coming for years. He had put her through hell, and deep down she blamed him for the death of her father. Ronnie had piled on so much pressure, constantly demanding her father pay what was owed, and extra of course, so that eventually he could see no other way out than to take his own life. And then the debt had fallen to her, and she had been forced to repay what was owed by marrying Ronnie, facing years of abuse and destruction at his hands. She shook her head in sadness. So much pain and loss over the years thanks to one man. She couldn't possibly feel guilty about her tormentor's death. He had taken enough of her life; she wasn't allowing him to take any more.

'Merry Christmas, honey.'

Renee jumped at the sound of Nancy's voice. As the New Yorker took a seat beside her at the bar, Renee couldn't help but notice her friend was dressed up to the nines in a bright red skirt-suit with matching heels and lipstick. Nancy's outfit was topped off with a little black pillbox hat and matching gloves.

'Merry Christmas to you as well, queen,' she replied, as she looked Nancy up and down. 'Where are you off to all dressed up like that at this hour?'

Nancy made a face. 'Thought I'd go over to the Regal. Say Merry Christmas to some of the regulars.'

'Really?' Renee thought for a moment. The idea had never crossed her mind. She'd thought that popping over the night before to wish everyone well would have been enough. 'Do you think anyone will be there?'

Nancy shrugged. 'Sure. A few folk are working hard for the community get-together this afternoon before coming back here.'

Renee nodded, distracted. 'Do you want me to come with you?'

A strange look crossed Nancy's face as she shook her head. 'No . . . honey. You stay here. I'll be back for lunch.'

'All right.' Renee couldn't say she was disappointed. She reached for her cup of tea. 'Did you see what happened with Archie and Temperance there last night?'

Nancy nodded and fiddled with her glove. 'I didn't see it, but Archie tore strips off that guy Stafford, I heard. To be fair, it's been coming for a while. Temperance might just think she's being friendly but it's clear Stafford wants more.'

'You've clocked that, then.' Renee raised an eyebrow.

'Hard not to,' Nancy replied. 'Temperance has been foolish, wanting her cake and eating it, too.'

'Still,' Renee said with a sigh. 'This won't be easy on Temp. She's obviously confused, poor girl.'

'You think she'll still come to Christmas lunch today?' Nancy asked.

'She'd better,' Renee muttered darkly. 'She's supposed to be helping me peel the spuds.'

Nancy laughed. 'Honey, you can't put her to work like that if her heart is broken.'

'It'll take her mind off it,' Renee said with a wry smile. 'Keeping busy is the best medicine when it comes to heartache.' She slid off the bar stool she had been sitting on and drained the last of her tea. 'I've got to get on. You'll be back in time to help me greet people, won't you?'

'You bet,' Nancy said, but Renee wasn't really listening. In her mind she was hoping Queenie wouldn't forget to bring the bird she'd promised to feed them all.

A couple of hours later Nancy was nowhere near the East End. Instead she was at the Rainbow Rooms, lying in John's cramped single bed. Resting her head on his shoulder, she felt exhausted but happy.

'Are you sure you can't stay?' he crooned.

He traced his fingers along the inside of her arm, making Nancy shiver at his touch.

'I wish I could.' She sighed. 'But I've got to help Renee with preparations for the meal.'

'And what about me?' John said softly. 'You're going to leave me all alone on Christmas Day?'

She giggled at the exaggerated neediness in his voice. 'We've spent the morning together, sweetie. That's going to have to be enough. Besides, it was hard enough getting away at all . . .'

Nancy trailed off, not wanting to go into the fact she had hoped she would be able to creep out of bed early enough that she wouldn't bump into anyone. She should have known Renee would have been in the bar – her friend had been struggling to sleep at all lately, and seemed to spend all the hours she could pacing up and down the Palais.

Nancy had had to think on her feet, of course. She'd told Renee she was going to the Bethnal Green dance hall. At seven in the morning? Who was going to believe that? It was the best she'd been able to come up with, though. The alternative was not seeing John at all on Christmas morning, and that had been unthinkable.

She turned to him now, wanting to drink in everything about his gorgeous face.

'It doesn't matter. Let's just say I had to play fast and loose with the truth.'

'I'm sorry,' John said softly. He planted a kiss on her cheek, coffee and sex on his breath. 'I know you hate lying to your friends. But I'm glad you did, Nancy. I can't give you up. I don't want to give you up.'

At the declaration, Nancy's heart beat faster. 'I don't want to give you up, either. You're becoming my world, John.'

John closed his eyes and breathed heavily. 'I hate this, too, you know. The lying. I have to tell my buddies I'm seeing some anonymous girl, but I want to tell them the truth. That you're my sweetheart.'

Nancy said nothing. She wanted the same. When Roger had seen them in the street a couple of weeks ago she had wanted nothing more than to tell him that John was her significant other, the man she loved. But of course she hadn't, and she couldn't. She had barely seen Roger since then, but on the brief occasions they had crossed paths he hadn't said a word. She very much hoped that she'd thrown him off the scent.

If only she could publicly declare her love for John, but it was impossible. They were both married, and although their relationships might be difficult, they were stuck with them.

'Where do your buddies think you are today?' she asked lightly.

'I told them I was doing some paperwork. Then said I might stop by some of the poorhouses.'

Nancy laughed. John's lie had been far too similar to her own.

'You think that's funny?' John asked.

'I don't,' Nancy admitted. 'I think it's sad we have to do all this sneaking around.'

John paused for a moment. 'I can't stop this, Nancy.'

Nancy couldn't speak. She didn't want whatever this was to end either. Yet she also didn't want to admit that it was becoming harder and harder to slip away for their trysts. The sometimes elaborate fibs, the time away from the Palais, not to mention the guilt of being dishonest with the kids. But she couldn't imagine a world without John in it, and she didn't want to acknowledge that one day he'd be gone.

'It's OK,' she said now, not wanting to spoil the time they had together. Glancing at her watch, she peeled back the thin cotton sheets, ready to get out of bed.

'That time already, huh?' he joked. 'You use me for your own wicked ends and then toss me aside.'

He snaked his arms around her waist and pulled her back

towards him. As his mouth travelled along her neck and down her body, Nancy moaned in pleasure. This was where she was supposed to be. As she allowed him to pull her back onto the bed, her eyes landed on a letter on John's bedside.

She didn't have time to read it all, but the parting words caught her eye.

Your loving wife, Myrtle.

And there it was. The stark reminder that he was married, as was she. They may want each other, but Myrtle and Alex had already staked their claims. She and John could never truly be together.

46

'Pass the spuds, Temp,' Violet asked from her place at the far end of the long table Renee had laid in the bar, as had now become tradition.

Temperance stared forlornly at the plate in front of her, not even bothering to pick up her knife and fork.

'Temp,' Violet tried again.

Still nothing.

'Temp!' she almost shouted now. Finally, Temperance looked up.

'Sorry, what?'

'The potatoes.' Violet nudged her. 'Can you pass them?'

'Oh.' Temperance finally came to as she handed them to Violet.

Violet shook her head as she popped a spud on her plate and one on Eamon's. Beaming at the baby sandwiched between her and Enid, she cut the potato into tiny places for her son, taking great pleasure in watching him pick up morsels and put them into his mouth. This year's Christmas was so different to last. Eamon was getting on for eighteen months old and Violet delighted in his every move. She could see how entranced he was in the paper lanterns, the newspaper chains and of course the shiny cutlery at every place.

'Mamamamama,' he crooned softly, as he picked up another piece of potato.

Violet's heart gave out a little. He had only just started using the word last week and she knew it was something she would never tire of hearing.

'Everything all right, Temperance?' Roger asked brightly from his place opposite her and next to Renee.

'She's fine,' Renee said, smiling at her. 'She's upset because she and Archie have fallen out.'

'We've done more than fallen out,' Temperance said sadly. 'We've broken up.'

Roger's face was a picture of concern. 'I'm so sorry to hear that.'

'Well, it's hardly a surprise, is it?' Queenie said, tactlessly. 'You were knocking about with that black fella more than you were with Archie. You can't blame him for getting upset. Blokes don't like having their noses put out of joint.'

'Didn't know you were the oracle on relationships, Gran.' Violet frowned, well aware that Temperance was feeling fragile.

'Never said I was,' Queenie said haughtily. 'But I've been round the block more times than you've had hot dinners girl, so less of the lip.'

Violet laughed at this, and was pleased to see that Temperance managed a smile, too. Enid looked over at her daughter, her eyes brimming with concern.

'Who is this other lad, Temperance?' she asked.

'That GI, Stafford,' Winnie said now, her voice booming across the table. 'He gave a speech at the LCP. He was the one who encouraged Temperance to do the same.'

'Oh.' Enid looked quizzical now.

'I think it's a good thing,' Winnie said suddenly. 'You need to mix with more black folks. Understand more about your culture, your Ghanaian heritage.'

Temperance closed her eyes, as though she was exhausted of hearing everyone else's opinion on her love life.

'Is Archie not coming today then?' Enid looked around hopefully as if she had somehow missed the butcher's presence.

'No.' Renee shook her head. 'He called in earlier this morning to wish me and Nancy well, but said he didn't think it was a good idea if he came. Said he'd be here for the New Year's dance though.'

'New Year's dance?' Roger asked.

Renee nodded as she swallowed a forkful of peas.

'We thought we'd hold it at Bethnal Green,' Nancy said. 'As a way of celebrating all we've achieved there this year. Betty's doing a spread, aren't you, honey?'

'I am,' Betty said proudly, then fixed her gaze on Roger. 'You should say a few words. It was your idea, after all.'

Roger looked abashed. 'I don't know about that.'

'Course you should,' Renee exclaimed. She laid a hand on his forearm and gave him an encouraging squeeze. 'I'll even teach you a few new steps if you like. Show the parishioners just what you can do.'

At the thought the vicar brightened. 'You know, although I can waltz, I've always wanted to be able to dance a proper two-step. As you might know, Renee, my mother used to cut quite a number on the dance hall up north all those years ago.'

'I remember,' Renee said fondly. 'It's not as hard as you think it is. Let me teach you.'

'All right.' Roger looked pleased. 'Thank you.'

'Who knows, play your cards right and you might give Archie a run for his money. Still, it's a shame he's not here today,' Queenie said, slightly forlornly, then brightening said, 'That mean there's extra spuds?'

'Queenie!' Betty admonished, while George sniggered.

'Steady, Ma, that's the sort of thing I'd say.'

Violet said nothing. She had been surprised when Betty announced she was bringing George to the Hammersmith Palais for Christmas lunch, but then again what else was she supposed to do with him? She could hardly leave him alone at home, more was the pity.

'Everything in order for this afternoon's Christmas lunch at Bethnal Green?' Roger asked Betty pleasantly now.

Betty nodded, her mouth full of green beans.

'The girls are coming to help as well,' she said, fixing her delighted beam on Temperance and Violet.

'I'll come and give you a hand as well, Bet,' Renee said now.

'And us,' Peter said, nudging his sister Ruth in the ribs.

Nancy smiled at them with pride. 'That's very kind of you both.'

Peter's face flushed with pleasure.

'Have you opened your Christmas presents, yet?' Roger asked the two of them. 'I know Nancy took a lot of trouble with getting them.'

Ruth and Peter looked blankly at the vicar, while panic flooded Nancy's face. 'It was so nice to bump into you the other day,' Roger went on. 'With that nice GI who helped us repair the Regal. How is he? I thought he might be here today, actually.'

Violet saw Nancy's scarlet cheeks and frowned. She looked downright disturbed. Surely there was no crime in going shopping?

'Oh? You didn't mention you'd gone shopping with John, Nancy?' Renee's tone was light.

'Didn't I?' Nancy shovelled a piece of chicken into her mouth and chewed furiously as she turned to Queenie. 'Honey, I don't know where you get all this meat at Christmas, and I don't want to, but I will say I'm very grateful that you do.'

Queenie laughed and tapped the side of her nose. 'Ask me no questions and I'll tell you no lies.'

'We could almost say the same about you, queen,' Renee addressed Nancy sharply.

Violet looked up at Renee in surprise. She never spoke to Nancy in that tone.

'I . . . don't know what you mean,' Nancy faltered. 'John and I just ran into each other while we were both out shopping together up west, that's all.'

'Course you did,' Renee said.

Then Roger turned to Violet. 'How's Alan doing, love? I hear he's been helping with the Regal?'

Violet was about to answer when George butted in. 'Alan Hopkins?' he said. 'What's he doing sneaking down to London?'

'He didn't sneak down here,' Violet said. 'He's only here till later tonight, he's got to get back to Birmingham for tomorrow.'

Betty glanced at George who looked like he was about to boil over.

'Flying visit, isn't it, Violet?' she prompted.

'That's right.' Violet hadn't intended on telling George that Alan had come to see her at the Regal, but she didn't want to lie, either. 'There's nothing cloak and dagger about it.'

She glanced at George, who had been tetchy since the moment he'd arrived at the Palais. She wasn't sure why. She wasn't aware that he and Betty had fallen out any more than usual, or that he and Queenie had exchanged words.

Roger smiled, trying to look friendly and appeasing. 'Has Alan recovered his spirits, after the bomb attack in Birmingham?'

'Well—' Violet began, before George cut her off.

'Ain't right, talking about *him*, not with me sat here. And at Christmas, too. It's a betrayal,' he spluttered, childishly.

'Do me a favour,' Queenie scoffed. 'What about all the times you betrayed your own family? Your wife? Once with the sister of a woman who is sat at this table.'

At the mention of her sister, Lizzie, Renee shook her head.

'Don't drag me into this,' she said sternly. 'My Lizzie was a fool and I've said as much, many times.'

'I'm not staying around here listening to any more of this,' George snapped.

With that he pushed his chair away and walked across the bar to the doors, flinging them open. Violet watched him go and wished she felt something, if only for the sake of her mother who looked broken at the exchange.

'It'll be all right, Betty,' Queenie said in a reassuring tone.

'George'll either calm down or he'll fall asleep and not remember a thing. One of the two.'

'Yes, I'm sure,' Betty said in a falsely bright voice.

Violet took a sip of water, wishing in that moment it was a port and lemon.

'Oh, dear,' Roger said, his eyes downcast. 'I didn't mean to cause trouble.'

Renee patted his hand soothingly. 'You didn't, love. It takes nothing to set that man off like a rocket.'

'I'm not very good at pretending, you see,' Roger went on. 'I'd rather treat people with respect and be honest with them. In my experience, secrets and lies only ever lead to trouble in the end.'

At Roger's words, Violet couldn't help notice the anxious looks on both Renee's and Nancy's faces, and then the look Renee gave Nancy. A piercing stare.

Violet frowned. What the heck is going on? she thought, picking up her glass. Something wasn't right between those two, that was for sure.

47

Two days after Boxing Day and Renee was in Roger's arms, leading him around the Bethnal Green dance floor.

'That's it,' she said encouragingly. 'Soften those knees. You've got it.'

Beads of sweat broke out across Roger's brow at the effort of concentrating so hard on his steps. Taking pity on him, Renee paused for a moment and allowed the vicar to take a break.

'You don't have to be perfect,' she said soothingly. 'It's only a New Year's dance. Nobody's expecting you to be Fred Astaire.'

Roger sighed. 'I want to do this right, Renee. It means a lot to me.'

'I know,' Renee replied. 'But Rome wasn't built in a day, love. You're doing well.'

'Not well enough.' Roger sighed. He ran a hand through his hair and Renee frowned. He'd seemed tired lately, as if he had a lot on his mind. She walked over to sit at one of the empty chairs. Patting the seat beside her, she encouraged Roger to join her.

'What's up, love?' she asked kindly.

Roger managed a weak smile. 'Is it that obvious?'

'Only to you, me and the gatepost,' she quipped. 'What is it?'

'I don't know,' Roger sighed. 'I suppose it's a funny time of year, isn't it? Can be a little maudlin – and this year it's bittersweet, because a year ago my brother died, but I met you, which has been wonderful. I hadn't seen Ronnie in over twenty years, and as you know, we were far from close.' He scratched his chin and looked thoughtfully at Renee. 'I suppose it's a time of reflection. You know, I've been holding these groups, Renee, for women like you, who've been treated badly by their husbands.'

'Yes, I know,' she said gently, though at the mention of Roger's groups she felt uncomfortable. So far she had shunned all attempts to get involved in them, citing the fact she was too busy, what with two dance halls to oversee. The truth was she didn't want to share her story with women like her, women who had seen what she had seen. She didn't want to open those floodgates, or worse, run the risk of confessing that she had finally got her revenge by killing her husband, even it had been self-defence. But the truth was, Renee could no longer be certain if that fatal act had been something she had done in the heat of the moment to protect herself, or something she'd wanted to do. After all, she had been running from Ronnie for years. Killing him seemed like the only way to free herself from his unyielding grasp. And she couldn't deny the euphoria she'd felt at getting rid of him, once and for all.

She took a breath and tried to shake the sight of his face that night from her mind. A face that might haunt her forever.

'What's the expression, God closes a window and opens a door?' she said, then. 'Maybe some things happen for a reason.' At Roger's intense expression, she added, 'But it's natural that you'd think about Ronnie now – as you say, it's been a year.'

Roger nodded and smiled. 'How are you feeling about it, Renee?'

'Me?' She gave a little laugh. 'I'm fine.'

'But are you?' Roger asked carefully.

'Course,' Renee said firmly. But as she did so the image of Ronnie's blood-spattered clothes, the shock in his eyes as he realised what she had done, flashed again into her mind.

Roger looked as if he was about to say something else,

when the unlikely appearance of Mick and Betty approaching stopped him.

'Hello,' he said cordially. 'You've just interrupted Renee trying to encourage me in a fruitless pursuit of dance.'

'Not fruitless at all,' Renee said loyally. 'You just need a bit more confidence on the floor.'

Betty wrinkled her nose. 'I'm not sure you do, Vicar. I'm not sure it's seemly for a man of the cloth to be making his way across the dance hall with vixens and evil all about.'

At the statement, Renee threw her head back and roared with laughter. When Renee had first met Betty she'd been a real God-fearing woman, who was terrified that her daughters would be guilty of moral sin by working at the dance hall. Over the years, though, Betty had softened, even if the idea of a vicar stepping out to a jive was a step too far for her.

'Calm down, queen,' Renee assured her with a wink. 'The vicar's steps are very appropriate.'

Betty flushed and said no more.

'What can we do for you, anyway?' Roger asked.

Mick rocked back and forth in his shoes and then put an arm around Betty's shoulders. 'This wonderful lady made me come and talk to you.'

'Oh?' Renee looked at Mick with suspicion in her eyes. The day before, she had finally plucked up the courage to tell him that she wanted nothing to do with his surplus stocks, wherever they may come from, and that she cared little for the consequences.

'I want to make the dance a bit special for you, Vicar,' Mick said easily. 'I've been offered a bit of beef.' He lifted an arm from Betty's shoulder and tapped his nose. 'Course, I'll give you mates' rates on it, as I said to Mrs Millington here, but she's insisted I talk to you.'

'We've already got a menu for the dance,' Betty said primly. 'I wasn't sure beef would fit in.'

Mick laughed. 'When does beef not fit in?'

'Well, I have to say it's a generous offer, Mick, but I think that as Betty has already planned a menu we wouldn't want to create extra work,' said Roger.

A flicker of relief passed across Betty's face as the vicar spoke. But Renee knew that wouldn't be the end of it.

'Come, come, Vicar,' Mick tried again. 'Bit of beef, be lovely. Ain't that right, Renee?'

Renee swallowed. Would this never end? But before she could say anything, Roger spoke.

'I don't doubt it would be lovely, Mick,' he said firmly. 'But I must insist that it's not right for us. I'm sure you'll have no problem finding someone else.'

'Just as I thought, Vicar,' Betty agreed. 'Come on, Mick,' she said, shaking his hand free from her shoulder. 'Let's leave these good people alone.'

With that, Betty marched Mick out of the door, not taking no for an answer. Renee smiled inwardly. Say what you like about Betty Millington: she wouldn't let a rogue like Mick get one over on her.

But just as Mick got to the doorway he paused, turned, and flashed a toothy grin.

'Hey, Renee!' he called. 'Don't forget to save me a dance at the New Year's ball, eh?'

And with that he was gone, earning a curious glance from Roger as he went.

Renee shivered. Like hell Mick wanted a dance. It was control, nothing more, nothing less. He was just a more pathetic version of her late husband.

'What was all that about?' Roger asked.

Roger's tone was light-hearted but Renee glimpsed an edge to his tone. Suddenly, she couldn't stand the situation she found herself in. She was sick of the lies. Sick of the pain. Sick of the years of lying, and running from who she was, terrified of what she had done catching up with her. No. There was only one way out – and that was to tell the truth.

Calmly, she turned to Roger and inhaled deeply before she spoke.

'Mick's blackmailing me,' she said. 'Or at least, he's attempting to.'

'He's what? Why?' Roger spluttered.

She paused. Could she really say the words aloud? Yes, she decided, she could.

'Because he believes I killed Ronnie. And before you ask, Roger, I'm afraid to say that I did, and I don't regret it. I killed your brother last Christmas, and I would do it again if I had to.'

As Renee finished speaking, she felt her heart race. Adrenaline coursed through her body as if it were on fire as she waited for Roger's reaction. It felt like an eternity before he spoke. But as she watched the shock register on his face and then slowly turn to anger, she knew she had made a mistake.

'*You?*' he whispered. 'You killed Ronnie?'

Renee nodded. She had come this far; she wasn't about to back out now. 'I had to. He would have killed me otherwise.'

Roger turned away from her, head in his hands. 'I can't believe I'm hearing this. Renee, what have you done?'

And in that moment Renee realised that although the burden of guilt had been weighing her down, she had now transferred a fresh round of pain onto Roger. A man who had been so good to her, and the rest of the Palais, he surely didn't deserve it.

'I'm sorry,' she said earnestly. 'I'm sorry I've hurt you.'

'But you're not sorry you killed Ronnie?' he asked, turning back to face her.

Renee couldn't lie. Not after all she had been through. 'No.'

Roger nodded. 'I see. Then, Renee, you leave me no choice. I will have to report you to the police. I appreciate you may not have meant to kill Ronnie, but this can't be covered up. You must understand that.'

With that he swept out of the dance hall and left Renee alone.

As she looked around her, the walls seemed to close in, and she struggled to breathe. What the hell had she just done?

48

New Year's Eve

It was a cold, dank day, but Temperance hardly noticed. All days now, as far as she was concerned, were dark and miserable. And the fact that it was New Year's Eve didn't make the slightest difference to her as she disembarked the bus at Bethnal Green and made her way to the new dance hall.

As the damp fog hit her cheeks and nose, she barely noticed. All she cared about was that Archie was no longer in her life. She missed him, she loved him: it had taken him leaving her to realise that.

Just after Christmas she had tried to apologise to him for any wrongdoing on her part. She had gone to the butcher's to try and talk to him, to try and make him realise that she'd been confused, but could now see what she wanted. But Archie wouldn't listen, he had just gently steered her out of the shop, told her he was sorry, and that he would always care about her, but that they both needed to move on.

The reminder of that terrible meeting brought tears to her eyes, but she knew she had to pull herself together. The first dance started in less than an hour – planned as a chance to thank the clientele and celebrate new beginnings. Temperance had a job to do, and she couldn't let her sad feelings about the past ruin her future. Not now.

As she rounded the corner, the Regal came into view, and

in the darkness Temperance made out the outline of a woman standing outside. With her head bent low and shoulders shaking, it looked as if whoever it was was sobbing.

Getting nearer, she could see clearly that it was Violet.

'Vi,' Temperance said, her voice full of concern, hurrying towards her friend. 'What is it?'

Violet lifted her head, and even in the gloom of the early evening December light Temperance saw that her eyes were blotchy and swollen. Violet said nothing, she merely shook her head, and Temperance caught the flash of something in her hands. A piece of paper.

'Violet, what is it?' she said again, 'What's wrong?'

When Violet still couldn't speak, only sob, Temperance gently steered her into the foyer of the dance hall. Thankfully, there was nobody about, so Temperance was able to get a still-distraught Violet neatly into the cloakroom, where she knew nobody would see them.

'What's this you've got, sweetheart?' she said, gesturing at the piece of paper Violet clutched. Temperance gingerly prised the piece of paper from her hand, and Violet finally found her voice.

'A little boy was waiting for me as I walked up to the dance hall,' she began. 'He said he had been asked to give me this note. I asked him who'd given it to him, but he shook his head then rode off on his bicycle. Then I opened it . . .' Violet's words were lost in a new rush of tears.

'Let me see.' Cautiously Temperance unfolded the paper and began reading.

Dear Violet Millington,
  Women like you should be ashamed of your-
selves. Whoring yourself about without a care in
the world. What you've done, bringing a baby into
this world, and a black one at that, out of wedlock,

is nothing short of disgusting. You're not fit to be
a mother, you're not even fit to walk these streets.
We don't want your kind around here so why don't
you sod off somewhere else and take your loose
morals with you.

Take this as a friendly warning. The next one
won't be as nice.

A friend

As Temperance finished reading, she was shaking with rage. Who the hell would write such cruel, hurtful things? And this wasn't the first time. Thank the Lord Violet had not seen the note Archie found before Christmas. It was plain evil.

'It's true, Temp. I am an unfit mother,' Violet said, her breath ragged from crying so hard.

'Don't be so silly,' Temperance scoffed. 'You can't possibly think that. Whoever wrote this is full of poison. They don't know you or anything about you.'

'But they're right,' Violet moaned. 'What sort of example am I setting my boy? I'm not married, I don't have a stable home life, I'm at work all hours of the day and night and constantly giving him to other people to look after. I mean, even now your mum and Winnie are looking after him. And I'm not black: that's plain as day. What if I can never understand my son in the way he deserves?'

'You will, and you do.' Temperance took a breath. 'Sweetheart, you can't believe this rubbish. I do think we ought to go to the police though. Whoever this is can't be allowed to get away with this.'

At the mention of the word *police*, Violet shook her head. 'No, Temperance. We can't. That'll just make things worse.'

'How can this get worse?' Temperance exclaimed. 'Violet, you can't let people intimidate you like this.'

'But maybe they're right—'

Just then the door opened, and Renee and Nancy appeared, their faces rich with concern.

'Oh, it's you two,' Renee said, looking relieved. 'We heard the noise and thought a cat had got stuck in here. I thought, that's all we need tonight—' But as Renee took in Violet's face, a shadow fell across her own. 'What the hell's happened?' she asked.

'Violet, honey, talk to us,' Nancy pleaded.

'This has happened,' Temperance said, pushing the note into Nancy's hands. She put then put her arm around Violet, as both Renee and Nancy read the vicious words. Temperance watched their expressions change from curious to disgusted. By the time they had finished reading, both women looked charged and ready for action.

'You cannot let this sick son of a bitch get away with this,' Nancy snarled.

'She's right,' Renee agreed. 'Whoever's doing this is not right in the head. They want locking up. You can't take any of this seriously, queen.'

'But they're right,' Violet moaned. 'I'm not doing the best for my boy. I'm not.'

'Honey, I know plenty of women who are married and doing a terrible job of raising their kids,' Nancy said. 'You have support, you have love. Any kid would be lucky to have you as his mom.'

'But I'm not black,' Violet persisted.

'But *I* am,' Temperance said firmly. 'And so is Winnie. And we can give him all the help he needs when it comes to working out his place in the world as a black man.'

'It's not enough,' Violet whispered. 'He needs his father.'

Temperance, Nancy and Renee exchanged looks. They could wordlessly all agree that there was no arguing with that.

'So, what do we do?' Nancy asked a few moments later, as Violet wiped at her eyes.

'We'll go to the police,' Renee said firmly, catching sight of Violet's look of protest. 'Two for one.'

Nancy looked at her quizzically. 'Two for one? What are you talking about?'

At the question Renee lifted her chin in the air with a hint of defiance, but Temperance could see a flash of real fear in her eyes. 'I told Roger the truth about Ronnie, and what I did that night.'

'What do you mean?' Temperance looked confused. 'What did you do?'

Renee let out a shaky breath. 'I mean that I killed Ronnie. I hit him with my shoe and the heel sliced through his flesh.'

Violet and Temperance's jaws simultaneously dropped open in shock.

'*You?*' Violet whispered.

'It was self-defence,' Nancy said quickly. 'He'd have killed Renee otherwise. She did what she had to, and if she hadn't done it, then I would have.'

Renee shot her a grateful look as the other two looked stunned.

'Oh, Renee,' Violet whispered, eventually. 'You must have been in hell.'

'And you've been carrying this with you all this time?' Temperance leaned forwards and pulled Renee into a brief hug. 'I'm so sorry.'

'I told Roger a few days ago,' Renee went on. 'I couldn't stand it anymore. And it was the only way to get Mick off my back – he'd been blackmailing me. Either I persuaded Roger to take his mate's surplus stock, or he'd open his mouth. But to be honest, the guilt of what I did has been eating away at me. Not because I regret it – I don't,' she said tearfully. 'I'd do it all again. But Roger's a good man. He deserves to know the truth about what happened to his brother.'

Nancy pinched the bridge of her nose and let out a sigh. 'I didn't know you'd told him,' she said.

'Well . . .' Renee gave her a wry look. 'You've been a bit tied up, lately, queen. There wasn't really the opportunity.'

Nancy swallowed. 'How did he take it?'

'Not well,' Renee admitted. 'He said he's going to report it to the police.'

'What? Why?' Violet spluttered.

'Because he believes in justice,' she explained. 'Accountability.'

'Renee, we have to stop him,' Temperance begged. 'I'll talk to him. We'll all talk to him.'

'I've tried,' Renee said shortly. 'But he's made up his mind.'

'Well, he's not heard from all of us,' Nancy said grimly. 'And I'd wager that if he hasn't gone to the police yet, there's a chance he can be talked round.'

'I don't think so,' Renee said. 'I've not seen or heard from him since. I don't even know if he'll be here tonight. You should have seen his face when I told him, though. The shock . . . the disappointment. He's been a good friend to me this past year, has Roger. I feel like I've betrayed him.'

'But he needs to realise exactly how much of a sick bastard his brother was,' Nancy insisted. 'Ronnie deserved what he got, Renee. We both know that.' She drew herself up straight. 'I'm going to find Roger and sort this out, once and for all.'

With that Nancy stalked down the corridor, flung open the doors and disappeared, leaving the three remaining women gaping at one another.

'Do you really think Nancy can convince Roger?' Temperance asked in a small voice.

'I can only hope so,' Renee said. 'Or it's the end for me.'

49

It was a full hour later that Nancy allowed herself the luxury of breathing normally. The moment she had heard what Roger had planned after Renee's confession, she'd felt a rage like no other possess her. Furious that their lives, all their hard work with the dance halls, were about to be ruined by yet another man. The Palais at least was theirs, hers and Renee's. It was their future, the crown of their achievements, but now it looked as if it were about to disappear. And all because of Ronnie son-of-a-bitch Newsham. Nancy shook her head as she sat in the corner of the dance hall sipping on a gin and tonic trying to think straight.

When she had walked away from the others, Nancy had half expected to collide with Roger, in which case she'd have told him exactly what she thought of him; how selfish he was being. But of course he was nowhere to be found. No surprise there. He was hardly likely to want to be anywhere near Renee after what she'd told him. Still, Nancy thought, as she took another sip of her drink and tried to think, where did that leave them? And, crucially, where did it leave Renee, who'd been fighting tooth and nail to rid herself of that terrible man for years. It looked now as if she were about to pay for that with her own freedom.

'Well, you look lost in thought,' boomed a familiar American voice.

At the sound of John's deep timbre, Nancy's heart beat a little faster. 'John,' she said, 'I didn't think you'd be coming tonight.'

John took a seat beside her and cupped her chin in his large, smooth hand. 'And miss seeing in the New Year with my best girl? Where else would I be?'

Despite her ragged nerves about Renee, Nancy quivered at his touch, her body naturally shifting towards him. 'How long can you stay?' she said.

'Honey, I can stay all night.'

As she held his gaze, Nancy's thoughts couldn't help projecting ahead to the future.

'You thought about what you'll do when all this is over?' she asked him.

A confused look passed across John's face. He leaned back and observed her. 'The dance? I guess I'll just go home and hope *someone* wants to keep me company,' he teased her.

Nancy couldn't help smiling. John could charm the birds out of the trees, and she knew she would fall for it every time.

'Not the dance. All this.' She gestured to the scores of men in military uniform dancing a lively waltz. Amongst them she saw Temperance dancing with Stafford, and frowned. There was a story that didn't have a happy ending. Whilst Nancy had always privately thought Temperance should do more to explore the black side of her heritage, she wasn't entirely sure that Stafford was the right person to help her do that. Archie would and should be the one to help. Or at least he would be, if he could get past his insecurities and take Temperance's race seriously. Of course, he and Temp were matched in pretty much every way that mattered, but their differences should be celebrated; Nancy was a firm believer in that. That was how it had been with her and Alex when they'd first met. She was the sassy New Yorker with an answer for everything; he was the well-spoken, quiet bartender from London. Together they'd made a good pair, or at least, Nancy thought they had.

Turning back to face John she tried to shake off thoughts

of her husband. Perhaps Alex was somewhere doing the same about thoughts of her? With a sudden sense of grief, Nancy knew then that her marriage was unlikely to survive.

'So . . . What did you mean?' John asked gently, pulling Nancy back to the present.

'Oh.' She smiled at John. 'I meant the war. What will you do when the war ends?'

'If it ever does, you mean?' he muttered darkly.

Nancy frowned and pulled away from him for a second. 'What are you talking about?' she asked, over the thrum of the music. Oscar Reyburn and his band had been invited to play at the Regal instead of the Palais for the evening, and it was comforting to see the familiar shape of the conductor in the distance.

John shrugged and took a sharp pull on his pint. 'Just that we've still got a long road ahead of us. Hitler's not backing down, and neither are we. Now it's been confirmed by both the US and Britain what the Germans are doing to the Jews, killing them like they're goddam cattle rather than humans, I dunno. It's hard to feel like there will ever be an end to this thing.'

Nancy fell silent. She too had read the statement Anthony Eden had given in parliament earlier that month confirming the mass genocide of Jews. Although what had been happening was widely known, this was the first time it had been officially confirmed. Since then, Nancy had felt displaced, unsure of her place in the world. How long would be it be before Hitler came for her? And for her family? Her thoughts turned to her cousin Rosa and her family. They had been missing now for over two years, and Nancy knew in her heart of hearts that Rosa was dead. Most likely killed by the Nazis.

But as she stared into John's blue eyes, this horror only made her more determined to enjoy life, to hold on to every drop of happiness she could find.

'Well, I believe this war will end, and that we'll end up on the right side of it,' she said firmly, reaching for her gin as John grinned back at her.

'You reckon, huh?'

'I know it,' she replied, and ran a finger along his forearm. 'And I know I'll be making the most of my life now and in the future.'

John leaned towards her. 'You sound like you've got plans.'

'I don't know about plans,' Nancy said. 'But I'd like to think I'll be living every day as if it were my last. I don't want to be unhappy any longer.' She took a deep breath and then threw back the last of her gin before she spoke again. 'And I'd like to think there's a future for you and me.'

John raised his eyebrows. 'A future, huh? You know we're both married.'

Alex and Myrtle. Nancy has to keep reminding herself that their spouses were real, and that her happiness, and John's, would come at the cost of other people's. But didn't she owe it to herself to be happy?

'What if we weren't married?' she said to John now, feeling fearless as the music started up again. 'What if we weren't married and we could live our lives as we wanted, together, you and me? I could come back with you to the States. Bring Peter and Ruth. Start all over again.'

'You'd really want that?' John asked. He bent down and kissed the inside of her wrist. 'To be with me? To face the stigma of divorce and all the upheaval that would bring?'

As Nancy felt his soft lips against her tender skin, she felt as if she had been scorched. She knew in that moment that being with John, leaving England and returning to her home country was what she wanted.

'I'd do all that and more, for you,' she whispered.

And then, because she was too weary to care what people thought anymore, she leaned forward and pressed her lips to John's. With that one kiss, she was convinced that when this war was over she was saying goodbye to London. Her present and her future were with John.

50

January, 1943

It was almost February, and Temperance was in the practice rooms at the Palais, polishing the men's shoes they lent out for dancing. It was an important part of her job, but it wasn't the only reason she was closeted away. Later that morning, Archie was coming to the Palais, and even though weeks had gone by since they'd split up, Temperance still wanted to avoid him.

Reaching for the polish and another pair of shoes, she rubbed furiously, trying to make sense of her feelings. She knew she ought to feel happy – the British war effort was going well with the Allied troops taking Tripoli from the Germans, and in the past couple of weeks she and Stafford had tentatively started courting.

With her heart still hurting over Archie, there had been something so comforting about Stafford's warmth and appreciation of her. Stafford wanted to be with her, even if Archie didn't, and that had really helped with the pain of rejection she'd felt in the days after Christmas and New Year. Besides, Stafford was wonderful company and it was refreshing not to have to explain all the time how the world appeared and felt to her, as she'd felt she had to with Archie. Stafford was kind, attentive, and there was the obvious connection she felt with him that she couldn't feel with Archie. So, she allowed herself to feel happy. And in time, perhaps, she might fall in love with Stafford?

But as Temperance reached for another pair of shoes, the sound of shouting in the dance hall pricked her ears and alarmed her. She rushed there to see Renee, standing with Violet, remonstrating with a group of regulars who always came to the Palais on a Saturday afternoon.

Temperance frowned. But at least it wasn't Roger, come with the law to arrest Renee. In the weeks since Renee had confessed to them about killing Ronnie, and Roger wanting to go to the police, Temperance had lived in daily dread of him coming good on his words, but it had all gone quiet on that front.

She rolled her eyes at the sight of the women. A formidable group in their early fifties, who'd been coming to the Palais for years. They were set in their ways and hated change. They had been upset when Bill Cain had announced his retirement last year, calling for Nancy to do something. They had even been cross when the tea at the Palais changed, with the ringleader – a stout woman by the name of Cynthia Harrington – demanding they make tea using the old stuff. Nancy had had had to remind them that, what with rations the way they were, they were lucky to get anything, but still they'd grumbled.

Renee seemed as if she were far from mollifying these women, though. Instead, she looked as if she was ready to tear their hair out, starting with Cynthia Harrington.

'Whatever's going on?' Temperance asked as she took in the scene.

'What's *going on*, Temp, love,' Renee said in a menacingly quiet voice, her eyes never leaving Cynthia's, 'is that these ladies want me to sack Violet.'

'Why?' Temperance demanded.

She looked at the women, in their uniforms of wool coats over floral aprons, hair pinned in curlers, with scarves tied over the top.

'Because they say I'm not fit to work here,' Violet said from behind Renee. 'They say my morality is in question and I'm not fit to walk these halls.'

'If the cap fits,' Cynthia said smugly. 'You ain't no better than you should be. You and your mother walk around here with all your airs and graces, when you're both a pair of cheap slappers.'

'How dare you!' Temperance bellowed. She turned to Violet, who was pale and clearly shaken. Violet didn't usually take rudeness from anyone, but for some reason her friend looked as if she were *unable* to say boo to a goose.

'I dare, all right,' Cynthia continued. 'Someone's got to do something about standards slipping. Don't you think we ain't seen what's gone on with the rest of you.' She turned to Renee. 'That so-called manager of yours, we all saw her canoodling with that American GI on New Year's Eve. A disgrace.'

'It was New Year,' Renee protested. 'People do kiss at New Year.'

'Not like that they don't,' Cynthia said firmly, earning nods of agreement from the women with her. 'If it weren't for you being friends with that vicar, we'd boycott this place altogether,' she finished.

Renee laughed. 'So now I'm a pillar of the community, am I?'

'For the moment.' Cynthia folded her arms and looked at her defiantly.

Renee shook her head. 'You lot are a disgrace. Coming in here telling me how to run me own business. Let me tell you something, lady. It's got nothing to do with any of you how I run things, or who I have working here at the Palais, or at Bethnal Green. And if you don't like it, you can sling your hook, as you lot like to say down here. Frankly, I wouldn't care if any of you never darkened my door again. You will not come talk about my staff like that. Violet and her mum have got more heart, more goodness, more soul than any of you lot have got in your tiny little fingers, so you can all sod off.'

With that, Renee put her hands on her hips and glowered at the women. Cynthia looked shocked, as if she had been slapped.

'Well, you heard me,' Renee said, taking advantage of her adversary's silence. 'Naff off!'

'We've been coming here for years,' Cynthia said furiously.

'And now you can go somewhere else for years,' Renee said in a firm tone, stepping closer to Cynthia to emphasise her point. 'You lot are barred, you hear me?'

Temperance, just as furious, moved closer to the women, too, to give Renee support.

'You cheeky cow,' Cynthia roared, and lifted her hand, aiming for Renee but getting Temperance instead.

As Temperance fell back against the wall, her cheek stinging, Renee took action. Drawing her right arm back, she clenched her fist and with one decisive, accurate punch, she launched it straight into Cynthia's face.

There was a horrific cracking sound and the next thing, blood was streaming from Cynthia's nostrils.

'You've broke my nose, you silly bint!' she cried, more in astonishment than anger.

Temperance stood in shock as Cynthia went on.

'The only reason I'll be coming back here is with the police, you mad cow!' she thundered at Renee.

'Good,' Renee fired back. 'I'll be sure to tell them why I had to crown you in the first place, and no doubt be given an OBE for me trouble. Now, for the last time, sod off.'

This time there was no argument and the women shuffled out of the Palais. Temperance's heart was still racing as she looked at Renee. 'Are you all right?' she asked.

Renee gave a wan smile. 'Shouldn't I be asking you that? Your face looks sore.'

Temperance touched her cheek. It was throbbing and hot. 'It's fine,' she lied.

Renee was just about to reply when the doors to the Palais swung open and in walked Roger.

'What on earth is going on?' he asked. 'I've just seen a group of extremely angry women walk out of here, and one had a very bloody nose.'

'Something and nothing.' Renee shrugged. 'What can I do for you?'

Roger looked anxiously at Temperance and Violet before answering her. 'Perhaps there's somewhere we can go to talk privately?'

'Whatever you have to say can be said in front of the girls; there are no secrets here.'

At that, Roger raised an eyebrow. 'Very well. In that case I've come to tell you that I no longer want you to have anything to do with the Bethnal Green dance hall. I've thought long and hard about this, and whilst I still haven't made up my mind about . . . the matter we spoke of a while ago . . . I simply cannot have you working in a church-associated venue.'

'What? You can't do that.' In disbelief, Temperance looked at Renee, who said nothing.

'I can and I will,' Roger said firmly. 'Given what's come to light recently, it's inappropriate for Renee to be involved with the Regal any longer. The rest of you, of course, can stay. But, Renee, I never want to see you on those premises again. Do I make myself clear?' Renee's chin may have been up but her eyes were dark with the pain of Roger's words and Temperance felt sadness and rage for her friend. But there was nothing anyone could do.

And with that, Roger lifted his hat to Temperance and walked out of the door.

51

February

The new month brought with it such a cold snap that Violet wondered if she would ever feel warm again. Lifting Eamon from his cot she felt his hands and feet, grateful that they were toasty in the blanket that Betty had knitted him last Christmas. Holding her son close to her chest, she kissed his forehead and was about to put him back down when a noise at the front door stopped her.

She looked at Eamon and smiled. 'Is that your granddad? He said he was coming back to London today, didn't he?'

Gently she placed Eamon in his cot and raced down the stairs, ready to greet her guest. Alan had written to her last week telling her he was coming to London for a few days, and asked if he could stay on her settee. After checking with Winnie, she had immediately written back and said yes, of course he could.

She was excited to see him. Although they had written regularly to one another, she'd only seen him briefly at Christmas and she was worried about him. He was lodging with a colleague of his from Howell & Smart now that he'd lost his own home in the blasts, and Violet was sure that couldn't be easy.

Walking along the hall, she was surprised to see that there was no figure looming through the plate glass door. But the window to the right of the front door had been smashed, and a white envelope had been pushed through her letterbox. Avoiding the broken glass, with a tremulous hand, Violet stooped to pick the letter up. Her name was scrawled on the front, in thick black letters.

Her heart beat faster. She recognised this handwriting from the last letter she had received. Tentatively she ripped it open and read.

Dear Violet,

I see you still haven't heeded my warning that you should leave. What will it take for you to understand nobody wants you here? You and your child are a disgrace. Why don't you go somewhere else, far from here, and never come back? Leave your child with someone who is worthy of bringing him up, who can give him a good and decent life – something you can't do with your filthy morals. You disgust us all.

A friend

Tears pricked Violet's eyes and she brushed them away with the back of her hand. The lengths this person was going to were escalating. Did people really despise her so much that they wanted to destroy her home? A home that technically belonged to Winnie, a God-fearing, upstanding member of the community. Who was doing this and when would they stop?

A loud rap on the door pulled her from her thoughts and made her jump. Looking up, she breathed a sigh of relief as she saw a familiar face peering through the broken window.

'What on earth's happened here?' Alan asked, looking in astonishment at the empty space where the glass plate had once been.

'Oh, it's nothing,' she said hurriedly.

'Nothing my eye,' he exclaimed, as she pulled the door open. He wrapped his arms around her, and she revelled in his warmth. For a second she wondered what it would have been like to grow up with Alan as her dad. She was sure she would have felt loved and protected in a way she had never felt with George.

'What's going on here?' he pressed, as he released her. 'Tell me.'

But Violet wasn't about to upset her father's arrival with her own problems. 'Just silly kids messing about,' she said, quickly stuffing the note into the pocket of her skirt. 'You should have told me which train you were getting. I'd have come and met you.'

Still feeling shaky, she walked into the kitchen and filled the kettle with water. Setting it on the hob, she gestured for him to take a seat.

'I got the bus,' Alan said, as he sat. 'I didn't want to bother you, love. You've enough on your plate. And if you don't mind me saying, Vi, you look done in.'

She smiled weakly, then sat down, too. Alan put a gentle hand on her wrist.

'Is everything all right, Violet?'

'Fine. Just tired,' she said, noticing the Howell & Smart carrier bag at Alan's feet.

Alan saw her looking. 'They're . . . er, for your mother. I thought she might like them.'

'Them?' Violet queried.

Alan reached into the bag and pulled out a beautiful pair of blue low-heeled court shoes. 'They were in the sale, in your mother's size. I had rations for them, and I thought how she never treats herself . . .'

This was such a beautiful gesture that it caused Violet's eyes to fill with tears again. Wordlessly Alan handed her the bag, and she nodded in understanding. 'I'll see she gets them,' she promised. Then, wiping the tears from her eyes, she got up to pour the boiled water into the pot for their tea.

When she turned back to hand Alan a cup, he was gazing at her anxiously.

'Are you sure you're all right, Vi?' he said. 'And don't give me another cock and bull story like you did about that broken window.'

Suddenly, the dam broke, and Violet found herself bursting into sobs.

'Oh, Alan,' she said, as the tears poured down her face.

'Oh, sweetheart, tell me,' he insisted.

Nodding, Violet calmed down enough to explain about the vitriol she and little Eamon had been exposed to over the past few months, including today's broken window incident and the latest letter. She fished it from the pocket of her dress and slid it across the table.

Grim-faced, Alan took the letter and silently read. When he'd finished his expression was aghast. 'Violet, you must to go to the police about this,' he insisted. 'Whoever is doing this wants locking up.'

Violet shrugged. 'That's what Renee says. But it's not that simple. Everyone here feels the same way. Only recently a group of regulars barged their way into the Palais to tell Renee she should sack me for my immoral behaviour. And then of course there were all the problems at the WVS last year. I'd hoped that break with you in Solihull might have helped things blow over, but if anything they've just got worse.'

Alan fell silent for a moment and then said. 'What do you want, Violet?'

'What do you mean?' Violet felt wrong-footed, as though Alan was asking her a trick question.

'I mean what do you want to happen with all this?' He tossed the letter to one side, giving it no more attention.

'I want to raise my boy in a way where he can be happy and accepted, and so can I. But most of all I want what's best for him. I want him to grow up in a world where he can be himself. I know he's going to have extra problems to deal with because of the colour of his skin and I don't want to add to those problems. I love my son, Alan, I'll move heaven and earth for him but this hatred . . .' she glanced at the cast-aside letter and shuddered '. . . it isn't going away.'

Alan nodded. He leaned forward and clasped his hands over Violet's. 'Your mother wrote to me and told me a bit about what's been going on,' he admitted.

'Did she?' Violet asked. She'd had no idea Betty even knew the half of what had happened. She had been doing her best to keep her out of it, not wanting to give her cause to worry, but apparently her mother had known all along.

'She asked me if I could think of any way to help . . . And that's one of the things I wanted to talk to you about,' Alan said. He inhaled deeply. 'What about starting again in Birmingham? Think about it, nobody knows you. You could be a widow left with a child.'

Violet was speechless. It had been talked about before, of course, but she hadn't really known her dad well enough then. But looking at this lovely, caring man, who she instinctively knew would do anything for her, Violet's mind raced.

Could a new start be just what she needed?

52

'That's it,' Renee encouraged her Palais dancers in the pen the following Saturday afternoon. 'Technique is key. Excellent. Maggie, remember your timing.'

Even though the official dancing bodies had declared ballroom lessons off the table until war was over, there were locals at the Palais who still paid a few quid under the table for secret sessions. They had held a Valentine's Ball last week, and lessons in the run-up had gone through the roof, with many of the women hoping to bag a handsome GI. Privately, Renee thought the American soldiers had brought nothing but trouble. Watching Nancy canoodling with John at New Year, she'd hoped it was a one-off. It was a special occasion and emotions were high. But with young Stafford now setting his sights on a newly single Temperance, Renee couldn't help feeling she would be glad when they all went back home. Whilst she knew it wasn't Stafford's fault that Temperance and Archie had split up, she also knew he hadn't helped matters. Archie and Temperance were made for each other, any fool could see that. Or at least anyone bar Archie and Temperance.

Renee shucked these thoughts from her mind and concentrated on bringing the lesson to a close. It didn't matter how many students Renee took on; she was always happy to spend her time teaching. Not just because the extra money was useful, but because she loved to share her passion. When she was dancing or instructing, her mind was only fixated on dance, and Renee loved nothing more than being transported into that familiar world where she could be truly free.

'That's it today then, girls,' she said, as the tango came to a natural end. 'We'll have a look at the cha-cha-cha next week, if you behave yourselves!' At the mention of the Latin American dance, there was a ripple of excitement amongst the twenty or so women Renee was teaching. 'And remember – tonight I want you lot showing the rest of 'em how it's done. Let's prove just how good our punters and the dancers are tonight, eh?'

There was a chorus of cheers as Renee spoke and the women filed out of the practice room and into the hallway, passing Bill Cain as they did so.

'Morning, Bill,' Renee said in surprise. 'Didn't expect to see you here this early.'

Bill waved her concerns away. 'I wanted a chat with Oscar. See if I could persuade him to come up east again one evening. I've heard some of the punters over there would like a big band of a night.'

Renee laughed. 'And did you?'

'He said to talk to you about it.' Bill made a face that showed his displeasure at the idea.

Renee turned away and walked across the room to the gramophone by the window. As she switched it off, she said, 'Nothing to do with me anymore, Bill. I'd have a word with Nancy, if I were you. She's running the East End outpost on her own now.'

'What a load of rubbish,' Bill growled. 'What's up with this bleedin' vicar that's got his cassock in a knot? You upset him?'

Renee turned to him and shrugged. 'No idea. You'd have to speak to him,' she said, pleasantly enough, but with a certain edge to her voice to let Bill know the matter was closed.

Bill said nothing to this, merely offering a grunt by way of reply. 'You think she'd let me do the odd night over there, then?' he asked.

At the question Renee hid a smile. Much as he was an old stick-in-the-mud, Bill obviously relished the idea of being somewhere new, with a new crowd who'd swell his ego and prove too much for him to resist.

'Have you spoken to Janice about it?' she asked lightly. 'You'd have to get her to come back here sometimes.'

'I was hoping you might talk to her?' Bill said.

Renee sighed. 'I'll talk to her. She's doing a grand job in Bethnal Green, though; I know that much. The crowd like her; she's a good set of hands to have about the place.'

Renee didn't want Bill thinking he could just waltz in and take up position as MC at the Regal, as if nothing had happened. Until she'd been banned from the Regal herself, it had been a pleasure having Bill at arm's length, and Renee wasn't sure she wanted him snaking his way in at the new place. Waiting till he was established and then slipping back into his old ways.

'Would you be happy with perhaps one weekend night and a weekday?' she asked.

'If that's all you can manage,' Bill said.

'Like I said, it's not up to me, but I'll put a word in with Janice.'

Bill practically puffed his chest out, and Renee gazed out of the window to hide her smile. She could see the legendary MC was pleased at the prospect, and the truth was Bill had always had a rapport with the punters, much as she was loath to admit it.

'Oh, there's Janice now,' she said, spotting her friend out the front. She was about to rap on the window, but Janice was in the middle of chatting to someone, although Renee couldn't see who it was.

'Get her in now,' Bill said, rudely rapping on the glass to get Janice's attention.

'Knock it off,' Renee hissed. 'She's not due in yet.'

But it was too late; Janice looked over to the source of the noise. And as she did so, Renee saw it was Mick she was chatting to. Renee frowned. What on earth was she talking to Mick about?

'Ah.' Bill peered over her shoulder. 'Thick as thieves, those two. Have been for months.'

Whirling around to face Bill, Renee stared at him in surprise. 'What do you mean?'

'I mean they're always chatting. Surely you've seen it?' Bill pointed out. 'I tried to warn Janice off him. Said he was a bad lot, but Janice weren't interested. Told me to mind me own business.'

'Did she?' Renee was astounded. She knew nothing of this relationship between Janice and Mick. She had always assumed that Janice was a bit of a loner, preferring her own company to that of the Palais staff during her time off. Certainly when they had worked together in Manchester, Janice had never made any secret of the fact that she liked time to herself, especially since she'd had family round every five minutes. But since she'd been here in London, building a new, albeit temporary, life for herself in London, Renee'd had visions of Janice wandering the capital alone, soaking up the culture. Lunchtime recitals or walks along the Serpentine. She hadn't thought for a minute that Janice was spending her time with a thug like Mick.

As she watched Janice bid Mick goodbye and walk inside, Renee was sure she saw a look of guilt pass across the MC's face. She frowned. Janice was well-liked and trusted at the Palais. So why did she look as if she'd been caught with her fingers in the biscuit tin?

53

March

For Temperance, Wednesday was often the busiest day of the working week and this first Wednesday in March was no different. Not only did she have the choreography to put together for Friday's weekly exhibition dances – for both Bethnal Green and Hammersmith, but she had also agreed to go east later on and help Betty and Nancy with a stocktake. Betty had assured them both it wouldn't take long, but Temperance had a feeling that without Renee's efficiency, it would take an awful lot longer.

As she danced a solo quickstep across the Palais's maple-sprung dance floor, Temperance tried not to dwell on the fact that Renee was banned from the Regal. She knew Roger was a man of principle, and hurt at what he must see as a betrayal, but Temperance also knew that Renee had a heart of gold, underneath the hard edges, and a sense of justice like no other. And, she'd suffered enough. They all had, what with one thing and another.

Temperance couldn't help worry about what Roger was going to do. He said he was undecided about going to the police and she could only hope that the fact he hadn't yet done it was a good sign.

She stopped dancing, and looked at her showcase of steps. She had paired Daisy with Archie, as that weekend they were hoping to put on a spring show and give everyone something to look forward to. Recent events in Britain had left everyone feeling as though there was precious little else to feel good about. The RAF had bombed Berlin at the weekend, and everyone was on tenterhooks waiting for the Germans' reprisal.

'May I intrude?' Stafford's voice rang out from behind her at the entrance to the dance hall, and Temperance jumped in surprise.

'You gave me a fright,' she exclaimed.

But as Stafford crossed the floor towards her, Temperance beamed up at him. No matter what had passed between her and Archie, Stafford still made her feel good about herself, and she was pleased he was here.

'Good to see you,' he whispered.

'Good to see you, too,' she said with a grin.

'What time d'you get off tonight?' he asked in his husky brogue. 'Thought we might go to the movies.'

Temperance frowned. 'Not until late. I've got to go over to the East End tonight.'

'Aw, come on!' Stafford wheedled, putting on his best puppy-dog expression. 'I want to take you to a real cowboy film. They're showing one at the Ritzy; it'll be fun.'

A giggle floated out of Temperance's mouth. Stafford always cheered her up. She was about to say as much when the sight of a figure hovering at the doorway made her stop. It was Archie, and her smile faded as she addressed her former sweetheart.

'Archie, hello.'

Archie shrugged, his mouth set in a firm line. 'I'm looking for Nancy. Have you seen her?' he said, in a slightly obstinate tone.

'She'll be upstairs. She's had a meeting with Janice and Bill but she should be free now.'

'Thanks,' Archie said coolly, then turned on his heel.

In that moment Temperance couldn't stand Archie's hostility any longer. 'Just excuse me a second,' she said to Stafford. And without giving him time to say anything, she rushed across the dance floor and pushed through the double doors to see Archie walking up the long wooden staircase.

'Archie, wait,' she cried.

Archie paused and turned. 'What is it, Temperance?' he asked.

The coldness in his eyes startled her. She had never seen him look at her that way before. She felt her confidence falter.

'I . . . wanted to clear the air,' she said hesitantly. 'I wanted to say I'm sorry the way things have worked out between us. I never meant for it to happen this way, but you're still my friend, Archie, and it seems crazy that we don't talk anymore.'

Archie let out a long whistle and shook his head.

'You've got more front than Blackpool, Temperance Adams,' he said. 'You gad about this Palais with your new fella, toss me aside like some old rag, but you still want to pick me up and use me when it suits?'

Temperance felt a flash of hurt. 'Stafford isn't my sweetheart, he's just my friend.'

'You must think I was born yesterday,' Archie scoffed. 'Sorry, Temperance, it doesn't work that way. You don't get to have me as a friend just because it makes you feel better. You and me are done. I told you that months ago. Now, I'm sorry if you don't like the way things are between us, but that's the way it is. You're not my friend, you were never my friend, you were always so much more to me than that. But now, Temperance, now you're nothing to me. Now, go back in there to lover boy and let him be the one to chivvy you when you're down and put his arms around you. We're finished, Temperance. The sooner you get that into your head, the better.'

And then, without waiting for a reply, he marched up the stairs, leaving Temperance feeling very much alone.

Later that rain-soaked evening – as she sat in the Bethnal Green dance hall listening to Betty list items that needed cleaning, throwing out, or repairing – Temperance found her mind wandering. Why couldn't she get over Archie?

'Temp, honey, did you hear me?' Nancy asked gently.

Temperance looked up from doodling on her pad and stared at Nancy expectantly.

'Sorry, I was miles away.'

'I can see that.' Nancy smiled benevolently. 'I was saying we should come back in the morning and help Betty clean up. Archie has offered to come, too.'

At the mention of his name Temperance's face fell, which was not lost on Nancy.

'Though I can see that's not necessarily a good thing,' she said with a sigh. 'Honey, I thought you two would have sorted this out by now.'

Betty, who was standing next to Nancy, dressed in a pair of beautiful blue court shoes that Alan had given her, rolled her eyes.

'When has young love ever been sorted?' she said, sagely. 'The pair of you are so miserable. Honestly, Temp, I don't know what you're playing at. Archie's a good lad.'

'I know he is,' Temperance said. 'But so is Stafford.' She got to her feet, suddenly tired of this conversation, and the hypocrisy that went with it. 'Anyway, you two should hardly be lecturing me about relationships,' she said hotly, giving a pointed glance at Betty's shoes.

As Nancy blanched, Betty drew herself up like the matriarch she was.

'Now just a minute, young lady,' she began. 'You've no right to stand there and tell us a thing or two. We're trying to get you to learn from our mistakes, not compete with them.'

'Well, you don't need to,' Temperance said sulkily. 'I'm fine.'

Nancy stepped towards her and reached out a hand.

'We're just worried about you.'

Tears pricked Temperance's eyes. Archie's words had hurt

her, more than she thought possible. All she wanted was to go home; the day had been long enough as it was.

'Can we just go home?' she begged.

Nancy and Betty looked at each other and Nancy nodded. 'Sure. Let me get my coat.'

Less than ten minutes later and the trio were walking towards the bus stop, Temperance treading determinedly. All she wanted was to get home and hopefully devour a bowl of the vegetable soup Enid had promised to make her daughter that morning.

Only, as they walked down Type Street, a familiar wail filled the streets, causing fear to grip Temperance's heart.

'Was that what I think it was?' Betty asked, clutching the neck of her wool coat.

'The air-raid siren,' Nancy said, frowning.

Temperance looked around, as if waiting for some sort of sign. Then came the familiar sound of the bombs somewhere, but strangely there was no plane overhead. A fresh wave of fear pulsed through Temperance. They all knew the Jerries would be on the attack soon, but why did it have to be tonight?

'Let's get to the Tube station for shelter,' she suggested. 'If we hurry, we can make it before the raid starts.'

Without discussing it further, the trio hurried towards the station, each woman hoping to find safe passage.

54

Betty could smell the panic in the air as they hurried towards the Underground. By now they had been joined by other people in their droves.

'We're not going to make it in time,' Temperance said, as she looked anxiously up towards the skies.

'Of course we're going to make it,' Nancy said firmly.

Though, as she said it, Bethnal Green Tube station had never felt further away. A sudden light beamed from overhead and Betty craned her head to look upwards. She saw it was the radio-controlled searchlight that always came on when the Allied forces had found an aircraft.

'Hurry,' Temperance said briskly. 'We don't want to be around here when Jerry drops another barrel-load of hate.'

The others needed no encouragement, but as they rounded the corner and the station came into view, they saw that hundreds had had the same idea. Everyone was heading for the landmark, seeking shelter.

'It's packed. What if we don't get in?' Temperance moaned.

'We're getting in,' Betty said firmly. She looked around and saw buses pulling into the station. 'Come on,' she said determinedly.

Crossing the road and walking towards the narrow entrance with a dim lightbulb suspended from the ceiling, Betty reached the top of the steps, flanked by Nancy and Temperance. She reached for the handrail and was just about to step off when the sound of explosions nearby made a deafening noise.

'Bombs,' someone cried. 'There's more bombs.'

Betty turned back to check Nancy and Temperance were behind her and saw the worry on their faces. They had all been in air raids before, but this felt different somehow. The atmosphere was highly charged; people seemed more desperate.

As the three women gave each other a silent but determined nod, they quickly made their way down the steps into the belly of the station. About midway down, Betty felt a sudden surge of people behind her, pushing her into the people in front.

'Stop it,' she called, a hint of desperation to her voice. 'There's room for everyone. Stop shoving.'

But her words fell on deaf ears. She looked around to see that Nancy had been shoved so far to the right by the scrum of people around her that her face was almost pressed into the wall. Temperance, meanwhile, had somehow ended up further in front and was desperately trying to remain upright. Betty tried to move her legs, get out of the way somehow, but she was stuck. She was completely hemmed in, and with every second that passed the people around her seemed to grow in number. Everywhere she looked, all Betty could see were arms and legs.

Shouts from the steps below overwhelmed her senses. There was a woman screaming for help, but Betty couldn't see what was happening to her. In fact, she could scarcely see anything more than a sea of coats and scarves. And the smell. The scent of wet clothes cooking amongst the steam of hot bodies was beginning to overtake her senses.

Betty could feel panic begin to envelop her and she took a deep breath, determined not to let her emotions get the better of her. People were just scared; there was no need for her to join in this hysteria.

'Temperance,' she called shakily. 'Temperance, are you there?'

'I'm here,' Temperance called from somewhere in front of her.

Betty felt relief flood through her as her maternal instinct to protect her daughter's friend took hold.

'Nancy,' she called above the maelstrom. 'Nancy, where are you?'

But there was no sound. All Betty could hear were the frantic calls from others. Everyone looking for their loved ones, mothers screaming for their children.

She craned her neck and managed to look behind her. More and more people were coming down the stairs. It seemed to Betty as if a sea of people were throwing themselves down the entrance, all desperate to get way from the Jerries and their bombs.

The familiar feeling of panic began to overtake her senses, and Betty felt as if her legs weren't her own, that they were moving without her will or control.

'Betty!' she heard Nancy call behind her. 'Betty!'

Thank heavens.

The Palais cook was able to look back and see that Nancy was quite a bit away from her, but there were even more people around her than there were around Betty, and Nancy seemed to grow smaller with every second that passed in the scrum of arms and legs.

Betty opened her mouth to call back to her, when she became aware of the fact her feet were now no longer touching the ground. Instead she felt as if she was falling, her arms and legs seemingly without power.

Next thing she knew, she was hoisted up high, and there was Temperance out in front of her, looking panicked.

'Temperance, it's going to be all right, love,' Betty bellowed, but her voice was lost in the din of people all shouting and screaming around her.

She tried to breathe while people in front of her fell like dominoes, one on top of the other. And then it was her turn. Everything seemed to happen as if in slow motion as Betty felt her legs buckle underneath her and she was propelled forwards, towards the heap of bodies lying on the station floor.

Fear gripped her heart. What was happening here? Why was there nobody around to help? Betty felt as if everything was happening in slow motion as she craned her neck and saw that there were no station officials. No guards. No police anywhere.

'Temp! Nancy!' she tried to call out.

But her words were lost in the screams and cries of those around her, and there wasn't time to think about what was happening next.

As she landed with a thud on a group of people, Betty managed to turn her neck, only to see a flood of people all tumbling towards her. Images of Violet, Roy and Maisie flooded her mind as she desperately tried to cover her face with her forearms. At the thought of never seeing her loved ones again, Betty did the only thing she could think of. She screamed for her life and all that might never be.

55

The sounds of screaming rang though the station as Nancy walked down the escalator now and towards a heavy steel door, which was being held open by a female air-raid warden.

'Hurry now,' the woman called briskly. 'Say nothing to anyone and keep walking.'

Nancy was too bruised and shell-shocked to do anything else but follow the other battered souls, all desperate for safety. Gingerly, she put one foot in front of the other and tried to make sense of what had just happened. One minute she had been walking down the stairs towards the shelter, next all hell had broken loose, with people falling and tripping over each other.

She looked around her and saw that she was surrounded by people, all cheek by jowl, chins lifted in defiance, determined not to let whatever was happening in the station break them.

The damage from what they had all been through was obvious. Coats were torn and ripped, stockings laddered, legs were bloodied and bruised. But still, everyone was stoically continuing on through the tunnel and onto the platform.

As the lines of bunk beds on the unfinished platform came into view Nancy felt a surge of relief and gratitude that she had made it to safety, along with the sea of people around her, all looking as confused and as discombobulated as she felt.

Heart hammering against her chest and her legs shaky, Nancy spotted Temperance, and somehow managed to weave her way through the crowds towards her, where she sat forlornly on the edge of a bunk.

'Oh, God, Nancy.' Temperance cried with relief at the sight of her friend.

'Oh, honey. What the hell happened?'

Nancy slid an arm around Temperance's shoulders and felt them shake.

'I don't know,' Temperance replied, looking as bewildered as Nancy felt. 'I was walking down the stairs along with everyone else and then suddenly we were all falling. I don't know why.'

Nancy shook her head. 'I don't either.'

She turned desperately to look back to the door, where the shouts and screams of those still in the entrance hall could be heard. Whatever was going on out there couldn't be good.

'A young woman fell,' an elderly man in the bunk next to them explained. 'A young girl holding her baby. She was rushing to get to the platform out of the way before the bombs dropped and she lost her footing on one of the bottom steps and fell.' The old man took off his wool cap as a sign of respect then shook his head before placing it back on his head. 'There were so many people up there . . . Well, you saw yourself. We all fell like dominoes.'

Nancy exchanged a frantic look with Temperance. She could tell that her mind had immediately strayed to Violet and little Eamon, too.

'Where's the woman and her baby now?' Temperance asked fearfully.

The old man shrugged. 'I dunno. Hauled out, I think, by someone. There are ambulances, someone said, coming to help all the injured.'

Nancy felt her head start to spin. She was cold and in pain. Her right side felt bruised, and the heel had come off one of her shoes.

She shook her head. Had the bombs stopped or had they just started? It sounded as if Jerry was intent on making London pay for Berlin tonight, but where had the aircraft been? Nancy had seen no sign of the familiar shape of the Luftwaffe.

'We didn't see any planes?' she said to Temperance.

'No. I wondered if the clouds had hidden them,' Temperance replied.

'It might be raining, but it's a clear night,' Nancy said, her mind working overtime now as she tried to make sense of the situation. 'We should have seen something.'

Nancy scanned the platform for the one person she couldn't spot, no matter how hard she tried.

'Betty . . .' she whispered. 'Where the hell is Betty?'

Temperance's face was a picture of worry.

'I last saw her behind me, just as the number of people started to swell. I turned to look for her but couldn't see her after that,' she said.

'But she must be here somewhere,' Nancy said, trying not to give in to the rising panic that had been threatening to envelop her since she arrived at the station. Something wasn't right.

For the next couple of hours Nancy sat beside Temperance, trying to push all thoughts of what was happening in the world beyond the platform from her mind. Whatever was going on, Nancy was powerless to do anything other than sit and wait.

But then the sound of footsteps walking along the tracks in the tunnel caught Nancy's attention. She looked up and saw police officers, air-raid wardens and firemen.

As they approached, a ripple of excitement spread across the crowd as everyone wondered what was happening. Since the raids had began, Nancy had frequently taken shelter in Underground stations like this, but she'd never seen such a collection of grave-faced officials.

'What do you think this is all about?' Temperance whispered.

'I don't know,' Nancy replied. 'But I think we're about to find out.'

The policeman cleared his throat as he reached the centre of the track and a polite hush fell across the crowd. Even the children who had been sobbing were now quiet, as if sensing the importance of what was coming.

'Ladies and gentlemen, please listen carefully,' the officer, who looked to be in his mid-forties said. 'We will have you out of here in the morning, and when we do you are to say nothing to anyone about what happened here tonight. You might be tempted to tell your family, your loved ones, your friends or even your neighbours, but you mustn't. Because what has happened here today is a matter of national security, and to say anything about it would give the enemy an advantage. I'm afraid I can't tell you any more than that.'

As he finished speaking, the crowd started whispering again, only for the female air-raid warden to now address them.

'I know you'll have questions,' she said. 'But we can tell you nothing further. Now I suggest you all quieten down and get some sleep. Tomorrow will be a difficult enough day as it is.'

With that, the team of officials wandered out of the platform and back through the steel door that Nancy had come through earlier.

As she watched them go, fear coursed through her. Something was desperately wrong.

The following morning, after a difficult night tossing and turning on a bunk next to Temperance, Nancy woke to find a steaming cup of tea being handed to her by the elderly gentleman in the next bunk.

'This'll help you face whatever's on the other side of that door,' he said.

'Thank you.' Nancy took it gratefully. Even though she was a confirmed coffee drinker it felt comforting to wrap her hands around something warm. She looked about for Temperance and could see the young woman was making herself useful handing out tea from a huge urn that had been wheeled in from somewhere.

She smiled. Temperance was just who you wanted in a crisis: calm, considerate and a safe and steady pair of hands.

Taking a tentative sip of her tea, Nancy tried not to shudder at the taste. She might be in dire straits after a night underground, but there were limits as to what she could realistically be expected to put up with. Drinking tea was a step too far. Setting the cup aside, she smiled at Temperance as she made her way back to the bunk.

'How are you feeling?' Nancy asked.

Temperance bit her lip. 'Worried. I've heard they're going to start letting us out any second.'

Nancy glanced down at her wristwatch and saw it was just after seven in the morning. With a start she wondered how Ruth and Peter had got on. She had never left them on their own for the night; she only hoped they had managed without her.

'The children . . .' she murmured.

'Peter and Ruth are good kids; they'll be fine,' Temperance said, intuitively. 'And please, God, so will Betty, Violet and little Eamon.'

'Amen to that.' Nancy smiled weakly and then saw a chink of light as the steel door opened. There was a sudden surge of activity, as everyone got to their feet and tried to leave.

'Single file, please!' the air-raid warden from last night bellowed. 'Show some respect for what you'll find in the stairwell on your way out.'

As Nancy passed the warden, she shot her a curious look, but the woman gave nothing away. After a night cooped up underground, the slight hint of cool air from the open door felt fresh and wonderful. Pausing to wait for Temperance, Nancy then wordlessly linked arms with the younger girl and they made their way forward to the staircase that would lead them to freedom.

It was only then that they saw the true horror of what had happened the previous night.

What looked like hundreds of bodies were strewn at the base of the stairwell. Eyes rolled heavenwards, skin ashen, faces contorted in fear.

'Oh, my God.' Temperance closed her eyes in horror.

Nancy didn't reply, but her free hand flew to her mouth as she took in the sight.

There but for the grace of God were all the poor souls who had been crushed in the stampede down to the station. Desperate to find safety, they had been killed in the process.

Nancy surveyed the scene. The feet of people who had not survived were sticking out as they lay on the floor. And, near the top, Nancy saw a pair of shoes she recognised immediately. A beautiful pair of blue court shoes, soles upturned to reveal the Howell & Smart logo underneath.

Nancy felt her heart contract unbearably. She quivered on her feet, as one hand clutched Temperance's arm.

'Temperance . . .' she whispered, as thick tears rolled from her eyes.

As they took in the horrific truth, both women then sank to their knees and sobbed . For one of those who hadn't survived was none other than their beloved Betty Millington.

56

It was three weeks since Betty's death, and Violet stared blankly into the mirror at Winnie's flat. Her grief had been overwhelming with every day that had passed. She had lost so much since the war had broken out: her brother Roy, her sweetheart Eamon, and now her own, beloved mother. Where was the sense? The justice?

As she peered numbly into the mirror, a beleaguered cry pulled her from the brink. Much as she felt like sleepwalking through reality just now, there was a little boy who wouldn't let her.

She walked over to Eamon's cot, pulled him to her bosom and hugged him as if her life depended on it. Feeling the weight of his mother holding him, protecting him, Eamon began to settle, and his cries were exchanged for contented gurgles.

It wasn't just Violet who felt broken, of course. Betty's death had the whole of the Palais beside themselves with grief. Temperance and Nancy blamed themselves for not doing more to help. One Saturday night Violet had spent hours consoling the pair as they begged for her forgiveness, wishing they could have done more to save her mother.

Violet knew they meant well, but her friends had no need to ask for forgiveness, certainly not from her. It sounded as though the two had been through enough of an ordeal as it was. And the truth about the attack on Bethnal Green that fateful night was still unclear. Bombs had gone off in the east, but no plane had been spotted. Yet 173 innocent souls had lost their lives. Crushed at the very station they hoped would offer them respite from Hitler's hate.

Violet rocked her baby in her arms and squeezed her eyes shut, bringing her mother's face to mind. She desperately hoped Betty hadn't been frightened, that she had known how much she was loved. The idea of Betty suffering in any way was too much to contemplate, but Violet had spent many a night lying awake. Tossing and turning, unable to sleep, she had sent fervent prayers and hope to the mother she hadn't always got along with, but had always loved, from the very bottom of her heart.

At the creak of a floorboard, Violet turned and saw Temperance, standing with Archie and dressed head to toe in black. Violet gave them both a quavery smile. The two of them had rallied around her over the past couple of weeks, trying to help her cope with the loss of her mother.

Even now, on the day of Betty's funeral, her friends were here, ready to do whatever she needed. For that alone, both of them would always hold a very special place in her heart.

'It's time to get to the church, Vi, love,' Temperance said softly.

Archie stepped forward. 'I can take Eamon if it's easier?'

But the well-meant gesture only made Violet hold her son tighter in her arms.

'I've got him,' she whispered, peppering his head with kisses. She would always have him.

Motherhood had not been easy for her or her mother, but today she would be honouring all that Betty had done for her, and for Eamon. Not just in the past, but in the legacy of love that she had surely left for them, and her little sister, Maisie.

She straightened up and despite her leaden heart, gave a small smile to Archie and Temperance. 'Shall we go?' she said. 'It's time to do Betty proud.'

At the funeral, Violet, flanked by the rest of the Good Time Girls and Archie, did just that. George had chosen to sit alongside her, and today of all days Violet didn't have it in her to fight with the man, so she had simply nodded and said yes. Their relationship had fallen into such disrepair that they hardly spoke anymore, but today was about Betty, nobody else, and if that meant she had to spare a kind word or gesture towards the man who had, in his own way, offered Betty safe passage when she had been at her lowest ebb, then Violet could and would do that.

Now, as she faced the altar, Eamon sleeping in her arms, the image of her mother's coffin haunted her as she stood ramrod straight. Her eyes never left the wooden box as she sang her heart out in tribute to the woman whose life had been snatched away so cruelly.

As she sang the closing verse to 'All Things Bright and Beautiful', her thoughts turned to Maisie. Her younger sister had been heartbroken when Violet had written to tell her the news, but she had been unable to get compassionate leave and so Violet had promised she would send extra love from Maisie to her mother, and of course, for Roy, too. She looked briefly heavenwards. After so much heartache, Violet wasn't sure she believed in God or an afterlife, but she found herself hoping that if there was a God, her sweetheart, Eamon, and her brother Roy were looking out for Betty, holding her steady as she made her final journey.

Shifting her gaze back towards the coffin, her eyes came to land on Alan. He looked desperate, Violet thought, as she watched him try to hold back the tears. Much as she wanted to respect George's feelings, Violet knew that Alan had been her mother's true love. For them there were no more second chances; that pathway to happiness had gone. It was heartbreaking to Violet. How she hoped nobody else would ever have to go through that pain. If only everyone realised that life was too short not to grab hold of the happiness it offered.

And now, as Roger delivered the final eulogy and the Good Time Girls trooped out of the church and into the graveyard for the interment, Violet felt as if she might break. Up until this moment she had some hopeless notion that her mother was not really dead, that Betty would appear behind them with one of her sage quips.

Sadly, her death was all too real and Violet watched the coffin lower into the ground. Suddenly, she couldn't hold back any longer and gave in to the great wracking sobs that had been threatening to overwhelm her for weeks.

'Oh, sweetheart . . .' Beside her, Enid gently took little Eamon from Violet, as she gave in to her grief.

Just as she thought she might shatter, her eyes blurred with tears, Violet felt two strong arms around her as someone pulled her to them. Looking up, she saw Alan's distraught face, as he held on to her for dear life.

'Dad . . .' She collapsed against him as he held her tighter.

'I'm here, love. I'm here,' he said.

She felt a warm hand grip hers, and turned to find Temperance smiling through her own distress. And then Archie, who put out a hand to squeeze her arm.

'We've got you, Vi,' Archie whispered.

'We've always got you,' Temperance promised.

And as Violet felt the love around her, she knew how lucky she was to have such wonderful friends, and Alan. Together, they would always look out for her. They'd always be by her side.

57

An hour later and the mood back at the Hammersmith Palais de Danse, though sombre, was also a celebration of Betty's life. Renee had gone to town, laying out paste sandwiches, sausage rolls – courtesy of Archie – and little plates of mock cheese on toast, but as she watched the guests tuck in with gusto, Renee knew that no amount of food could fill the very large space in her heart that Betty Millington had filled.

The grief Renee felt when she'd learned Betty had been killed had taken hold of her in a way that was completely unexpected. She had always been fond of the Millington matriarch, but the impact of her friend's death had knocked her for six.

Since then, Renee had gone out of her way to do things in tribute to Betty. She had not only offered to take on the food and drink for the wake and given Violet all the time off she needed, she had also tried to find a more spiritual solution. She knew that she was no longer welcome at the Palais in the East End, but she remembered how Roger had asked her to talk to the battered women groups he had been running at the dance hall, and how she had always put him off, not wanting to touch on the raw emotion that a life with Ronnie had left her with. But Betty's passing had focused her mind. She knew that although George probably imagined he'd loved Betty and done his best by her, he hadn't. Betty, too, had been a victim of a form of abuse, and Renee wanted to honour that.

And so, just a week after the Bethnal Green attack, Renee found herself making preparations for a forthcoming talk she was planning to give to a group of women she had invited to the Palais, in the hope that she might encourage them to talk of their own experiences with violent or mentally abusive men. She owed it Betty, and she owed it to herself. She was living and breathing for now, she'd told herself, but soon, depending on whether Roger finally went to the police, she could be facing the hangman for Ronnie's murder.

As she stood amongst the mourners now, Renee tried not to think about what might happen to her. Today was about Betty, not her. She took a large gulp of her gin and tonic to try and numb the feelings that were threatening to take over.

'You all right?' Nancy asked, as she stood alongside her.

Renee gave her friend a wan smile. Nancy looked resplendent dressed in a fitted knee-length black dress that showed off her curves. It was a little glamorous for funeral attire, but then Renee spotted John milling about the throng of people, and knew who the dress was for.

'I'm fine,' she said wearily. 'But I worry that you won't be if you carry on with this affair for much longer.'

At the mention of the word *affair*, Nancy coloured. 'I don't know what you're talking about.'

Renee sighed. Life was too short for these games. 'You knocking about with that GI is common knowledge.' She softened her tone a little. 'Nancy, you're not the first woman to have a fling when the old man's away but . . . at least show a bit of dignity. You're throwing yourself at the lad wearing that dress.'

'I am doing no such thing.'

Renee laughed. 'And I'm the queen of Sheba, love.' Her humour faded, as she took in the hurt on Nancy's face. 'I don't mean to be unkind . . . But you're married, and you've two kids to think about.'

'One has left school and the other's about to,' Nancy said obstinately. 'Besides, you know my marriage to Alex is over. You saw what he was like when he visited last year.'

'That's as may be.' Renee sighed. 'But you can't make your

unhappy marriage a reason for your affair.' She paused. 'And you can't go thinking about a future with John. This is very likely just a bit of fun for him. If you take my advice, stop acting like a lovelorn kid and be the strong, confident woman I know you are.'

Without waiting for a response Renee walked away. She'd been brutal. But, as much as she understood why Nancy was carrying on with John, she couldn't tell her it was a good idea, or listen to Nancy's excuses about why this affair was different. They were both too long in the tooth for that.

As Renee moved across the room smiling and nodding at mourners, her eyes fell on Temperance, who was standing next to Stafford, but with her gaze fixed firmly over his shoulder at Archie. Renee sighed again. Another couple playing silly beggars. When would they all realise that life didn't last forever and you had to make it count?

Before she knew it, she was walking towards Temperance and linking her arm through her dance instructor's. As Renee guided Temperance across the room she said, 'When are you going to stop mooning about with Stafford and admit to yourself that you're still in love with Archie?'

Temperance gasped. 'What are you talking about?'

'Temperance, love.' Renee raised an eyebrow. 'I've had more than enough of this from Nancy.' Another flicker of protest passed across Temperance's face, but Renee waved it away. 'Surely our Betty's passing has taught you something?' she said. 'And don't give me that "we're just friends" rubbish. I've seen the way you and Archie look at each other. I was with him the night you were stuck in Bethnal Green. The lad was beside himself on firewatch duty. He couldn't concentrate on anything he was so worried. The moment you stepped through that door the following morning with Nancy I've never seen anyone look so happy. Loves the bones of you, he does.'

Temperance shook her head. 'I don't know—'

'I do,' Renee cut in firmly. 'Tell me, if Archie was black, would you feel as if you had differences?'

Temperance looked shocked. 'What do you mean?'

'You and Archie. What exactly is it that divides you? You've got more in common than you haven't. It's not just the way you can't take your eyes off each other. It's the way you've come together to rally round Violet these past few weeks, to help her and care for her. Now will you stop playing silly sods and sort this out?'

Just as she said that Archie walked past and raised an eyebrow at Renee's choice of language at such a sombre occasion, before he broke out into an involuntary grin at both Temperance and Renee.

'Right, that's it!' Renee said hotly. 'Archie, it's time you forgave Temperance for feeling confused about who she is. It's time you supported your differences and showed her how much you love her.'

'Now wait a—' Archie began, but Renee held up her hand.

'I haven't finished yet, lad.' She turned to Temperance. 'And you, it's time you stopped pratting about with GI Joe over there and made a life with this man, who's clearly right for you. I can't stand to see the two of you mucking about like this.'

As Renee brought her speech to a close, Archie and Temperance gawped at each other.

'It's . . . not that simple,' Temperance said hesitantly.

Archie looked at his shoes. They were his dancing shoes, Renee noticed, the only black pair he owned.

'No. It's not,' he said softly. 'Though I do love you, Temperance. Renee's right about that.'

Temperance looked at him and Renee could see her expression soften. 'And I love you. But—'

'I know I've been stupid,' Archie cut in. 'Not taking your feelings about our differences seriously enough. And, no, I will never know what it's like to be you, Temp, but I will support you, always. And I'll listen . . . Honestly, Temp, I was so terrified that night you were at Bethnal Green. The thought of losing you . . .'

At this point, Renee slipped away. This was a private moment between the two of them. Besides, she wanted to mingle with more of the people she cared about, while there was still blood in her veins and oxygen in her lungs.

58

'You given any more thought to what we talked about when I was last down, love?' Nancy heard Alan ask Violet.

Keeping her head low, Nancy concentrated on the bar takings. She had invited Alan to stay with her while he was in London for Betty's funeral, but in the two days he had been here she could see he was bereft. At first Nancy thought it was because he was devastated over the loss of Betty. But though his grief over the loss of Violet's mother was evident, as she had spent more time with the department store manager, Nancy had come to realise how much he cared and worried about Violet. Nancy had tried not to pry; she had more than enough on her plate as it was. But she worried about Violet, too. The notes the poor girl had been receiving, not to mention the abuse from Palais regulars, it was all getting out of hand. Even at Betty's funeral, Nancy had intercepted what turned out to be a poisonous message left for Violet in the foyer.

As Nancy had steamed the letter open she had seen straight away what kind of note it was, and that it was anonymous, and it had made her blood boil. Poor Violet didn't need anything else to worry about, so Nancy had hidden it behind her toaster until she could work out what to do with it.

Now, she glanced across the bar and looked at Violet who was sitting opposite her father, staring into her tea. 'Not without my son.'

Startled at this, Nancy's arm knocked a glass off the bar, and the noise caused Alan and Violet to turn to look at her. She felt her cheeks colour. 'I'm sorry,' she said. 'I couldn't help overhearing . . . What's this about going somewhere without Eamon?'

Violet smiled. 'Alan suggested when he was here last that I move to Birmingham. He thought it would be a good chance for me to make a fresh start.'

'And leave Hammersmith?' Nancy gasped. 'Honey, no. You can't leave.' She turned to Alan, feeling cross. 'Violet's got a life here, with friends, people who love her.'

'I know that.' Alan nodded in understanding. 'But there's quite a few who can't forgive Violet for having a baby out of wedlock, and they're making her life hell.' He shook his head. 'At least in Birmingham, where no one knows her past, she wouldn't have to put up with abuse. Then, when she's settled and her story is straight, she could send for Eamon.'

'I see,' said Nancy, though she couldn't see how that would work. Little Eamon needed his mother.

'I haven't worked out all the details, yet,' said Alan. 'All I know is that she can't stay here.' He gave his daughter a pained look. 'Tell Nancy what you found when you got back to Auntie Winnie's flat last night.'

Violet looked down, ashamed.

'It's not you who should be embarrassed,' Alan said firmly. 'You have done nothing wrong.'

'What's happened now?' Nancy asked.

Violet exhaled sharply and said in a small voice, 'Someone posted human excrement through the letterbox.'

'What?' Shocked, Nancy clutched the gold chain around her neck.

'There was a note on the outside of the box,' Violet continued. 'It said, "If you are shit, you should roll around in shit."'

Nancy recoiled, her nostrils flaring with rage. She had never heard of anything so disgusting in all her life.

'I never knew people could be so vicious,' said Alan, turning to Violet. 'It's why I want you to get away from all this. You're still grieving for your mother, and being surrounded by such hate . . . It's not good for you or Eamon.'

Violet said nothing, but Nancy didn't need her to. She could understand having so much love in your heart that you would do anything for your child. Although Peter and Ruth hadn't been in her life for long she would do anything for them, that much she knew, even if it hurt her in the process.

A few hours later, across town at the Rainbow Rooms with John, Violet was still on Nancy's mind, as well as the conversation she'd had with Renee.

Nancy knew Renee had her best interests at heart, but she was wrong about John. Nancy was sure he felt the same as she did about their future, that it was only the complication of their marriages to the wrong people that stood in their way, for now.

John traced a finger lazily down her forearm as they lay curled up in bed together.

'I don't feel like you're with me today.'

Nancy returned his smile and snuggled in closer, and decided to tell him half the truth.

'I'm here. Just worried about a friend,' she said.

'Anything you can do to help?' John asked.

Nancy thought for a moment. Could she do anything for Violet? 'Not at the moment. Though I'm working on it.'

John smiled and kissed her forehead. 'That's my girl,' he said, throwing the covers back and getting out of bed.

The tender touch of her sweetheart made Nancy smile as she watched him. She was grateful to the universe for sending John to her; she would be truly lost without him. And after this war was over, they would find a way to set up a new life together.

Nancy lay back in bed, a lazy smile spreading across her face.

'What are you looking so happy about?' John asked, having put his trousers on. He picked up his white vest from the chair.

He walked over to the bed with it and stood over her, waiting for her answer.

'Oh, nothing much,' Nancy said, stretching her arms above her head and admiring her lover's torso. He was so groomed and chiselled in a way Alex never was. 'Just thinking how lucky I am to have you.'

John raised an eyebrow as he slipped on the vest. 'Oh, yeah?'

'Yeah,' she agreed. 'And I can't wait for all this to be over, so we can spend the rest of our lives together.'

John laughed and planted another kiss on her forehead. 'Keep dreaming, honey,' he said, turning to go the neighbouring bathroom.

Nancy shook her head, but threw off his comment, wanting to savour the luxury of being wrapped up in sheets in the middle of the afternoon but she had to get back to the Palais soon. Not only did she want to check on the kids and make sure everything was in order for the evening dance, but she was also going to try and talk to Violet. Maybe a new start, or at least a temporary new start, was what was needed, and Alan was right.

As she rolled onto her side and reached for a glass of water on John's nightstand, she thought that a new start could be just what everyone needed.

She took a sip, but as she set the glass down, her eyes landed on a letter, with familiar handwriting. John's wife. Nancy couldn't help herself; she picked it up and started reading.

My dearest John,

It was so good to get your last letter. I miss you so much, honey, and just hearing from you when you can write means so much to me. I can't imagine what life must be like for you in England. All I know about London is it's cold, wet and the food is bad. I'm happy to know you're in the

Rainbow Rooms getting decent food and drink,
at the very least. We're all well here, and yes, I am
looking after myself. You are so sweet to ask. Baby
Jefferson is doing mighty fine. Can you believe he's
six months now? Months without ever once seeing
his daddy. But I know you can't wait to meet him,
and you'll be back soon. I tell him that every day—

Nancy abruptly put the letter down, her hands shaking. She didn't need to read any more. She sat upright in bed, shock and nausea coursing through her. John had never once mentioned he had a young baby. It wasn't a lie as such, but it was dishonest, that was for sure. Suddenly his comment, 'keep dreaming, honey' was no longer harmless. He had no intention of leaving his wife, yet so far he'd gone along with her plans for their future. While she had fallen in love, to John it had just been a game. Nancy thought back to Renee's warning words. She had been bang on the money.

'How could I have been so stupid?' she whispered now, just as John walked back through the door holding two bottles of Coca-Cola. At the sight of Nancy sitting on the edge of the bed shaking, he stopped in his tracks.

'Honey, what's wrong?' he asked carefully.

Nancy lifted her head and gave him a cold look. 'You never told me your wife had just had a baby,' she said sharply.

John's expression changed in a heartbeat. 'You never asked,' he said, coolly.

Nancy gaped at him. 'Are you serious?'

John had the audacity to yawn before adding, 'It's none of your business, Nancy.'

'It is when I'm sleeping with you,' she fired back. She stumbled out of bed and grabbed her dress, pulling it over her head. She couldn't be in this room, with him, any longer. 'I thought you were different. Those jokes people in England make about

GIs being oversexed and over here – I thought you were the exception to all that. I thought you cared about me,' she said, anger and hurt in her tone.

'I do care about you,' John said.

She shook her head as she found her shoes and put them on. 'You don't care about me. I was just a bit of fun, until you went home to your wife.'

Anger flickered across John's face. 'Hey, we both knew what this was.'

'You know that's not true,' Nancy countered. 'You knew I had fallen in love with you. And you let me believe that you felt the same way . . .' She gulped back the tears that were coming. 'How wrong I was. You had no intention of making a future with me. You were just stringing me along.'

'It's not like that, Nancy,' John said with a sigh. He set the bottles of Coca-Cola down. 'But surely you know it would never have worked. We had a lot of fun, and you're wonderful. But it could never have been more than a fling. A glorious break from reality. We're both married, for Chrissakes.'

Humiliated, Nancy reached for her coat and pushed her way past him, heading for the door, only turning when she got there.

'You won't be seeing me again,' she said, trembling from the effort of not breaking down. 'If you've any sense, you'll stay away from both of my dance halls. We don't need your kind in there.'

And with that she left the room and walked out of John's life forever. As she wrapped her scarf around her neck to keep out the March chill she hurried along Piccadilly, letting the tears finally roll down her cheeks. There was no fool like an old fool.

59

April

It had been a month since Betty's funeral, and in that time Temperance had found a new truce with her former love. She and Archie were no longer the young sweethearts they had been, but instead had become something else – something more grown-up, she supposed.

Ever since the terrible Bethnal Green attack, Archie had been a constant support. Gone was the stubborn coldness of recent months, and in its place had come a genuine caring and comfort. It had been Archie who'd held her while she cried for Betty and for her friend Violet. Archie who'd silently let her know that his love for her was real. And together they'd been there for Violet.

The night of Betty's funeral, when, instigated by Renee, truths were finally spoken, the two had really begun to understand one another. Temperance had realised that Archie's blindness, as she had chosen to see it, wasn't a bad thing. It was just Archie had seen the whole of her. To him the colour of her skin hadn't been the thing that necessarily defined who she was.

As he had explained, it was a bit like her seeing him as a butcher and nothing more.

'I'm much more than a highly skilled meat cutter,' he'd quipped.

Temperance had laughed at that, and they'd started talking

about what had gone wrong between them. Archie had been so sweet and tender when she'd opened up about how hard life had been for her parents as a mixed-race couple, and that it had been difficult for her when he hadn't taken her concerns seriously. He'd sat there, his eyes full of regret, and told her how sorry he was to have made her feel like that. From now on, he'd told her, he would be what she deserved him to be.

And so, since that day when they'd laid Betty to rest, Archie and Temperance had tentatively started seeing each other again, learning to understand one another in a new way, and Temperance had felt a new kind of happiness.

There had of course been one casualty of their reunion – Stafford. Once he'd seen the two of them growing closer again, the handsome GI had told Temperance it was better if he stepped back. With his customary honesty, Stafford had said that though he'd always hoped there would be more than friendship between them, he wished Temperance well and had no hard feelings.

Though Temperance felt sad, she knew she had to let him go, too. But as she watched Stafford walk out of the Palais, she knew he would always have a place in her heart.

Now, however, Temperance was relying on Archie to help her with something tough – a return to Bethnal Green. She hadn't been back since that fateful night, and she needed all the strength and support she could get to return.

Every time she closed her eyes Temperance was haunted by the screams of those poor people who hadn't made it to safety. And afterwards, the harrowing images of all those bodies piled up on the pavement . . . Betty's blue court shoes.

She knew she had to move on, even though none of them who'd been there could talk about what had happened; the authorities had seen to that. The newspapers had merely said there had been an accident at Bethnal Green. There was no mention of the true horrors that had unfolded that night. Nor had there been mention of enemy raids, dropping bombs, not even in Bethnal Green where Temperance had heard them with her own ears.

It made no sense, and she had lost track of the hours she had fretted and worried about all she had seen, with only Nancy to talk to about that night. Which was why she was grateful that Archie had offered to accompany her and Violet that morning for their first trip east.

Disembarking from the bus, the trio wordlessly made their way past the park and up to the Regal. As the building came into sight, Temperance gripped hold of Violet's hand, while Archie slipped his arm around her shoulder. Giving him a quiet smile, she allowed him to guide them both inside the dance hall.

The three of them stood in the foyer, and Temperance half expected something to have changed or shifted, but everything looked the same. A reminder that life carried on.

'Shall we go through?' Archie suggested. 'I'll get the kettle on if you like.'

'I don't know if there'll be any tea,' Violet said. 'Betty was always in charge of supplies.'

'There's tea, don't you fret,' Queenie's voice boomed unexpectedly.

Glancing up, Temperance couldn't help smiling as the older woman walked towards them, arms outstretched in welcome.

'Didn't think I'd let your mother's legacy fall to nothing, did you?' Queenie said gently, planting a kiss on Violet's head. 'Some of the women your mum helped feed and water have taken charge. Said it was their honour to help. So come and have a brew and a think before you start back at work.'

'Thanks, I'd like that,' Violet replied, her voice low.

'So would I,' Temperance said warmly. 'Thanks, Queenie.'

'Pleasure.' The older woman led them into the bar where a pot of tea was already waiting. 'So,' she said, as she handed out the cups. 'I know Renee's not allowed to cross the threshold, but is Nancy not with you? I thought she said she was coming along.'

'Said she was busy with something,' Temperance replied.

Queenie frowned. 'She's licking her wounds, more like. Broke it off with that John didn't she. Found out he wasn't going to leave his wife. As if the rotten swines ever do,' she added with a growl.

'I didn't know she was courting him,' Archie said in disbelief.

'If you can count carrying on behind your husband's back as courting, Archie, then yes, she was,' Queenie said, with a hint of self-righteousness.

'That's not fair,' Temperance said. 'Nancy's been through a lot, and she's been so unhappy with Alex. I think she saw John as a fresh start.'

'Men who have affairs don't have just the one, love,' Queenie said. 'They tend to make a habit of it. Take my George for example.'

Temperance lowered her eyes uncomfortably, while beside her Violet snorted.

'I agree with Gran,' she said darkly. 'You can't ever trust men like that.'

'You seen much of George?' Temperance asked.

'No.' Violet shook her head. 'I asked him if I could come back and stay at the house for a bit, after that excrement was shoved through my letterbox, but he said no. Said he couldn't afford to house me and my child, and not only that, he didn't want that sort of thing shoved through his door.'

While Archie was speechless at this, Temperance's eyes narrowed.

'Pig,' she said.

Nobody could argue with this, including Queenie.

Temperance turned to Violet and could see the worry etched on her face. She looked haunted, the bags under her eyes showing she was getting very little sleep. The poor girl needed help, and for the life of her Temperance wished she knew how to give it.

'You read him the riot act, though, didn't you, Queenie?' Archie finally put in.

The matriarch nodded. 'I did. Said I'd gladly take Violet back and sling George out on his ear, but he put up a fight and I'm just too old to keep battling like I used to.'

Queenie took a sip of tea and Temperance thought for a moment.

'Nancy said something about Alan offering you a fresh start in Birmingham.'

Violet let out a little laugh. 'Yes. His solution to all this is that I go and live there with him. Find a new life.'

'Sounds wonderful,' Archie said. 'Birmingham's lovely, all those canals. I'd fancy it myself.'

'No, you wouldn't,' Temperance said playfully. 'You'd be lost the moment you set foot there. In fact, you're lost the moment you leave Hammersmith.'

Archie blushed, then smiled. 'True.'

'But why not think about it?' Queenie said. 'I mean, what's to keep you round here?'

'You! My son! They're just a couple of things, Gran,' Violet exclaimed. She shook her head. 'I'm not leaving.'

'But you can't keep putting up with this either, love. It's not even as if we can say it's just one person behind it all.' Queenie sighed. 'It seems to be the whole community. Because if it was just one old cow I'd knock 'em into the middle of next week.'

So much for being too old to fight, Queenie was back to her warrior self, cheeks puffed red with anger. She looked around the assembled group expectantly.

'You could clear off for a bit, though, Vi. Just until the dust settles,' she said.

'I'm not leaving Eamon,' Violet said obstinately. 'I can deal with this; I know I can.'

'Nobody's saying you should leave him forever, love,' Queenie said gently. 'But no matter how much you put up with, who's to say how much Eamon can cope with? It's not fair on the poor little mite.'

As Violet fell silent for a moment Temperance felt a hand rest on hers.

'We could care for him for a while, me and Temp,' Archie suggested. 'Give him a bit of stability until you find your feet.'

'Don't be daft, Archie,' Violet snapped. 'Eamon belongs with me. I'm his mum.'

'And we'd make sure he always knows that,' Archie continued. 'We could make sure he always knows his mum loved him, but she's just making her way in the world until she can have him back with her. And you'd know Eamon would be in the best possible hands.'

Temperance felt as if she were on a merry-go-round. What on earth was Archie doing? 'We can't look after him,' she said. 'We've no home, we've no stability—'

'Temp,' Archie cut in, earnestly, and to both her and Violet's shock, he slid off the chair and got down on one knee. 'Will you marry me? I love you, and together we can give Eamon a safe, temporary home, with the very best possible start in life, until Violet is ready to have him with her.'

60

While Violet, Temperance and Archie were across town, Renee and Nancy remained in Hammersmith, preparing for a very special event. That afternoon, instead of a ladies' tea dance, Renee was getting ready for a different kind of tea party. One where she, Nancy and assorted local women, would all sit, chat, and find comfort in one another's words. Renee hadn't been sure what to call the event, so had advertised it as a 'ladies' get-together'.

Renee was sure that her days as a free woman were limited. At any moment, the police could come for her.

'Personally, I'm not convinced about that,' Nancy said firmly. 'If Roger was going to go to the police, he'd have done it by now.'

Renee shook her head as she arranged the chairs in the bar. 'He's just biding his time. He knows I'm hardly likely to do a moonlight flit with all this going on. Besides . . .' She stood up and arched her back. 'I killed someone, Nancy. Even if it was in self-defence. That's how the law will see it, anyway. And you know what the sentence is for that. Before I meet my maker, I want to have done something for other women like me. Made a difference.'

Nancy sighed. 'That's commendable, honey. But we both know that Ronnie deserved to die, and you don't. What he put you through all those years doesn't bear thinking about. Roger has to see that.'

'Well, he doesn't. And honestly, I can see why.' Renee sighed. 'What I did was a sin, according to Roger, even if he couldn't stand Ronnie.'

'What *we* did,' Nancy said gently. 'I was there. If you're going down for this, honey, I'm darned well coming with you.'

The gesture, which Renee knew to be true and heartfelt, was said with so much love that she reached out and squeezed Nancy's arm. 'Thanks, doll,' she said, just as the first few women began to file into the bar.

Immediately, Renee got to work, handing out teas and coffees and generally making everyone feel welcome. But one visitor took Nancy by surprise. Edna. As her mother-in-law came in and made her way to a seat at the back, she gave both Nancy and Renee a nod.

'What the hell is she doing here?' Renee murmured to Nancy. The last thing she needed was Edna chipping in with her judgemental comments.

Beside her, Nancy shook her head, mystified. 'Damned if I know,' she murmured back.

They decided to focus on the job in hand, and once everyone had come in and was seated, Nancy took centre stage at the front of the bar.

'Welcome, everyone,' she began in her broad New York accent. 'We're so glad you could be here today, for what we hope will be the first of many afternoon teas where you can all get together and chat about the things that matter to you. We want you to find comfort and hope, no matter what sort of situation you may find yourself in.'

At that, Nancy paused and glanced nervously at Renee. They had agonised over how to word the event, knowing that if they said this was a tea party for battered women, chances are folk would be too embarrassed to attend.

'What are we all here for, then? To gossip about how to serve up him indoors something better than Potato Jane and Mock Duck?' one woman called, to a chorus of laughter.

'Or the holes I'm sick of darning in his socks,' called another.

Renee smiled. 'Ladies, if that's what you want to talk about,

I'll not stop you. But to start things off, I want to tell you about myself, and how wonderful it feels to no longer be married to an abusive bully.'

At this startlingly blunt statement, the women fell silent, watching agog as Renee stood beside the bar.

'Many of you know me as Renee Hammond, chief dancer at the Palais, manager and all-round Scouse loudmouth,' she said, earning herself a ripple of laughter from the assembled women. 'But for years I was also married to a man who made my life hell. He abused me, hit me, and tried to control me.'

There was more sombre silence, as Renee's honest words hit home. She could already see the recognition in some of the ladies' faces.

'But, you know,' she continued, 'the beatings weren't the worst of it, despite me getting them for anything so much as forgetting to pair his socks, or daring to wear bright lipstick to work. I got a beating from Ronnie Newsham on an almost daily basis. But I learned to live with the bruises and cover them up with make-up – and, being a dancer, well, I'm used to pain for hours at a time, so I could deal with that, too. What was harder was the battering me self-confidence took. A little piece of me was rubbed away every time he laid a hand on me, or mocked me for what I was doing, or wearing. By the end, I couldn't think for meself, and my confidence was that low, I didn't think I were capable of living a life on me own. He took everything from me, day in, day out. I was so ashamed of what was happening to me, I never talked to anyone about it. See, somewhere inside me, I thought it was my fault. Something wrong with me. That I'd made him do what he did to me.' She paused. 'Can you believe that?'

Renee looked at the crowd. She could see Nancy, her eyes glistening with emotion, smiling at her in support. And to Renee's surprise and relief, some of the women, including Edna, were nodding knowingly.

'I've had the same with my husband,' one woman called out, timidly. 'I know it's terrible to say, but I was so relieved he got called up, 'cause now I no longer dread going to bed each night, wondering whether he'll beat me or force himself on me.'

There was another murmur of sympathy and agreement from the crowd.

'I'm the same,' another woman said. 'My fella's gone, and my daughter keeps telling me we should just scarper. Leave and never come back. For years I've been telling her she's got it wrong, that all married couples have barneys every now and again, but she doesn't believe me. And she's seen the bruises I can't hide.'

Renee nodded, and smiled in solidarity as the experiences came thick and fast. These stories, so many of them, were hard to hear. But Roger had been right. These women needed to hear each other's stories and find support in each other.

'I'm so sorry to hear what some of you've been through,' she said. 'But that's why I want you all to feel as if you can come here, to the Palais, whenever you want. Not just for a dance and a natter, though you're always welcome to do that. But to come and find support with each other. We're women, we might not like airing our dirty drawers in public, but we should always be there for each other and that's what I want for all of you.'

She was about to say something else when she saw Edna stand up.

'Edna?' Renee said respectfully, wondering what was coming.

'You and I have never got on, Renee, dear,' Edna began. 'You've always been too loud for my tastes—'

Nancy got to her feet. 'Edna. You can air your grievances with Renee later, in private—'

'I was about to say, Nancy,' Edna said quickly, turning back to Renee, 'that marriage is hard, but you've had it tougher than most. My husband and I hadn't been married many years when he died. But that's not to say things were idyllic just because we were together a short time.' She paused. 'What I mean, is that I understand how marriage can leave you feeling lonely and misunderstood, but as women, we often do what we have to in order to survive. Thank you, Renee, for bringing this subject out into the open, because I believe that too much is left unsaid, and too much goes on behind closed doors . . .'

As Edna sat back down, Renee was momentarily speechless. In those few words, the former Palais matriarch had said everything that needed expressing.

'And thank you, Edna,' she said, just as a flicker of movement at the back of the room caught her eye. It was Roger, dressed in a large grey overcoat over his black suit, and flanked by two police officers. Renee felt her heart plummet, like one of Jerry's bombs. She had been waiting for this moment – and was almost relieved that it had finally arrived.

61

While Nancy served tea and coffee and made polite conversation with the ladies, her mind really wasn't on the job at all. All she could think about was Renee, and what was happening.

When Roger had arrived with the police, Renee had gone as white as a sheet and merely followed the vicar as he gestured for her to come with him to the office.

Since then, Nancy had been on tenterhooks, desperate to find out what was happening, but knew she couldn't leave these ladies in the lurch.

And it didn't help that Edna was in the background, hovering with intent as she helped herself to a cup of tea. Nancy knew she couldn't avoid her mother-in-law any longer, so with a heavy heart she walked over to her.

'Didn't realise you were stopping by today,' she said.

Edna took a sip of tea. 'I was intrigued to see what this ladies' get-together was all about. Not what I expected, at all.'

'No?'

'No,' Edna echoed. 'But I'm glad. Women now aren't taking a bad marriage lying down, and I think that's right.'

'Did you mean what you said about your own husband?' Nancy asked softly.

'I did,' Edna replied as she held Nancy's gaze. 'I realised fairly early on we weren't right for each other, but I thought maybe once we'd got through a few years, we'd settle down. But then he died, and I'm grateful I didn't have to find out.' She took another sip of her tea. 'Marriage isn't for everyone. And some marriages shouldn't last a lifetime. I know you've often thought

I didn't think you were good enough for my son, Nancy, but that wasn't the case. I've always admired you: your tenacity, your wit, your wisdom, your go-getting attitude. And I wanted you to succeed. I merely thought you and my son weren't right for each other.'

'Right,' Nancy said, taken aback. This speech from Edna was so unexpected that she didn't know what to say.

'Which is why I've written to Alex and told him of your affair with the GI,' Edna added.

'You've done what?' Nancy's mouth dropped open in shock.

'Now, I know you'll think what I've done is cruel. And I also know you'll find it hard to believe that I did it for you, Nancy. You're too young to continue living a lie, and you both deserve more, but from other people. Perhaps, with the truth out there, you can both find joy with someone else, or you can go your separate ways and find happiness apart. Either way, Nancy, you can't stay in an unhappy marriage. I for one can tell you that.'

With that, Edna moved quietly away from Nancy to mingle with the remaining guests.

As she watched her mother-in-law chatting, Nancy didn't know what to think or feel. Edna had always interfered in her marriage, and this time she had taken it a step too far. Yet, Nancy believed her when she said she had the best of intentions. Perhaps it really was better for the truth to come out. Then, no matter what happened with her and Alex, at least they would continue on an open footing.

It was relief she felt most of all, she realised.

As the place rang with the sounds of conversation, Nancy's thoughts turned back to Renee. She had to find out what had happened to her friend. She rushed out to the foyer to see if she could find out anything. But instead all she found was Janice, who was busy making notes behind reception.

'Janice, honey,' Nancy said, surprised. 'Are you OK?'

At the interruption, the MC looked confused. 'I'm fine,

flower. Just trying to make some notes for the police while it's all in my head.'

'The police?' Nancy echoed. 'Whatever for?'

At the question, Janice sighed. 'Sit down, Nancy, love. There are a few things you need to know.'

Wordlessly, Nancy did as instructed.

'Thing is, flower, I haven't been completely straight with you. My husband hasn't been called up. He's in prison for robbery.'

'What?' Nancy cried out.

'When Renee offered me this job, I didn't just take it because I wanted to work with Renee, though I did, of course. And I didn't take it because I wanted to work at the Palais de Danse, either, though I couldn't believe I'd got so lucky. No, my old man's gone to prison for theft. I was wracked with shame when he tried to turn over our local tobacco shop.'

'Honey, no,' Nancy cried. All of this was news to her. She'd thought that Janice was biding her time until she and her husband could be reunited. She had no idea that this was something she had been forced into.

'It's true,' Janice said. 'When the Crystal, you know, the old dance hall me and Renee worked in back in Manchester, was bombed out, I was out of work and devastated. Me old man told me not to worry, that we'd cope. But his way of coping was to go on the rob. Course, the silly sod was caught and sentenced to five years in Strangeways.'

Nancy's head was spinning at these revelations, but Janice hadn't finished.

'So when Renee offered me a fresh start down here, I took it, grateful to escape the wagging tongues and make a bit of extra. But things weren't as simple as I hoped they'd be. I knew they wouldn't be the moment I saw that thug Mick.'

Nancy frowned. 'Mick?'

'Yes.' Janice nodded. 'Mick was the one that got my old man caught up in thieving. He stole to order, you see, for Renee's husband. When he saw I was working here, Mick tried to recruit me, too, but I hated him for what he'd got my husband drawn into and I hated him even more when I saw what he was doing round here.'

Nancy shook her head. How far-reaching Ronnie's poison had been. It had wrecked the lives of so many. As she reflected on what Janice had just said, something struck her.

'What do you mean, exactly? What Mick was doing round here?'

'You didn't know?' Janice said.

Nancy shook her head. 'No idea.'

'It was him that was writing all those letters to Violet,' Janice said softly. 'And it was him that delivered that charming parcel, and it was him that broke her window.'

'But, why?' Nancy was reeling. What did Mick have to gain from upsetting Violet in this way?

'He wanted what was his due in the deal Ronnie was arranging before he died. Mick thought he was getting a share of the Palais when Ronnie sold it, so when it all went to the vicar, he went on the warpath. Mick's plan was to create so much upset and torment amongst the Palais staff that the people who'd held it together – Renee, you, Temperance, and Betty Millington, God rest her soul – would all leave. When that wasn't working as he hoped, he ramped up the blackmail with Renee. Telling her he would go to Roger about her killing Ronnie if she didn't do his bidding.'

'You knew about that?' Nancy exclaimed.

Janice chuckled. 'Not a lot gets past me, flower. What Mick didn't know when he tried to lure me into his web, was that all I wanted was revenge.'

Thinking back over the past few months, Nancy recalled that she had seen Janice and Mick talking a couple of times and thought it was odd.

'I pretended I was happy to go along with him,' Janice

said. 'But the truth was I went to the police about it all. The poisoned letters, the thieving, the damage he was doing to Violet and her home, and, of course, the blackmail. I wanted him to pay for his evil, and I think right now that's what he's doing.'

'So, the police aren't here for Renee?' Nancy exclaimed.

'I don't think so,' Janice said.

'But, Roger,' Nancy put in. 'He's threatened to go to the police and tell them Renee's guilty of murder.'

Janice looked pained, then sighed. 'I had no idea about that. When I saw Roger with the two police officers I assumed they were here to talk to Renee about Mick.' She thought for a second. 'We can't let that happen, Nancy. Ronnie was a cruel, violent thug who'd have killed Renee before she killed him.'

The two women eyed each other, before Nancy spoke.

'Right. Let's go and sort this, honey,' she told Janice, assertively. 'Enough is enough.'

At that, both of them hurried across the foyer and up the stairs to the office, just in time to see the door to the office open and the two policemen walk out.

'I'll see you out,' Roger said, as he followed behind them.

'No need, sir,' one of them said. Turning to Renee, he tipped his hat at her. 'Thanks for your time, madam.'

The officers then walked past Janice and Nancy, who were agog.

'What is going on?' Nancy demanded, as soon as the police were out of sight.

'Not here. Let's talk in the office,' Roger suggested, gesturing to them both to follow him and Renee back inside.

Within a few minutes the little group was sitting around the desk Renee and Nancy shared.

'The police were here about Mick,' Renee said shakily, as Janice looked triumphant.

'They have enough evidence to charge him with the poison

pen letters he sent Violet and hopefully he'll be in prison and out of the way.'

'Thank all that is good and holy,' Janice said, making the sign of the cross against her chest. 'Maybe now Violet will feel life's not so bad here after all.'

Roger frowned. 'I don't know. The damage seems to have been done. I tried to talk to the parishioners about this the other week after service – turning the other cheek, offering a neighbour a kindly hand. But many of them seemed to believe that Violet was no more than a modern-day Mary Magdalene who should be punished for her sin.' He shook his head. 'Unfortunately, Mick just managed to make a bad situation even more cruel and miserable.'

'Well, I hope he rots in prison,' Renee said vehemently, as the others agreed.

'And, Renee?' Nancy said, looking expectantly at Roger. 'You've been keeping us all in the dark long enough, Vicar. If you're going to the police about Renee, for our sakes, do it soon.'

There was a pause as Roger fiddled with his dog collar.

'I was going to. When I came here with the police, my intention was to have them arrest Renee for Ronnie's murder. But then I heard your speech, Renee.' His eyes met hers and Nancy could see empathy in his gaze. 'The way you revealed your own experiences to those women, the way you gave such an account of all you had been through. I can't say as I can ever forget the fact that you were responsible for Ronnie's death, but God believes in forgiveness and you have suffered enough. As far as I'm concerned, the matter ends here.'

Relief flooded Renee's face, and Nancy got to her feet and threw her arms around her friend.

'Oh, thank God,' she cried into her shoulder.

'It's over,' Renee replied. 'It's really over.'

'Is it?' Janice said in a flat voice. Nancy and Renee broke apart and looked at her in dismay. 'Mick knows,' Janice went on.

'When he's in prison he'll tell them what he knows in exchange for a softer sentence.'

Renee shut her eyes in despair.

'But who'll believe him?' Roger exclaimed. 'A known liar and fraud. They'll put it down to the fact that he's a desperate man looking to say anything to get out of trouble. He has no proof or any witnesses to back up his story.'

'But *you* know, Roger . . .' Janice said in disbelief. 'You really won't say anything if the police come calling?'

He shook his head. 'My lips are sealed. Renee has paid a high enough price for a lifetime with my brother, and she is now doing God's work in helping others with their pain. It's time to put it in the past.'

62

July

Around three months later, as Violet turned nervously in the church pew and watched the bride walk towards the altar, she felt her eyes pool with tears. Temperance looked so beautiful in her simple white dress with its sweetheart neckline. She could see there were tears in her friend's eyes, too, but, unlike Violet, Temperance had her gaze fixed on one person only – her beloved Archie.

Flashing Violet a sweet smile, Temperance walked up the aisle – past Violet and the rest of the Good Time Girls who were standing beside her, and took her place beside her groom.

As Temperance cast a shy glance at Archie, Violet saw her radiance, the love in her eyes, and thought her heart would burst with joy. Temperance deserved this happiness in her life and Violet was delighted that she had found it.

'Welcome all on this wonderful July day.' Roger's voice rang out loud and clear as he addressed the congregation that had gathered in the little church in Hammersmith to witness the happy event of Temperance and Archie's marriage.

Violet exchanged a glance with Nancy, who was sitting beside her, looking as keyed up as she felt. As Roger continued addressing the congregation, Violet glanced around the church, taking care to drink it all in. The church, though small, was packed to the rafters with friends and family, not to mention Palais regulars who all wanted to celebrate the couple's love. Even Roger had got involved, offering to marry the couple since he knew them personally, as long as the vicar of the Hammersmith church agreed, which thankfully he had.

'And so, let us begin,' Roger said, once the first of the hymns had been sung and the congregation had settled.

Sitting on the hard pew, Violet watched the happy couple turn to one another and hold hands.

'Do you, Archibald Ledbetter, take Temperance Adams to be your lawful wedded wife?' asked Roger.

'I do,' Archie replied solemnly, his eyes shining with tears now.

'And do you, Temperance Adams, take Archibald Ledbetter to be your lawful wedded husband?'

'I do,' Temperance said.

As Roger continued through the rest of the vows, the quandary Violet had been in for so long faded. She knew without doubt that Archie and Temp would make the perfect stand-in parents for little Eamon, until she could be together with him again.

Her eyes travelled down to meet her son, who was asleep in his basket on the other side of her. She looked at him tenderly, memorising every last detail of his beautiful face. His long dark lashes, his warm smooth skin, his dark curls and Cupid's bow lips. Violet knew she would never tire of looking at his face, but for the moment at least she would need to rely on memories alone to remind her of the joy he gave her.

'I now pronounce you man and wife,' Roger said, triumphantly.

At that, there was a roar of approval from the congregation and Violet turned to exchange happy smiles with Nancy and Renee who, like her, were crying with joy.

A wedding had been a lot to plan in just three months, but Temperance and Archie, who were determined to wed, had taken it in their stride. In the end, it had taken Temperance all of thirty seconds to say yes to Archie's proposal. She had got on the ground with him, flung her arms around his neck, and peppered his face with kisses as she screamed yes over and over again.

Once the excitement had died down a little, the subject had once again turned to Violet and Eamon and Archie's suggestion that they might be the perfect stand-in parents for Violet, just until she sorted out her new life. Violet had agreed to think about it.

Truthfully, at first she was not keen at all. The thought of being without her son for even a moment made Violet want to curl into a ball and never get up. But then, when she got the news that it had been Mick who'd been sending all those vile things to her, Mick who'd vandalised her home, something hit home.

Attitudes around Hammersmith, and the East End probably, would never change, with or without Mick's involvement. Whilst the letters weren't being pushed through her letterbox any longer, and her windows weren't being smashed in, she was still drawing stares and looks of contempt everywhere she went. The word *whore* was often whispered by regulars under their breath whenever she was near. And although Violet knew she could withstand it all, she wasn't sure if it was fair to ask her boy to grow up with this sort of torment.

There was nothing really left for her in Hammersmith now. Not now that Eamon, her brother, and her mother had died. Maisie was in the ATS – hopefully she would return one day, but with the way the war was going who could say when. There was, of course, Queenie, but she had her own thoughts on the matter, which she shared when Violet had popped round to discuss the situation a month earlier.

'Don't you go putting your life on hold for me, girl,' she'd said briskly. 'I'll be brown bread myself soon.'

'You can't say that!' Violet had said, shocked.

Queenie just shrugged. 'It's true. And you don't want to waste any time thinking about what could have been when there's a chance to create something wonderful for you and that boy. So go on, take your father up on his offer and start again, Vi. You deserve it.'

And so, after much pacing of Winnie's flat, Violet had decided to do just that. To start again in Birmingham, where nobody knew her, she could put the heartache of the last few years behind her. Violet had thought back to the promise she had made in Solihull. How she would move heaven and earth to protect her child. Giving him up, even if it was only temporarily, was just that.

'Enid and I will come and visit often, don't you worry about that,' Winnie said, giving her a wink.

And so she had written to Alan and told him of her decision and he had delightedly set the wheels in motion, arranging for her to move into a new house with three women who worked at Howell & Smart. There was no job for Violet as yet, but Alan had assured her that he would help find her something, and in the meantime at least she would have a roof over her head away from prying eyes and gossip. He had also booked her on a train leaving soon after Archie and Temperance's wedding.

An hour later and the celebrations continued back at the Palais, which, for the first time in its history, had closed that Saturday night so the reception could be held in style.

As ever, Renee and Nancy had done the couple proud with three trestle tables pushed together, all groaning under the weight of cheese-and-onion sandwiches, sausages and even a ham. Violet couldn't remember the last time she had seen a spread like it, and dreaded to think how the food had been found.

Nancy grinned as she sidled up to Violet. 'Isn't this wonderful, honey?'

'It's lovely,' Violet breathed, as she took it all in.

'We had lots of regulars offer to give up their rations, in case you were wondering where it all came from,' Nancy explained. 'Temperance and Archie are so well thought of.'

'As it should be,' Violet said, as Temperance and Archie glided towards them, joy radiating from their faces.

'Congratulations.' Violet beamed as she leaned in to kiss the happy couple. As she did so, Eamon gurgled contentedly in her arms.

'Don't you want to put him down somewhere?' Archie said gently. 'You can have a drink and a dance, then.'

Violet shook her head and held Eamon closer to her chest. 'He's all right where he is for the minute.'

Thankfully, neither Temperance nor Archie pressed her on it, and Violet was glad. She knew her time with her baby was coming to an end for now. She didn't want to be deprived of a second longer than she had to.

'So how does it feel to be Mr and Mrs Ledbetter?' Nancy gushed.

At her new name, Temperance giggled. 'It hasn't sunk in yet. I don't suppose it does for a while?'

'I always stuck to my maiden name for work,' said Nancy. 'I never really gave it up. And who knows, maybe that'll be what I'll be doing for the rest of my life now.'

'What do you mean?' Temperance looked at Nancy sharply.

Nancy sighed. 'I had a letter from Alex last week. Edna wrote to him about my affair with John. Alex said that when he comes home, we have a lot to discuss. That he doesn't think he'll ever forgive my betrayal.'

'I'm so sorry,' Archie said softly. He reached for Nancy's hand and clasped his fingers around her palm.

'You know what, it's fine,' Nancy said with a smile. 'John clearly wasn't the love of my life, and I don't think Alex is, either. Edna's done me a favour, funnily enough – she's set me free. But you two, on the other hand, are a world away from me and Alex. You two are made for each other; any fool can see that.'

At the compliment, Temperance and Archie laughed.

'We've been through enough bumps in the road,' Archie said.

'And it'll only make you stronger for it,' Renee said authoritatively as she joined them, glass of port in her hand. Raising the drink, she touched it against Archie's and Temperance's then Violet's and Nancy's. 'Here's to all of us. To Archie and Temp and a long, happy marriage. To Nancy for continuing to be the strong woman she is. To Violet, who deserves the world, And to me, for having more lives than a cat.'

At that, everyone laughed and sipped their drinks.

'And, to Betty,' said Violet. 'Wherever she is.'

'I'll drink to that, queen.' Renee squeezed Violet's arm with her free hand.

As Violet lowered her glass, she saw Alan at the door. Catching sight of her, he gave her a little wave and though she was happy to see him, her heart sank. It was time.

'Well, then,' she said with a false brightness. 'Looks like it's time for me to go.'

'Already?' Temperance gasped. 'We were just about to have our first dance. You'll stay for that, won't you?'

'I can't,' Violet said, and then suddenly tears were running down her face. 'I can't miss my train.'

'We'll be thinking of you,' Archie said sombrely.

'And I you,' Violet said through her tears.

Looking down at her son in her arms, whom she cherished more than life itself, Violet stared into his eyes and tried to convey everything she was feeling in her heart. That this pain, this parting she was inflicting on him now, was all for his happiness later. That her motherly love ran that deep. That she'd die for him.

'It's not forever, Vi,' Temperance said fiercely. 'It's just until you get settled. Then you can have him right back with you.'

Violet nodded, and glanced at the clock on the wall. There was no more time for goodbyes, and the truth was, she'd said everything she needed to say over the past few days. Taking Eamon to the park, delighting in his new words and milestones. Now it was time to hand him over to the couple who'd love him and care for him while she couldn't.

'Bye, bye, baby boy,' she said now, kissing him gently on the forehead and handing him to Temperance. 'I'll see you soon. Remember, your mummy loves you.'

'He knows,' Temperance said softly.

'He'll always know,' Archie added.

Turning to Renee, Violet threw her arms around her. 'Thanks for everything.'

'Don't be soft,' Renee said, though there were tears in her eyes. 'I'll be seeing you in Birmingham before you know it. I'm thinking of opening another dance hall up there.'

Laughing, Violet opened her arms to Nancy next. 'Thanks for taking me on. For giving me a job all that time ago and changing my life.'

Nancy squeezed her tight. 'Honey, it was one of the best decisions I ever made. And this move will be one of the best decisions *you* ever make.'

'Never got to have that career though, did I?' Violet said forlornly. 'I had such high hopes for myself when I started working at the Palais.'

'And you can still have those hopes, Vi,' Nancy said fiercely. 'You're smart. You have a future, don't forget that. This is just a small step on a new journey.'

As Nancy let her go, Violet took a step back and looked at them all. There was nothing left to say apart from a few words. Turning to Temperance and Archie, she said, 'Thank you. For looking after Eamon.'

'We'll love him as if he were our own,' Temperance promised.

And then, before Violet could change her mind, she smiled at them all and turned to walk away.

As she passed through the doors of the Palais, Violet heard the band playing the opening notes to 'We'll Meet Again'. Stopping for a second, she turned around and watched everyone she loved and adored take to the floor and dance to Vera Lynn's anthem. She had loved and lost in the Palais; she had learned everything she needed to about life, and more. She had made the best of friends, and the worst of enemies, but most of all the Palais had been there for her whenever she needed it. As she stepped outside with Alan, Violet knew for certain that she would meet them all again.

Acknowledgements

I feel I always start these things listing all the people who helped write this book, but that's because it truly does take a team, rather than one person, to make a novel become a reality. I've been blessed to have two phenomenal editors in Cara Chimirri and Hannah Bond who understand the saga market so well: their insight and perspective have truly helped make this book shine. Equally, my agent Kate Burke from Blake Friedmann is a real guiding light and I'm grateful for all she does and continues to do. I'd also like to thank the wonderful Embla team, Emilie, Jen, Jane and Anna, for helping bring these stories to life, and of course the copy editors and art department who create these fabulous covers – thank you!

As I hadn't been thought about in wartime I am once again indebted to the Fulham and Hammersmith Historical Society and everyone from the Hammersmith Palais – Old Skool and You're Probably from W12 if . . . social media groups, who have all been a huge source of help. Any mistakes within this book are entirely my own.

I must also extend a huge thanks to my family and friends who patiently read, listen and put up with so many wartime stories they'd be forgiven for thinking Uncle Albert from *Only Fools and Horses* had entered their midst – I am grateful, and I can talk about other things, promise.

Naturally, the biggest thanks of all must go to every single reader out there who has picked this book up and taken a chance. Thanks for reading this. There are a lot of sagas out there and I'm delighted you have chosen this one.

About the Author

With a passion for reading from practically the moment she was born, it was inevitable Fiona would become a writer. Sure enough, after studying English Literature at university, Fiona became a journalist before making her move to books where she began ghost writing fiction for celebrities (too famous to name, of course). One day, some bright spark suggested she write her own stories and, suddenly, an idea was born. She lives in Berkshire with her husband and two cats, and has an unhealthy attitude towards exercise and chocolate – believing one must surely cancel out the other.

About Embla Books

Embla Books is a digital-first publisher of standout commercial adult fiction. Passionate about storytelling, the team at Embla publish books that will make you 'laugh, love, look over your shoulder and lose sleep'. Launched by Bonnier Books UK in 2021, the imprint is named after the first woman from the creation myth in Norse mythology, who was carved by the gods from a tree trunk found on the seashore – an image of the kind of creative work and crafting that writers do, and a symbol of how stories shape our lives.

Find out about some of our other books and stay in touch:

Twitter, Facebook, Instagram: @emblabooks
Newsletter: https://bit.ly/emblanewsletter

www.ingramcontent.com/pod-product-compliance
Lightning Source LLC
Chambersburg PA
CBHW050543260626
47157CB00002B/417